SKY STAT

The Human Spirit Series Book 4

ANDREW HARRIS

ALSO BY THE AUTHOR

The Human Spirit Series

The C Clef
A Litany of Good Intentions
More

First published in 2024 by Faithful Hound Media
Copyright © Andrew Harris 2024

ISBN 978-1-3999-8441-6
Also available as ebook.

Published by Faithful Hound Media Ltd

www.andrew-harris.net

For Lynne

PART ONE

"Genius always finds itself a century too early."

Ralph Waldo Emerson

CHAPTER 1

A growing sense of unease had dripped doubt into her mind all night. Dry sleep drowned in her private water torture. Was this *really* the right time? Should she wait? After all, the handover was only weeks away. Yet patience had never been one of her virtues. She was in this exalted position because of her positive attitude and unwavering decisiveness. Now *was* the time. She must take the risk.

Wanting to get things moving, she'd tried for an early meeting, but the Reptile Queen foiled her once again. Bernard Mertens, former Belgian Foreign Minister, and lifetime politician was allegedly busy with conference calls at his residence all that morning. He was not due in the office until eleven thirty at the earliest, she'd been told, in no uncertain terms. He had a tight window before an important luncheon engagement downstairs.

Reluctantly, she took the appointment. Twenty minutes would have to be enough. She'd vowed to herself there and then that the Reptile Queen would be the first casualty after the handover. Thick scales, slimy to the touch, denizen of the shadows with a poisonous bite and spitting forked tongue, the Reptile Queen's nickname was well deserved.

Eucabeth Ava Gachuhi was simply known to her many friends and colleagues across the diplomatic community as Betty. New York had become her adopted home through necessity, yet the pulsating rhythms in her soul would always remain Kenyan. Despite breathing the rarefied air reserved for ministers, representatives, politicians, and lobbyists after all these years, Betty still retained the playful exuberance of the young intern, committed to making the world a better place.

As she waited for the elevator on the ground floor amongst a silent congregation of dead-eyed bureaucrats and clerical staff, Betty rehearsed the opening scene in her mind. *Come*. The command he always used, as if she were a black Labrador. He would be sitting with his back to the window, the East River shimmering behind lace curtains like a ribbon of mirrored glass.

He would offer her an armchair around a low table far away from his oversized mahogany desk. The drab watercolour of Brussels Town Hall would not be quite straight on the wall. The tired, old clock would be marking out the final heartbeats of his disappointing regime. A silver tray would be carefully positioned on the barren table, the weak coffee as tepid as his demeanour.

Her sin, however, would not be the intrusion itself. He knew she would be asking difficult questions and, worse, demanding he take action. He'd warned her that, a Secretary-General who took action, never got re-elected. The role was political and meant to be symbolic, he'd explained, on numerous occasions. We'll see about that, she reminded herself.

As the elevator doors slid shut, she could imagine him making his slow, deliberate way over to join her. He would be carrying the notepad that would remain blank throughout their awkward exchange. One of the most influential men on the planet, surrounded by the sharpest minds humanity had to offer, all of them bursting at the seams with the most creative and ingenious ideas, yet he never had anything to write down.

Her fellow travellers drifted off at various floors until she was alone for the final whispering ascent. The muted ping as the doors slid open, the lush carpeting beyond, grabbing at her heels, the triple-glazed silence; she had entered a privileged world and immediately felt out of place. Guard up, stomach queasy, caution guiding each careful step. She had been here before. It felt wrong the first time she met him. It felt just as wrong today.

It's Your World was proudly emblazoned above the blue and white flag, neatly framed on the wall ahead of her. It couldn't have been less like her world or the world of the people she knew, including the people who must have voted her in.

The United Nations had become a post-war relic, established with the best of intentions but now broken on the wheel of power politics; brow-beaten into conformity, submission, and toothless compliance.

"I'm tight for time." He sighed, the notepad on his knee, a dormant fountain pen sleeping on the polished table in front of him, its white, snow cap staring at her in disbelief like an unblinking eye.

"How can I help you?" His lips moved, but his bloodshot eyes remained steady and distant.

In the elevator rehearsal, she had meticulously followed the presentation skills training module. State your objective: produce evidence to support your case: argue the benefits: finish on a clear call to action, with well-defined next steps: and don't forget to smile.

Despite her best intentions, she abandoned protocol and let the words pour out. Betty's infectious enthusiasm was arguably her greatest strength but also a weakness when it came to logical, structured argument, especially in the flint-hard world of diplomacy and political horse trading.

"We had some respite from climate change during lockdown." She blurted out.

He recrossed his legs in irritation. The notepad slipped but was caught in time. He took a mouthful of cold coffee as he made a point of lifting his gaze towards the clock on the wall behind her.

"The aviation industry was hit hard. Many airlines went under, never to fly again. With no international or domestic flights, the upside was a huge reduction in carbon emissions while the virus raged." She saw him adjust his watch strap. "Now that's all changed."

"Of course, it has. Normality has returned. People need to travel, it's perfectly natural." He was holding her eyes. What hair-brain scheme was she proposing this time?

She pressed on. "We've lost all we gained. We've resumed our disastrous journey of polluting the skies and overheating the planet."

"Betty, you know as well as I do that aviation is one of those tricky problems. We've been over this before. I've sent you the reports. Sustainable aviation fuel and green hydrogen are the future, but the technology isn't there yet. It will take time. For now, people need planes, and planes need fossil fuels. What more can I say?"

He put the pad on the table, freeing up his arms, as if by waving them around he would force home his argument. "Besides, offsetting must be given time to work. Newly planted trees will soak up some of the emissions. It's all we can do."

She blew out her cheeks. Now to test the water. It was bound to be ice cold, but it would at least expose his line of resistance and help her prepare for the battles yet to come. Battles she would have to fight when sitting in his chair, after he was long since put out to grass. "I don't think it is. I have an idea I wanted to run past you."

He rolled his eyes then leaned forward in his seat, preparing to stand. She asked him to hear her out. He suggested she put it in an email or, better still, wait until it was her office, then discuss it with her own team of advisers.

It would only take a few minutes, she assured him. The future of humanity was at stake. He reluctantly slumped back, picking up the notepad and pen this time, implying he would at least pretend to give her idea his full attention. He ran a lazy finger over the snow-capped peak.

"I was reading the biography of Charles Lindbergh." Her eyes widened with excitement. "He was the first man to fly non-stop across the Atlantic in May 1927."

Mertens interrupted. "His plane was the *Spirit of St. Louis*. A huge crowd turned out to see him land in Paris. What's your point, Betty? I haven't got time for a history lesson."

"Lindbergh was competing for the Orteig Prize. $25,000 was big money in those days, enough to get other aviators interested. Some paid with their lives. Lindbergh became a national hero. Technological advancement in aviation would never have happened unless there was big prize money or national pride at stake."

He shifted in his seat. "So, what're you saying?"

"I'm saying we need competition to create change. There'll never be an aviation industry without fossil fuels, as things stand. Sure, they're making all the right noises about sustainable aviation fuels, but I'm hearing numbers like 60% mix with kerosene by 2050. We haven't got that long. The oil companies will find ways to slow this down and block the investment needed."

Betty continued. "We need to challenge our best scientific minds to solve the problem. I'm proposing a race, organised by the United Nations, with huge prize money for the winner, funded by a grateful world. Imagine the excitement it would create. The first commercial airliner to fly actual passengers non-stop around the world without using fossil fuels. What do you think?"

9

This time Mertens was on his feet. It followed a light tap on the door, which opened to reveal the Reptile Queen holding a copy of his lunchtime speech. The one about the need to work together to continue our fight for world peace, to think about the homeless and refugees, and to help others less fortunate than ourselves. The audience may change, but the speech stayed the same. He didn't really need the script – he knew it off by heart.

Mertens paused at the doorway. "What happens if no one takes up the challenge? We'd look silly."

Clearly, he hadn't thought of a good enough reason yet to say no. She was encouraged.

"Raymond Orteig issued his challenge through the Aero Club of America in 1919. There were no takers for five years, so he issued it again in July 1924. By then the technology had advanced. No one ever said he looked silly."

Mertens waved away the Reptile Queen's protestations that he would be late. He slipped the speech into his jacket pocket. "How would you know they didn't cheat?"

"I've worked out a route. The planes would be photographed from the ground and the time recorded. We'd have observers on board and at the Sky Stations. They'd fly west to east over landmarks like the Golden Gate Bridge, the Great Pyramid at Giza, and the Statue of Liberty before landing back where they took off."

Mertens searched her eyes, looking for a weakness. "A commercial airliner, you say?"

"We can make the rules. There must be at least fifty passengers on board, with a further payload of two thousand kilos. It would have to be a normal plane with proper toilets, safety features, hot meals, drinks trolley, cabin crew, inflight entertainment, the works. People must be convinced the new technology is safe to fly."

10

"And what is this new technology? I believe an Airbus A320 would need a fully charged lithium-ion battery weighing sixty tonnes just to get airborne and fly for seven minutes. Are you suggesting recharging points at fifty thousand feet? What did you call them, Sky Stations?"

"A Sky Station is a fixed point 2000 feet above a chosen landmark. Each plane must pass through this point to complete the race and be photographed from the ground with the time recorded." Betty explained. It was the first smile he'd offered in the last half hour.

The fact he was still listening was a breakthrough, although he hadn't moved from the open doorway. The Reptile Queen had slithered back to her nest.

Betty continued. "The first electric cars appeared in the 1890's. Advancement in battery technology has been painfully slow. Only now are lithium-ion batteries threatening an oil industry made rich by the automobile. We need to offer a big enough prize to show we're serious. I think US$10 billion would be a small price to pay to save our planet."

"US$10 billion? You're joking, right?" Mertens eyes widened in disbelief.

"No, I'm serious. We always find the money when we have to. Besides, most GDPs make that figure look small. Think of the positive environmental impact of electric planes. It's huge."

She watched with satisfaction as he slowly returned to his seat. "You're saying the future of commercial air travel rests in battery technology?"

It was Betty's turn to take a spin around the room, the energy pulsing through her, the ideas sparking. She was trying to restrain herself, knowing that at some point he would run true to form and pour cold water on the proposal.

She pulled aside the lace curtain to take in the majestic view and made another mental note. After the Reptile Queen, the lace curtains would be next to go.

"Not necessarily." She went back to her notes. She didn't want to get this wrong and give him the excuse to wriggle out.

"In 2016, Solar Impulse 2 circumnavigated the world using solar power, but it could only carry two people. We have electric planes, but payload and range are limited. The technology for zero carbon emissions across the aviation industry is there, but there's no urgency to change, given the comparatively cheaper fuel prices. I think a race would focus minds, create a real buzz, drive the change we need."

"I can see you've given this a lot of thought." He smiled again. She surmised that he'd found his way out.

"I'm sorry to dash your hopes about this race, as you call it, but it simply wouldn't work. Competition divides people, sets one organisation against another, one country against another. The future of humanity must lie in collaboration, pooling resources, and working together in harmony. This idea is too divisive. Maybe you should talk to the aviation industry. I don't think they'll buy it. Sorry, Betty, I must go."

The silence that followed began to press in upon her. She had just been put down by the Secretary-General of the United Nations. She was trespassing in his private office, standing alone by the dirty lace curtains. At first, she wanted to scream out against the negativity. Her ideas dismissed out of hand, making her feel foolish and naïve.

Suddenly, beyond the heavy glass window, a strong ray of sunshine pierced the low clouds, finding her spirit and lighting up the room. Instinctively, she leaned against the glass and looked down.

At street level there were cars moving around like remote-controlled toys. People congregated on the sidewalks, waiting for a green light to cross. They were ordinary people, living in an increasingly uncertain world.

The list of global problems seemed endless. Incurable diseases, famine, climate change, ruined economies, poverty, earthquakes, forest fires, mindless wars, refugees fleeing from natural and man-made disasters, even the threat of nuclear war was still present.

Now, more than ever, there was a need to rebuild confidence and restore faith in the human spirit. People needed to be inspired once again. They craved leadership and direction, a new hope for the future. This was her chance to shine, to lead the way.

Very soon, this would be her office. She had a clear mandate. Stop playing games, quit the politics; make the world a better place, while she still can. Time is running out. It's now or never.

Her mother was Kikuyu. She used to tell her stories as a little girl, filling her head with wonder and wisdom. *We do not inherit the earth from our ancestors; we borrow it from our children.* One day it will be your earth, she would say. Treat it with respect and use it wisely. The next generation will thank you for it.

Betty decided to call the race *The UN Crystal Clear Skies Challenge.* It would be one of many initiatives she would introduce when she became the first female Secretary-General of the United Nations: the youngest: and, God willing, the best loved and most successful.

She picked up her things and made her way to the door. Her mother's voice was still with her. *If you want to go fast, go alone. If you want to go far, go together.*

13

Betty wanted to go all the way. For the sake of our children, and grandchildren. We must go together, she reflected.

If this race was to take off, she clearly had some resistance to overcome, some serious persuading to do.

CHAPTER 2

Dr Hannah McGlynn was listening to footsteps climbing the old wooden stairs that led up from the street. She knew there would be a loud creaking sound when they reached the middle stair. The octave gave away the person's weight; the deeper the sound, the heavier they were. This tread was slight, possibly a woman or a youngster.

Although the job seemed to be going well, Hannah felt frustrated at her lack of real progress. She always knew it would take time to settle in. It was a newly created job after all. Success would come with persistence and determination. And patience. She had to learn patience. Change had always been an unwelcome stranger in the Roman Catholic Church and was always met with suspicion.

Despite her current frustrations, it was still an exciting career move and the right decision to have made at the time. She had loved being the CEO of the Klinkenhammer Foundation in New York and had many happy memories of the place and its people. Instinctively, though, she knew it was time to move on.

The footsteps stopped outside the front door. Hannah had positioned her desk so she could see who was coming and going when her office door was open. A silhouette was etched onto the frosted glass. If it was a woman, she must be very tall and slim. Judging by the delay in turning the handle, she must also be quite nervous. Yet if anyone should be nervous, it was Hannah herself. All her staff had gone for the day. She was alone in the office with no other means of escape.

15

This was her main office, in the heart of Vatican City. Her other office was in Geneva, but time had not allowed her to visit it yet. Whenever she needed to be in New York, she could hot-desk at the United Nations.

She had accepted the role of Papal Legate to the World Health Organisation when it was offered to her by the Pope himself. She met him briefly during a whirlwind honeymoon in Rio de Janeiro.

She'd been allocated vacant first floor offices in an old building opposite the Vatican News on Via del Pellegrino. The rooms were light and spacious, well equipped, and comfortable, with some quirky touches including an ancient coffee machine that made a noise like a waterfall yet produced the best macchiato she'd ever tasted.

A Lucas F.L. Ribeiro floor safe, dated 1878 and believed to have come from a church in Lisbon, stood proudly in the corner. It was locked. No one had a key, not even the white-haired *bidello* who had looked after the place for almost forty years. Rumoured to be full of gold and precious stones, it was now an ornate table for the Xerox machine.

Hannah's role was to represent the Pope at the World Health Organisation: to act on his behalf and make the organisation more effective: to co-ordinate resources to find a cure or means of preventing currently incurable diseases: to provide healthcare for everybody, not just Roman Catholics, and to make the world a better and safer place.

As part of her new responsibilities, Hannah inherited four postgraduates who mostly spoke English. One bright spark, Fabio, had appointed himself her deputy. Cheeky, sharp, and quick on the uptake, he was proving to be an invaluable assistant who had accumulated an amazing

16

array of passwords and could somehow patch his way into all the Vatican library systems and archives.

The figure behind the frosted glass was not moving. Hannah's curiosity got the better of her. She stepped purposefully across the office and opened the door, startling the woman who turned to scurry back down the stairs.

"No, please wait, I didn't mean to frighten you. Would you like to come in?" Hannah spoke softly, opening the door wider as if to show they were alone and there was nothing to fear.

Hannah moved back inside and waited. At first there was no movement, no footsteps, and no creaking noise. The top of the stairwell remained empty, bathed in electric light from the main office.

Into the void came a head, followed by a woman's body clad in a brightly coloured cotton dress. Jet black hair was collar length and braided with beads and metal tokens that jingled as she moved. Dozens of thin necklaces were coiled around her long neck, accentuating the strength of her jawline, and adding yet more reds, blues, yellows, oranges, and vibrant greens to her dazzling appearance.

On her feet were leather-strapped sandals, well-worn and covered in dust like she had walked to Rome from her homeland, which, Hannah surmised, was somewhere in Africa.

Her skin was coal black, obsidian smooth and glistening in the warmth of a late summer's evening. Being so tall, she almost had to stoop as she entered the room. Cautiously she made her way over to where Hannah was standing. She took a seat in front of Hannah's desk and nodded acceptance for a glass of cold water. The windows were open, allowing a refreshing breeze to filter through.

They both sat in silence for a few moments, sipping mineral water. Despite the dazzling array of colours and the mystical aura surrounding her presence, it was her restless eyes, Hannah decided, that drew the most attention. Almond shaped, with clear whites making an impossible contrast to their dark retinas. Her eyes portrayed a disturbing turbulence churning deep within her.

Hannah realised the woman needed time to compose herself. Clearly whatever she wanted to discuss was very important. Could she speak English? Where had she come from? Why was she here? This would be another good test for her patience.

"My husband, he dies." Her gaze was suddenly fixed and unblinking, holding Hannah's, not letting her move, soft tears starting to flow.

Hannah could feel her pain mixed with fear and uncertainty. On closer inspection, she saw tell-tale lines etched across her forehead with crow's feet moistened by fresh tears. Hannah guessed early to mid-forties but could be wrong.

"Grandchildren dead. Baby boy and my princess dead. Four others sick. Many people gone. Animals dying in village. You must help."

Hannah had a thousand questions. Take one at a time. "Where is your village?"

"By the lake, beautiful lake. But lake going, no more fish. People move away."

"Which lake? What country?" Hannah was guessing Zimbabwe or maybe South Africa. Her former colleague Kitty at the Klinkenhammer Foundation was originally from South Africa. Kitty's skin was more burnished bronze. This woman's was pure black. Who is she?

"I'm Turkana. Lake named by my people. In Kenya."

"Kenya? How did you get here?"

18

"I come see you. Father Patrick tells me. Hannah good woman, he said. My last hope."

Hannah picked her way through the broken English. Her name was Agnes Nyanga. She did indeed have a son, two married daughters and six grandchildren. The first grandchild died some weeks ago, the second last week. No one knew why. One day they were healthy then they grew sick and died only days later.

Hannah established that her husband worked as a fisherman on the lake. The fishing had become harder. Lake levels had fallen and the water itself was increasingly salty. The big fish had moved away.

Agnes had become Catholic many years ago but still believed in the religions of the Turkana peoples. They called their God Akuj. He looked after her people and the lake. But Akuj had fallen under the evil spell of Ekipe, she said, who had brought darkness to the land.

"He gave me this for you." Agnes pulled out a crumpled envelope from the folds of her cotton dress. Hannah noticed she was trembling as she passed it over.

The envelope had been addressed by a clear, steady hand. It was to be delivered in person. Hannah opened it, smoothed out the letter and sat back in her swivel chair. The letter looked authentic enough and gave all the contact details of its author below his signature:

Dear Dr McGlynn,

I hope you don't mind me writing to you directly, but it seemed the best thing to do, given these very difficult circumstances. There was a recent blog about you and your new role at the WHO on the Catholic News Agency website. It has given us all much hope. The Lord will guide you in the blessed days and weeks ahead.

I would like to introduce Agnes Nyanga. She is a very special woman. Considered a spiritual leader amongst

19

the Turkana people, she is respected as an Emuron, one of a group of religious priests and faith healers collectively known throughout the region as the Ng'Imurok. Only they can communicate with Akuj, their Supreme God, and Father of Creation.

All the other Ng'Imurok are male and mostly village elders. Agnes has earned their respect and been accepted into their ranks through the accuracy of her predictions, healing powers, and prophecies. Trust me, this woman can work miracles, I have seen her do it.

Agnes claims to have been visited in a dream by Ekipe himself, the Devil-God. He intends to punish the Turkana for straying from their traditional way of life. Increasingly they are becoming westernised, welcoming tourists, moving away to the towns and cities in the south and abandoning the lake, their land, and cattle.

The families that remain will suffer a great plague and pestilence that will destroy them. Ekipe told her about this prophecy in a dream. The people are very frightened as her predictions are starting to come true. Even when we have some success converting them to Catholicism, they still hold tight to their ancient beliefs.

My diocese has funded her trip to Rome to see you. I pray for your help before it's too late. The local authorities here are not interested in her claims and deny there is a problem. They blame global warming for the salinity of the lake and over-fishing for falling stock levels. The lucrative pull of jobs in Nairobi is drawing people away from the villages, especially the young people. Lack of investment in irrigation schemes and agriculture projects is behind their failing crops.

In Kenya, the people are very willing but there is sometimes a lack of co-ordination and preparedness for any kind of health crisis. I just hope and pray that, in your new role, you can help save the lives of these good people

who have lived on the shores of Lake Turkana for thousands of years. I don't know who else we can turn to. Please help them if you can.
May the Lord walk with you and keep you safe.
Yours in the True Faith,
Father Patrick Thomas Kelly.
Parish Priest,
Roman Catholic Diocese of Lodwar,
Northern Kenya

Hannah felt at a great loss. She looked across at Agnes who was gazing down at the floor in despair. Hannah wanted to do something but felt powerless to help her.

"How long are you staying in Rome?" Hannah didn't know what else to say. Was she looking for a way forward or a way out of this? She genuinely felt for Agnes and her people but what did they expect her to do?

"Long as it takes." The eyes lifted, a half smile, a ray of sunshine, inviting more conversation.

"Where are you staying?" Hannah noticed the clock on the wall. Lawrence would be getting hungry and a little worried.

"Many Kenyans in Rome. I sleep there." Agnes rose gracefully to her feet. Out of another pocket she produced a lock of braided hair. The stiff black strands, twisted and pulled into a tight figure of eight, were adorned with silver beads, pink ribbons, and tiny, colourful eggshells. She presented it to Hannah with both hands.

"For me? Thank you, I will treasure it." Hannah admired the simple gift and placed it respectfully on the empty desk in front of her.

"It from my princess. Very lucky for you."

They embraced and held each other for a few moments. Then Agnes disappeared as quickly as she had come. Hannah watched through the open window as she melted into the evening crowds, making her way towards the ancient church of Sant'Egidio A Borgo. She wondered if Agnes was going there to say a prayer. She felt like saying one herself and asking for guidance as to what to do, even though, in truth, her faith had lapsed many years ago.

The church was dedicated to Saint Giles, one of the Fourteen Holy Helpers invoked as protection against the Black Death in the fourteenth century. Maybe this was some kind of sign, a connection with Ekipe's evil prophecy in Agnes's dream.

Hannah put the letter and the lock of hair in her bag before calling Lawrence. She told him about Agnes and the plea for help. They agreed to discuss it over dinner. Lawrence was preparing Aventine Chicken Pasta, his new signature dish, as he called it. Table laid, candles lit, and a bottle of Chianti Classico was breathing gently on the dining room table. He sounded bored without her.

She didn't remember the drive home. Despite the bustle and noise of the late rush-hour traffic, all Hannah could hear were Agnes's final words as she left the room.

"Father Kelly bring you to us."

CHAPTER 3

Dinner in an hour please, Hannah requested, breezing in through the kitchen. She approved of his complex yet tasty pasta sauce which needed a bit more kick. She slurped a mouthful of ice-cold, pinot grigio then stripped off in stages as she headed towards the shower. She needed to check a few things out online before eating. *Lentamente*, she advised the chef, take it slow.

This gave Lawrence time to take his beloved Trigger for a short walk. The golden retriever sensed the opportunity and brought a scabby old tennis ball for entertainment. The park nearby had just enough lighting to get around and back before returning to the kitchen and donning his chef's apron again. Trigger found some cool tiles over in the corner and quickly returned to his slumber.

The food was delicious. Helping himself to the last spoonful of pasta, Lawrence reported that he'd had a most productive day, working from their rental apartment on the Aventine Hill, not far from the Tiber. The wi-fi was behaving itself at last now that the new router had turned up.

Lawrence had accepted the Pope's offer of a research job within the Vatican. So far it was going well. He'd been able to link his research studies with the Faculty of Medicine at Sapienza University and was now building modules towards a PhD. He loved the idea of being Dr Lawrence McGlynn.

His tutor had called to discuss his dissertation and he was making good progress researching the possible causes of Parkinson's. Whilst working in New York for the Klinkenhammer Foundation, he'd made a promise to his old Rotarian friend Toby Stanton and his wife, Wanda, who was slowly being crushed by this insidious disease. Lawrence would find a cure; he would give her a life worth living. He intended to keep his promise.

"So, tell me about this mysterious Lady of the Lake. I'm intrigued." Lawrence topped up their glasses. The chianti was a good choice to go with the pasta and was proving quite painless.

"She's a miracle worker, an Emuron, according to Father Kelly. We'd call her a witch doctor, I suppose. Agnes told me they see illness as part physical, part spiritual. If you're ill, an evil spirit has entered your soul. She drives away the badness and treats the illness with herbal remedies." Hannah drained her glass.

"And this Father Kelly? What's he doing in Kenya? He's a long way from the Liffey."

"As you're finding out, the Catholic Church works in mysterious ways. It's a religion that uses fear to control the faithful, yet it functions on favours, gratitude, and arm twisting."

"Favours?" Lawrence was smiling. A better word might be obligation.

Hannah wiped away some sauce with a napkin. "The Holy Trinity of Catholicism: Incense, Implication, and Inference. You suddenly find yourself doing things for people without ever actually agreeing. Catholicism is more about who knows you than who you know. I guess Father Kelly's a good man just trying to help his flock and save a few more lost souls along the way."

"Well, he's got to find something to do out there. It sounds a bit remote. Did you google this lake? I've never heard of it." They moved over to the couch.

"It's known locally as the Jade Sea, the largest desert lake in the world. One hundred and eighty miles long,

24

twenty miles wide and nearly four hundred feet at the deepest point." Hannah nodded her agreement to the second bottle. Lawrence made his way towards the kitchen.

"Three hundred thousand people live on its shores and twenty-two thousand crocodiles call it home." Hannah announced as she plumped up a cushion.

"Who counted the crocodiles?" Lawrence returned with another bottle of the 2012. The Gallo Nero crowed at him. The cork offered little resistance.

"When the Aral Sea disappeared, Turkana became the fourth largest salt lake in the world. Now there's a real danger it will go the same way. It could dry up in the next ten years." Hannah continued.

"Dry up, why? Climate change?" Lawrence did the honours. Somehow the second bottle always tasted smoother. Settling back, he snaked an arm around her shoulders.

"Less rainfall and higher summer temperatures increase evaporation which makes the water saltier, apparently. The article said the biggest problem, though, was the new dam."

"What dam?" Lawrence started to massage around the scar from an old bullet wound at the base of her neck. It seemed to relax her. Hannah curled up deeper into the couch like a contented cat.

"The one across the Omo River."

"Omo? That's a washing powder. My mum preferred Daz." Lawrence laughed at the confusion on her face which was starting to flush nicely under the healing effects of the chianti. Omo was another example of a joke not travelling well across the Atlantic. "Please start the dam story from the beginning. Take as long as you like."

Hannah took another slurp then pushed her head back onto his playful fingers. "Eighty percent of the water comes into the lake from Ethiopia down the Omo River. The Ethiopians have just built the Gibe III Dam across it to generate hydroelectric power and irrigate new plantations for cotton, sugar cane and palm oil across their southern regions."

"Good news for the Ethiopians I guess, but a disaster for the Turkana people. Funny way to treat your neighbours." Lawrence shook his head.

"I haven't read the rest of the article yet but there seem to be all kinds of other issues connected to this dam." Hannah could feel her eyes starting to close as the heat from the massage deepened.

The telephone ringing brought her out of the trance.

She climbed off the couch and tried to sober up as she moved carefully towards her mobile which she'd left charging on the sideboard. The call was mercifully short. She was soon back on the couch and returning to the wilds of East Africa.

"Who was that?" Lawrence checked his watch. It was getting late. Loading the dishwasher would have to wait.

"Monsignor Guido Moretti. Or is he Padre? I'm not up to speed yet with all the elaborate titles. He's Vice Camerlengo, the Pope's diary secretary. Guido is one of the friendly ones. He's not too precious about getting his kennel club name right. I wish I could say that about some of the others." Hannah tried to relax back into the massage, but the spell was broken.

"Bit late for office calls, isn't it?"

"His Holiness apologises but he's had to cancel my audience with him for tomorrow morning. Urgent church business, you understand. That's the third time. Disappointing, but I can live without a meeting tomorrow. I'll really need to talk to him before presenting to the United Nations in New York. You're still coming, aren't you?"

"Wouldn't miss it for the world. My favourite girl's inaugural speech telling the UN it's time they got their collective fingers out. I want a ringside seat please." Lawrence had stopped rubbing her neck but hadn't given up all hope for later. He knew he was up against tiredness, a formidable enemy.

"Guido's been asked to set up a meeting instead with Cardinal Dominic Maina. He wanted to check with me first. I said fine. I've never heard of him. But I bet there'll be something magically coincidental behind it all. I could look him up tonight, but I suspect you have other plans, Mr McGlynn."

Lawrence was going to put the cork back in the bottle, but his mind was on other things. The chianti could wait as well.

* * *

Hannah woke early, showered, and made fresh coffee with toast which she crunched as she flicked through the church directory. She used one of Fabio's passwords to access the inner sanctum. The directory was very helpful, but Hannah was learning you had to read between the lines to understand what was really going on in the Vatican.

After a lifetime of providing pastoral care in and around his birthplace, Nakuru, Kenya's third largest city, Cardinal Dominic Maina was appointed Archbishop of Nairobi, a post he held for fifteen years. He was called to the Vatican six years ago as President Emeritus for the Pontifical Council for the Unity of Christian Worship, the biography proclaimed. This was obviously a good career move and brought his rising star into the Catholic political firmament. He looked quite austere in the photograph. Maybe he'd be warmer in the flesh, she wondered.

It was a beautiful sunny morning as she zipped over the Tiber and headed towards the majestic white dome of St Peter's Basilica. She was driving herself even though her job held high enough diplomatic status to come with a chauffeur. After careful consultation with her born-again student husband, she opted out of the official car.

Instead, they found a fully reconditioned Alfa Romeo Spider in a car showroom down the road. Stunning red with a pull-up black vinyl roof, Series 2, vintage 1978, 2.0 litre with twin-cam, it even had a retrofitted CD player.

Hannah didn't know what the technical specification meant but the car turned heads and still managed electrifying acceleration when she could find an empty stretch of road long enough. Buying the car brought them a bit closer to the dream of *La Dolce Vita.*

As she slowed for a red light, Hannah was going to change *A Little Touch of Schmilsson in the Night,* Lawrence's favourite CD, for something more upbeat but instead found herself singing along. Somehow, after their gratuitous bedroom gymnastics last night, *Making' Whoopee* hit just the right note.

Lawrence was still a work-in-progress in that department, she reflected. At times, he was too direct and clumsy. At others, he was hesitant and insecure. Despite his bedroom failings, she'd never laughed so much with anyone during the delicate art of lovemaking, which somehow added a more intimate dimension to their relationship.

Harry Nilsson was still crooning away as she slipped into the underground car park and killed the engine. The bay next to hers was empty. She couldn't resist putting her foot on the floor sensor and punching the air with delight when the green light above her turned red.

Childish, Hannah, *better put your game face on for Cardinal Maina.*

Her high spirits gradually cooled as she made her way through the labyrinth of marble corridors within the lofty Palace of the Holy Office. She had to show her Vatican pass four times to gain access to the upper floors. Each security guard looked more intimidating than the last. They were all male, dressed in black suits and would have made credible extras in a Godfather film or, perhaps, a spaghetti western.

The Cardinal's heavy wooden door was protected by a young priest also dressed in black who spoke little English. She was expected, he confirmed, grudgingly, having fiddled with his keyboard. He made her wait. There wasn't a seat available. No drinks were offered. She was getting the message.

Eventually the phone buzzed, and she was shown into the lion's den. Cardinal Maina was a giant of a man. He was squeezed tightly into an enormous chair behind an impressive rosewood desk. He lumbered to his feet yet stayed rooted to the spot. He held out his arm which Hannah mistook as an invitation to shake hands, but a turn of his wrist indicated a straight-backed wooden chair facing his desk. His features remained fixed, with cold eyes watching her every move.

"I requested this meeting." He opened without any foreplay or small talk. "I want you to know that you are not welcome here. Most of the Cardinals agree with me. We see your appointment as totally unnecessary and potentially destructive. My job is to make sure you do not damage us in any way. Am I making myself clear?"

He sat down squarely behind the wooden barricade and placed both hands on the desk in front of him, arms fully stretched, fingers splayed. A tiny bead of perspiration had the insolence to trickle down his temple before being

29

swatted away. An open window behind him allowed cooler air to infiltrate his palatial office. Muffled sounds carried up from the street below. Otherwise, there was stony silence.

Hannah felt insulted but curiosity afforded her some composure. This was not the first hostility she had faced but it was the most direct so far. On the other occasions, she put it down to her being a strong woman in a secretive world of insecure men. This reaction was far more sinister and threatening. What was he trying to hide?

"Perfectly clear, Your Eminence." She spat the words.

"You have been granted the rank of apostolic nuncio, a papal representative of the Holy See. A nuncio is merely a messenger, that's all. For the time you are here, you will take your orders from us, the guardians of our true Faith. We hope it is a short time."

"I'm not planning on going anywhere. My mandate from His Holiness is quite clear. So long as He wishes, I will do what is required of me. Do *I* make myself clear, Your Eminence?" Hannah was trying to contain her anger. If she was to find out who or what he was protecting, she needed to open him up.

Cardinal Maina leaned back in his chair which groaned under the strain. "This building houses the Congregation for the Doctrine of the Faith, the oldest of the nine curial congregations and the most important. Since the sixteenth century, we have defended the church from heresy and promoted Catholic doctrine. I understand you no longer share our beliefs, Dr McGlynn, let alone swear to defend our faith. You are a threat to us and a disgrace to our church. You cannot and will not represent us."

Hannah took a deep breath and stared into his eyes. Why was he even bothering to tell her this? There was something important she didn't know, yet sensed she needed to. Ignore his protestations and push him for answers, see what falls out.

"Part of my brief is to make the World Health Organisation more effective in providing healthcare for everybody. How does this impact on your role within the Pontifical Council for the Unity of Christian Worship?"

"I can see that you are out of date and ill-informed. From next month, I will be President Emeritus for the Pontifical Council for the Pastoral Care of Doctors and Medical Professionals. Among other duties, the Council is to spread the church's teachings on the spiritual and moral aspects of illness as well as the meaning of human suffering. We talk about the *apostolate of mercy*. I doubt you even know what the words mean."

Hannah studied him carefully. She didn't blink. As with all bullies, attack was the best form of defence. "In my lifetime, I've watched millions of people die from viruses, sickness, and incurable diseases, including thousands of doctors and medical professionals. Instead of pontificating about the *meaning of human suffering* or the *apostolate of mercy*, I want to know how you intend to provide healthcare for all and make the world a better place, Your Eminence."

The trickle of sweat had returned. The Cardinal's face was flushed. Folds of dark skin looked prickly and uncomfortable, spilling over his starched white collar. He held up the flat of his hand to signify their meeting was at an end. He rose awkwardly to his feet and pointed towards the door. Hannah averted her gaze and crossed the room in silence. She was just about to leave when he called out.

"One more thing. I was visited by a parishioner from the Diocese of Lodwar. She told me she had given you a letter from her parish priest. I told her she must not contact you again. She is to go home immediately and

31

tend to her sick husband and family. I have since reprimanded her priest. Stay out of this. It is a church matter and nothing to do with you. You have been warned. Now close the door behind you as you leave."

Hannah needed three tours of St Peter's Square before she'd calmed down enough. The Saints above her gave silent counsel as her anger swirled then slowly evaporated. At this early hour few tourists were about, otherwise they would have been treated to some choice Brooklyn expletives. How dare he!! Who the hell does he think he is?

No doubt Cardinal Maina would deny their conversation in front of the Pope. Hannah knew His Holiness was not universally popular because of the liberal views he espoused on such thorny issues as birth control, abortion, and homosexuality.

He had been described by one critic as a butterfly collector, filling Vatican City with a dazzling display of brightly coloured academic, media and commercial specimens from around the world. Another called Him a magpie, gathering whatever shiny new ideas and trinkets caught His attention.

But Hannah saw Him as a leader working hard to clean house and distance the church from the scandals and intransigence that had haunted it over recent years. To make it more forward looking and relevant to the lives of all people, not just the one point two billion Roman Catholics.

Indeed, one journalist described her own appointment as an investment in an exciting new world that was yet to come. She could not fail. This was just the beginning. She would silence Cardinal Maina and the others like him. Action was the antidote to their threats. She had work to do.

With her head clearing, she walked in the direction of her office, passing between the ancient Tower of Nicolas V, the home of the Vatican Bank, and the Barracks of the Swiss Guards. She turned onto the Via Sant'Anna before veering left onto the part-pedestrianised boulevard of the Via del Pellegrino.

Above the Church of Saint Anne of the Palafrenieri, the October sky was a perfect azure blue and cloudless. Strong sunlight enriched the ochre shades of the old buildings nearby. The air was freshly scented by many flower beds and window boxes along the way. They helped to remind her that, despite the bitterness and anger of some people, the world was still a beautiful place.

She turned off the street and skipped up the old staircase, carefully avoiding the middle stair so as not to alert her team. She wondered if they'd all be busy working or simply occupying themselves on YouTube or Instagram. She'd only just opened the door when Fabio stepped out in front of her, a puzzled look on his face.

"There's someone here to see you."

CHAPTER 4

"She's in your office." Fabio nodded towards the open doorway.

The timing wasn't good. Hannah was still preoccupied with angry thoughts about Cardinal Maina. She would prove to be an asset to this Pope and bring about the changes necessary within the World Health Organisation, changes humanity needed if it was to survive.

Hannah was surprised to find Agnes Nyanga sitting in her office, especially after what Cardinal Maina had said. Agnes immediately stood up and turned towards her. Her eyes were bloodshot and puffy. She looked like she'd been crying all night. Her clothes were dishevelled. Some of the braids had fallen out of her hair which was now greasy and unkempt.

Hannah just had time to close the door before Agnes leapt forward and collapsed into her arms. Through uncontrollable tears, she managed to utter a few words. "He gone. My husband, he dead."

Hannah held her tight, Agnes's head on her shoulder, drawing the pain out of her, feeling the strength ebb from her body. Hannah closed her eyes and let her own feelings off the leash for a few moments. She could imagine Cardinal Maina glaring at her and was fighting back the tears. Her own emotions were churning inside, an unhappy maelstrom of sadness, anger, love, gratitude, and determination.

After they both regained some composure, it transpired that Father Kelly had been visiting her village yesterday when he discovered a body lying in a boat by the lakeside.

He recognised Agnes's husband, even though he looked so emaciated.

"Father Kelly calls me. He must bury. It very hot." Agnes explained they followed the ritual of wrapping the body in a white ox hide and burying it in the goat pen behind her hut, facing east.

Agnes continued. "Women from village lay branches of esekon tree over him. It sacred to us."

The body was laid to rest under handfuls of soft earth, while the women averted their eyes and Father Kelly said a prayer. Then the goats were brought back in to trample the ground flat.

"When did Father Kelly call you?" Hannah was curious about the timing of it all and how Cardinal Maina had got involved.

It took a few more questions before Hannah discovered Father Kelly had telephoned Agnes with the bad news late last night at the home of the priest she was staying with in Rome.

Earlier, the same priest had accompanied her to evening mass where they spoke afterwards to Cardinal Maina, as the priest had arranged. They hoped he could open some doors with the Kenyan authorities. They were disappointed by his cool reaction.

Hannah could see Agnes was just as upset about not being there to say goodbye to her husband as she was about grieving at her loss. This was combined with the worry that her husband would not be the last to die. Until they knew what was causing this disaster, others would surely follow.

Agnes desperately wanted to return to her family and friends but knew things could only get worse without the promise of outside help. Clearly Cardinal Maina would not lift a finger for them. Agnes now believed Hannah was their only hope.

"You in my dream." Agnes was looking her full in the eyes. "You must help us. Our only chance. You save my people, my village."

Agnes was due to leave for Nairobi that very afternoon. Overnight, Cardinal Maina had arranged her return trip with Kenya Airways. He'd managed to upgrade her to super economy. Was this a guilty conscience at work, Hannah wondered, or perhaps he just wanted to soften the blow that she would be fighting this tragedy alone.

"You come, I see you." Agnes managed a weak smile as she hugged Hannah one more time then made her way slowly towards the door. A few moments later, the middle stair creaked. Was that the last time she would hear from her?

Hannah rubbed her face with both hands and brushed away a strand of hair from her eyes. She would call Father Kelly and explain that, while she wanted with all her heart to help them, she needed to be in Rome and New York over the next couple of weeks. She was sure he would understand and break it to them gently. The idea of saying a prayer for Agnes wouldn't go away. Maybe it was the least she could do.

She sat in silence staring out of the open window. Nothing seemed straightforward. How could she get involved? What she hadn't realised, when she took this job, was the degree of politicising that went on. In her previous job, Hannah had many dealings with the World Health Organisation. She found them quite brittle and somewhat confused about what they saw as their role.

Their narrative was monitoring, collating, advising, recommending, consulting, and analysing rather than resolving, leading, controlling, managing, taking ownership, co-ordinating resources and, quite frankly, banging heads together.

People want to believe global healthcare is being taken seriously by sensible, highly skilled, and responsible professionals who can take decisive action when needed. This heart-felt belief is especially true amongst people living in countries being run by tyrants, dictators, and power-crazy politicians who consider healthcare as little more than an opportunity to make money at the expense of the poor and needy.

Now Hannah was beginning to understand that the World Health Organisation was constantly walking a tightrope between ideologically opposed players who ultimately controlled their purse strings.

It was impossible to keep everyone happy. They continually ran the risk of falling into political firestorms. Meanwhile, they were trying to battle global healthcare crises with both arms tied behind their backs.

She pulled out Father Kelly's letter and dialled the number. He answered on the second ring, almost like he was expecting the call.

"Father Kelly, I wanted to apologise for getting you into trouble. I met with Cardinal Maina this morning. He told me about your reprimand. I'm so sorry." Hannah felt a bit better having said this but couldn't see that it was her fault.

"Bless you, my child. You've no need to apologise. If anything, I should be apologising to you for writing the letter in the first place and dragging you into this mess." His accent was a rich Irish brogue you could cut with a knife. His words were buttered with genuine, heart-felt warmth and came singing down the line. Hannah could feel a wave of relief wash over her.

"And don't worry yourself about His Eminence. Our paths have crossed many times before. He's a right, royal pain-in-the-arse if you ask me, pardon my French."

37

Father Kelly told her that he'd seen the blog about Hannah's appointment and forwarded it to all and sundry, not only across East Africa but to his many friends in Ireland, the United Kingdom and America.

He believed it was an inspired appointment that gave hope to the civilised world and put the Catholic Church back where it belonged, in the cauldron of public debate on healthcare and providing help for people in need.

His Irish brogue was engaging. Please call me Pat, everyone does. And may I call you Hannah, Dr McGlynn? He knew many McGlynn's back in his former parish near Galway on the west coast. They were good people, salt of the earth; give you the shirt off their backs, as no doubt your husband Lawrence would as well. He'd looked him up too, from a family of fish-fryers who crossed the Irish Sea and settled in Yorkshire.

Hannah was impressed about how much homework he'd done and wanted to tell him so but couldn't get a word in edgeways. She sensed her new-found Irish friend had taken a bit of the Blarney Stone with him to Kenya. But after the heavy conversations of the day so far, it was good to share a bit of what they called *the craic* with a genial Irishman.

"Lawrence said you're a long way from the Liffey. What are you doing in Africa, Pat, if you don't mind me asking?"

"Not at all, it's a fair question." Pat offered to ring her back and put the cost of the call on the Lodwar Diocese budget which made Hannah smile. She was confident that no one in the Vatican Bank, with total assets more than US$8 billion, would be worried about her phone bill.

Pat gave her the shortened version of his life story. "We had a family from Kenya come to settle in Dublin which was my last posting. They were lovely people, good Catholics, who'd fled from poverty and suffering.

Apparently, the husband had some Irish ancestry on his mother's side which helped them get visas. He spoke so highly about his homeland I decided to visit. Kenya won me heart. It was meant to be. I knew then what I must do."

His first posting was to Nairobi where he met Cardinal Maina who was still an archbishop at the time. "He was a nasty piece of work then and still is. Nobody liked him. He was conniving and devious, always linked to various scandals but never implicated. We nicknamed him *Teflon Dom* as nothing ever stuck."

Hannah listened intently. A picture was forming. She would have to break the disappointment about Agnes soon, but she knew any dirt on Cardinal Maina could be a political lifesaver at some point.

Pat was in full flow. "We did high fives when he was called to Rome, but we laughed too soon. He still controls things here and now calls the shots in Rome. I'm not surprised you've had the gypsy's warning. He'll see you as a threat. He doesn't like any women and certainly won't like you. What did the article say? *A sassy American professional with a razor-sharp mind and strong shoulders.* Maina broke several government officials here who got in his way, so be warned."

Fabio stuck his head around the door and disappeared again when he realised she was on the phone. Hannah checked her watch. She knew Fabio was leaving early today. She needed to talk to him before he went.

But Pat hadn't finished the story. "There's something else I should tell you, Hannah. It's bound to come out if the Cardinal knows we've had this little chat."

"How will he know? I won't tell him." Hannah sounded surprised.

"Don't worry, he'll know, he always does. His spies are everywhere, trust me." Pat's voice went quieter. Was it shame she was sensing or the potential relief of his confession? "It worked out well for me coming to Kenya. I've been able to defeat one of my demons."

"Demons? How do you mean, Pat?" Hannah had already guessed he was running away from something. What did Lawrence say? He'd be remote from civilisation out there, with very few temptations or distractions.

"In Ireland, I was struggling with a man called Jameson. He'd taken over me life. I can see now how it happened. He was there all the time. Everywhere I went he would tempt me. At every gathering, it was always understood I would partake of his finest. In the end, I couldn't live without him. I was possessed and powerless to resist." Pat's voice was no more than a whisper, occasionally broken by momentary interruptions as no doubt painful memories flooded back.

Jameson, Hannah thought. Does he mean the whiskey? She smiled as she remembered they spelt it with an e in Ireland, so Lawrence had told her. Her mind was full of useless information.

"Hannah, despite all me years studying the Bible and the Gospels of the Saints, the most profound prayer I ever heard was written by an American theologian in the 1940's. I repeated his words every day for years. It changed me life. Do you know it?" Pat enquired.

"I know of it but not the actual words." Hannah checked her watch again. This was all well and good, but she had more pressing matters to attend to. Patience, Hannah, hear him out.

"God, grant me the serenity to accept the things I cannot change, the courage to change the things I can, and the wisdom to know the difference. I like to think I've learned the wisdom to know the difference. But it's taken me a long, long time."

"Pat, look, it's lovely to talk to you and thank you for sharing all this with me. I can see this prayer has a deep

40

meaning for you. I will reflect upon the sentiments behind it. It applies to all of us." Hannah took a deep breath. She had reached that point. "My heart goes out to Agnes and the people in her village. I would dearly love to help them but I'm struggling to see how I can. I will ask the World Health Organisation representatives in Kenya to investigate this, but I can't see what else I can do."

She explained about her itinerary over the next few weeks. Even as she elaborated, it sounded a feeble excuse. Pat remained silent throughout. In conclusion, she asked him if he could apologise on her behalf to Agnes next time he visited and wish them all the best of luck.

Still silence. She wondered if she'd upset him. After all, he'd just bared his soul to her. She hoped he didn't think she'd brushed it off like a matter of no consequence. It was a few more seconds before Pat replied. She expected anger or disappointment but didn't anticipate what he was about to say.

"Hannah, can I ask you a personal question?"

"By all means, Pat, fire away."

"After you met Agnes and read my letter, what was your heart saying to you?" Pat was speaking quietly again. She felt as if he was standing next to her.

"It said help her. Go to her village, find out what is killing them and stop it."

"Hannah, that voice in your heart, that's the voice of God. He is telling you what He wants you to do but He cannot force you. Agnes was sent to you by God, Hannah, not by me or the Catholic Church. I was just His instrument. We all have choices to make. We live or die by our decisions. You must choose. *Accept the things I cannot change and the courage to change the things I can.* If your role is not about healthcare for all and using

41

your influence to save people's lives, then what is it about?"

The words struck home like tiny arrows, releasing a narcoleptic potion deep into her veins. She had been wrestling with this dilemma ever since taking the job. Lawrence had warned her. The idea of righting the world's wrongs in healthcare through influencing the World Health Organisation had excited her. But an analogy, he suggested at the time, warned that, although she would be driving the train, it would still only go where the rails took it.

Had she just joined the political establishment; another snout in the trough, making a living out of looking like she was trying to bring about change but in fact just playing games like everyone else? She'd vowed to get her hands dirty, yet here was evidence that she had no intentions of doing so, despite the most important of causes.

Hannah felt the room starting to move, objects losing focus, sounds from the office and the street outside becoming muffled. Pat's words echoed around her head. *The courage to change the things I can.* Am I being brave enough? Or am I staying on the beaten path and risk failing the way others have failed before me.

The phone was still in her hand. Pat's voice was now a distant whisper. She struggled to find the right words to thank him. She would reflect on what he said and call him back. She missed the receiver for the handset three times, eventually steering it home with both hands.

Her eyes closed as she leaned back in her swivel chair. *Accept the things I cannot change.* Am I fooling myself? Maybe this is just a job like any other. Enjoy *La Dolce Vita*, Hannah, pick up the rewards, drive the Alfa Romeo round the back streets of Rome and just do the best you can, given the constraints you're working within. No one would think any the worse of you.

She drifted into some kind of waking dream. She was standing by a lake on a beautiful sunny day. It was surrounded by green rolling hills. Above the blue waters, by the edge of the lake, a large bird of prey was circling.

She watched its majestic wingspan catching the sunlight, piercing yellow eyes fixed on the shoreline below, feathers ruffled by a light breeze. The bird flew over and landed in front of her, transforming itself, as it did so, into a beautiful, young tribal girl, partially clad in brightly coloured clothes.

The girl smiled at Hannah as she stepped purposefully through the tussock grass towards her, fluorescent white teeth gleaming in the sunshine, sharply contrasted against flawless, chocolate-brown skin.

She stopped just a few feet away and stretched out her long arms in greeting. Hannah moved into her welcoming embrace; a sweet-smelling fragrance laced through her beaded hair.

Hannah could feel warm lips being pressed against her right ear. The girl spoke just a single word.

Amani.

CHAPTER 5

It had been many years since Max Hartley had been inside the hallowed halls of the Houses of Parliament. He was reading a magazine in the reception area to stave off boredom. Ten minutes late already. Was his host playing games again?

The article advised that the correct name for the building was the Palace of Westminster, which was owned by The Crown. There had been a Royal Palace on this site since the 11th Century, the article droned on. With over 1100 rooms, the sprawling complex covered eight acres, about the size of four rugby pitches, Max calculated.

The majestic Victorian edifice, standing near Westminster Abbey on the north bank of the Thames, played host to the House of Commons and the House of Lords, hence being known collectively as the Houses of Parliament. It was a British institution, the spiritual home of government and the rock on which an empire was built. And lost, Max added, for his own amusement.

The security procedures had been elaborate on entry, with full body-scans, metal detectors, and even a brief interview with an ashen faced guard who kept flicking his eyes towards a hidden screen. Why did they always make you feel guilty?

Passport Control and police officers must be specially trained to unsettle their victims, Max decided, as he tried unsuccessfully to stick the visitor's badge to his lapel. The printed label displayed a bar code and security number but no name. All this state-of-the-art technology yet the adhesive didn't work.

44

Minutes later he was being whisked through a labyrinth of corridors and passageways, up flights of stone steps and through a series of unmarked doors. He saw one heavy wooden door marked *Private - No Entry. Underground Access Only.* He'd heard rumours that secret tunnels existed in case senior ministers had to escape in a hurry but never thought they were true. Not until now anyway.

His escort, walking two steps ahead, was an androgynous civil servant dressed in a dark trouser suit. The creature had uttered few words so far and obviously wanted to keep things that way.

Max had always been proud of his reputation for being something of a ladies' man. In his younger days, he cut quite a dash in an RAF pilot's uniform. *Now I can't even tell the girls from the boys,* he sighed to himself.

Suddenly he was alone in a small meeting room, the trouser suit having quickly closed the door on leaving, to the whispered command, wait here. At the centre of the bare room sat a wooden table with four straight-backed chairs, all clad in green leather, embossed with the familiar gold portcullis emblem.

He moved across to the open windows which looked out over the murky waters of the Thames. It was warm for early October and the welcome breeze brought with it delicious lunch smells from the Terrace kitchens, two floors below.

"Max, my dear fellow, how good to see you again." A voice boomed through the opening door behind him. The tall, slim figure gave clear instructions to the departing trouser suit: fresh coffee for three with a plate of dark chocolate digestives. Three? Who else was being drawn into this little mystery, Max wondered. There was no apology for tardiness.

If it had been some years since Max had been inside the building, it was even longer since he'd seen his host, yet Quentin Fitzgerald-Manning, OBE, hadn't aged at all. His stylish black hair was centre parted, neatly combed back, and just the right length above his collar. He must be mid-fifties now, similar age to me, Max thought, yet there were no hints of silver or grey. He made a mental note - never trust a man who dyes his hair.

A dark blue, bespoke Saville Row suit flashed open with the handshake, revealing a distinctive Cambridge blue silk lining. The button-down cream linen shirt sported gold cufflinks and an RAF Club tie. The colourful lanyard around his neck was clipped to a House of Commons Pass - *Access All Areas*. A gold lapel badge was too elite even for Max to recognise.

"I've had to schedule another meeting, I'm afraid, so I don't have long today. Milk and sugar?" Quentin was doing the honours, now that the coffee had arrived, and the pleasantries were out of the way. No sugar, thanks. This was a second put-down after being kept waiting. Sorry Max but I have more important things to attend to, you're lucky I could squeeze you in at all. But Quentin had requested this meeting. What does he have in mind? Who is the third person?

Max took a careful sip from the overfilled cup and placed it gently on the green, leather-inlaid table. From memory, Quentin had never been in the RAF. His grandfather had been a fighter ace in the Battle of Britain. Max remembered a wonderful evening sitting next to former Group Captain Harold 'Ginger' Manning during an otherwise routine dinner at RAF Duxford.

Max was introduced to Quentin when he came to pick up the old boy. He was late then as well. They'd met several times after that but most of their dealings had been by phone and email. Max had many genuine friends, but

46

Quentin had never been included amongst them. Their relationship was strictly for business. There was something about him Max never quite liked, beyond his lack of punctuality.

"I've got a favour to ask." Quentin continued. The smile had gone, his deep blue eyes were steady and penetrating. "Well, not so much a favour, more like a business proposition, if you're interested."

"Quentin, I'm listening."

"What do you know about *Comet 5*?" Quentin was unclipping a tan leather attaché case he'd brought with him.

"Is this something to do with an air race? I heard it on the news recently. Like the good old days, Schneider Trophy, Brits versus the Yanks, fastest plane wins. Is that it?"

"That sort of thing, yes, but it's less about speed and more about endurance." Quentin handed him a report marked *Top Secret*. "*Comet 5* is to be the first commercial airliner to fly non-stop around the world without using fossil fuels."

"Not if the Americans can help it, no doubt." Max fingered through the slim report looking at the pictures mostly. The artist's impression of the plane was very sleek. One heading caught his eye: *nuclear propulsion systems*. He was going to continue but Quentin was in full flow.

"We're up against a plane called the *New Spirit of St Louis*, being backed by a consortium calling themselves Lindbergh Aviation Inc. It's a hybrid, we think, running on green hydrogen with enhanced lithium-ion batteries, but it could be methane as the main fuel source."

"We? Who's we, Quentin?" Max was intrigued but not sure where this was going.

Quentin checked his watch. "For my sins, I'm now CEO of Comet Aeronautics Group, a European consortium with some powerful friends. For once, it's not been a problem getting sponsorship. Airbus has come to the party along with several of their suppliers."

"A couple of universities and research outfits have chipped in and, of course, the atomic energy brigade has appeared with cheque books at the ready. They've always wanted to be the good guys and win popular support for the nuclear industry, especially after Three Mile Island, Chernobyl, and Fukushima."

"A nuclear-powered plane, is that it?" Max couldn't believe his ears.

"*Comet 5* will make history, taking 55 passengers and crew around the world non-stop using a nuclear propulsion system. It's perfectly safe. After all, we have nuclear subs and nuclear ships, so why not nuclear commercial airliners?"

Max's head was spinning. This guy was serious, judging by the impressive list of sponsors in the report and the detailed timelines. "As you mention it, what about the nuclear safety record?"

"I knew you'd ask that." Quentin checked his watch again. "I'm going to introduce you to the very man who can answer that question. He should be here any minute."

The third cup. He must be late or enjoys cold coffee. Max pressed on. "Quentin, what's this got to do with me? I know we've worked together before, but things have moved on. Being a test pilot was in my younger days. I'm running a successful IT company now."

Quentin paused, put down his cup and locked eyes with him. "Not that successful, I hear."

"I beg your pardon? What did you say?" Max could feel the colour rushing to his cheeks.

48

"Max, I said I've a business proposition for you, so calm down and listen. I know your IT company is suffering and your markets remain soft, given the global uncertainty surrounding long term investment. My people have crunched your numbers. Your company, Kampion, needs some lucrative, new work, pronto. I might be able to help you. More coffee?"

After he'd received the invite out of the blue from Quentin last week, *Coffee at the House?* Max had done his own homework on the man sat confidently before him. When they first met, Quentin was a procurement adviser to various commercial airlines around the world. He also bought from military aircraft manufacturers.

He often hired Max as a test pilot to try out some prototypes on behalf of his shadowy clients. Maybe that's where the mistrust stemmed from.

Quentin's OBE was for 'services to the aerospace industry', he discovered. Nowadays, Quentin was a senior adviser to the British government on matters relating to aviation, which Max interpreted as selling fighter aircraft, probably under the table. Poacher turned gamekeeper, or was it the other way around?

Either way, it was enough for Quentin to have a full pass, an office at the outer reaches of the building, a trouser-suited servant who made good coffee and, most importantly, to have the opportunity to worm his way onto every imaginable committee, Quango and government agency connected, in any way, to aviation, including, most recently, travel and tourism, he noted.

"I'm still listening." Max swallowed a large mouthful of cold coffee and sat back, with growing anticipation. Some lucrative government contract work would certainly help their bank balance.

"The race is the brainchild of the new girl at the United Nations. They're stumping up $10 billion for the winner.

The UN Crystal Clear Skies Challenge. It's put the cat among the pigeons in my industry. 'Bout time the UN shaped up', people are saying."

Quentin continued, dangling a large, juicy carrot. "When we win, it will be a huge breakthrough in aircraft design and capability. The skies will literally be the limit. The whole industry is watching. Indeed, given the high stakes for controlling climate change, the whole world is watching."

"I read somewhere that this race wasn't going to happen. Competition is old-school these days, too divisive for a world of teamwork, inclusiveness, and collaboration." Max probed.

"Betty Gachuhi, the new girl, is passionate about this. She's winning the argument against the flat earthers in the industry. It's time for a shakeup. Competition brings out the best in humanity, she reckons.

"I spoke to her last week and have another call scheduled later today. She pointed out that this very building, the Palace of Westminster, was the result of a competition after the old palace burnt down in the 1830s. We're sitting inside the Gothic Revival brainchild of the winner, Charles Barry. Whatever her ideology, $10 billion is my kind of prize money. Bring it on."

"And my part in this?" Max was starting to see possibilities. But there was still the risk factor. Nuclear energy had dirty connotations.

"*Comet 5* is an Airbus A350, currently under conversion at their test centre in Bristol. I need you to fly the plane over to St Louis Lambert International Airport in Missouri. In return, I'll pay you handsomely for your troubles and offer you a VIP passenger seat for the race. Afterwards, you fly the plane back to Bristol. Piece of cake, as you used to say in your RAF days." Quentin looked satisfied with his offer.

"Fly the plane? Why me? I haven't flown a commercial airliner in years. Surely you have other, more capable pilots?" Max remembered he'd flown a prototype A350 when it was first being touted around the bazaars. The engineering and build-quality were superb but the on-board computer systems had a mind of their own. Very French, was his verdict at the time. Factor in a nuclear power plant and things could get messy.

"It's simply a matter of trust, Max. We have an experienced aircrew for the race itself, but any skulduggery will happen well before the wheels leave the runway. I need a man who will deliver the plane without any hiccups or interference. There's too much at stake if this goes wrong. Will you do it?"

Before Max could reply, Quentin added. "The race has to be completed within a 50-hour window. You're flying west to east, passing over eight Sky Stations, as they're calling them. San Francisco, Japan, China, India, Middle East, Europe, UK, over the Atlantic, New York and back to Missouri. The UN will have observers on board and at the Sky Stations. I won't bore you with the rules now. You'd be away for less than a week."

"And when's this supposed to happen?" Max was warming to the idea. No doubt conversations about government-backed IT projects would be easier to have once the prize money was in the bank.

"Tomorrow soon enough? I'm told the plane is ready to go. They've done all the engine tests, simulations, and a few spins around Bristol. Nothing like getting her up and stretching her legs though, is there?"

Max was going to ask again about the question of risk when a gentle tap on the door broke his concentration. Trouser Suit showed the other guest into the room. She'd thoughtfully brought a tray of fresh coffee with her, but no more biscuits.

Quentin was on his feet, pumping the man's hand like he was trying to breathe new life back into him. Max gave the man a tick for having successfully attached his visitor pass to the lapel of his aging, tweed jacket, even if it was upside down.

"Max, may I introduce Dr Robert Stannard."

CHAPTER 6

Stannard was tall, well over six foot, with wild, grey hair, tangled beard, and black rimmed glasses, all askew. One of the arms was clumsily held together with tape. His jacket was well worn, had a couple of holes in it, with the collar half turned up.

His fawn-coloured slacks had what looked like a paint stain down one side. He wore old leather sandals over red, woollen socks. He had the look of a man never quite able to cope with the mundanity of day-to-day life.

"Dr Stannard is Professor of Nuclear Physics at Brandon College, Oxford." Quentin proudly announced, "And is Chief Scientific Adviser to the Comet Aeronautics Group. He designed the propulsion systems."

It must be more like Bedlam College, Max smiled to himself. If this man designed the nuclear reactor, there were some serious questions to be answered. Max wouldn't have sent him out with a shopping list on his own, let alone design a potentially lethal power generator at the cutting edge of science.

"We worked together on the design and build of the new Achilles-class submarines for the Indian Navy some years back. And there was that nuclear powered aircraft carrier project as well, Robert, for the French Navy." Quentin sounded like he was trying to reassure himself, Max thought.

"Aircraft carrier? I don't remember that." Stannard looked puzzled.

"Well, yes, it didn't get off the starting blocks once the designs were finished, too expensive in the end." Quentin composed himself. "But money is not a problem for *Comet 5*, I'm pleased to say. Robert, please explain the propulsion systems to our friend here."

"Yes, very well, you see, Rex, we've opted for thorium as the main fuel source."

"Max, my name is Max."

"Sorry, Max, I'm not good with names."

"Never mind, please continue. What is thorium?" Max had been ready to say yes to this project but now Stannard was worrying him.

"Thorium is a weakly radioactive metal, discovered in the nineteenth century by Scandinavian scientists who named it after Thor, the Norse God of thunder. It has some applications today, but it lost out to plutonium after the Second World War as it couldn't be weaponised."

Stannard was talking while fishing in his briefcase. When the handful of scruffy notes finally emerged, he couldn't find the pages he was looking for and tossed them all onto the table in disgust.

"Thorium has three big advantages." Quentin interrupted, trying to move things along. "Firstly, it's safe. There is little or no threat of a radiation leak as our fast-neutron reactor uses molten salt, not water, as the coolant, enabling any chain reaction to be switched off instantly, if needed."

Max noticed that Stannard had found some graphs he thought might help but Quentin had stolen his thunder, literally.

"Secondly, it's naturally abundant and therefore cheap. We all have trace elements of thorium in our bodies. There's enough thorium in the USA today to meet the country's energy needs for the next thousand years, at current consumption rates." Quentin added.

Stannard put down the graphs and cut back in. "And thirdly, it's environmentally friendly. Zero carbon emissions, thorium decomposes in three hundred years compared to plutonium 94 with a half-life of twenty-four thousand years. Even a plastic bag will take a thousand years to fully decompose."

"Tell him the best part that will really get the tree-huggers excited." Quentin took the *Comet 5* report from Max and slipped it back into his attaché case, preparing to leave.

"Oh yes, Rex, we've found a way to mix thorium 232 with some nuclear waste products that improves efficiency and reduces cost even further."

"So, you could start re-using some of the nasty stuff we've got buried in disused mines?" Max didn't bother correcting him again. He'd settle for being called Rex for now. But the big questions remained. For that, he addressed Quentin.

"How safe is the plane, Quentin? Thorium is still radioactive. What shielding is there for the passengers and crew on board? And what about range? How much thorium do we need to cover the journey?"

Quentin grabbed Stannard by the arm, indicating he'd answer the first part. "The reactor is contained in a protective shield made from a combination of polyethylene, lead crystal and carbon-enriched concrete. Tests have shown no leakage. We've got radiation monitors on the plane that will shut down the reactor automatically. And, before you ask, we have lithium-ion batteries as back-up that will give you six hours flying time, long enough to get down safely."

Stannard took his cue. "And as for range, thorium is energy efficient. One ton of thorium produces the same amount of energy as two hundred tons of uranium or three million tons of coal. We'll need very little thorium to power *Comet 5*, probably a few kilos. You could fly round the world non-stop for years. And the whole propulsion system weighs less than a grand piano."

"All of which data we'll be happy to share with you before you fly." Quentin was on his feet. "I must dash, Max, so tell me. In or out?"

"In."

"Excellent news, welcome on board." Quentin started pumping Max's right hand. Stannard joined in by grabbing his left hand in an awkward manoeuvre. The three men beamed at each other like they'd achieved something momentous.

Quentin explained he would send Max some documents to sign, background papers on things he needed to know, a non-disclosure agreement, a confidentiality contract and a proposal regarding remuneration for his services. Stannard would walk him through the actual propulsion system details for *Comet 5* if he had time now, which he did.

After Quentin left the room, Stannard became far more relaxed. He slipped his jacket off, poured more coffee and put his papers into some semblance of order. He even snaffled the last chocolate biscuit which, by now, was starting to melt.

"I'm afraid all this politics and arm twisting is not my thing." Stannard explained. "I suppose as an RAF pilot you had to be diplomatic and polished in the social graces. Even more so now as a CEO."

"How much do you know about me?" Max was curious to see what Quentin had told him.

"You're the man to have in a crisis, is what he said. You're used to adapting. If things went wrong, as they must have done with prototypes, the pilot had to improvise and maintain calm in the cockpit. Quentin was very complimentary. He'll be delighted you said yes. I've a sneaky suspicion having you as one of the race

56

passengers will give him a sort of insurance policy in case something should go wrong during the race itself."

"Are you one of the VIP's?" Max enquired.

"Yes, wouldn't miss this for the world. Theoretical physics is fascinating but seeing your ideas come to life, that's something special indeed."

"Is Quentin among the VIP's? Is he coming round with us?"

"You know, I don't think he is. Not wanting to hog the limelight, I suppose. He said he sees it as a chance to impress potential clients, given such limited capacity." Stannard replied.

This seemed somewhat unusual. Quentin was a peacock, after all. Max half expected him to have soundbites ready for when he stepped out in front of the world's media, a victory speech akin to *one small step for man*.

"So, what are your plans?" Max was starting to think about the arrangements he'd have to put in place to cover his CEO role if he was going to disappear for a week.

"The timing works well for me. I'm giving a lecture to the US Atomic Energy Commission at Columbia University. The following day I'm addressing the Annual Conference for the Global Nuclear Forum in Manhattan. Then I'm heading over to St Louis."

"By which time I will have delivered the plane, no doubt."

"Yes, there are some engineers joining you on the flight across, as well as PR, marketing and UN people cadging a free ride, I believe. You will have a capable co-pilot and cabin crew. All creature comforts, no expense spared." Stannard explained.

"And in St Louis?" Max thought he'd better ask these questions now if Stannard was going to be preoccupied with his speeches. The man seemed to be permanently preoccupied.

"We've chartered a hangar on the far side of the main runway, away from prying eyes, as Quentin put it. We'll be able to fine tune the engines and get her ready for final FAA inspection and certification. We've already had the nod so it should be a formality."

"Last question, how different is flying the plane with a nuclear propulsion system?" Apart from the bleeding obvious, Max reflected. Sitting on top of a molten-salt reactor with enough radioactive fuel on board to keep the plane airborne for the next 30 years, that's going to test even his powers of adaption.

Max was starting to get excited about this venture. His initial mistrust for Quentin, a hare-brained plan to fly a nuclear plane round the world and the sudden arrival of an absent-minded Oxford professor, all these obstacles were fading away.

Fundamentally at heart, Max was still a fighter pilot who thrived on pushing the envelope, testing things to the limit, and seeing how far he could go. He loved the adrenalin rush when opening the throttle, not knowing what was about to happen. This was the sharp end of aviation. Risk and reward. His blood was already pumping. He was ready to give it a go.

"Basically, there's very little difference, from the pilot's perspective." Stannard reported calmly. "You'll have a few more instruments showing how the reactor's performing and the capacity of the power storage units. But you won't have to monitor fuel consumption or the flying time you have left.

"The actual thrust output is very similar, slightly enhanced actually. You'll find the jet engines respond much quicker." Stannard smiled for the first time. "We still call them jet engines even though they're electric.

58

The terminology isn't keeping pace with the technology, I suppose."

"And exhaust fumes? Noise levels?"

"Thing of the past. It truly is a whispering jet. Bit disconcerting at first but you'll get used to it. We've been working on this propulsion system in the lab for some time. I never thought we'd ever get the chance to see it in action. It's robust and quite a clever bit of kit. You can't break it if that's what you're thinking. Anything else?"

"Yes, what about take-off weight?

"Not really an issue. There have been electric planes flying since the seventies, running on little more than a car battery. For them, range is limited, and take-off weight is a crucial factor. The race organisers have stipulated it has to be a normal plane, with normal people having a normal flying experience with drinks trolleys, luggage, and proper food, well airline food, at least. If the public is to trust electric commercial airliners, they must see them as normal not prototypes."

The door opened with immaculate timing. Trouser Suit showed them out in perfect silence, down the stone steps to the main reception area and helped them exit through security. Stannard managed to get his visitor badge stuck to his fingers. In frustration, he scrunched it up and slipped it into his trouser pocket rather than placing it in the receptacle provided.

"It's a pleasure to make your acquaintance, Robert. I'm looking forward to working together. Meet me in St Louis." Max nearly burst into song as he shook his new friend's hand again. "You're heading back to the dreaming spires now?"

Indeed, he was, via Paddington Station. Stannard hailed a black cab which quickly melted into the traffic crawling round Parliament Square. Max decided to walk back to the office in Blackfriars along the Embankment.

The fresh air would help him think. And plan. He needed to rearrange his diary. But did he need to update his will?

As he strolled past the Royal Air Force Memorial opposite Admiralty House, one question kept nagging at him.

There had been nuclear submarines and naval vessels for decades. So why hadn't nuclear-powered planes been tried before? Or had they?

CHAPTER 7

The lace curtains had gone. Brussels Town Hall had turned into a colourful African print showing hot air balloons over the Serengeti at sunrise. The Reptile Queen was no more, although her evil spirit still haunted some of the darker corners of UN Headquarters.

Betty Gachuhi was feeling frustrated. Although many of her new projects were starting to bear fruit, especially regarding famine relief, refugees and peacekeeping initiatives, the narrative was very much, *moving towards* and *early days*, *making progress* and *heading in the right direction*. We'd heard all this before, was the cynical response. She called it *creating the illusion of progress*.

The one success so far was the *UN Crystal Clear Skies Challenge*. She had successfully won over the flat earthers by arguing that fossil fuels could be phased out more quickly once a proven, financially viable alternative was available. The race merely speeded up the technological advancement.

Also, competition didn't have to be divisive. There was ample opportunity for good ideas to be explored and tested. It may well be, she argued, that the money being invested in the race would enable new thinking to flourish that otherwise might never have got off first base. The cream will always rise to the top, especially when pride and big prize money were at stake.

Betty was delighted two consortia had stepped forward. They had deep pockets and had already pumped millions in getting two very different commercial airliners up to the starting line.

The Americans had converted a Boeing 787 Dreamliner to run as a hybrid on green hydrogen with greatly enhanced power storage capabilities. Betty had been impressed by her visit to Seattle and was given a short test flight.

Entrants were required to give seven days' notice prior to making their attempt. An entry fee of $250,000 was also required to cover administration costs. Five UN observers would need to be on board. The attempt was to be made within a 50-hour time window, starting and finishing at St Louis Lambert International Airport. Observers would be positioned at the eight Sky Stations.

We are already past the 1st October, she reflected, staring out at a cloudburst driving heavy rain against her office windows. Technically, the race was on. Media interest was growing.

The *New Spirit of St Louis* was just waiting for FAA approval then they would file for entry and bring the plane down to Missouri. Amid tight security, the Lindbergh Aviation Inc. PR machine was creating quite a buzz on social media, with their website getting over a million clicks for the first time yesterday.

But Betty wanted more. The reports she was getting about the need to reduce carbon emissions were disturbing. Glaciers melting, sea levels rising, wild weather across Europe, floods and droughts in Africa, hurricanes and tornadoes causing havoc in the mid-west, it appeared nowhere was safe. Even her native Kenya was suffering the driest spell since records began.

A sharp knock on the door. Betty turned to see the smiling face of her new assistant, Chantelle. "I've got 007 on line 2. He says it's urgent."

Betty shook her head as she moved back to the mahogany desk and reached for the phone. Chantelle was the antidote to the Reptile Queen. Always cheerful, accommodating and infinitely flexible, she anticipated problems before they appeared and had the innate capacity to defuse even the most explosive situation. Best of all, though, she cared. This wasn't a game to her either. Working together, they would really make a difference.

"Please don't call him that, you'll get me into trouble. He's not that good looking, anyhow." Betty waved her hand to say she had the call, now leave before you embarrass me.

"Quentin, what can I do for you?" Betty had spoken to him several times during the build-up. He'd used his cool English accent and persuasive diplomatic demeanour to good effect so far in squeezing some minor concessions out of her. Whilst she wanted to help any entrant if she could, she had been around the diplomatic community long enough to watch out for any potential allegations of bias or favouritism. Help yes, negotiate no.

"Betty, just wanted to let you know that *Comet 5* is flying over to Missouri tomorrow. We have some final tweaks to make before the FAA inspection the day after." Quentin announced, setting the scene for some arm-twisting to come, Betty surmised. *Always lead in with good news*.

"I'm delighted to hear that, Quentin, we look forward to welcoming her to the race."

"A couple of suggestions, if I may." His voice was calm. Here it comes, she smiled to herself.

"You intonated when last we spoke that the other consortium is nearly ready for entry. Is that still the case?"

"Yes, we expect to receive their documentation shortly. Why?"

"I've got several corporate sponsors looking to take advertising space if the global TV audience is big enough covering the race start. I know it's not stipulated that both planes take off together, but it would make it feel more like a race, don't you think?"

Betty pondered this. If both planes are ready, then why not? It would certainly focus media attention. "What do you have in mind, Quentin?"

"I'm suggesting an Americas Cup type start. Both planes take off, enter a starting box then cross the line when you fire the gun, so to speak. We'd need some rules about safety and distance but I'm sure they could be worked through. No starboard tacks at two thousand feet or whatever."

Betty liked the idea. After days of persuading numerous lobby groups who were trying to get the race postponed or even cancelled, it was refreshing to hear someone excited about her brainchild. Better still, that someone was the CEO of one of her entrants. And a very handsome CEO as well, she had to admit.

"I'll give that some thought and get back to you. Was there anything else?"

"Yes, I've been thinking about the prize money." Quentin continued.

I bet you have, Betty thought. $10 billion had certainly created the impact she hoped it would.

"I wondered if you'd consider splitting it into a first and second place. I'm proposing $7.5 billion and $2.5 billion. If the planes get round with no mishaps or nasty emissions, it would prove that both technologies offer viable alternatives to fossil fuels. If we don't win but complete the race, a second-place fee would at least help cover our costs. What do you think?"

Betty had considered this idea previously but decided consolation prizes were not in the true spirit of competition. Maybe she'd consider it next time she used the competition approach to address global problems facing humanity. She told him the answer was no, it was

64

winner-takes-all but thanked him for the suggestion. Quentin was disappointed but accepted it in good grace.

Betty was about to disconnect when Quentin added. "Betty, did I read that you're due in London for a meeting with our PM soon? Downing Street is just down the road from my offices here in the House."

Indeed, she was. A series of meetings had been arranged with several European heads to discuss the worsening refugee crisis. London, Paris, and Berlin were on her initial agenda, but she was trying to squeeze in Rome and possibly Warsaw.

With widening inequality over the distribution of wealth, an energy crisis and worsening living conditions in many countries around the world, some of which were the result of pointless conflicts, the tide of refugees flowing into Europe was in danger of becoming a tsunami.

Quentin was clearly angling towards a meeting which she thought wouldn't be appropriate. But if she was in London when the race went over, that could be a big PR coup and get masses of media coverage. She would check her diary with Chantelle later.

"I have a busy schedule, Quentin, so it may not be possible. Thanks for your call. Best wishes for the race." Betty disconnected.

The more she thought about the *race for the starting line* idea, the more she liked it. Chantelle came in carrying two mugs of earl grey tea, extra hot. Perfect timing as usual, how did she know? They discussed the start idea. It sounded like a winner, especially if it generated more media interest. They agreed that Chantelle would circulate it to the judging panel and add it to the agenda for the next online meeting tomorrow.

"I was chatting to him before you came on the line." Chantelle had a gleam in her eyes. "He's divorced, lives in a pied-a-terre overlooking the Thames, has just bought himself a vintage Aston Martin DB5 and likes to go rowing. I think you'll deserve a little R&R in London with 007 after all this, don't you? You've achieved more in weeks than your predecessor did in years. The UN is back in the thick of world politics. Give yourself a pat on the back, girl. No one else will, that's for sure, apart from me, of course."

* * *

Quentin was pacing his office like a caged hyena. Her dismissal of the suggestion to split the prize money left him with a problem. The growing irregularities in the Comet Aeronautics Group accounts had not yet surfaced. He had to keep it that way.

His appointment as CFO of a Harvard Business School graduate who majored in financial analysis and fiscal policy got past the board unnoticed. Quentin was greatly relieved they thought he was a clean-cut, young American with lots of future potential.

His New England pedigree and Ivy League credentials, coupled with his private pilot's licence, film-star good looks and educated taste for the finer things in life, made him a perfect choice, Quentin decided. The fact that he had no accounting qualifications, knew little about UK tax laws and had only a passing interest in double entry bookkeeping clinched the deal for him.

Quentin knew things had gone past the point of no return. Even if he could pay back the money he'd siphoned off, there were deep enough holes in the accounts to bury his reputation. Maybe even jail time if the press got hold of it. It had been just too tempting and too easy. He'd cleared all his gambling debts at the casino and with the bookmakers.

66

He'd reasoned it all out but still had the problem. If *Comet 5* wins the race, the auditors will quickly find the irregularities. There would be an investigation and Quentin would be ruined. Sure, he would pick up a bonus along with his salary, but it wouldn't be enough to plug the gap. Winning the race would be disastrous for him.

Whereas, if *Comet 5* loses or doesn't return, the investors might write the whole thing off as bad luck. Spending more money on an audit report wouldn't be appealing. The $2.5 billion might have sweetened the pill but that wasn't to be. The whole venture would be written off, the losses offset against tax and *Comet 5* would just become a case study in failure for future MBA courses. This would give him a chance of getting clear.

Quentin had considered taking out an additional insurance policy. It could cover most of the expenditure costs in the event of failure. He had a friendly broker who would take his money, no questions asked. It was starting to look like a realistic option but not without risk. If the existence of the policy became known, after it paid out, Quentin was back to square one and the finger of suspicion would be pointing at him.

There was, of course, another possible solution. He stopped pacing and picked up his phone. He'd put the number in the directory only the other day. He hesitated. It was also a huge risk.

Maybe it was a risk he had to take.

CHAPTER 8

Tonight's delicacy is king prawn surprise, the chef announced with a flourish as Hannah stepped through the door. He handed her a large glass of chilled pinot grigio, adding, with a smile, she looked like a woman who needed it.

Hannah had to ask, her curiosity being too much. Where had he got the prawns from as she'd had the car all day and he was supposedly working from home? Had he taken the bus into town?

"It's grilled pork, from the freezer. That's the surprise."

She should have known. Lawrence's British sense of humour could be a blessing and a curse. She went through to freshen up. It took longer than usual to shower as she kept seeing the young girl's face in the steam, hearing her whispered voice. *Amani.*

Hannah dried off, wrapped the towel around herself and padded through to the laptop in the spare room. In a few moments, she'd found what she was looking for.

"It means hope in Swahili." Hannah took the last piece of pork. The chef had truly excelled himself. It turned out to be a very tasty surprise.

"What does?" Lawrence had struggled throughout dinner. Hannah seemed distracted, with him one minute then gone the next, back into her own private world.

Since arriving in Rome, the spiritual Hannah had all but disappeared. Lawrence had seen many times over recent years how she could connect to other worlds using her sixth sense. He wondered if she had somehow muted these powers on account of her new job. He guessed being a female psychic in the male-dominated halls of the

68

Vatican wouldn't have featured much in the job description.

"*Amani*. It's what she said to me in the dream. It translates as hope, peace, or harmony. It's a sign. Other forces are at work here."

"Swahili, you say. Well, Miss Smarty Pants, *I've* been doing some digging today as well. Swahili is the language of the coastal plains of Kenya, not the interior. Your dream girl must be shy of the mark." Lawrence fingered the air in victory, 1-0.

"Then you didn't go deep enough, lover boy. You'll have to go beyond Wikipedia if you want to be the second Dr McGlynn in this apartment."

Hannah had a few surprises of her own. "Lake Turkana was once connected to the Nile. The watercourse was disrupted thousands of years ago by lava flows and earthquakes, that's why it's full of crocodiles and Nile perch. Arab traders went up the river as well as down the coast. The Turkana are a Nilotic people who speak a language of many different tongues, including Swahili."

Although he had to concede defeat over this language point, with a PhD in his crosshairs, Lawrence wasn't finished showing off his online research prowess just yet.

"Talking of volcanic rocks, did you read the article about the burglary at the Natural History Museum in Vienna? Apparently, most of Crown Prince Rudolf's mineral collection was stolen, including some rocks from the 1888 expedition." Lawrence beamed triumphantly. Clearly Hannah wasn't up to speed with this story.

"Vienna? Crown Prince who? What's this got to do with the Turkana?" Hannah shook her head. In the dream, the bird of prey had been quickly followed by other images far more troubling. Death, disease, and famine: a village littered with dying animals and helpless people begging for mercy. It had left her shaken.

"Everything, my dear girl. The first Europeans named it Lake Rudolf after their patron, the Austrian Crown Prince. He stumped up the dosh for their expedition to explore East Africa. His hobby was geology, so they brought him some lumps of rock back from the shoreline. The specimens were so unusual they took pride of place in his collection. When he died, the collection was donated to the museum in Vienna. Someone nicked them a few months ago."

"Nicked? Were they precious stones? Just lying by the lake? Surely not." Hannah was only half listening. She kept thinking back to Agnes, the dream girl, and the meeting with Cardinal Maina. It had been a very strange day. By the time she had awoken, her team had gone home, including Fabio, who left her a note. He would update her tomorrow, it said.

"That's the thing. The rocks had no real value, according to the article. The police were baffled. The thieves ignored precious gems on display nearby. They only took these worthless rocks. Another unsolved mystery surrounding your lake."

"So, it was called Lake Rudolf? When did the name change?" Hannah mopped up the last of the sauce with some crusty bread.

"After Kenyan independence in 1975. The Turkana are the biggest tribe so it was named after them but there are plenty of others. Most of them are still fighting amongst themselves. It sounds like a bit of a wild frontier."

Hannah barely registered his reply, her mind still combing over other more important dilemmas. Lawrence noticed she'd drifted away again.

"Dr McGlynn, I know you well enough to know you're struggling with something. Spit it out, please." Lawrence led the way to the couch and resumed last night's

70

massage, hoping to hit the right spot again, a portal to a world of sinful pleasures.

Hannah tried in vain to get comfortable. "I want to help her. Agnes looked so lonely, so desperate. I'm her last hope. I checked the airlines. There's a direct flight tomorrow morning, Kenya Airways, gets into Jomo Kenyatta International at seven p.m. local time. I've got seats on hold. Overnight in Nairobi, there's an early flight to Lodwar the following day. We can be in her village by the day after tomorrow."

"Then what's stopping us?" He'd guessed this might be what was on her mind. Kenya had always been on Lawrence's bucket list, but he was thinking Maasai Mara, Mount Kilimanjaro, and the coastal resorts of Malindi and Mombasa. The prospect of visiting a crocodile-infested lake in a desolate war zone just wasn't doing it for him.

"But, well, you see.....it just doesn't work. I need to stay here and get ready for the UN presentation. New York's my big chance to make an impact. I don't want to blow it." Hannah twisted round to face him.

'So how long are you thinking?" Lawrence's fingers had found the spot. He applied some gentle pressure. She moved rhythmically under his fingers but still couldn't relax.

"A week, maybe less."

Lawrence was running through practicalities. They'd recently had booster jabs. Their diaries were relatively quiet. Airlines and hotels were offering great deals. They could pick up currency at the airport, but heaven knows what they'd spend it on. Lake Turkana was a long way off the beaten track and miles from any tourist destinations. And what about visas? He'd have to check.

And availability at the local kennels. At the mention of the word, Trigger was sat by his side, resting his head on

71

Lawrence's knee. Although they did look after him, being spoilt in kennels wasn't the same as being spoilt at home.

"If we need longer, we can always go back." Hannah managed a weak smile. Maybe this was do-able after all. But it still left the big stumbling block.

"OK, I hear this, so what's the real problem?" Lawrence was already imagining herds of wildebeest coming down to drink at sunset.

"Politics." Hannah was suddenly on her feet, pacing the floor. "To go through proper diplomatic channels, I'll need to notify the local World Health Organisation office, the Kenyan Government, even the Catholic Church hierarchy above Father Kelly. That will lead me back to Cardinal Maina who'll have our passports confiscated at the airport, no doubt."

Lawrence smiled and patted the couch beside him. He topped up her glass to tempt her back. She acquiesced and sat down. As soon as she reached for her glass, she leapt to her feet again, pacing backwards and forwards, continuing to think out loud. "I'll just get bombarded with official statistics, proving there's nothing wrong. The defensive barriers will go up. I'll be shepherded around or kept under house arrest in Nairobi before being sent back to Rome with a flea in my ear. Either way, I'll never find out what killed Agnes's husband."

"Then don't go through diplomatic channels." Lawrence struggled to his feet and stood next to her, his arms folding around her shoulders. Slowly she realised what he'd said. This was the answer. A broad smile flashed across her face.

"In all your confusion, you've forgotten you're a McGlynn now. Remember our family motto?" He smiled.

"I didn't know we had one."

"*Ignoscentia non Probatio*. It loosely translates as *Seek forgiveness not approval*."

72

"I didn't think the Romans got as far as Ireland." Hannah took his hand and led him back to the couch.

"They didn't. But I'm sure that's what they would have said if they'd met my family. It's always been good advice." Lawrence resumed the massage.

"Alright then, what do you have in mind, Mr McGlynn?" Hannah closed her eyes, trying to unwind.

Lawrence was happy to point out she'd been so uptight with feelings of guilt, political correctness and worry, that she'd missed the bleeding obvious. "We take a week's holiday. Tell the office I've secretly booked a short break, to make up for the honeymoon we didn't get in Rio. You knew nothing about it until I presented you with the tickets over dinner tonight. How does that sound?"

"Sounds perfect, but what about when we get there? Without access to official records, how will we find out what's going on?"

"You said yourself, official records won't tell us anything. As far as anyone knows or cares, we're lounging by a pool somewhere. We'll hire a local guide and do some digging. From previous experience, we don't need any help getting ourselves into trouble, Dr McGlynn."

"OK, I'm in. Let's do it." Hannah suddenly felt relieved. The decision was made. It was the right call. *The Voice of God.*

They agreed on a plan. Lawrence was to confirm the flights Hannah had reserved, sort out the hotels and arrange visas if required. Hannah would call Father Kelly on his mobile, just in case anyone in the Vatican was listening.

Lawrence quickly discovered the Turkana Lodge. He showed Hannah the website. It looked amazing. He called them to check availability. His holiday budget would stretch to a week at discounted rates in the luxurious

73

Lotikipi Suite, a colonial-style villa with panoramic views over the lake. The dawn hot air balloon flight with champagne breakfast was tempting.

They regrouped back on the couch half an hour later. Hannah was tingling with excitement. *The courage to change the things I can.*

Father Kelly was delighted at her decision. He would meet them at Lodwar Airport and drive them over to Agnes's village, Hannah reported. He believed the holiday cover story would work. He knew a local guide who spoke good English and would sound him out. He also gave the Lodge a vote of approval, from what he'd heard, even though he'd never stayed there himself.

"They've lifted visa restrictions to encourage more tourism." Lawrence announced jubilantly. "We get our passports stamped on arrival. We can stay or return within three months. The receptionist at the Lodge was charming. She said they'll send a boat to collect us from the village. If we're struggling to find a guide, they can recommend someone. The flights are booked but there's only fifteen kilos allowance on the local plane, so we'll need to travel light."

"That's what I had in mind anyway." Hannah smiled.

"We'll just need one set of decent clothes, for dinner at the stopover hotel in Nairobi. I think they're more relaxed these days from when Ernest Hemingway stayed there." Lawrence kept his face deadpan, to see if she was listening.

"Really? Hemingway? You know how to treat a girl." Hannah was fizzing. The indecision was over. She didn't know what to expect from this trip but if she could save lives, it would be the most worthwhile thing she'd achieved in this job so far.

Lawrence gave her the details for The Stanley Hotel. Hannah explained that Father Kelly was keen for them to have dinner with some very special friends of his in Nairobi. He was going to see if they could make it.

As she was talking, her phone pinged in its charger. Father Kelly's text confirmed they'd arranged a babysitter and could meet them around 9.00pm. Lawrence called the hotel and booked a table for four in The Thorn Tree restaurant.

Lawrence drained the bottle. No more tonight, he decided. It would be an early start. They chinked glasses. Lawrence looked puzzled. "Who are these friends? Did Father Kelly say?"

"He was quite secretive. I suppose he didn't want to let us down if they couldn't make it. But he did promise we'd find them fascinating and possibly helpful, whatever that means."

"Don't tell me we'll get dragged into another Catholic Church conjuring trick?" Lawrence added.

"We won't have time for that. People are dying. We need to find out why."

CHAPTER 9

In his heart of hearts, Detective Sergeant Steven Mole had to admit their relationship was falling apart. Worse, he didn't know why. He'd spotted some tell-tale signs. She'd seemed happy enough with her new job. It was a real challenge, she'd said, her dream job, exactly what she was looking for. But now he was beginning to doubt she'd been telling the truth.

It was the sudden mood swings that surprised him. They were getting more exaggerated. Happy one minute, homesick for Britain the next. He would find himself in an argument over trivial things. Who should unload the dishwasher or take the rubbish out? He didn't like the word trash. And he never even wanted a dishwasher; it just came with the apartment.

Things had been so good when they first moved to New York. They hadn't lived together before. In fact, they hardly knew each other. It just felt so right. Thrown together in unlikely circumstances, they soon found they had so much in common, with similar tastes and an aching desire to make more of their lives. She had grown on him to the point where he couldn't imagine life without her.

For Sophia, it was second time around. She'd lived alone since the pain of divorce. For Steve, he'd been married to the job for too long. The idea of a steady relationship hadn't featured on his radar until they met. Her soft, oatmeal-blonde hair and electric-blue eyes enticed him. Being an ex-policewoman added to the intrigue. He felt they had a shared sense of purpose. He wanted to know what made her laugh, made her cry, what excited her, what adventures lay ahead. He was hooked.

The offer of a secondment was totally unexpected but came at just the right time. The *crossroads dilemma*, he called it, when he was feeling a bit lost. He was approaching his mid- thirties with no career direction. She appeared like an angel, as if sent to him. The secondment meant moving from Surrey to the Big Apple. It was a risk for both of them. She didn't hesitate. Neither did he.

Soon they were choosing curtains and combing the flea markets across Tribeca, Soho, and Chelsea. They preferred old furniture and quirky, character pieces. He allowed himself a smile, recalling the day the Victorian brass bed was delivered and how they christened the mattress. The bed arrived before the sheets. The stain never did come out, a permanent reminder of their spontaneous and sublime lovemaking.

He'd left the office early and was waiting impatiently for her in the lobby of the Rokelle International Hotel and Conference Centre on 5th Avenue, opposite Central Park. She'd said five thirty. It was almost six. The place was heaving with trolleys full of luggage playing catch-up behind self-important guests in a hurry to check in.

To add to the melee, the ground floor conference rooms had disgorged an army of thirsty delegates, desperate for a drink before facing the rush hour traffic and the stifling heat outside.

It had been forecast as the hottest October day on record with the mercury expected to touch a hundred. The hotel's air conditioning was struggling to keep the huge lobby area bearable. Steve could hear sighs of relief from sweaty visitors when they spun into the crowded space through the revolving doors.

He thought it ironic Sophia wanted to meet him here. The Rokelle International Hotel was next door to where the Klinkenhammer Foundation building had stood. It was his work on that case whilst in Surrey CID which brought him to the attention of the NYPD and ultimately led to the secondment.

There had been tough times after they relocated, but they'd pulled together and got through it. Now one of his bosses was talking secondment extension or even a permanent transfer. Steve loved New York and was excited at the prospect.

At first, he'd been directly involved in complex homicide cases connected to the Klinkenhammer incident. It was high profile detective work. The pace was relentless yet engrossing. Once the criminals were finally brought to justice and the workload dropped off, Steve was transferred to his current role in fraud investigation.

It was a very different kind of policing, he reflected. He was getting great exposure to the FBI, city law and accountancy firms, the IRS and even contacts on Wall Street. But it was dry, number crunching, analysis work, sat behind a desk all day, with cases sometimes dragging on for years. Although it was important, fraud lacked the adrenalin rush of homicide.

One such case was proving problematic. He'd been trying to speak to Constance Pemberton for weeks. She refused to return his calls or emails. It could all be resolved quickly, he felt, if she'd just answer a few simple questions. With fraud, there was no easy way to create urgency which only added to the frustration.

Earlier that day, Steve had spoken to his boss about getting a green card. It didn't seem to be a problem. We have friends in the right places, he'd said. But when Steve asked about getting a transfer back to homicide, he didn't get a proper answer. The implication was, if you scratch my back, I'll scratch yours. Do a good job for me, keep your nose clean in fraud and I'll see if a transfer is possible, sometime in the future.

Standing there in the hotel lobby, it wasn't the job or the green card that worried him. Fraud, homicide, it didn't really matter. He still got a kick out of police work, bringing the bad guys to justice. Steve knew the big challenge was going to be Sophia. He'd planned on discussing everything over dinner tonight. He was just thinking about how best to play it when his phone rang. He didn't recognise the number.

"Steve, is that you?" English accent, female, Steve thought the voice sounded familiar.

"Yes, who is this?"

"It's me, Maria, you haven't forgotten me already, have you?"

Steve had been watching a group of delegates as they spilled out of one of the smaller conference rooms. They all looked a bit weird, like mad scientists on a day trip from the lab. One stood out. He seemed to be the centre of attention, slightly taller than the others but just as awkward. They started grouping around him after they'd finally got their drinks.

"Maria, it's great to hear from you again. Long time, no speak, how the devil are you?" The signal wasn't strong enough. Her voice kept fading in and out. Why can't they invent things that work? He tried moving over by the revolving doors. Only marginally better.

"So, so. Look, Steve, have you got a minute?" She sounded quite upset. He could sense hesitancy in her voice. Some years back, she was introduced to him as a forensics expert by his ex-boss in Surrey, Detective Inspector David Lonsdale.

Maria Li turned out to be a civilian with attitude. She thought like a police officer and shared his passion for bringing criminals to justice. She'd been seconded to the NYPD at the same time he had. They worked together through the Klinkenhammer caseload, but when it dried up, she moved offices, and they lost touch. It was good to hear a friendly voice.

"Sure, always time for you, Maria. What's on your mind?"

She told him about her transfer to the Forensics Department, initially based in Downtown but last year she was moved over to Yonkers. "I'm the department's eyes and ears in a serial rape case. We're piecing together tiny fragments of medical evidence. It's highly sensitive work and involves a TV celebrity, so I can't talk about it. Most of the technical stuff has been outsourced to a specialist laboratory. That's where I spend most days."

"So, you're babysitting, is that it?" Steve suggested.

"Exactly." Maria sounded almost in tears. "I just check they're doing what we've asked them to do. They're getting paid a fortune and there's no urgency. Sometimes I think we're just going through the motions, to make it look like we're investigating, with no real intention to get to the truth or bring a prosecution. Well, ticking boxes is not my style, you know that."

"Not your style or mine, Maria. I'm in a similar situation in the fraud team. I seem to be doing the grunt work no one else wants to do. Being on secondment means you can't really argue with them. I still love New York and don't regret moving here but I miss homicide."

"That's why I called, Steve, just curious, I guess, to see how you're getting on. I'm thinking of going back to the UK unless something changes. I'm bored and wasting my time here."

Steve arranged to meet her for a coffee the following week and disconnected. He'd never heard her sound so emotional. Maria had been the voice of reason, the cool, calculating professional who asked the sharp questions and got straight to the heart of things. This sounded like a huge waste of her talent.

He remembered she'd trained as an electrical engineer and moved into police work later in life. It suited better for her young family. Steve couldn't recall what her husband did, he didn't feature much in her conversation. She loved Sudoku, crossword puzzles and playing Scrabble. They'd have some serious catching up to do. He was looking forward to that coffee.

He checked his watch again. Twenty past six. No messages from her. There was nothing to do but wait. He looked across at the mad scientists who were well into their evening drinks. He moved towards the tall man who was now holding court.

Steve noticed his drainpipe trousers were quite short. He was wearing old leather sandals over white tennis socks, which didn't entirely seem out of character. His tousled grey hair and bushy beard hadn't seen scissors or a comb for a while.

Suddenly Steve's phone chirped into life again. It was Sophia and about time too. She was nearly an hour late. He could hardly hear her over the background noise. He discovered the quietest place was over by a sculpture near where white socks and his entourage were gathered.

"I'm in the lobby, next to a bloody awful statue. I think it's a nun carrying the severed head of a lion." Steve had to raise his voice above the growing crescendo as the drinks lubricated the minds of the great, the good and the hangers-on. "Don't ask me what it means. The lion doesn't look very happy. I know how he feels."

Sophia apologised for running late. She had one more room to finish. Steve was going to ask finish doing what but thought better of it. Now wasn't the time. Another argument would just delay her. Instead, he told her to take her time as he was in no hurry. He would call the restaurant and push back the reservation.

He disconnected and noticed a sign next to the sculpture. *Find Your Courage Through Love* was a modern piece in marble and steel by Etienne de la Paix, symbolising the intrinsic bond between man's desire to love and his need to control the world around him. Worth every dollar, Steve concluded, shaking his head.

"Excuse me, but I couldn't help overhearing your British sense of humour, so refreshing. Which part of England are you from?" The small group of scientists had dissipated, leaving white socks alone, clutching an empty glass. He introduced himself as Dr Robert Stannard, holding out his left hand until Steve removed his empty glass and put it on a table next to the sculpture.

Steve always thought it amusing that two Englishmen would studiously ignore one another walking down Oxford Street, yet the same people would engage like long, lost friends when meeting in a foreign land.

"Surrey, born and bred." Steve replied. "How about you?"

"Actually, I was born in Bombay, my father was in the army, you see. We moved to Oxford when I was eight. I'm still there, can't get away from the place. He's long dead, of course. They call it Mumbai. Different world nowadays."

"And what brings you this side of the pond?" Steve was warming to the man who was doing his best to act normal but clearly had been off school the day they covered chit chat, human interaction and generally being sociable. Like many people blessed with huge intellectual horsepower, Steve could see Stannard was struggling to untangle his many thoughts as they raced into his mind.

"I've been presenting a paper at an Annual Conference. I say annual but it didn't happen last year. So much has changed, it was difficult to know where to start." Stannard did his best to explain. "Anyway, that wasn't why I

82

interrupted you. I've been in New York three days and I'm desperate for some pub grub. Is there anywhere decent to eat where they don't dish up fried food by the bucket-load?"

Steve smiled. He knew exactly what Stannard meant. It had taken him some time to realise that a small portion meant extra-large and super-size was a one-way ticket to the diabetes clinic. He'd put on seven pounds himself in the first month. Even the salad options were dripping in calories and the homemade bread contained more sugar than a Victoria sponge.

"There's a pub called *Shine The Light* on the corner of East 28th and Lexington. They have Fuller's London Pride on tap and some great guest beers. There's one from your neck of the woods. I think it's called Heavy Metal or something like that. Full bodied with a big head, if you like that sort of thing."

"You mean, Heavy Water Bitter? Really? Here in New York? Well, well. It's brewed down the road from me. They use styrian golding which is much more refined than the fuggles hop variety it was originally cloned from. It's one of my favourites, goes well with meat or fish."

Steve saw his face light up and thought he would add to his lip-smacking expectations. "The pub got a special mention in the CAMRA guide, international section. The menu is all steak and kidney, Yorkshire pudding, proper haddock and chips, spotted dick, the works. There's even real malt vinegar on the tables. You'll be right at home."

Stannard had already forgotten the name of the pub and the address. Steve found one of his old Surrey CID business cards in his trouser pocket and scribbled the details on the back.

Stannard couldn't thank him enough. "Heavy Water. That's how I came across the brewery. I was such a good customer they sponsored my work on fast-breeding reactors."

"Where are you staying?" Steve was happy to fill time with this man while scanning the room behind him. No sign of her yet. Did he say fast-breed reactors?

"A hotel off 7th Avenue called *Sixty-Nine*. It describes itself as boutique which means the rooms aren't big enough. I'm meeting someone there at seven thirty." Stannard pulled back his crumpled shirt sleeve to reveal the most impressive gold watch Steve had ever seen.

"That's some timepiece. May I?" Steve helped him as he fumbled to slip it off. According to the engraving on the back, this limited-edition Rolex Oyster Perpetual 22 was presented to him by none other than HRH Prince Charles, in recognition for his tireless work in nuclear energy.

"I've had it for years. It keeps excellent time." Stannard added as he slipped it back on. "It's been a pleasure to meet you, but I must be off. Thanks again for the recommendation. I might try the haddock."

They shook hands. Steve watched him weaving his way clumsily towards the revolving doors, bumping into several guests as he did so. Over his shoulder, he spotted Sophia coming across the lobby towards him.

He could tell by the flustered expression on her face that their dinner conversation was going to be hard work.

CHAPTER 10

The city was heaving. They had to wait outside in the sweltering heat for twenty minutes before getting a cab. The journey passed in painful silence. Steve knew he had to bring things to a head. This was no way to live. He still didn't understand what the problem was. There was only one way to find out.

When they finally got to the restaurant, they'd been squeezed into a corner near the kitchens which further darkened her mood. It was the only free table. The restaurant had been unhelpful when he called. Now he could see why. It was even busier than the hotel. A lethargic air conditioning unit above them was circulating warm air and looked none too clean.

Sophia had complained she was starving as they waited for the cab, yet now she wasn't hungry. The mood swings continued during the meal. One minute it was a playful smile and holding hands across the tablecloth, quickly followed by a complaint. The water wasn't cold enough. A glass was dirty. She was playing ice hockey with her colourless, vegetarian bake.

"How's your day?" Steve ventured, hoping she'd tell him what she'd been doing. Apply my detective training. Get her talking, the clues might come out. He had no such luck.

"OK, I suppose. The hotel manager was as rude as ever and my corporate client said I couldn't come in as I was late."

"Were you late?" Steve was enjoying his salmon and trying to find the right moment. There were glimmers of hope, but it wouldn't take much to start the next argument. He was getting tired of walking on eggshells.

"Only twenty minutes. The heat caused a systems failure or something on the subway. I lied and said the plants would all die and start smelling if I couldn't tend to them. He let me in but didn't so much as offer me a glass of water. What a total jerk."

Of course, Steve remembered, that's what she did. In her previous life, Sophia had studied horticulture. Her employer had contracts with clients all over New York to supply flowers, evergreens, and shrubs, mostly in hotels, offices, or top end residential properties. Her job was to keep them alive and make them look pretty. It seemed a good fit.

"Sophia, what's wrong?" Steve heard his own words without realising he'd actually spoken them. It was too late now. Attack was the only form of defence. "Is it the job? Is it New York? Is it me? There's something annoying you. You're not the same girl I moved here with. I just want you to be happy, us to be happy. What can I do to help? Please talk to me."

Sophia went very still. She put her knife and fork down, wiped a napkin slowly over her full lips and raised her stunning blue eyes to meet his. He got the sudden feeling he was on a film set and about to receive a rehearsed speech. "Steve, you're a very sweet man. Lots of girls would envy me. It's not you. I'm the problem. I thought living in New York would help me make a fresh start, you know, find myself."

Her eyes took a sudden interest in the bread roll. After a few moments, she found a quieter voice. "I don't know, I just feel…. trapped, I suppose. I can't breathe. The job's OK but I've got so much more to give. I need to express myself. Look, Steve, New York isn't for me, I realise that now. After Scotland, it's just too noisy, too full on. I haven't wanted to say anything. I know you love living here. I really don't want to hurt you. You deserve better and so do I."

Steve could see the tears welling up. Her eyes were still radiant when she looked up but softer, some of the light having dimmed. "Sophia, I've never said this before. I don't know, maybe I've never felt it before but I…. I love you. I'll do whatever it takes. If living here is the problem, let's go somewhere else. I don't want to lose you. Can we make this work?"

His phone sprang to life. He'd left it on the table, vibrate only. It started rattling against the wine bottle. He kept his eyes fixed on hers, ready to ignore it and apologise, but she turned away. He looked down at the illuminated screen.

Constance Pemberton. Perfect timing. Duty calls. He'd no choice, he had to take it.

Minutes later, they had left the restaurant and were heading back to their apartment in Yorkville. The cab driver tried to make chatty conversation but they both remained silent. The traffic was heavy which made it slow going. Sophia was gazing out through the tinted windows.

As they turned a corner, Steve's hand accidentally brushed her thigh which made her recoil. After apologising, he tried to explain that the woman was only in town for tonight. He'd arranged to meet her at her hotel off Broadway. Her husband was back in Chicago. She said it would be easier to talk without him being there.

Steve realised the possible implication and added, rather incongruously, the woman must be pushing seventy. The comment got no reaction. He feared Sophia was already somewhere else.

She didn't look back as she climbed out of the cab and slammed the door. He would try to reason it out with her when he came home. He didn't want the evening to end like this. As they pulled away, they drove past the florist on the corner. Steve remembered they stayed open all night. It was worth a try, for later.

Constance Pemberton appeared much younger than he'd imagined. No blue rinse, floral patterns, tweeds, or pearls. Instead, she stood six foot in her sneakers and wore skin-tight blue jeans, a designer white polo with a little gold motif on the arm and very little jewellery or make up. She could have passed for mid-forties.

Her striking silver and white hair was towel dried and shoulder length but it was her sharp, green eyes that caught his attention. He felt she could look straight through him. Her long face and high cheekbones were comparatively smooth skinned. Cosmetic surgery? Possibly. The overall effect was quite stunning.

Her elegant, youthful appearance may be for show, but Steve could sense this was a confident woman used to getting her own way. Within minutes the thin veneer of control started to crack. Her eyes became restless, unable to focus, a nervous fidgeting betrayed her inner turmoil.

She'd taken a booth off the main lobby where they couldn't be overheard. An empty glass on the table was soon replaced by another large gin and tonic. Steve ordered mineral water. He asked if he could make notes as they talked. At first, she hesitated but quickly relented and told him to proceed.

From their small talk, he could tell she'd agonised about meeting him at all. He kept losing eye contact as she scanned the lobby area behind him. He needed her to relax.

"You're not from New York, Detective Sergeant." It was a statement not a question. He liked her directness.

"No, I'm a British police officer on attachment to the fraud team. Please call me Steve."

"OK, Steve, you may call me Connie. So, I'm curious - is the NYPD so short staffed they're drafting in foreigners who don't know the turf?" The ice tinkled in her glass as she drank.

"Mrs Pemberton, sorry, Connie, you asked for this meeting."

"I didn't expect them to send a boy along?"

"Can we cut the snide remarks? It won't help either of us. I need to talk to you. I take it you ignored my messages." Steve didn't expect this reaction from her.

"You've been a nuisance for weeks. Why are you stalking me? Haven't we suffered enough? What do you want?" Her expression was a confused mixture of anger, frustration and despair, Steve decided.

"I want the truth. Let me come to the point. Why did you sell out so cheaply?" Steve kept fixed on her eyes which had started to moisten. Was it the drink or the conversation? It didn't matter which so long as she levelled with him.

Connie leaned back, took another mouthful but stayed silent, seemingly lost in thought. Steve kept pushing. "You sold Pemberton Electronics earlier this year to a start-up company for less than five million dollars. The IRS estimate it was worth ten times that amount. They smell a rat. Believe me, Connie, they know what they're talking about. I've got all the numbers."

Still silence but Steve noticed patches of colour flushing around the base of her neck.

"The website says you're a third-generation company, manufacturing world-class products for a growing customer base. Your recent market penetration is impressive, especially into Asia. So why sell up at all?" Steve noticed the colour was spreading over her upper chest. She was still fidgeting. Her glass was empty again.

"I know what the website says, Steve. I wrote it. It was my company, my family's company, I'm angry as hell. It was stolen from us. We had to sell. Do you understand me?"

"No, I don't understand. How was it stolen? Tell me." He put his notepad down. He needed to listen. The notes could come later.

"Because we had no choice. Look, can I trust you? I mean, really trust you. I don't want this going any further." Somehow, she must have ordered more drinks, maybe a nod to an unseen waiter. Steve didn't want the fresh mineral water when it arrived.

"I can't make any guarantees, Connie, you know that, especially if a crime has been committed."

"Well, a crime has been committed. A fucking big crime. Todd thinks we should count ourselves lucky and walk away."

"But you don't."

"These bastards must pay for what they've done." The flush had reached her cheeks and forehead.

"Which bastards? What have they done?" Steve drained the first glass, more for breathing space than a need for hydration. "Connie, can we start this from the beginning. Tell me about Pemberton Electronics."

She reached forward for the gin and tonic but decided against it. Steve thought he saw her take a deep breath and compose herself. Her eyes focused on his again. She exhaled slowly. Maybe now this would make more sense.

He tried not to think about Sophia and what she might be doing. Sleeping, he hoped. But was this yet another triumph for hope over gut feelings? There was nothing he could do about it anyway. This conversation was more important right now. He needed to concentrate.

"I married Todd du Prez thirty-two years ago. Second time around. My ex turned out to be a gold digger. Only thing he gave me was a son. Todd's different. He's an engineer by training. We made him CEO, a unanimous family vote. For once we all agreed. He did a good job too. It's not easy running a family-owned company. When he retired, we bought out the other family members which gave us a majority shareholding. Then we hired a general manager. He runs things for us. Sorry, ran. The factory's in Joliet, Illinois, that's where we're from. But you know that."

"You kept your name." Steve needed her to stay on track. The flow of information was increasing as she relaxed, as she began to trust him.

"Yes, I'm proud to be a Pemberton. My granddaddy was a genius. He started making power cells in his garage. He got frustrated when lead-acid batteries lost their charge with no warning. He sold an order for twenty rechargeable units to our local golf club for their carts. He'd no idea how to make so many. Grandma went nuts. He had parts in the kitchen, the bedroom and all over the house. She said take premises or get divorced. That's how we got started."

"And the company grew." Steve sipped the water. It was time to make some notes. Clearly, she didn't mind.

"Lithium-ion batteries had just come onto the market. It was boom times. Over the years, we branched out into forklifts, security systems, anything that needed a reliable power supply. It was all custom made. We sold good products and we cared." The colour was fading. She'd stopped fidgeting and arranged for a large bottle of still mineral water and two clean glasses, with ice and lemon.

"Your profits jumped forty percent in one year." Steve couldn't remember which year. He didn't have his files with him. It didn't matter, she didn't challenge him.

"It was 2014. We broke into the residential market. It was a remote housing development in California. Way off the grid. They needed solar power storage. It was our single biggest contract ever. We built an extension to the factory on the back of it. It stretched us financially. A friend of my father's worked in raising finance. He introduced us to Slaker Nadzy."

Steve had read an IRS report on them. A venture capital firm based off Wall Street, they had offices in London, Paris, Toronto, Kiev, and Tel Aviv. They specialised in private equity investments for discerning, international clients, or so the blurb said.

The IRS considered them kosher but raised question marks over their ownership. That wasn't unusual for venture capital firms, as Steve was finding out with other fraud investigations. Their ability to protect people, hide behind a cloak of secrecy and move money around the world without paying tax was legendary.

"So, you sold equity to raise capital."

"We'd been one hundred percent family owned until then. I was against it. I had friends who'd sold the family silver and found they'd lost control. I knew it was a slippery slope, but I was outvoted. Todd wasn't sure but the rest of the family could smell big money."

"Tell me about new products." Steve had read a report that said Pemberton overstretched itself. Big players had moved into their markets. Pemberton needed new products just to keep up. It must have meant borrowing more and more.

Connie stood up and announced she needed the bathroom. While she was away, Steve tried ringing Sophia but got no answer. It was getting late.

Maybe it was already too late.

CHAPTER 11

Connie seemed more composed when she returned. Most of the colour had gone. She must have swilled her face, Steve decided, as some of her fringe was a slightly darker shade.

"We were approached by a car manufacturer. *Quicker, longer, lighter*. That was the phrase Todd used. They needed lithium-ion batteries that were quicker to recharge, with a longer lasting power supply and didn't weigh too much. We launched into it without thinking. We raised more capital through Slaker Nadzy and expanded our research team. I knew it was dangerous."

"Dangerous?"

"Over half our income was tied into automotive. It's regular work but they squeeze the little guys, pay when they feel like it, demand the earth and show no tolerance. Just-in-time means just in their time, not yours."

"So, what did you do?" Steve sensed she was still holding back. There was real fire in her eyes when they first started talking. *These bastards must pay for what they've done.* Was she skirting round this? He may need to drag it out of her. Be patient, let her keep talking.

"We were running to stand still. Sure, we were making good money, but breaking into automotive meant our product development had pretty much stopped. Other markets were falling away. We had to diversify, come up with something new. It was our chief engineer who thought of it."

The colour had returned. It was getting tough for her again. Keep pushing.

93

"Like so many good ideas, it was simple, practical and had been tried before but without success. No one had joined the dots. We called it an *ecodrivetrain*."

Connie topped up their glasses then waved the bottle in front of his eyes. "Water. The answer was good old H2O. After a year in the lab, we made a combined electrolysis system, power generation unit and advanced storage cell. You pour water in one end and out comes green electricity at the other. The only emission is pure oxygen. It's a climate activist's dream ticket."

"Did you patent this technology?" Steve was thinking industrial espionage, maybe. But there was something else. Tiny beads of perspiration had appeared over the colour on her forehead.

"Todd decided we must protect ourselves, so he filed several patents. It was all about the unique design of the polymer electrolyte membrane, he said. I didn't understand it, but suddenly new markets opened for us. We needed to raise more capital."

"Through Slaker Nadzy again?"

"They had clients in Israel looking to invest in green technology. We had no choice but to share our plans with them. That's when this all started."

Steve had been making copious notes. He asked her if she needed another break. She was fine to continue. Whatever was on her mind, needed to be said.

"Out of the blue, our Slaker Nadzy contact in New York asked if we would consider selling Pemberton Electronics. They had another client ready to buy. We could name our price, he said. No, we bloody well didn't want to sell. We told him so and thought that would be an end to it. Todd started looking at other avenues to raise finance. We didn't trust them anymore."

"But they came back to you?"

"They started to get angry. Would we sign a non-disclosure agreement? Would we meet them at their New York offices? Could their accountants talk to our accountants? Do we want to see what the offer is? It was harassment. Todd took legal advice and was ready to go to the police. And then, suddenly, it all stopped. We didn't hear from them for weeks. It's all in my diary."

"I'd like to see that, if I may."

Connie recalled how it happened. She'd been at a meeting in Chicago, sometime before Easter. It was driving rain and cold. The other committee members had gone. She was about to make a dash for the car when her phone rang, caller's number blocked. She thought it was going to be a sales call, for health insurance or double glazing.

"His accent was very distinct. Caribbean, definitely Caribbean. We owned a condo in St Lucia, back in the day. I recognised the lilt in his accent but couldn't tell which island. Then, suddenly, he swore at me, called me a white bitch. He spoke very slowly. I was terrified. *If I wanted to see her again, we must take the offer.* At first, I didn't know what he was talking about. It was awful."

Connie could hold back no longer, tears flooding, her body shaking, all composure gone. Steve offered her his handkerchief which she took but couldn't stop the tears.

"Who, Connie?"

"Our precious angel, Chicory, our only grandchild. They'd snatched her from a friend's house. She was sleeping over. They must have followed her. He said no harm would come to her if we did as he said. No police, no investigators or she was dead."

Connie said he called several times over the coming weeks. Number blocked. She noted all the calls in her diary, times and dates, duration and what was said. Todd wanted to hire a private detective, but she said no, it wasn't worth the risk.

"He said it was the only blackmail where the target received money. It made him laugh out loud. Evil bastard. He said five million was a fair price as we'd already made our fortune. Once we'd signed over ownership of the company, the money would be transferred, and Chicory would be returned."

"And that's what happened?"

"Yes, she had a few cuts and bruises but was otherwise fine. We quizzed her about where she'd been and who she saw. She's eight years old, Steve, there was nothing solid, no leads. She'd been blindfolded. They wore masks."

"Did you go to the police when you got her back?"

"No, I was too worried. If they'd taken her once, they could do it again. Next time we may not be so lucky. They had nothing to lose by then. I've never been so scared. They were ruthless but they knew what they were doing. Todd was right, we had to let it go."

"But you haven't, have you?"

"Since I got your first message, I've been going over and over it in my mind. Should I tell you this? Todd has closed the door on the whole thing. He'd be furious if he knew I was here. *We got her back, it's over, leave it,* he said repeatedly. But for me, it's not about the company or even the money, come to that. It's the injustice I can't live with. This isn't the America I grew up in."

"And what about the company now?"

"The new owners seem decent people. They're doing all the things we would have done, so we hear. I don't believe they had anything to do with the blackmail."

"They must have been suspicious, buying a company well below market cap, surely." Steve made a note to dig further into the new owners.

"The rumour going round was that we were strapped for cash. The markets were tightening up. We were facing tougher competition with more stringent regulation. Add to that we were supposedly tired, had enough already salted away and needed a quick exit, no questions asked."

"And was that the case?"

"Some of that was true but we still wouldn't have sold out. The rumour would have made sense to the new owners. We got lucky, they must've thought, right place, right time, I guess. It's just business."

"I'm shocked by what you've told me, Connie. It can't have been easy. As you said, a crime has been committed. I will get to the bottom of it. I'd like to go through your diary notes and everything else you can remember. Pull all this together, one piece at a time. It may not bring your company back, but it might stop others suffering the same ordeal. Besides, I want this guy behind bars."

Steve wondered if his budget would stretch to a return flight to Chicago. Collect the diary, meet Todd, and perhaps corroborate her story. As he discovered, there was no need. Connie told him she was now due back in New York the day after tomorrow. She would bring the diary with her. Steve decided to start the investigation from there.

"How did the kidnapper know when the sale was completed?" Steve had closed his notepad.

The question took Connie by surprise. Clearly, she'd not considered it. "Somebody must have told him. We certainly didn't."

"So, the new owners could have been involved."

CHAPTER 12

Hannah could tell Lawrence's imagination had gone into overdrive. He'd bought a Lonely Planet Guide to Kenya at Rome Airport and read it from cover to cover during the flight. As they were landing, he proudly announced that the ballroom was named after Winston Churchill who stayed at The Stanley Hotel in his early years.

According to the guidebook, it was common practice for guests to leave notes for other guests on the actual thorns of an acacia tree growing out of the middle of the restaurant floor. The current tree was third generation but nowadays a noticeboard complied better with health and safety regulations. Hannah could see in his eyes Lawrence was hatching a plot to carry on this tradition.

On the way to Rome airport, Hannah had contacted the office to let them know about her impromptu holiday. Fabio was delighted for her and said he would sort out her diary, rearranging any meetings she had booked. The preparatory work for her New York speech would continue in her absence. He would keep in touch by email but suggested she should switch off the laptop and enjoy the adventure.

The kennels had sent a text message and photo of Trigger playing with the other dogs quite happily. It came through when his mobile connected to the local telecoms network. Lawrence loved it when a plan came together.

After a quick shower and change into her smart clothes, Hannah was now waiting for their dinner guests in the Exchange Bar, as Father Kelly had arranged. A large gin and tonic, with ice and lemon, was clinking around a tall glass in front of her. Lawrence had slipped away to check on the restaurant booking. She had a few minutes to herself as they had somehow managed to be early.

From the outside, the floodlit hotel looked a little tired and uninspiring. Their bedroom was perfectly adequate but no more than that. It wasn't until they explored the older parts of the hotel that its historical significance really came to life.

Built in 1902 and named after the legendary Welsh explorer, Sir Henry Morton Stanley, the hotel became the traditional meeting place for those going on safari. The Exchange Bar replaced the original Long Bar in 1932.

Hannah noticed the bar had retained most of its colonial charms. Dark wood furnishings, leafy aspidistras, scattered leather settees and plush tribal-patterned carpeting provided a serene backdrop for numerous hushed conversations.

Ornate ceiling fans made lazy circles overhead. Hannah was particularly taken with the rows of linear fans moving in unison like obedient line dancers. A pianist in a white jacket was teasing Lennon & McCartney classics out of a baby grand near the tiled bar area. *We can work it out* seemed uncannily appropriate.

"You must be Hannah." The voice was molten chocolate, pouring over the back of her armchair, from an unseen source. She stood and turned to face a tall, slim man in a pale blue jacket and dark trousers. Henry Gachuhi introduced himself and held out his right hand.

The other was clutching a stunningly beautiful woman in a leopard-print dress. Heavy gold jewellery decorated her perfect, mahogany skin. They both wore stylish glasses. Her eyes were alive with playful curiosity, while his retained a touch of wariness and restraint.

A few minutes later, a waiter brought their drinks and confirmed the table in the restaurant was ready. Hannah could see Lawrence weaving his way over towards them.

99

They waited for him to arrive before drinking a toast to good health and new friends.

Henry's wife was introduced as Fara, short for Farashuu. "It means butterfly." Henry explained. Hannah could see they were very much a couple, well matched, clearly on the same wavelength and deeply in love. She guessed they were similar ages, late thirties, or early forties perhaps, judging by the light touches of silver grey in their hair.

They took their drinks through to the restaurant and ordered light suppers with two green salads to share. After some badgering, Henry acquiesced and passed the wine list to Hannah who insisted on making the selection.

She'd had a good day. She was officially on holiday. The food on the plane was tasty. The flight was thankfully uneventful. Now she was looking forward to finding out why Father Kelly had been so keen for them to get to know each other.

"We met him in this very room, sitting over there by the tree." Henry recalled, pointing to an unoccupied table. "He'd just arrived from Dublin and was still getting his bearings. Thankfully, everyone can find this hotel. In many respects it was quite a strange meeting really, wasn't it, honey."

Fara agreed without elaboration. Hannah was curious. They were pinning many of their hopes on the Catholic priest for the success of this trip. If there were any shadows hanging over him, she'd prefer to know now. "Strange? How do you mean?"

Henry paused while he chewed over some rocket. "Well, it was as if we'd known him all our lives and were catching up over lunch, yet it was our first meeting. What's more, we had to discuss a student I was having problems with. He was a Catholic boy from a single parent family. It was a delicate matter, and I was cautious

100

about discussing it with a stranger. But Father Kelly engendered so much trust from the outset. Sorry, I've given up trying to call him Pat. It seems disrespectful somehow."

Hannah established that Henry was a science teacher at The Alliance High School in Kikuyu, a few miles to the northwest of the city. Although founded on an alliance of Protestant churches, the school today, known locally as Bush, taught boys from all over Africa. Catholics numbered amongst the other Christian religions and there was a growing population of Muslim and other non-Christian students.

"Father Kelly dived straight in." Henry was starting to relax. The jacket had been abandoned over the back of his cane chair. He'd undone a second shirt button to reveal a heavy gold chain nestling on smooth, dark skin underneath. "The boy was missing a father figure, he believed, and needed some genuine pastoral care. He was tirelessly working with the boy and his family. Within a few weeks the boy was getting top marks in physics and even won an award for a chemistry project. The man's a saint, really."

"He's picking us up at the airport tomorrow morning. We're looking forward to meeting him." Hannah added.

The restaurant had quietened off since they first sat down. Only three other tables were now occupied. Most people were casually dressed, apart from two white men in dark suits over by the terrace doors. Engineers, she guessed, or perhaps accountants. They were drinking a bottle of mineral water and eating very little, she noticed.

"Hannah, is this your first trip to Kenya?" Fara had finished her Red Snapper Zanzibari which, she pronounced, was delicious.

"Yes, we're very excited to be here." She gazed across at Lawrence and squeezed his hand. "It was an impulse

101

thing, really. I'd been contacted out of the blue by Father Kelly about a church matter. He was telling me what a wonderful country it is. Kenya's somewhere we'd always wanted to visit so, we thought, why not? And here we are."

"And you're off to Lake Turkana? Most tourists go to the game reserves or the coastal resorts." Henry offered, an element of caution returning to his voice.

"We're not most tourists." Lawrence bounced in, deciding some light-hearted good humour was needed as a deflection. "We want to see the real Kenya, immerse ourselves in its culture and meet the people who've made this great country what it is. We don't mind roughing it a bit, do we, love of my life?"

"Roughing it? You must excuse my husband. He gets like this after a few drinks." She leaned over and punched him lightly on the shoulder, amid ripples of playful laughter.

Before Henry could pursue his line of questioning, Hannah took the initiative. "I recognise your surname, Ga-chuhi. Is that how you pronounce it?"

"Perfect." Henry nodded. "It's quite common in Kenya. We're both Kikuyu. It's a local tribe."

"So why do I recognise your surname?" Hannah poured the rest of the wine. A 2016 Leleshwa Sauvignon Blanc was crafted from grapes grown in the Rift Valley, according to the label. Hannah had no idea they made such excellent wine in Kenya. Another good decision.

"That's probably why Father Kelly wanted us to meet tonight, especially given your new job with the World Health Organisation." Henry continued. "I'm guessing you'll know my older sister, Betty."

Hannah looked at Lawrence for some inspiration, but none was forthcoming. Gachuhi? World Health

Organisation? No, she apologised, she couldn't make a connection.

"I'm delighted to say my big sister is the new Secretary-General of the United Nations." Henry raised his glass. The others did the same. Betty Gachuhi was the toast. "She's just taken over. To say she's excited is an understatement."

Yes, of course, Hannah remembered as soon as he said it. She recalled how she'd been at a function in New York the day after it was announced. Betty was the guest of honour. The room was so packed Hannah never managed to get introduced.

"Pardon my ignorance." Fara interrupted. "Is the World Health Organisation connected to the United Nations in some way? I've never been sure."

"The World Health Organisation's an autonomous agency within the UN." Hannah explained. "The UN is a huge organisation these days with many other agencies within it like the International Monetary Fund, the World Bank, and the World Trade Organisation. Betty's going to have her hands full running this lot."

"She'll be fine. Betty's been in the diplomatic community for years. Lawrence, you'll be pleased to know your UK taxes paid her salary for a while." Henry smiled before reaching for his glass.

"Money well spent, I'm sure." Lawrence had followed Hannah's eyes over to the two dark suits in the corner. They kept glancing over which made him nervous. Were they being watched? But, this was a business hotel as well as being a tourist refuge. He reminded himself he was sat with two very attractive women who would always get male attention in any restaurant.

"We're due to be in New York for a UN meeting. I've been invited to speak. I'll make sure to say hello."

Hannah was curious to know how two siblings could have taken such radically different career paths.

Henry enlightened her. Their parents had both been maths teachers at the Bush, before retiring to the coast. Betty excelled in political studies and economics. After graduating from university in Nairobi, she was awarded a scholarship to complete a Masters in African Studies at Cambridge, Henry explained. "She moved away and never looked back.

"She joined McKinsey's in Manhattan and was soon promoted to the government consultancy team in London. After getting her UK citizenship, she was headhunted by the Foreign Office and posted to Cairo before being sent to the embassy in Washington DC. She ended up back in New York as the UK's Permanent Representative to the UN, the youngest ever. Now she is the first female Secretary-General. We're very proud of her."

"And what about you, Henry? Did you consider a career in the diplomatic service?" Lawrence had to ask. He guessed it must have been difficult growing up in her shadow.

"No, that wasn't for me, but I'm delighted for her. Her career took her overseas. I love what I do here and get job satisfaction every day. The boys are a pleasure to teach. Not only that but I'm married to the most beautiful woman in Africa and have two wonderful kids. Being Betty's brother, I get to meet all kinds of fascinating people, including you guys. Hannah, Lawrence, our new friends, welcome to Kenya."

Another toast and chinked glasses. Fara completed the picture. Their children were fourteen and twelve; the eldest, Giles, was at the boys' school, and spirited Phoebe was ruling the roost at the Alliance Girls' High School, down the road.

"Fara, do you also teach at the school?" Hannah needed to know. Fara didn't look like a teacher, but it seemed the most tactful way to find out what she did. Fara had kept quiet all evening, which might have been her personality but, given the true reason behind their trip to Kenya, it would be good to know where she fit in.

"No, I'm not, thankfully. There're enough teachers in this family already." She smiled but quickly realised, in the silence that followed, that she hadn't really answered the question.

"I'm a research scientist, working in a lab at the university, here in Nairobi. We met when Henry was doing his teaching practice. I helped him out running some tests for one of his classes."

"What kind of science, if you don't mind me asking? It's always helpful to know a good lab in my line of work." Hannah was trying to feign a passing interest, but Fara could prove to be a useful contact, if she could trust her.

"Medical research. We try our hand at most things but tend to specialise in degenerative and cardiovascular diseases, sports injuries and immunotherapies."

"Does that include Parkinson's?" Lawrence interrupted.

"Yes, we've a team investigating the neurological implications. That's what I've been doing today. It's fascinating work. Why do you ask?" Fara looked curious.

"It's a subject close to our hearts. We've a friend we want to help. I'm doing a PhD into the causes of the disease. Maybe I could connect with you professionally when we get back?" Lawrence suggested.

"I'm sure that would be fine. I can check with my head of faculty if you like?" Fara seemed happy with the proposal. Lawrence was pleased with her positive response.

"So how often do you all get together as a family? Do you see much of your sister, Henry?" Hannah felt sorry for senior UN people. Like political eunuchs, they had responsibility without the wherewithal to make any real decisions. Everyone expected the UN to act but they were often fighting a losing battle against international power politics. Maybe Betty would be more successful.

"We keep in touch by social media mostly but it's not the same. Once she gets this air race off the ground, she might have a bit more time to come home. I tried to get her to re-route it over East Africa then we could catch up. The nearest they'll come though is Egypt." Henry explained.

"What air race?" Lawrence looked as puzzled as Hannah. They knew nothing about it.

"She's calling it *The UN Crystal Clear Skies Challenge*. Betty believes in competition. She always pushed herself to be top of the class. By offering a big enough prize, she's hoping to eradicate fossil fuels from the aviation industry. It would be a huge step towards reducing carbon emissions and slowing down climate change."

Henry talked them through the planned route. "I'm surprised you haven't heard about it. The media are saying it's the boldest move by the UN in generations and has really put the cat amongst the aviation pigeons, or lame ducks, as one reporter described them."

"I love the concept. Why haven't the UN tried something like this before?" Lawrence was working out if the planes would fly over Rome. From Cairo to Paris, there was a good chance. Or perhaps they might be in New York when the race passed over the Statue of Liberty.

"Betty said some in the media think competition is divisive." Henry shook his head. "I think it's a brilliant

106

idea. Once she's proved this approach works, Betty has other plans to incentivise medical and scientific advancement. How about putting up a prize to find a cure for Parkinson's?"

Lawrence and Hannah loved the idea. What had anyone to lose? It would focus attention and maybe lead to greater urgency in pushing for a cure. Millions of people worldwide would benefit. The healthcare savings would far outweigh the prize money. They all agreed to discuss it further, perhaps over the next dinner.

A waiter brought the sweet menu, but they agreed it was time to go. Henry and Fara had to relieve the babysitter. Lawrence and Hannah had an early flight. They exchanged contact details, embraced each other, and promised to keep in touch.

After their guests had gone, Lawrence remarked what a charming couple. "I see why Father Kelly wanted us to meet them. Henry's sister Betty sounds like a real live wire. She'll make a nice change from the stiffs they usually pick. Maybe she'll shake things up a bit."

As they made their way across the restaurant floor, past the acacia tree, Lawrence tried to tell her about the message he'd seen pinned to the noticeboard, but Hannah was distracted. She kept glancing across at the men in dark suits. They were still talking. Hannah didn't want to carry on their conversation until they were out of earshot.

"They've hardly eaten anything all night." Hannah whispered when they were round the corner.

"It's a restaurant, Hannah, lighten up. It might just be a business meeting. Besides, if they were following us, they weren't exactly dressed as spies."

"Maybe you're right." Hannah agreed, stifling a yawn as she did so.

She spotted the note pinned to the noticeboard, addressed to her. It was from the Rt. Hon. Winston

Churchill. With a broad smile, she announced that she'd read it when they got upstairs. First, she wanted to see if they were being followed.

Hannah didn't notice anything immediately suspicious, but a closer inspection of the lobby area would have revealed a young businesswoman in a slate grey suit reading a newspaper. The woman was keeping a close eye on the elevators.

Once back in their room, Hannah sat on the bed, opened the note, and kicked off her shoes at the same time. It was in Lawrence's handwriting. *You can always count on Americans to do the right thing - after they've tried everything else.* **Winston Churchill**. She smiled at the sentiment without agreeing with it, her Brooklyn heritage tugging at the heart of her patriotism.

Lawrence emerged from the bathroom dressed only in the hotel robe which was much too small for his corpulent body. From where she was sitting, Hannah could smell the new aftershave he'd bought at duty-free. God loves a trier, she thought, admiring his persistence.

"Fancy a crack at doing the right thing before we turn in, Dr McGlynn?"

CHAPTER 13

Hannah insisted on the window seat in the hope of getting her first glimpse of Lake Turkana, or the Jade Sea as it was known locally, due to the vivid aquamarine colour. The fifty-seater turboprop left on time, around three quarters full. The two spies, now dressed for a day in the bush, were the last to board. They sat together near the front and continued their conversation for the duration of the one-hour flight.

Hannah pointed them out, but Lawrence was cocooned with the in-flight magazine. She knew to expect a full report on what he had learned. His boyish enthusiasm had been at full throttle since they left the hotel.

"It's the biggest wind farm in Africa, over three hundred turbines, built by the Danes." He suddenly announced. "Loiyangalani is one of the windiest places on earth, it says. A Spanish company went bump before they could connect it to the grid, so the Chinese finished the job. For such a remote part of the world, this lake's attracting a whole lot of international attention."

"Do you think these guys could be wind farm engineers?" Hannah nodded towards them.

"I'm not sure. They'd need a helicopter or a private plane to get there from Lodwar. Moving around can't be easy in this country." Lawrence added before diving back into the magazine.

A few minutes later, a dune-covered desert, dotted with thick green patches, was rising to meet them. Disappointingly for Hannah, there was no sign of the Jade Sea, despite a cloudless blue sky. A heat haze made the distant horizon shimmer. It had been warm when they left

Nairobi. The afternoon forecast for Lake Turkana was pushing forty in the shade, and there didn't seem to be much of that.

Hannah stepped out into a blast of dry heat as she left the plane. The spies had joined a crocodile of fellow passengers sidling towards a new terminal building across the apron. Amongst them was an anonymous young businesswoman, no longer wearing a grey suit.

As Lawrence reached the bottom step, Hannah grabbed his arm and pulled him to one side. She was pointing to a conical hill overlooking the runway. In disbelief, they were staring at the figure of Christ the Redeemer on the hilltop, arms outstretched in its familiar welcome.

The statue was obviously much smaller than the one in Rio, but the similarity was uncanny. Hannah could only hope it was a good omen. The last time she saw Christ the Redeemer, she nearly lost her life.

Inside the terminal building there were people everywhere. It was a riot of colour and emotion, reunions and partings, tears, laughter and shouting, baggage being collected and deposited. There were young children selling bottles of water. Some taxi drivers were touting for business while others were clutching signs displaying names almost impossible to pronounce.

As Lawrence joined the scrum in the baggage reclaim area, Hannah was watching her spies carefully. They had retrieved a mountain of luggage, which was handed to a liveried porter. He was wrestling to stack an under-sized trolley while they made their way outside again, strolling towards an unmarked helicopter on the far side of the apron.

The rotors were turning expectantly. Two impatient ground crew looked daggers at the porter while they waited to load the cargo bay and get out of the sun.

"That's not fifteen kilos each, I'll bet." The rich Irish accent was unmistakable. Hannah smiled to herself. The adage remained so true. The quietest voice was often the loudest.

She turned to find herself staring into the beatific face of Father Patrick Kelly, his glasses having steamed up in the brutal air conditioning. He offered her his hand which seemed awkwardly formal, given the circumstances. They were meant to be on holiday, after all. Taller than him by a good few inches, Hannah stooped to his level and hugged him instead. "Who are those guys? Why do they get special treatment?"

"My dear Hannah, they are the chosen ones." Pat replied, mopping the last droplets of sweat from his brow with a handkerchief before attending to his glasses. "Oil company glitterati. I've seen them before. They'll be heading for Lokichar. It's two gruelling hours by road or twenty minutes by air."

They watched as the chopper rose majestically into the azure blue sky, hovered momentarily, dipped its nose in salute then sped off due south, climbing as it went, back the way they'd flown in.

Lawrence appeared beside her; their bags safely recovered. This time handshakes were exchanged, and introductions made. After some pleasantries, they headed towards the main exit and quickly found the 4X4 in an unmade section of the parking lot.

"How long's there been an oil industry here, Pat?" Hannah had taken the front seat on Lawrence's insistence.

"They discovered oil years ago, but it will be some time before it reaches full production capacity, apparently." Pat replied. He needed to collect some things from the office before heading over to the lake. He handed them small bottles of ice-cold mineral water. Hannah checked the seals hadn't been tampered with. They'd been warned not to drink the water.

"Why so long, for the oil I mean?" Lawrence chipped in from the back.

"Welcome to Africa, Lawrence. No disrespect intended but you need to understand the complexity of politics in this country." He smiled across at Hannah. "The people who've lived here all their lives call it the *land of broken dreams*. The historical pattern is long established. The oil industry is just the latest chapter."

The streets around Lodwar were bustling with people of all ages, along with goats, camels, motorbikes, and donkey carts loaded with everything from fresh vegetables to furniture. There were cars and trucks in varying degrees of dilapidation mixed in with brand new, all-wheel drive vehicles. It looked to Hannah like a town on the up, although obviously coming from humble beginnings.

As they twisted and turned deeper into the back streets, she was encouraged by the growing evidence of civilised infrastructure. There were metalled roads, streetlights, some new civic buildings shining amid corrugated iron dwellings and shops that had seemingly grown out of the dry earth.

Pat swung through an open, filigree ironwork gateway into a tree-lined compound, past a sign proudly announcing their arrival at *St Mary's Pastoral Centre, Diocese of Lodwar*. It was an oasis of calm amid the heat and frenzy outside. A cool fountain was playing over smooth pebbles as they strolled through an adjoining courtyard into an unremarkable, single-storey building.

"How do you mean, Pat, broken dreams?" Hannah pulled up a spare chair in a cramped office, the unseeing eyes of the Virgin Mary looking down on her with great pity. "Lodwar looks like a boom town to me."

112

Father Kelly was rummaging through a pile of papers on his desk. "The local people were told oil would be their salvation with new jobs and a share in the huge profits to come. That became ten percent of the profit, which became five percent. A proposed Ugandan–Kenyan pipeline taking the oil to Mombasa was shelved when the Ugandans switched allegiance to Tanzania.

"Now the British and French oil companies involved in the project are pulling out. With the unpredictability of oil prices and seemingly ever-increasing production costs, it's not economically viable for them to continue. Or so they say."

"A minor setback, surely? Oil prices always go back up. The world seemingly still can't live without it." Lawrence had found a breeze off the courtyard drifting in through an open window. Keen as he was to get this investigation moving, the thought of a long, bumpy drive over to the lake didn't fill him with much enthusiasm.

Lawrence continued. "According to the in-flight magazine, Turkana's the happening place right now. A growing oil industry, the hottest new tourist destination in Kenya and they've just discovered two huge aquifers near here with enough water to supply the whole country for the next seventy years."

"I love your optimism, Lawrence, it's so refreshing." Pat was pushing papers into an old leather briefcase that had been sleeping next to his desk. "The aquifers were also discovered years ago, by satellite. The water will need desalinating then pumping to the surface. There's no budget to exploit this resource. The government will eventually partner with an international company who'll smell big profits and think they can pull a fast one over them, only to come unstuck themselves in a quagmire of local politics."

"I thought you said you loved this country?" Hannah, on the other hand, was ready to get moving. They had a job to do. Sitting here being cynical and picking over failed business ventures wasn't helping. "With so many broken dreams, as you call it, why have you stayed?"

"I love the country and its people. They are the constant in all these stories. Never complaining, never questioning, they just get on with their lives while outsiders exploit them, drain their lake, and steal their land. Talking of the lake, remind me to show you the fish processing plant built by the Norwegians in the eighties. Politics unravelled their little game as well." He was packed and ready but remembered something he kept in a locked cupboard. A fumbling of keys ensued.

"So, what about tourism? I read the main road from Kitale to Lodwar is nearly tarmacked all the way." Lawrence had intended to take the magazine with him as he left the plane but forgot. "Turkana is called The Cradle of Humanity, boasting the oldest human fossils ever found, along with stone tools dating back over three million years. Tourism must be a winner here, surely? One dream that can't be broken?"

Father Kelly, much to Hannah's surprise, produced a sleek, black handgun with a box of ammunition. In one smooth motion, he checked it over, loaded it, flicked on the safety catch and offered the handle towards Lawrence, who was equally shocked.

"There'll never be tourism without security. And I'm not just talking inter-tribal skirmishes over cattle or border disputes. That's gone on for generations and always will. I mean full out carjacking, muggings at gunpoint, organised crimes by cross-border gangs from Ethiopia and South Sudan. It's not as bad as it was but you'll need this to protect yourselves."

"That's a very kind thought, Pat, but I don't think so." Lawrence held up his hands in refusal. "We'll put our trust in the local police force. I saw a new station up the road. Presumably they're well protected?"

"They are but, you must remember, they can sometimes switch sides. I don't want your first trip to Lake Turkana to be your last. If you change your mind on this, just let me know." He unloaded the weapon and returned it to the cupboard. He checked it was locked and slipped the bunch of keys into his pocket.

A Catholic Priest with a handgun? That was another intriguing insight into Turkana County that Hannah wouldn't forget in a hurry.

Twenty minutes later the 4X4 bounced off the hard surface onto a sand-coloured dirt track. A dashboard light told them the outside temperature had touched thirty-eight degrees. Clouds of dust spiralled out behind them into the heat. The road ahead was deserted. Apart from the odd acacia tree, the flat horizon was featureless and barren.

"I forgot to mention, the guide I had in mind let me down, sorry." Pat swung the wheel to avoid the remains of a dead animal of some sort, possibly a goat. There was nothing left but bleached skin and bone. Hannah could see that life was fragile here and death, a constant companion. Maybe Father Kelly was right: they weren't ready for mass tourism just yet.

"That's not a problem, thanks for trying, Pat. The hotel said they could help us with a guide." Lawrence replied from the back seat.

"How are you going to get around? I wish I had more time to spend with you. I'm needed further north in Loki for a few days but might be able to catch up over the weekend, if you like."

115

He sounded hesitant and somewhat vague about his movements. Father Kelly added that, if they wanted to meet up, he'd need a couple of days' notice at least. Text was the best way of reaching him although the signal was often weak or non-existent. For Hannah, one thing became perfectly clear. Once he'd dropped them off, they'd be on their own.

Lawrence checked his phone screen. He had a signal at last, dialled the number and got through on the third ring. The receptionist was as helpful as before. Their room was ready. She reconfirmed the boat transfer for later. It was bright orange with Turkana Lodge painted on the hull, they couldn't miss it.

He asked about a guide. She said the best was Josphat and that she would arrange for him to meet them after breakfast. They could agree an hourly rate with him directly. His English was good, he spoke several local dialects and knew the area well. The hotel had no hesitation in recommending his services.

Lawrence asked if she could also arrange a 4X4 for the week. Could it be delivered early tomorrow morning? That was not a problem, she replied. She would need a copy of his passport, driver's licence and credit card or it could be charged to their room. He opted for the credit card and thanked her profusely. At least they had a base, a guide, and a means to move around. But where would they start?

"Tell us about Agnes." Hannah had formed a mental picture what her life would be like. She was already a remarkable woman, in her eyes, being able to move between such vastly different worlds. Hannah felt strange enough landing in Turkana directly from the sophistication of Rome. For Agnes, the prospect of going the other way must have been very daunting. Yet she accomplished her mission to get help. Admittedly, she had the belligerence of Cardinal Maina to thank partly for that.

"You must forgive me if I've already told you this. Agnes's husband was also married to another woman. She lives in the next village. It's quite common here, although I don't think the Holy Father would approve, if he knew." Pat crunched into all-wheel drive and slowed to negotiate a series of deep, powder-dry ruts.

"Another woman?" Hannah exclaimed, her mind suddenly racing. No, he hadn't told her this before. Hannah didn't appreciate surprises and Father Kelly was producing too many for her liking. Two wives could mean many more children involved. She wondered if the other wife's children were also suffering any illness. Add it to the list of unanswered questions.

"Then how did they know where to bury him?" Hannah probed.

"It's tradition. Whoever he marries first is usually the senior wife, so to speak."

"Usually?" Hannah was puzzled.

"Well, if the other wife has more cattle or goats, or bears him more sons, then things can change. Sons are valued, daughters are not. Their view of the world is very different to ours, I can assure you, Hannah."

Another vehicle was heading straight for them. If there was a middle on this road, they both owned it. Hannah quickly realised there must be a code that came into force in such situations whereby the right of way belonged to the larger vehicle. They slowed and squeezed past each other, leaving behind only scraps of paint on the acacia thorns.

They rounded a corner and were suddenly on a hard surface again. Pat picked up speed, but it was short-lived. The tarmac ended as abruptly as it began. A deep crack in the road surface and an ocean of loose sand and gravel drew them back down.

Lawrence had worked out that if he sat up straight to look out of the windscreen then he kept banging his head against the grab handle as they bounced through the potholes. He slid further down. There was nothing to see anyway. Another half hour and they should be there. He swigged some water which had become quite tepid.

"Her Banda is just outside the village of Kalokol, which used to be on the shoreline."

"Used to be? Where's the shoreline now?" Hannah was struggling to make sense of it all as more and more of Agnes's story was revealed.

"About two kilometres away. The lake's quite shallow at this point. With water levels dropping, it's a good walk for them, especially carrying fish."

"Do they have any refrigeration?" Hannah realised her mistake as soon as she asked the question.

"My dear girl, they don't have electricity. The village only got solar-powered streetlights a couple of years ago. The fish processing plant ran off generators. The Norwegians built this road otherwise we'd never get there. It's falling apart as you can see. They planned for electricity in phase two. Of course, it never happened."

"So, what do the local people live on?"

"They try to grow some crops but, due to climate change, there's been a severe drought for years. Only goats and camels can survive. Cattle need too much water. Anyway, they kept getting rustled by neighbouring tribes. Mainly they live off the lake. I hope you don't mind the smell of fish."

"How about water? And wastewater, come to that?" Hannah hadn't really thought about all this until now. She started bracing herself for more shocks.

"You'll see." Pat veered off the main track as they reached the outskirts of a village. In the near distance, a small group of reed huts clustered in a circle. Some children were playing in the dirt outside. Two dogs were eyeing their approach carefully.

As they got closer, Hannah could see several goats in a corral to the side of the largest hut, fenced off with brush and twigs. Not much of a burial place. Poor bastard, she thought.

They pulled up near the entrance. Father Kelly suggested they leave their bags in the trunk. He would drop them off later, down by the water's edge. He said he wanted to make sure they had a signal to call the hotel. Hannah suspected he had other concerns for their safety. Having pretty much invited them to his parish, Father Kelly was taking his duty of care seriously, for now, at least.

What Hannah hadn't noticed was the car that had been following them at a discreet distance since they left Lodwar.

CHAPTER 14

Shemmy Biwott parked well away from the reed huts and killed the engine, the green 4X4 quickly lost in thick bush. Her sat phone had good signal strength. Through the binoculars, she had a clear view of the settlement, or what she called a manyatta, being originally from the coastal plains.

"They've just reached the huts." She reported. "I can see the woman. She's surrounded by people. Children are running about. They're talking to her now."

"No guide?"

"No, just the three of them. They've come straight from town." She put down the binoculars and made a note, as he'd asked her to do.

"Good. That meddling parson can't speak the language. They'll learn nothing. We must keep it that way." His words were clipped.

She could picture him behind his polished desk, an 80's poster of the Twin Towers in New York on the wall. *A constant reminder that we can't drop our guard.* No doubt there'd be a large glass of Jack Daniels not too far away. *White man's burden*, he'd said, with a crooked smile. She didn't understand the meaning of that either.

"I called my friend Marianne at the Diocese." Shemmy added.

"The postulate?"

"Yes. She overheard the conversation. They trust the police to keep them safe. The weapon's still in the cupboard." She could hear his laughter.

"That the British guy? Probably thinks they still got Kenyatta in jail up the road. I bet he's wondering where

120

the cricket ground is. Limeys, huh? No wonder they lost their empire."

He told her to keep on their tail, but at a safe distance. They mustn't leave the hotel tonight and if they do, follow them. If they had any sense, he explained, they'd head back to the airport tomorrow. He didn't tell her anything else.

"What if they don't, Joel? What if they find out? What am I supposed to do?"

"Whatever it takes. They can't jeopardise our work."

She had responded to a job advertisement six months ago. It was a start-up operation, owned by a consortia of venture capital and investment houses, part of a global network, they told her.

The job description was fluid, to say the least. Some marketing, some IT support, special projects, they were looking for an all-rounder, right attitude, a taste for adventure, flexible on hours and location.

At interview, he said ideally single, no dependents and physically fit, although he would deny it, if ever asked. Her martial arts training could be put to good use, he suggested, shaking hands to seal the offer over the dinner table, the following evening.

She'd seen very little of him in the first few weeks. She sold her apartment in Nairobi and moved to a company-owned house outside Lodwar. The job got off to a slow start. But one thing she did learn. Don't double-cross him. Two of the management team had already disappeared.

She found him tough to deal with. A man of few words, he demanded total commitment and loyalty. He paid her well, as he said he would, and expected her to do whatever he wanted. Things had been kept above board so far, but his drinking was getting heavier which worried her.

She could see exciting career prospects that would hopefully lead her away from him, away from Africa but there were limits. It was still just a job. For now, she had to keep him sweet. And this was home.

Joel Chernick had no home and no life outside making money. He went where he was sent, usually to kick-start a project, put things in place then train the locals. It was called turnkey project management in the trade.

He would get things moving, hand it over and bank the cash. Most projects went according to plan but occasionally the exploration team got it wrong. He was guided by his one golden rule - unless it made money, don't do it.

Increasingly this took Joel to ever poorer, more desperate, dangerous, and remote hell holes. They were running out of decent places to exploit. *If the world had an arsehole, it would be in Turkana*, he'd told her on her first day.

But Shemmy struggled to process the logic. If they create a sustainable and profitable business that generates employment, builds infrastructure, pays taxes, and helps improve the quality of life for local people, then that must be a good thing, surely? He didn't see it that way.

He cited examples of projects in other parts of the world where terrorist groups or local agitators tried to shut them down or take over their operations. Death threats, car bombs, hostage taking, blackmail and spurious prohibition orders issued by corrupt government officials came with the turf. Joel knew how and when to grease which palms, to keep the wheels turning.

Joel had been warned by a reliable source that these two jokers were sticking their noses in to cause trouble, he told her. He omitted to tell her the source was a certain Cardinal in the Vatican. Joel firmly believed in the *only what you need to know* principle. They couldn't be trusted and must be stopped. She got the message.

As Shemmy watched, the three of them shook hands with Agnes and the other adults. Hannah cuddled a few of the children before waving goodbyes and climbing back into the car. Marianne, her postulate friend at the Diocese, whom she'd known since school, had said Father Kelly would be dropping them off somewhere, but didn't know where. He might be taking them to their hotel, but it was a good distance away, further down the lake.

The sun was starting to dip towards a distant horizon, taking the edge off the sweltering heat. Shemmy was surprised when their car turned towards Kalokol instead of going back the way they'd come. She stayed back as far as she dared without taking the risk of losing them. In the village, they took a sharp right down a dirt track heading for the lake. Clearly, he was not going to their hotel. She slowed to a crawl.

Women were walking past carrying baskets of fish on their heads, children scampering round their feet and playing with stray dogs. Some men were carrying nets and fishing lines from the boats. Happy faces bathed in the glowing embers of day. Some young men were singing and dancing to impress the girls. Others were filleting fish and stacking them to dry. The scene had a timeless, almost biblical, magic about it, Shemmy thought.

As she got closer to the lake, there were fewer and fewer trees. The vegetation had thinned out into scrub bush. There were no other vehicles near the shoreline. Shemmy decided to leave the 4X4 and cover the rest of the way on foot.

She took a cheap camera from the glovebox, leaving her watch and jewellery in its place. No need to draw attention. To complete the tourist look, she grabbed a baseball cap, sunglasses and a flimsy map from the door pocket.

She smiled at the steady stream of people walking towards her. Up ahead, the priest had pulled over near some boats that were being wiped down. Father Kelly helped unload their bags.

Shemmy took shelter behind a group of fishermen. She peered round and took some photos on full zoom. The pictures were poor quality but at least they showed what was happening. The fishermen took no interest in her and carried on haggling over today's meagre catch.

Father Kelly shook both their hands before he drove away. He spun the wheel and was suddenly heading straight for her. She dipped her head as he sped past, the dust cloud making her cough in the aftermath. The fishermen took no notice.

Shemmy watched as the tall woman she was following started to take pictures of the lake on her phone. She was stalking a group of flamingos dancing in the shallows nearby. The last rays of sunlight tinged their bright plumage with an orange glow. Her male companion was zipping and unzipping bags whilst fiddling with his phone. He looked up in time to snap a squadron of pelicans crashing like overladen flying boats into the calm waters offshore.

She heard the boat before she saw it. The high-pitched whine indicated it was moving at speed up the lake towards them. The engine tone noticeably dropped as it rounded a corner and came into full view. *Turkana Lodge* was emblazoned along the orange-painted hull in bold black letters. A single occupant by the outboard caused the nose to rise high above the spray. The resulting bow wave made it rock as he cut the engine to idling speed.

A few minutes later, Shemmy watched as they loaded the boat, climbed in and sped away. She made her way back to the 4X4 and took the inland route, back through the village. The sun had almost gone as she flicked on the headlights. Given the state of the track that led to the hotel, they would be there long before her. She buckled up, tossed her sunglasses into the tray, and resigned herself to the treacherous terrain. Duty calls.

* * *

Hannah and Lawrence quickly established his name was Thomas. He'd worked at the Lodge since it opened. They declined his offer of lifejackets as he'd assured them it was only a short ride, and they would be hugging the shoreline most of the way. He knew the lake better than anyone and had grown up fishing these waters.

"This a stunning place." Hannah was clinging to the side of the boat as it crashed through low waves, occasionally throwing up welcome sprays of cooling, lake water. "I've never gotten so close to flamingos before. They seemed almost tame."

"Same for the pelicans. I saw a boy feeding them fish scraps. It's like everything has a place here. The ecosystem is delicately balanced. Humans, birds, animals, plants; they've all found a way to live in harmony." Lawrence burst out laughing as a big wave broke over them, drenching the boat. It tasted like soapy water.

"Well, they have for thousands of years. But now I sense the balance is being disturbed." Hannah nodded behind them towards Thomas. "Let's talk over dinner. I'm not sure if he can hear or even understand us. No point in taking the chance."

Hannah was scanning the water's edge when she saw a huge swirl, followed by another. None of the fish they'd seen piled by the boats could make a splash that size. She spun round to Thomas then pointed to where a third splash was sending shock waves into the shallows.

"Crocodiles, Missy." Thomas pointed to calm waters in the lengthening shadows of a clump of trees. "More there. They shy. Come close to shore to feed this time."

The boat swerved further out into deeper water, the silty brown quickly changing to cloudy blue. Lawrence pointed to a distant, offshore island, rising like a volcanic peak from the lake, the rugged cliff tops now painted nipple pink by the sunset. Thomas confirmed it was Central Island, very beautiful place. He would take them, but not tomorrow.

"Why not tomorrow?" Lawrence asked.

"Weather very bad, sir, storm coming. See." Thomas indicated a patch of sky way out to the east. All Lawrence could make out were the first few stars ducking between wispy high clouds.

He looked back at the lake. The changing colours and distant shoreline were amazing. The sun was setting quickly behind them now. He hoped they would get to the hotel in time. He could tell by the look of growing unease on Hannah's face that being out in the dark on the lake was taking *roughing it* a bit too far.

Hannah heard a mosquito-like whine coming towards them. A small boat was heading across from the island at high speed. It was the only other craft she could see. Two spotlights were picking out the tops of the bigger waves they were ploughing through.

If they were tourists visiting the island, they were cutting it fine to get back before dark. Looking the other way revealed very few lights on the shore to guide them. She hoped its skipper knew what he was doing.

126

It was too far away to see how many occupants. The boat had been aiming for the village behind them when it swung sharply in their direction, the distance closing rapidly. Hannah couldn't see any navigation lights.

Their own lights seemed brighter now as the daylight faded. Suddenly the main spots on the approaching boat blinked out, making it disappear momentarily, apart from the spuming bow wave and chain-saw engine noise.

Lawrence was watching too. He drew Thomas's attention to it, but he seemed unperturbed and carried on nosing out into deeper water. Immediately ahead was a patch of shallows with some rocks breaking the surface. Lawrence pointed to a large crocodile sleeping on a stretch of sandy beach nearby.

Hannah began to feel uneasy. As the boat drew nearer, she could see it was much bigger and faster through the water. A figure was crouching to the side of a small cockpit. They were only a hundred yards away now and showed no sign of slowing down. They must be able to see us? She turned to Thomas. He was still intent on edging out into deeper water and keeping away from the rocks.

Suddenly there was a popping sound, followed by splashes in the water ahead. It was like hailstones hitting the lake. This got Thomas's attention. "Get down, get down!!" He ducked as low as he could and killed the navigation lights. He powered up to full throttle, but with three passengers and luggage, the increase in speed was marginal.

"Bigger boat, Missy, too fast for us." Another burst of gunfire, this time pockmarking the hull. A line of bullet holes traced their accuracy, splinters flying off in all directions. Hannah screamed and dived for cover, clinging tightly to Lawrence who had barricaded himself behind the bags. The boat was bouncing around. They heard a scraping noise as the keel slid over a rock.

The other boat had fallen in behind them. The crouching figure was sitting up to get a better shot. Another drilling burst brought a cry of pain from Thomas, bullets searing his neck and shoulder. He slumped over the steering arm causing the boat to lurch, missing a large dark shape in the water by inches.

Hannah shouted to Lawrence. "We must go faster. Shall we ditch the bags?"

"It won't help. We can't outrun them. Thomas said he knows these waters better than anyone. I hope he's right. Stay down. Hold tight."

Blood was smeared all over Thomas's shirt. His face was wracked in pain, eyes intermittently rolling upwards into the darkening skies. Hannah wanted to help him but moving would unbalance the boat again and expose her to the next shot.

The other boat was bearing down hard on them. The crouching figure had been joined by two others, both carrying rifles. They were no fishermen. One moved to the other side of the cockpit and took aim.

More gunfire, more holes, this time below the water line. One round hit the outboard, making it growl like a wounded animal. Hannah could feel cool jets of lake water streaming into the hold. Their engine tone changed. They were slowing down.

Thomas had regained some control but the fear in his eyes told her they were running out of time. He shook his head, a downcast expression, as if to say sorry, he had failed them. They were sitting targets. No lights on the shore, no other boats on the lake, no sign of help, no means to fight back.

Hannah thought about using her phone but who would she call, even if she had a signal? Father Kelly? A gun-packing priest, could she trust him? Maybe he'd arranged this reception party. But if he had, why had he brought them to Turkana in the first place? Nothing made sense.

She wanted to shout to Thomas but didn't know what to say. This was the end. But why? Who were these people?

"Hold tight, Missy, Ferguson Bay. Best chance." Suddenly Thomas sat up, gripping the steering arm tighter. He swung the nose round towards a dark strip of land jutting out into the lake. The water between them and the shore was dotted with pointed rocks and breaking waves. Dark shapes were moving through the shallows, others slid beneath the surface as they approached. There were crocodiles everywhere.

Hannah looked back to Lawrence who was now wearing a life jacket. He passed her one that she clipped on. He tossed one down to Thomas who nodded his thanks, without averting his eyes from the water ahead. It wouldn't stop a bullet, Lawrence told her, but it might frighten off a crocodile or protect her against an underwater rock if they hit it at speed. She squeezed his arm for reassurance.

Gunfire split the air above them. A few more seconds and they'd be gone. They struck a rock with a sickening thud. It was a glancing blow but enough to pierce the skin. Water was pouring in. Lawrence tried to plug the gap with an old rag.

Thomas yelled for them to hang on tight. He'd managed to pull the outboard half out of the water, giving them a shallower draft but still powering along at a fair lick. They were almost on the beach.

"He must know some deeper channels through the Bay." Lawrence shouted above the engine noise. "Let's hope they don't."

"Surely they'll just shadow us from deeper water and pick us off when they like." Hannah was cupping water out over the side, but it was several inches deep now and getting worse.

"Maybe we can land somewhere and run for cover." Lawrence managed a smile of encouragement.

Hannah knew by his eyes he was just trying to keep her spirits up. She was wishing they'd taken Father Kelly's advice. What she wouldn't give for that handgun, if only to make them think twice. They were holding all the aces.

More shots, one splintering the deck nearby. Then an almighty bang like a bomb going off. The dark shape behind them lurched high into the air and spiralled like a breaching whale, amid terrifying screams. It came crashing down, breaking its back on a huge rock, sending bow waves surging out in every direction.

As she watched in horror, Hannah could see the chasing boat had split in two. There were bodies in the water. Suddenly a jet of flame pierced the night sky, the heat searing her face. The surface of the lake was ablaze as diesel fuel spilled out. One of the crew was on fire. He jumped into the churning waters, a hissing sound coming up with the steam.

Thomas slowed and looked towards Lawrence for instruction. Keep going, as fast as you can, he shouted, take us to the hotel. We can't help them. And we don't want to.

It did cross Hannah's mind to stop and go back. Who were they? Why were they trying to kill them? The thought was short lived. *Fuck them.* Besides, their boat was sinking. And Thomas's shoulder was in a bad way. He needed proper treatment.

Hannah found a first-aid box floating around in the hold. There was a tube of antiseptic, some pain killers, and a bandage. It was too dark to see if the bullet had

130

passed through the wound. She strapped his arm up and made him as comfortable as she could. Once a doctor, always a doctor.

Thomas dropped the outboard to normal depth and started manoeuvring the boat out into deeper water, following an invisible channel between certain large rocks.

Suddenly the engine began to splutter. Lawrence passed him a torch. A beam of light quickly found the problem. Fuel was leaking out through a bullet hole at the back of the tank. Thomas managed to plug it with a cloth, but the damage was done. They'd lost most of the fuel, he said, and would have to crawl home. They may need the oars for the last part of the journey.

With the darkness came a chilling breeze off the lake, churning up the waves and making the boat difficult to steer. Hannah and Lawrence had managed to bail out most of the water and secure more padding over the leaks. But it was still touch and go if they'd make it.

The temperature had fallen sharply. Adrenalin levels were dropping also. They'd found some warm and reasonably dry clothes in their luggage. They agreed to remain silent until safely back on dry land.

Hannah pointed to a light emerging over distant hills across the lake. A sultry moon was fingering its way up into a star-lit canopy. The wispy clouds had gone, for now. This was the magic of an Africa she'd dreamt about.

She clasped Lawrence's hand. The evening could have worked out very different. We must be grateful, she suggested, a steely look in her eyes. "I'm determined to get to the bottom of all this."

Twenty minutes later the lights of the hotel came into view. With one last cough, the engine gave out, leaving the boat gliding into the shallows. They broke out the oars and rowed the last hundred yards. Thomas was nearly asleep. They dragged the boat up onto a sandy beach. Hannah ran off to get help.

They reported the incident to the hotel manager who said they would notify the police and look after Thomas. He wanted to make sure Hannah and Lawrence were none the worse for their ordeal. Nothing like this had ever happened at the Lodge before, he assured them. There would be a full investigation. They would send Thomas over to the hospital in Lodwar to be checked out. He hoped it wouldn't ruin their holiday.

They thanked him for his concern and made their way along the boardwalk to their villa near the beachfront. Once inside, Hannah double-locked the front door and checked that the doors leading out onto the veranda were also secure.

Before settling down for the night with hot baths, room service and the strongest drinks the minibar could offer, Hannah shivered at the thought at what had just happened.

"I get the feeling someone's running scared tonight."

* * *

"You fucking idiot! I said scare them off not wipe them out."

"The boys got carried away, Boss. What do we do now?"

"Stay there. I'll send the supply boat at first light. Take the wreckage out into deep water and lose it. Bury what's left of the bodies tonight. Leave no trace, understand?"

The American told him to disappear once he'd cleaned up the mess. He would call him in a few days. They disconnected. It had seemed so straightforward. Now Joel needed to divert any potential police involvement. No doubt there would be media interest, especially with

132

tourists being attacked and a local man in hospital with gunshot wounds.

He would think about getting Shemmy to concoct a cover story. An attack by bandits from across the lake? A terrorist group from Ethiopia trying to grab the headlines? Maybe poachers on a hunting trip fuelled up on drugs and booze?

He reassured himself. They still knew nothing. No one would help them. Even so, he should take precautions.

CHAPTER 15

Steve found himself walking aimlessly. He needed to untangle everything and think more clearly. It was well after midnight yet still very warm and quite humid. *The city that never sleeps*. Traffic was busy; bars were open, music blasted from a nightclub up some metal stairs.

Numerous cab drivers pulled over and offered to take him somewhere. A well-endowed blonde woman in a sparkly crop top and short leather skirt appeared from an alleyway and offered him whatever he wanted, for a price. All he wanted was to be alone.

He made his escape and found himself in an all-night diner, eating a bowl of french fries and drinking an Americano. He was hungry. He never did finish the salmon. It seemed a long time ago. The Sophia conundrum had been parked for now. He should be tired, but his mind was alive with questions. Was he really responding to this mental stimulation or just avoiding going home?

He did consider walking to his office and doing some research. Who owned Slaker Nadzy? Who else was involved in the sale of Pemberton Electronics? There must have been legal advisers, accountants, bankers. Or was there a company insider working with the kidnapper. Maybe the insider was the kidnapper.

And what about this kidnapping? Did it even take place? He only had Connie's word for that. Perhaps he should go to Chicago, talk to her husband Todd and her son Theo, Chicory's father. Steve got the feeling Connie didn't get on with Theo or her daughter-in-law. She didn't talk about them much. Was she called Sarah? Suzanne? It was in the notes.

Also, this diary of hers might hold some clues. He'd soon find out. One thought kept recurring. Was he looking for a crime to relieve his own frustration, perhaps turning this into something it wasn't? Maybe Connie dreamt up the kidnapping story. If Pemberton Electronics had been about to file for bankruptcy, the smart option would be to take the money and run. A kidnapping almost creates an alibi.

Another possibility surfaced as he sipped his refilled Americano. Lonsdale used to say, if you're going to hide something, put it where everyone can see it. Was Steve missing the obvious? They could have sold the company for much more than the five million to avoid tax. The rest of the money could have been paid offshore and never declared. The IRS may genuinely have been short changed.

There were too many questions for one night. He was back on the street and yawning. Another yellow cab appeared and, this time, he climbed in. The traffic thinned out as they got closer to Yorkville. Steve asked the driver to pull over at the street corner when he saw lights were still on.

The florist had just received a delivery of helianthus plum sunflowers, fresh in an hour ago from North Dakota, the lady said. They were Sophia's favourite. The bouquet looked beautiful with some greenery, gold paper and a ribbon. Steve walked the rest of the way home, crept into the apartment, and put the flowers in a vase in the middle of the dining room table. That's when he saw the note.

It was mercifully short. He checked the rooms. All her clothes had gone, along with the photos, toiletries and personal items. She'd finished off with a single kiss. Despite this sign of affection, he instinctively knew there was no point in keeping hope alive or going after her. *Life without Sophia* would have to start right now.

He just had time to set the alarm and turn off the bedside light before closing his eyes. Sleep came instantaneously but was short lived. He got up and drank some cold water. *Three am.* Back in bed, he read for a while but wasn't taking in the words. *Life without Sophia* was going to need some adjustment.

He must have been asleep again as he could hear what sounded like church bells. He woke with a start. Not church bells but his phone ringing on the bedside table. It was a different tone to the alarm. He leaned over sleepily and checked the screen.

His boss.

After taking the call, he slumped back into a sodden pillow. His hair was drenched in sweat. The duvet was damp to the touch. He fumbled for the light but kept his eyes half closed at first.

It was still dark outside. *Five thirty am.* No wonder he felt ragged. Little more than four hours sleep.

The cool shower didn't really help. Neither did the strong black coffee. He tried a slice of toast but couldn't eat it. He needed to concentrate.

His boss was normally a man of few words. Today's call was no exception. It was urgent. Be there in an hour. Ask for Tony on the second floor. That was it. Steve tried to tell him about his conversation with Connie Pemberton but didn't get very far. He said this was more important and disconnected.

Steve thought about taking the subway but didn't really know the Lenox Hill area where the 19th Precinct station house was. At that time of day, a cab was the best option. The daily grind of rush hour had started but the traffic was still flowing. They sped across town, the wheels splashing through dirty puddles left by the early morning rain.

He paid the driver and stood for a moment on the sidewalk, looking up at the old brick and mortar building on East 67th Street. The brightening sky confirmed it was just before dawn. Thinning clouds overhead were rippled in pinks and greys. The rain hadn't cleared the air. It would be another warm October day.

As he drew closer, he recognised the renaissance-style façade. He'd been here once before, just after he arrived in New York. He'd met Detective Apicella who was running the Klinkenhammer case. Of course, Tony Apicella. This was his office. Good guy who got promoted to fourth grade when the investigations closed. Somehow Steve sensed that being here again wasn't a coincidence.

Ask for Tony on the second floor. He made the mistake of doing what he was told. It turned out there were two Tony's on the second floor. Steve was introduced to a real geek in tech support. Once the confusion was untangled, Steve found himself sat across the desk from the familiar, if somewhat chubbier, face, of his former boss.

"Good to see you again, Steve." Apicella was shuffling a pile of photos. "I need your help. I lost two officers recently; another had a breakdown and my best guy resigned yesterday. He'll be making more money as a security guard at the mall, you know. Go figure. What's gone wrong with people?"

Before Steve could ask what this was all about, Apicella handed him the photos then added. "They fished a woman out of the East River last night with multiple stab wounds. Haven't had chance to open a file on that case and now I got this. What do they expect me to do?"

Steve was flicking through the photos. They showed mostly close ups of a torso with two bullet holes. It was the body of a man, taken front and back. He must have been shot in the chest at close range as the exit wounds across his back were particularly gruesome.

One bullet passed clean through his heart. The cadaver was naked, Steve couldn't see a face. Apicella was looking for more photos buried in the rat's nest of paperwork on his desk.

"Tony, I'd love to help but I'm stuck in Fraud. My boss won't transfer me. I've tried." Steve placed the photos carefully on some case files.

Apicella gave up the search. The other photos would turn up. "I spoke to him, he said he would, you know, provided you carry on with the big fraud case. He called it multitasking or some shit like that."

Be careful what you wish for. When Steve asked about a move back to Homicide, he hadn't imagined they'd double his workload. How could he handle both cases? Suddenly he had an idea.

"Tony, remember in our Klinkenhammer team, there was a British woman called Maria Li."

Apicella pulled out a buff file, shoved the photos in, then dumped it back on his desk. "Oh yeah, the pretty Chinese girl, she was smart. What about her?"

Steve liked Apicella. No frills, he had a big heart and would stick his neck out to nail the bad guys, even if it meant ruffling a few feathers upstairs. It was worth a try.

"OK, here's the deal. Give me Maria and I'll take this case. You'd need to pull some strings with Forensics."

"Forensics? That all? Consider it done, Steve, they owe me big time." Apicella moved towards the door. "Come on, I'll show you where the coffee machine is."

They did a tour of the second floor. There were some empty spaces. The others in Homicide seemed a friendly enough bunch. Steve didn't recognise any of them, but he'd been working across town on the Klinkenhammer case, so it wasn't surprising.

Apicella said he had an unmarked car he could use. Steve managed to negotiate an empty corner cubicle with a window. It had amazing views of a tenement slum next door. Most importantly, there was enough space for a second desk, a wipe board, and lockable cabinets. The kitchen was close by, and the coffee smelled good.

Steve was starting to feel at home. They were back in Apicella's office. "Tony, what made you think of me? You couldn't have known I was looking for a transfer. Also, why this case? Why not give me the woman with the stab wounds?"

Apicella smiled. He'd found the other packet of photos on top of a filing cabinet and handed them over. They showed the murder scene with close-up images of the victim. Steve felt a shiver run through him. Now he understood.

"When we searched the body, we found a card with your name on it."

CHAPTER 16

The police station in Lodwar looked like it had just landed from another world. Pristine symmetry, elegant lines and smoked-glass windows that sparkled in the morning sun. Hannah remarked that it was the cleanest building in town.

The parking lot stood empty, save for a solitary police car incongruously needing a serious wash. More layers of dirt were being sandblasted onto it by a howling gale blowing in from the east. The wind had been ferocious all morning. They'd even seen a dust devil whipping up the desert sands on the way over from the hotel.

Josphat sat in the middle of the back seat of the rented Land Cruiser like royalty. He had presented himself after breakfast, as planned, and impressed them immediately with his calmness and good command of the English language.

He was wearing a Cambridge blue polo shirt emblazoned with the Lodge's crest in gold. Pressed khaki shorts and leather sandals completed the ensemble. All he needed was a pair of Oakley Radars. Somehow, Hannah hadn't expected him to be the mirror image of a Kenyan golf professional.

"And whereabouts did this alleged incident occur?" Constable Wanjiku unfolded what looked like a treasure map on the counter. Lawrence couldn't help smiling to himself at its simplicity. There's nothing like a comprehensive ordinance survey map, he concluded. And this was nothing like one. Their hotel didn't appear on it at all. At least the words Ferguson Bay were etched near

140

an outline of the lake, next to a child's stick drawing of some tents.

"Right here. How many times do we need to tell you?" Hannah was losing patience. Lawrence was going to come to her aid, but he knew it wouldn't do any good. The young constable clearly didn't believe them.

"And approximately when did this occur?" He wasn't making any notes. It was the third time he asked.

"Between six and six thirty last night. Constable, this was a serious incident. Are you going to investigate it or not? We could have been killed. One man is in the hospital. It was a brutal attack. Automatic weapons were discharged. There were no other witnesses but there is evidence right there," Hannah stabbed at Ferguson Bay on the map with her index finger. "And plenty of evidence at our hotel. The boat was shot to pieces."

Constable Wanjiku, the name clearly visible on his badge, had been joined by a colleague who looked even younger. He didn't have a badge, or a name. They conferred in their native tongue then realised Josphat, who was standing behind Hannah and Lawrence, was well within earshot. They exchanged words with him. Hannah assumed they were warning him not to repeat anything they'd said. She turned in time to see his eyes lower in acquiescence.

"We'd like you to come back tomorrow and make a statement. We're understaffed today so it will take time to investigate your claims." Constable Wanjiku's face never changed but Hannah sensed a subtle blend of contempt and amusement. "It was most likely an accident. Some hunters had too much to drink. It happens all the time. Crocodile skins fetch a good price in Nairobi these days."

Hannah was just about to let rip when Lawrence grabbed her by the arm. He frogmarched her to the door, thanking the constable for his help and promising to return the following day with some photos to support their claims. Josphat shuffled along behind them out to the car in silence. Clearly, they could not expect much support from him.

The visit to the hospital added more frustration. The ward nurse was highly suspicious and would only confirm that Thomas had been discharged earlier that morning. She was not able to comment on his state of health and what treatment he had received, for reasons of patient confidentiality. They tried getting Josphat to ask her, but she was just as unhelpful in her own language.

The one success in Lodwar was to stock up with groceries for Agnes and chocolate for her grandchildren. It was more of a general store than a supermarket, but Hannah knew the food items would be appreciated by their hungry mouths. At the same time, they bought bottled water, tea bags, instant coffee, long life milk and some items for the hotel room. They filled up the tank before heading off back towards the lake.

"Did you really expect the police to zip over to Ferguson Bay?" Lawrence had finally managed to get the seat, mirrors and steering wheel adjusted to his bulky frame. He'd wrestled with them on the way into town. Now he was comfortable. Most of the instruments were in Japanese. So long as the ancient Land Cruiser kept going, he'd be happy. If it broke down, getting roadside assistance could be an interesting challenge. He set the trip meter just in case he needed to tell someone how far they'd come from Lodwar.

"Well, yes, quite frankly. I know Father Kelly said security was an issue, but no way were they drunks on a shooting spree." Hannah looked across at him, nodding towards the back seat.

Lawrence was more relaxed about whatever Josphat would hear. He let her know he was prepared to take the risk. "So, do you think we should go back for the handgun? What's the expression? Tool up?"

Hannah paused. They had been in some sticky situations over recent years, not unlike last night. No doubt having a gun could have tipped the odds more in their favour. But she still believed, deep down, guns just attracted more trouble and increased the risk of being killed. Live by the sword, die by the sword. She continued her belief in brains over firepower to win the day.

They found Agnes sheltering outside from the hot, scouring wind. She was mixing a poultice with ingredients she'd collected that morning, Josphat explained. Hannah was told there were purple boxwood berries, acacia pods and some orange Momordica flowers. Also, there were black seeds, strange-looking bush plums and a mixture of green and yellow leaves. The whole concoction was being ground into a paste using water from a plastic canister.

Agnes had already prepared a bowl of herbal tea which was dark brown in colour and had bits of bark and leaves floating on the surface. It looked terrible and smelled even worse.

They learned that her friend's child was sick with diarrhoea and had been vomiting most of the night. The villagers were gathering outside a large communal hut nearby. Their mood was sombre as they filed inside. The strong wind blew dust into their faces and dishevelled their loose clothing. Agnes invited Hannah, Lawrence and Josphat to join the ceremony that she was leading.

Inside, the room became hot and sticky once the flimsy brushwood door was closed behind them. There were no windows, just reed walls and a dirt floor that must have housed some animals in the last few days, probably goats, Hannah decided, judging by the smell.

A space was cleared in the middle where the child was laid down on a goat skin. Hannah guessed the child was no more than eight or nine. She looked very weak and was crying intermittently. There was spittle around her mouth and her eyes looked swollen and sore. Her mother knelt beside her and kept soothing her fevered brow.

Suddenly Agnes started to chant and clap her hands, swaying to a rhythm only she could hear. The villagers quickly found the beat and joined in, the pace quickening. The room was filled with the joyous sound of African voices in rich harmony. It was music as old as time itself. Hannah could sense spirits lifting, as if the Gods had joined them.

The dancing became more liberated, hips swinging, arms raised on high, feet stamping on the dry earth. Hannah noticed Agnes's eyes were rolling upwards as she went into a trance. Others soon followed. The room was a swirl of colour and heat and life, with an energy that made the walls pulsate. Lawrence and Josphat were swaying along, big smiles on their faces, rivulets of sweat pouring down their cheeks, feet moving in unison, hands clapping in time to the beat.

Hannah kept her eyes on Agnes. Her chanting became more like a murmur, drowned out by the singing. She began flicking water from a bucket over the child and her mother, using a long-haired brush. Josphat leaned across and explained to Hannah that Agnes was now in touch with the spirit world. The spell she was casting would drive away the evil that had possessed the child, while the water would cleanse her soul.

Next, Agnes applied liberal amounts of the poultice to the child's belly and lower abdomen. She massaged it in with soothing hands, all the time murmuring the same words, over and over. When the poultice was gone, Agnes and her mother coaxed the child to sit up and drink the herbal tea. It made her cry and spit out the first few mouthfuls. Eventually she drank the remainder until the bowl was dry.

By now, many in the room were lost in the trance. Some rolled on the floor while others danced as if the bones had been removed from their legs and they were struggling to remain upright. Mostly it was women and girls but some of the men were equally lost in a spiritual world.

The child was being comforted by her mother when Agnes resumed centre stage. She was pumping up the frenzy as if to create a united deterrent against the forces of evil and darkness, Josphat added.

Hannah found herself swimming in a sea of communal warmth, embraced by the sheer outpouring of human emotion. Her eyes closed as she became lost in trance herself. She imagined the reed walls melting away around them. She could see a vast plain in a sepia half-light, acacia trees dotted against a sienna skyline.

Hundreds of people were walking towards them from every direction, in small groups and large. There were men, women, and children, in families and alone, warriors and tribes' people of all ages. Their feet kicked up dust that hung in the still air. Some were driving goat herds, others had strings of camels. There were cattle feeding all around her.

Hannah noticed the ground was no longer a desert but had become lush and thick with vegetation. She could smell a sweet freshness in the air brought about by recent rains. In the distance, beyond fields of crops, beyond the trees, Hannah could see great herds of zebras and wildebeest grazing on swathes of grassland.

Occasionally they were disturbed by a lion or a cheetah, causing them to scatter, only to regroup again and carry on gorging themselves on the rich, green shoots. Amongst the herds she could make out the unmistakable profiles of elephants and giraffes.

All the time, the crowd of people was growing larger. They joined in the singing and dancing as they reached the spot where the reed walls had stood. Hannah could clearly see their shining faces now. It was a truly joyous spectacle. They looked so real and yet this was all part of the magic Agnes had created: a privileged insight into another, much older, reality.

Hannah realised Agnes had summoned up her ancestors to protect the child. They came from a time before any drought when the land and the lake provided everything the local people needed. Water was abundant. The people of the village honoured those who had gone before them. They worshipped their Gods and the Gods looked after them.

Life was simple and in total harmony with Nature. It was an Africa before the white man came, Hannah reflected. Agnes's ancestors suffered none of the hardship of today. Whatever killed her husband, and was killing her children and grandchildren, must, in some way, derive from interference by people from so-called western civilisations.

The history of Africa was a dark tapestry woven with the threads of colonialism, slavery, exploitation, and the misappropriation of mineral resources. It justified the rape of the land and its people as well as the collateral damage caused by European diseases, for which the local tribes had no defence. They paid the price with their lives for the profits of their conquerors.

Hannah could now see that climate change, through its bastard children of drought, flood, heat and cold, was a

146

modern-day extension of colonial superiority and exploitation. It brought blight and pestilence to their land as a direct consequence of greed by people living thousands of miles away who did not even think about the death and destruction they were spreading.

Added to this mix was the religious brainwashing and manipulation of local people who had been persuaded or coerced into passive obedience to the politics and control of the Christian church. It had become their way of life, yet it never had been.

As she stood amongst the crowded shadows of the ancestors, Hannah suddenly felt ashamed. She understood what was happening and it was wrong. These were good people, genuine people who wanted nothing more than to be left alone to live their lives in peace.

Yet Hannah could see she was part of their problem. She did not belong here. Her very presence was polluting their way of life. She had appeared and would disappear, yet would leave behind traces from a distant world that cared nothing for them.

The Turkana people had unwittingly become pawns in somebody else's game, powerless to stop the encroachment by people never satisfied with what they had and constantly greedy for more.

The local people did not understand why their lake was disappearing, why healthy people were dying, why the rains did not come, why the crops no longer grew, why it was getting hotter or why they were increasingly short of food and water.

They prayed to their Gods, but the Gods weren't listening. Their ancestors had no answers either. Now, in desperation, they were asking for help from the very people who had caused the problem in the first place. Hannah felt it was a kind of madness that had no end. She likened their situation to a drawing by Escher. It looked

147

perfectly feasible but, on closer examination, it was impossible, reality playing a trick on the eye.

Yet a solution must be possible. Whatever had been done could be undone. Hannah had a job to do. The little girl in front of her was seriously ill and could die. She had to prevent that and ensure others did not suffer the same way. The ethics and philosophising could wait. She could feel the expectations of the ancestors upon her. She needed to step up and confront this man-made evil. Step up right now.

Hannah's eyes flickered open. The walls had returned. She was back in the heat of the room. The singing was louder than before, the dancing more frenetic. Lawrence and Josphat were embracing some of the villagers and seemed to have learnt the words of the song. The little girl was sleeping in her mother's arms. Agnes was jumping up and down, shaking her arms at the ceiling.

Suddenly Agnes stopped and turned towards Hannah. Her mouth was closed yet her eyes were on fire. Her unblinking stare chilled Hannah to the core. Without opening her lips, Agnes spoke only to her.

"They killing us. Help me. They killing us."

CHAPTER 17

After the ceremony, they returned to Agnes's hut to share out the groceries with her and the children. The chocolate was a huge hit, and warm embraces were exchanged. Hannah noticed that Agnes, on closer inspection, didn't look well. Her eyes were red-rimmed and itchy sore.

Now that she'd come down from the trance, her body was listless, all the positive energy having seeped away. She told them she hadn't slept and had been vomiting most of the night but didn't want to say anything in case Hannah got worried.

Josphat was translating without any emotion. Hannah could feel her irritation growing towards him. These were his people, yet he somehow passed it off as another day in the office. So, more people were sick and dying, he seemed to imply. In Africa, people die every day. But not if Hannah could help it. Not good, healthy people dying needlessly. And not on her watch.

They spent time going through Agnes's daily routine. Hannah made some notes. The food they ate; the water they drank and the places she went to collect the ingredients for her herbal remedies. This included daily trips to the lake to barter for fish. Agnes brought back mainly dried fish which looked and smelt awful, but this part of their diet hadn't changed.

They made a list of places to check out. Lawrence asked about the toilet arrangements, being as diplomatic as he could. His acting demonstration of bowel movements brought much-needed laughter. Why were men always fixated on toilets? Hannah wondered.

It turned out most of the village used a communal soak-away surrounded by brushwood screens for privacy. The warriors found their own places, Agnes explained through Josphat. They find it by their noses, she suggested, offering a weak smile.

Hannah picked up on the word nose. *Pua*, in Swahili. The answer they were looking for must be right under their noses. But what? They had discussed this at length on the journey over. Something must have changed in their routine to bring about the illness they were all suffering. But what could cause so many people and animals to die? Two more goats had died overnight, they discovered.

Agnes said she had been helped by Father Kelly to take one of the children to the hospital in Lodwar some months ago. Their tests drew a blank. The doctor was newly qualified and didn't know the area or its people. He apologised when he told her he had limited resources and was as baffled as everyone else. He gave her some medicine to ease the stomach pains. It didn't help. The child died several days later.

"How about mercury poisoning?" Lawrence suggested in a whisper, having taken Hannah outside. The wind was dropping but they still needed to shelter behind the Land Cruiser.

"Maybe mercury has leaked into the lake somehow. The Nile perch and tiger fish they eat are predators. Tiny doses in the small fry could have built up in the food chain. It's just a thought."

"Good thought. I suppose if it were mercury in the fish then other people would be dying around the lake. I haven't seen or heard any reports of the illness being more widespread. Father Kelly said even some of the villagers on the other side of Kalokol were largely unaffected. It's worth checking out though. Let's ask

Agnes for a small piece of fish and get a sample of lake water for testing." Hannah realised what she'd said. "Testing where?"

"I know a good laboratory in Nairobi." Lawrence smiled. "Not sure if she'll play ball but we can only ask."

"You mean Fara? Can we trust her? If this got out, I could be in real trouble back home. Cardinal Maina could bury me with this. Holidaymakers don't usually test water samples for mercury contamination." Hannah looked concerned. Things were developing too quickly for comfort.

"Let's find out. No time like the present. I think we should take the risk before more people die. At least if we know what we're up against, we can look for a cure." Lawrence had put Henry and Fara Gachuhi's contact details into his phone. He moved away to where the signal was stronger and called her. He got straight through.

She'd be delighted to help, understood the sensitivity of the situation and was happy not to ask too many questions, Lawrence reported back a few minutes later. If it could save lives and make sick people better, then why not, Fara had said.

"We might get the results back while we're still here. Good call." Hannah calculated. For better or worse, it was another big decision taken. Now it was time to get moving.

"Fara asked if we had any sample jars. I told her we hadn't thought of that so she's couriering some to us on the afternoon flight. They'll be at the Lodge when we return. I'm beginning to love this country. The people are so helpful." Lawrence beamed as their plan started to take shape.

"Not all of them, remember?" Hannah reminded him of their adventures on the lake the previous evening. "Someone doesn't want us here. We need to be careful."

Hannah noticed a small group of young girls getting ready to go and collect water, their colourful plastic containers swinging about in the breeze. Josphat was chatting to some of the other women while Agnes had disappeared inside, maybe to get some rest, Hannah hoped.

"Let's go with them." Hannah indicated for Lawrence to let Josphat know. "I'd also like to see where they collect their vegetables and herbal remedies. I'm guessing you want to find the latrines?"

"Not just find them." Lawrence crossed his legs which made her laugh. Was it the early onset of old man urinary syndrome? She could live with it if it was. Lawrence was quick to add. "We can always come back tomorrow and take samples, if you think it worthwhile."

The small group of water carriers soon picked up a few stray dogs along the way and a couple of old men out from the village who were looking for a lost goat, according to Josphat.

Hannah could smell the latrines long before they reached them. There was little privacy, but no one seemed to care. Lawrence opted to go behind a tree instead, much to the amusement of the young girls.

"I think definitely worth taking some samples tomorrow." Hannah concluded. "Human waste is always very revealing. If people have eaten any nasties, they'll be in there somewhere."

"I'm guessing the sort of nasties you're thinking about go way beyond tummy bugs, e coli, that sort of thing?" Lawrence added.

"If it's killing people and animals, it must be extreme. Don't forget, this outbreak is all quite recent. Something must have changed in their diet or the local environment." Hannah suggested. "It's under our noses."

152

Along the way, the girls pointed out where Agnes collected her berries, herbs, and medicinal plants. The bushes looked healthy enough, but Hannah decided to take cuttings. She had brought clippers and a bag from the Land Cruiser for that purpose.

The wind had dropped to a stiff breeze and the heat was rising. Lawrence was struggling to keep up, the pace of the girls quickening as they sang songs and used the empty plastic containers to beat out a marching rhythm. He felt embarrassed as the girls were barefoot and he was wearing stout walking shoes, which should have made it easier to cover the harsh terrain.

Josphat was engrossed in talking to the two old men who seemed to have forgotten about the goat and were just enjoying the walk. Suddenly all three stopped dead, Josphat holding up his hand to warn Hannah and Lawrence who by now were some paces behind.

"Bafe!! Bafe!!" Josphat announced in a loud whisper and pointed to a patch of rocky ground near some acacia trees ahead. "Be careful, go round."

Hannah and Lawrence speeded up until they were tucked in behind the three men. Hannah followed the line of where Josphat was pointing but couldn't see anything. The girls were almost out of sight now up ahead, just the harmony of their voices catching the breeze.

"Bafe? Josphat, what's a bafe?" Hannah found herself instinctively grabbing Lawrence's arm.

"Snake, Missy, very nasty. Follow me." He took them in a wide circle around the rocks.

After this encounter, Hannah could see snakes everywhere. Every leaf, branch or clump of grass had piercing eyes and a venomous tongue. They were in the trees, lying under bushes, tucked away in the rocks. She knew it was ridiculous, but fear *was* ridiculous, she kept telling herself. At least that settled one debate - Josphat would be coming with them if they decided to collect samples tomorrow.

"I didn't see anything." Lawrence whispered to her when the danger had passed. "I'll have to look that up tonight. Bafe, he said. Or maybe it's best not to know."

They pushed on through some thick bushes, the girls' voices growing louder. In the middle of a clearing stood a large, metal hand pump, set high into what looked to Hannah like a concrete plinth. As they got closer, the concrete turned out to be baked earth, the browns and reds' reflecting the colours of the dry ground.

The ancient pump was a relic from British colonial days, Lawrence proudly reported, pointing to an engraving on the front which said *Benjamin Shepherd and Sons, Birmingham, 1903.*

The girls were working as a team, taking it in turns to pump the long handle, fill the containers, and screw the tops back on to stop spillage on the return journey. They'd walked for nearly an hour. It made Hannah appreciate the luxury of turning on a tap. She would never complain again about poor plumbing.

Lawrence thought about cupping his hands and drinking from the pump, but Hannah reminded him of the dangers and passed him a little bottle of mineral water instead.

Hannah moved over to talk to Josphat while the girls took a rest under a tree, before the heavy lifting on the journey back. Clearly this was routine for them, something they did most days.

"Many people use this well." Josphat responded to Hannah's question. He involved the old men in the conversation who nodded when asked if people from Kalokol came out this far for their water. "Easy pump, fill quicker. Pump in village many times break. This better."

154

"I'd like to come back here tomorrow and take samples of the water. Can you help us with that, Josphat?" Hannah noticed the girls were starting to load the containers on their heads and get ready to leave.

"Yes, Missy, as you wish."

One of the two old men spotted what he thought were fresh animal tracks leading deeper into the bush. They made a point of saying *kwaheri* and shaking hands with the three of them before carrying on their search for the elusive goat.

The girls had just set off when Lawrence caught Hannah by the arm and pulled her to one side. "Can you hear that?"

"Hear what? I can only hear the girls singing." Hannah looked puzzled.

"No, in the distance, it's coming from that direction." Lawrence pointed just to the right of where the old men had gone. "Can you see, over there, above the trees, a dust cloud? Sounds like heavy machinery."

"I can't hear anything. The dust could be wild animals or old men wrangling goats, I suppose." Hannah offered a smile.

"I'm being serious, Hannah, there's something going on." Lawrence's persistence convinced her to investigate it tomorrow. She made another mental note.

The return journey was slower, the girls taking it in turns to carry the heavy containers. It was hot and dusty. The flies had multiplied and were enjoying some tasty white flesh for a change.

As well as being sweaty, tired, and irritable, Lawrence was feeling guilty. He offered to carry the water but got short shrift. It was woman's work, Josphat explained, even though he did make the offer. The look on the girls' faces confirmed this. At least Lawrence's conscience felt easier.

"Josphat, did Agnes tell you about her husband's other wife? I'm keen to meet her if that would be possible." Hannah was keeping pace with her guide. She had left Lawrence struggling along behind. Her bag was full of berries, leaves, a few meagre roots, and some dusty vegetables. They were nearly back at Agnes's home.

"Yes, she lives other side village. I know the place. Her name Layla. She has three children. Other men bring her fish now." Josphat's beaming smile told Hannah all she needed to know. So, the poor man toiled all his life on the lake to provide for Agnes, Layla and two families, only to end up dying in agony alone and being buried under the goat pen. Hannah appointed herself his avenging angel. May he rest in peace.

Agnes was sleeping when they got back. Hannah didn't want to wake her but was assured by Josphat that it would be fine for them to visit Layla without talking to Agnes first. The two women knew each other well and got along fine, he explained.

They got back in the Land Cruiser and set off, Josphat resuming his regal position in the middle of the back seat. Had Lawrence checked his mirror, he'd have noticed a green 4x4 with one occupant pulling out of some bushes and following them at a discreet distance into the village. The young, female driver was wearing wrap-around, reflective shades and talking into her satellite phone.

* * *

"Bafe is a puff adder. It's one of the most common and deadliest snakes in Kenya. Tends to feed at night on small rodents but will take whatever it can get its fangs into." Lawrence duly reported.

He had told Hannah he needed to do some serious online research when they finally got back to the Lodge.

156

While she was collecting a parcel from the concierge desk and checking flight times, Lawrence fell fast asleep at the screen, the exertions of a long day proving too much. He resolved to pace himself better tomorrow.

Showered and changed, they were now enjoying dinner on the terrace surrounded by the magical sounds of Africa at night. Squadrons of bats swooped in and out of the garden lights, feasting on the abundant insect life. David Attenborough would have felt right at home.

"How deadly?" Hannah didn't really want to know but felt she had to let him show off.

"During its lifetime, each snake will produce enough venom to kill five adult males. You've a fifty-two percent chance of dying if not treated within a couple of hours of being bitten." Lawrence was savouring a sirloin steak, medium rare. He'd decided against the grilled perch, at least until they got the test results back.

"I didn't even see it." Hannah blinked in demonstration.

"That's why we have Josphat." Lawrence continued. "He's our eyes and ears. He was very helpful with Layla too, I thought, quite sensitive and diplomatic."

"You think so? Matter of fact is the best I could give him. Still, we found out what we needed to know. No health problems with Layla, her family, or neighbours. Yet she only lives a few miles away. And she's eating the same lake fish. The boys were queuing up to supply her, weren't they?"

"I could see why." Lawrence smiled. "She wasn't without her charms, I thought."

"One track mind. Typical male." Hannah tutted but couldn't resist a smile. "I'd still like to get samples from the well Layla uses and the one in Kalokol itself. It was kind of her to give us some vegetables. I'll include them for testing as we've got enough jars. Thank you, Fara."

157

"Are you feeling any better about her now?" Lawrence topped up their wine glasses.

"Fara? The jury's still out but she delivered on the parcel, so fingers crossed." Hannah put down her knife and fork having cleared her plate. "I'm pleased we had spare groceries left over. Layla was very appreciative. I don't think her kids had seen chocolate for a long time."

"Ironic as they grow cocoa beans in southern Kenya. Talking of which, split a brownie with me for dessert?"

Hannah didn't hesitate. "Why not, the chicken was delicious, and we are supposed to be on holiday, after all."

Lawrence ordered; one brownie with yoghurt and two spoons. "What's the plan for tomorrow?"

"Early start, I reckon." Hannah pulled out her list and cleared a space on the tablecloth.

"There's a flight back to Nairobi at noon. If we can get the samples over to Fara by early afternoon, she might be able to run the tests for us tomorrow: lake water, the three wells, roots and vegetables and a fish sample, that should do it."

"Don't forget the latrines." Lawrence smirked as the brownie duly arrived and was presented with a flourish by the effervescent waitress. "We're not just going through the motions with this, Hannah."

She looked at the brownie, picked up her spoon but then thought better of it. Lawrence made short work of the rich, brown chocolate delight.

"So, what's your hunch, Dr McGlynn?" Lawrence hoped to distract her while he scooped up the last of the yoghurt.

"Hunch about what?"

"What killed Agnes's husband and all the others."

"And may be killing Agnes herself." Hannah added. "She looked terrible. We've got to act fast. We must catch that flight and hope Fara comes good for us."

"I'll call her again tomorrow morning and let her know the plan." Lawrence resisted licking the plate clean. "Come on, I need a hunch."

Hannah looked him full in the face, their eyes locked together. She took a moment to consider. "I don't think it's mercury in the lake. It's more localised."

"What then?"

"My best guess is whatever's going on beneath your dust cloud."

CHAPTER 18

Steve felt decidedly weird. He didn't like coincidences. Only the previous evening he was chatting to the man about fish and chips in the lobby of the Rokelle International. What would Stannard give for a pint of heavy water bitter now, he wondered. He'd seemed a decent bloke and didn't deserve to die in such a brutal fashion.

The CCTV camera in a jeweller's shop across the street caught the assault. Stannard appeared to be the victim of a random mugging that went wrong. Two men, both wearing ski masks, gloves, and anonymous dark clothing, came out of the shadows and pulled him into an alleyway. There was no one else on the street at the time. It all happened in less than two minutes.

Steve worked out Stannard must have been walking from the subway station to the *Shine The Light* pub. They pushed him against a wall, there was a struggle, and the gun went off. He'd have been dead before he hit the ground.

The gunman was much taller than the other man, in fact taller than Stannard himself, who, Steve recalled, was maybe a tad over six feet. He surmised two men, given their size and physicality. It could have been a man and a woman. He made a mental note.

The video ran on. After the shooting, they frisked his pockets, removed what looked like a wallet and some cash. A car going past clearly spooked them. They ran off down the same alleyway into darkness. It was some time before a pedestrian spotted the body and called it in. Steve switched it off, he'd seen enough.

160

As homicide investigations go, this one had started well. Unusually, Steve knew something about the victim. He saw the crime being committed and had some leads to follow up. Although it was a tragic situation, Steve felt the adrenalin buzz again. A homicide had taken place, and he was going to solve it.

An autopsy report would confirm the cause of death but that was clear. A ballistics report was being prepared after the two bullets were dug out of the bloodstained wall. He didn't expect to learn much from it.

Apicella had passed over the case file together with a clear plastic bag containing Stannard's phone, room key, Steve's old business card and some bits of paper. Also in the bag was the Rolex which surprisingly survived the robbery. Steve tried the phone, but it needed a six-digit pin. No wonder they didn't take it.

He got a message from the front desk to say the victim's clothes were ready for collection at the morgue. Forensics were too busy to run any tests. No help there either.

Steve took the pool car over to the Fraud office and cleared his desk. He updated his laptop with notes from the interview with Connie Pemberton. He googled Stannard and read his profile on LinkedIn and the Oxford University website. There was even a Wikipedia page on him and links through to some of his published work.

Exploring Applications for Thorium-based Propulsion Systems utilising Molten Salt Reactors proved impenetrable. The man obviously had more brain cells than all the 19th Precinct put together, Steve included. What a waste of a human life, he reflected.

On the way out, he saw his other boss at the water cooler. He thanked him for agreeing to the transfer, promised regular reports and told him about Connie Pemberton. They decided to keep the IRS in the loop but

161

not mention the kidnapping yet. Steve wanted to be certain.

As he readjusted the seat in the pool car, Steve got a call from a very excited Maria. She couldn't wait to get started and was on her way over. No need for coffee next week. They arranged to meet at their new office then go together to Stannard's hotel. He wanted her to see the CCTV footage of the assault first.

His next stop was the morgue. Steve wasn't required to ID the body, but the morgue attendant asked him to sign anyway. The clothes, including the bloodstained shirt, white socks, and leather sandals, were neatly bundled up inside a heavy-duty, clear, plastic bag.

Driving back to the 19th Precinct, Steve replayed his brief conversation with Stannard. He'd said he was visiting New York to give a couple of talks. Copies of the presentation slides and lecture notes could be helpful.

Was Stannard flying straight home or going somewhere else? The air tickets could be on his phone or in the room. Was he married? Were there next of kin to be notified? He must have a diary. Presumably his passport was at the hotel. Also, Steve remembered he'd said he was meeting someone at seven thirty. Unlikely that person was connected but it was worth checking out.

Stannard, a brain the size of a planet; all that knowledge and experience; a leader in nuclear physics yet his life was snuffed out in two minutes by a couple of street thugs and for what? Steve couldn't help but feel guilty. Stannard was only in that part of town because Steve had recommended the pub. He owed the man justice. He would put these two behind bars for a very long time.

* * *

"Have you been through these bits of paper, Steve?"

They were in Stannard's room at *Sixty-Nine*. The timeless art deco fixtures didn't compensate for the fact that Stannard was right. The room was way too small. A laptop sat forlornly on a polished bureau, access by password only. No diary: must be electronic. No sign of any air tickets either. There was a handwritten note on hotel stationery near the laptop. *MH @ SLLI 10.30,* meaning unknown.

Stannard's passport was eventually recovered from behind the reception desk. The concierge was most unhelpful, pointing out they had to respect the privacy of their exclusive clientele, I'm sure you understand, officer. Steve put him straight on the importance of his cooperation and asked to see the CCTV footage of the lobby area for the past twenty-four hours.

It was all too much for the concierge and the manager was at a conference, could he come back another time, next week perhaps. Amazingly, the manager appeared after the concierge was reminded about the implications for obstructing a homicide investigation. Immediately the footage was being saved onto a USB stick.

"Bits of paper?" Steve turned to Maria. "Not yet, I needed my forensic specialist. What are they anyway, I'm guessing receipts."

Steve smiled at her, the chemistry sparking between them once more. He always felt Maria complemented him so well, covering his blind spots. He knew her attention to detail and ability to analyse things systematically would prove invaluable once again. The devil was always in the detail.

"There are some receipts including one for a return journey from Oxford to Paddington last week, with taxi fares to and from Westminster. Stannard must have been meeting someone at the House, there's a scrunched-up visitor badge." Maria held it up.

"Does it say who?"

"No but there's a security number and a bar code. It must be traceable."

He looked at Maria and realised, by her expression, she was thinking the same thing. They wouldn't get far with this investigation without some help from across the pond.

"I worked with Oxford CID some years back. They're a bunch of show ponies and think it's all like Inspector Morse, intuitive policing, brilliant ideas over a pint in the pub. Getting their hands dirty and doing grunt work is for ordinary plods." Steve checked his watch. Still early evening over there.

Maria was putting the receipts into chronological order. "Then maybe we could start in London. Get someone to follow up on this visitor badge. You got any contacts in the Met?"

"I have someone in mind." Steve dialled the number. They hadn't spoken for some time but if anyone could help, it would be his ex-boss. The question was, did he have the time? Come to that, was he still a police officer?

"Lonsdale."

"Detective Inspector, good evening, I hope I'm not disturbing you, it's…".

"I know who you are, Detective Sergeant. *An Englishman in New York*. And I know you well enough to know this isn't a social call. Come on, out with it." Lonsdale sounded his usual blunt, direct yet calm and composed self. But Steve detected a slight hint of something else in his voice. Was Lonsdale pleased to be getting this call?

Steve explained the circumstances surrounding Stannard's death, his connection with Oxford University and the House of Commons visitor badge in his pocket. Lonsdale said he had an old friend who was now a

164

professor at the university. When Steve mentioned he was working with Maria again, she leaned over and shouted hello.

They had little to go on and needed boots on the ground in the UK. Steve was unsure how best to proceed, given the protocols around Lonsdale being a superior officer.

"Don't dance around the handbags, Detective Sergeant, this is a possible murder investigation, there's no time for niceties." Lonsdale interrupted, much to Steve's relief. "If you're asking me if I could work with you and Maria from this end, the answer is yes."

Lonsdale explained that he had been seconded from Surrey CID onto a national task force, set up to establish positive discrimination methodologies within the police and promote the benefits of greater cultural responsiveness and diversity.

"The Super said I'd been chosen as it would broaden my horizons, enhance my network of internal contacts and help me align my outdated values with the more progressive society we now serve."

Steve couldn't help but smile. "And can I ask, sir, how are your values these days?"

"I'll let you know once I've finished my sessions with the police psychiatrist, Detective Sergeant."

Lonsdale had relinquished his office at the Surrey Force Headquarters in Guildford and was now hot-desking in the bowels of New Scotland Yard. His subsidised bed-sit in Millbank was within walking distance. He described the recent approval for his own car parking space as the ultimate Pyrrhic victory.

"We may need you to go to Oxford, would that be a problem?" Steve was still hesitant. Although he sensed Lonsdale was itching to get his hands dirty, Steve knew the politics could get heavy. He didn't need Apicella getting a bill for Lonsdale's time and expenses.

"Detective Sergeant, travel is part of my new job. Oxford CID are on my list of people to be indoctrinated, sorry, made aware of the error of their ways. No one knows where I am or even cares. Your call couldn't have come at a better time. Send over the notes, and I'll visit the House first thing in the morning."

Steve disconnected. He didn't know why but he suddenly felt relieved, even quite tearful. It had been an eventful couple of days. Maybe it was the lack of sleep, losing Sophia, feeling guilty about Stannard or, perhaps, sensing the warmth and encouragement again emanating from Maria and Lonsdale. His real police family.

Maria purposefully clamped the receipts into a large bulldog clip, placed it on the bureau next to the inert laptop then spontaneously threw her arms around him. They embraced in silence. Steve could feel hot tears soaking through his shirt front. His own tears had started without warning.

Somehow this priceless moment helped clear the air, draw a line under the frustrations they had been feeling over recent weeks. They had a new sense of purpose. There was a job to be done. With Lonsdale coming on board, the old team was back in place and ready to get moving.

They bagged up Stannard's laptop, papers, and anything else in the room that looked helpful. On the way out of the hotel, they collected the USB stick and some other papers from the concierge, who had obviously benefitted from some corrective indoctrination himself, while they'd been upstairs.

They agreed to play the lobby footage when back in the office. Maria said she also wanted to watch the assault video again. Something was bugging her. She smiled as she pointed out that her perspective might pick something up that Steve had overlooked. He couldn't agree more.

166

Back in their office, Maria got the coffee while Steve powered up his laptop. The footage from *Sixty-Nine* wasn't ideal as the camera was understandably pointing at the reception desk. It did show Stannard collecting his room key then disappearing into an elevator. It was pictures only, no sound.

The digital clock in the recording showed seven thirty when Stannard came back fifteen minutes later. Shortly afterwards a man in a suit appeared in the lobby area. They shook hands then Stannard passed over an envelope. They talked for a few minutes before moving towards some chintz-covered armchairs.

Steve sat up straighter. "I recognise that man. He was at the Rokelle, in a group, talking to Stannard. He could be another scientist. He must have been at the lecture. Pity we can't get a photograph."

Maria turned the laptop towards her, pressed several keys then disappeared behind the screen, heading towards the kitchen area. Steve wondered if she was going for more coffee. It was getting late, and he didn't need any more caffeine today. They could pick all this up again tomorrow morning.

Maria returned clutching several sheets of paper. Somehow, she had enhanced the imagery, the colour photograph clearly showing the man's face. She put one copy in the case file and a second in a plastic sleeve. Her smile said it all. Steve was going to ask how she did that, but he'd have been none the wiser if she did explain. So long as she was on his team.

"Tomorrow morning, I may be late getting in. I must follow up this fraud investigation." Steve announced apologetically. He suggested Maria could go over the lobby footage in his absence.

"Steve, you've saved me from the tedium of my forensics job. I'm only too happy to help you. Earlier, did you mention a possible kidnapping?"

It hadn't occurred to him she might be interested in this case too. Given her passion for electrical engineering, she would know more about the technology behind Pemberton's product range than he did. Connie Pemberton was due to hand over her diary which would need some careful, forensic analysis. He made the decision.

"OK, meet me here at eight, we'll go together. I'll warn you now, Connie Pemberton is a handful. It's quite a story."

"Before we go tonight, Steve, can we just run through the assault footage again? I think there's something we've both missed.

"It will still be here in the morning, Maria. We need fresh eyes. Let's make it seven thirty."

CHAPTER 19

Steve slept better that night. He couldn't face breakfast. Back in the office, the hot coffee was hitting the right spot. Maria's mug was empty. She'd been in for nearly an hour. He could tell by the sparkle in her eyes she'd found what she was looking for.

They watched the assault again in silence. Maria kept rewinding and playing over the part where the gun went off and Stannard plummeted to the ground. Then she fast-forwarded to the car going past and both assailants running off down the alleyway.

Steve glanced at the clock on the far wall. They'd need to leave soon to meet up with Connie Pemberton. He'd got the files ready this time.

"There, just there." She pressed pause. "He's limping. The gunman, his right leg. See, his knee gives way slightly, here, and he switches his weight to his left leg, here. Then watch again, they run off into the alley. There, and there, he's carrying his right leg."

Steve had to agree, the gunman did appear to favour his left side. She rewound to the beginning and, sure enough, as the two assailants lunged at Stannard from the darkness, the taller one kept the weight off his right knee.

It was a start, but only that. The injury could be temporary. They knew nothing about the gunman or his accomplice. Steve congratulated her on spotting it, something he'd failed to do. Although the answer was always in the detail, you needed the hunch to know where to look. Maria had demonstrated both. They could talk in the car. Now they had to leave.

"OK, Steve, let's imagine we're the two assailants." The traffic was heavy. They were crawling closer to Connie's hotel. Maria was also looking out for a parking space. "Our plan seems to be, wait in the darkness until someone comes past, drag them into the alleyway, point a gun at them until they hand over their money, cards, whatever, then run away. Is that it?"

Steve wasn't sure where she was going with this. He would play devil's advocate, a role he'd understudied with the grandmaster, his ex-boss, Lonsdale. "We're two muggers, we don't have a plan. We need heroin and don't have any money. A guy walks past and bingo, we got what we need."

She spotted a parking space just down the block. It was a tight squeeze, but Steve was getting used to the heavy steering. He killed the engine and gathered his files. A blast of sticky heat hit them as they got out. It was going to be even hotter and more humid today.

Maria continued. "We couldn't see the guy until he walked past. We didn't know the street was deserted. And we didn't know he had any money. You say it was a mugging, but we missed his Rolex?"

Steve waved to Connie as they entered the lobby. She was in the same booth, on her phone. No glass on the table this time, just a cup and saucer alongside a book he took to be her diary.

He pulled up out of earshot and turned to Maria. "What are you saying?"

"Steve, I'm not saying anything yet. Maybe it wasn't a random mugging. Maybe it was a deliberate hit made to look like a mugging. There's something about the whole incident that doesn't feel right."

"If you're right, then I must be a suspect."

"How come?"

170

"I knew where he'd be around that time. I'd given him the address."

"You've got alibis." She reassured him with a smile. "Anyway, he could have told someone else where he was going, the man in the lobby, for example. Maybe he'd arranged to meet someone in the pub. I'm not saying it was a set-up but there's a funny smell. Surely, they'd have taken his watch?"

"She's off the phone. We'll need to pick this up later. Come and meet Connie."

Steve made the introductions. Maria was a colleague in the Fraud team. Connie didn't seem to notice. No more snide remarks. She had come to do business. They ordered a bottle of mineral water, with three glasses.

"His name was Ethan Bronstein, one of the directors, or so he told us. There were others within Slaker Nadzy, but Ethan was always there. We trusted him, up until then. He knew the buyers, found their seed corn capital, helped them get started, he said. He introduced us to them. What a meeting that was. They were just kids, fresh out of college, so naïve. Ethan made the deal."

"What was the connection to Israel?" Steve was going to make notes, but Maria was ahead of him. She was listening intently and tapping into her laptop.

"We were told the funding came from Israel. The buyers were a start-up here in New York. Herzl Power Technologies. They'd only been going three years. They've renamed our company Herzl Pemberton Electronics, not very original, but what can you expect from a bunch of wannabees." Connie failed to keep the look of disgust from spreading across her face.

"And what did Herzl make, prior to the acquisition, Connie?" Maria found her voice without looking up from her screen. "Why did they want to buy you?"

Connie was trying to find the appropriate layman's language until Maria explained her background was in electrical engineering before joining the police. Connie seemed to brighten at the prospect of talking to someone who understood what she was saying.

"Herzl made vanadium redox batteries. They were a spin-off from the business incubator at Princeton. Three pretty-boy, PhD students from Upstate New York. They thought they could take the market by storm. Their parents helped with some of the funding, Slaker Nadzy found the rest." Connie explained.

"And that's the Israeli connection?" Maria added.

"Yes, but we were never told who these Israeli investors were." Connie confirmed. She was keen to press on. "They'd seen a gap in the green energy market and patented an electrolyte design using a clever alloy of vanadium, bromine, and gadolinium. Their rechargeable flow batteries were intended for the solar and wind farm markets. Sadly, that's where their dream ended."

"How come?" Maria had stopped tapping. Steve took over the note taking as he could see she was being drawn further and further in. He was very glad he'd invited her now.

"The problem was their membrane. It wasn't semipermeable or reliable enough, Todd said. It kept failing. Their credibility was being destroyed; unit costs increased, and delivery times blew out. Customers were deserting them. The company was on the point of collapse when some bright spark suggested buying us. Our membrane technology was world class. That's what they wanted, Maria."

"And buying you solved their problem overnight?" Maria added.

"Yes, and it got them into the automotive and other more lucrative markets."

172

"And that bright spark, you reckon, was Ethan Bronstein." Steve prompted.

"He knew all our trade secrets. He had access to our business plans. He'd convinced investors to put money into Pemberton Electronics. There are too many coincidences." Connie swallowed some water then leaned back, like a weight was being lifted off her shoulders.

That word again. *Coincidences*. Steve could see the sense in what Connie was insinuating but he still didn't feel they had the full picture. Insider dealing, industrial espionage, illegal trading - this was bread and butter stuff for a fraud investigation but was a far cry from kidnapping and the possible homicide of an innocent child. Steve wondered if there wasn't something more sinister behind all this.

"I've got to ask, Connie, sorry for being so blunt. How do we know you weren't in cahoots with the guys at Hertzl?" Steve needed more evidence than the flash of anger that shot across her eyes. "Ethan arranges for five million to go through the books while the other fifty million changes bank accounts somewhere in Switzerland. When the dust settles, you and Todd fly over to the superyacht and head for the Adriatic."

Instantly the weight was back on her shoulders. Connie hunched forward, sipping more water while she played through the options. "I'm happy to make a full disclosure, Steve, open the books for Pemberton and our personal finances. We've nothing to hide. The sale was legal even if the threats behind it were criminal. We don't have any offshore accounts or investments, never did have. I've let Todd know I'm talking to you. It seemed only fair. He was surprised but assured me of his full support. We'll provide everything you need."

173

Steve looked across at Maria. She was on the same page. It was all that Connie could do at this stage. Full access was a good place to start. Steve could assemble a team of financial sniffer dogs, as he called them, to uncover any skeletons buried in the numbers. But it still left the question of the kidnapping.

True to her word, Connie's diary was a treasure trove of times, dates, personal comments and verbatim accounts of the numerous telephone conversations they'd had over many weeks with the Caribbean kidnapper. Her shorthand for him was PD, after Papa Doc Duvalier, the brutal leader of Haiti in the 60's and 70's.

"I think it was timed around the end of the spring semester." Connie was flicking through the pages. "Chicory only missed the last two days at school, so her absence went unnoticed. PD held her until the sale went through, August 14th. It was the worst time of my life. He called us twice a week. We spoke to her several times. *When am I coming home, grandma?* I just melted."

"Tell us about her release, please." Steve softened his voice. Connie was fighting back the tears. He noticed Maria also looked ready to cry, no doubt wondering what she would have done in the circumstances, if it had been her own children.

"He emailed a photo of her holding that day's newspaper. We were to sign the final paperwork transferring ownership at Ethan's office. Our lawyer was there. He couldn't understand what we were doing. He didn't believe the press release about us intending to retire. Todd wanted to tell him the truth, but I stopped him. The fewer people who knew, the better. All the time, I could just see her beautiful, little face. We had to go through with it." Connie dabbed away the tears.

"When did you know she was safe?" Maria interrupted.

174

"They'd arranged for the money to be held in escrow and paid in two equal stages. Todd refused to sign until we had confirmation that she was unharmed and free. It was all a blur: people coming in and out of the room, papers to be signed and numerous calls to the bank. Todd was very calm throughout, but I could feel his heart pumping."

Connie finished the water. "Once the second payment was in our account, I got a text from PD. It gave the registration plate of a blue rental van in an underground garage near Central Park. We raced across town. The driver's window was partly open. They'd scotch taped a key in the arch above the rear wheel. She'd been sedated and was sleeping. I cradled her frail little body and cried all the way home."

In the weeks that followed, Connie continued, Todd tried to piece it all together. Every lead went cold. The van was driven in and out of the garage by a guy wearing a mask. The rental company couldn't divulge customer information. The phone company couldn't help in tracing the calls or the texts.

"All the time I was conscious he'd said no police. We had her back. I couldn't bear the thought of her disappearing again or even worse. Todd was right to leave it at that, but it still hurt." Connie handed the diary to Maria. They could keep it if they liked. Connie offered to arrange meetings with whoever they wanted to talk to within the family, including Chicory herself. Steve promised to get back to her when they'd been through her notes.

Connie had told them everything she could remember. She was returning to Chicago later that day but could be contacted anytime. They wanted to give her a hug as she moved off towards the elevators, but thought a handshake was the proper British thing to do.

After Connie had gone, they sat down again, waiting for the check.

"There must be a connection between our kidnapper and this guy Ethan." Steve announced.

"The kidnapper must have known where they were up to in the acquisition. Only Ethan had the full picture, by the sound of it."

"Not necessarily Steve, there were plenty of other people involved. It could have been someone at the banks or law firms, but I agree, the finger points at Ethan. We should have a word with him for sure."

"Well, there's no time like the present. His office can't be far from here. I've got all the files. Maybe, as Lonsdale said about the homicide investigation, we need to stop dancing around the handbags. It's time to shake things up.

Steve held the door open. "Let's go and point that finger."

CHAPTER 20

The New York office of Slaker Nadzy was more difficult to find than Steve had anticipated. His satnav had seemingly developed a sense of humour and was proudly telling him they'd arrived at the destination, when clearly, they hadn't. It may well have been the back of the right building but that didn't help, especially given the myriad of alleyways and one-way streets running across the city's financial hub.

Finding the right building was only the start of their frustrations. Steve felt they'd walked into a parallel world with more smoke than mirrors. It was Maria who eventually saw the name etched into the frosted glass on one of the many doors dotted down a long, second floor corridor. Steve quickly realised these were shabby rental offices, designed to attract start-ups and wannabe financial services companies aspiring one day to bathe in the commercial limelight on Wall Street itself.

Whoever signed the lease for this office wanted the address, first and foremost, Steve concluded. The young receptionist had been happily engaged on Facebook when they entered. It took some minutes for her to understand that, no, they didn't have an appointment and, yes, they wanted to see Mr Ethan Bronstein right away, on urgent police business. Her attempt to persuade them he was on vacation failed miserably when the man himself buzzed through for some fresh coffee. It was the only thing buzzing about the place.

"I don't seem to be making myself clear." Steve had taken the nod from Maria. She looked tired of the stonewalling too. "There's two ways this can play out, Mr

Bronstein. You can cooperate with this routine investigation, answer our questions voluntarily, and provide us with the material we need. Then we disappear and life carries on as normal. If you've nothing to hide, then you've nothing to worry about. That would be the sensible thing to do."

"Or else?" Bronstein had barricaded himself on the other side of a large, empty desk and was trying to cower behind his two computer screens.

"Or else I will bring in two teams of investigators and forcibly extract the information we need." Steve noted some confusion on his face which by now was several shades paler than when the meeting had started.

"The main team will be crawling all over this office and will remove anything we deem connected to the investigation. The second team will be at your home, going through everything with a fine-toothed comb. Getting search warrants for both premises will not be a problem." He lied.

"This is harassment, you can't do this. I have rights, you know."

"Indeed, you have, Mr Bronstein, and we will be happy to uphold them. Of course, if you make things difficult for us, we'd need to notify the District Attorney's Office and the Department of Financial Services. They may wish to send in their own teams as well, although I'm sure that won't be necessary. Now, let me ask you again, Mr Bronstein, which is it to be?"

"Did you say routine investigation? Has this case been chosen at random?" Bronstein had swallowed hard and adopted a more conciliatory demeanour. "Before you answer, could I offer you both some coffee or water perhaps?"

"I think you've just answered my question, Mr Bronstein. I'll take an Americano, please, no sugar."

"And just a glass of water for me. Thank you." Maria had her laptop open, ready to capture his every word.

Bronstein retrieved a thick manila file from another room. Steve was reassured that, in this digital age, when all transactions were seemingly electronic, there was still a need occasionally for someone to sign a piece of paper.

"It's all above board, as you can see. Signatures witnessed, legal advice given, monies transferred from escrow, even keys and passwords handed over on the day." Bronstein was passing him the documentary evidence. "This file has been reviewed by an independent auditor, in line with our security protocols. He's a qualified CA, I've worked with him since I got here. Here's his final report."

Maria picked up the questioning while Steve was reading through and photographing certain documents on his phone. She saw him smile and shake his head at one point as he snapped a copy of the CA's invoice. Maria continued. "And when *did* you get here, Mr Bronstein? To New York, I mean."

"Please call me Ethan, only my bank manager calls me Mr Bronstein." The attempt at humour fell flat. Steve asked to see the whole file which was reluctantly handed over.

"Our records show you were given a green card five years ago and that you hold an Israeli passport." Maria enquired.

"Yes, I was born in Haifa. My wife's originally from New York. We met on a kibbutz after university and moved to Tel Aviv when I started with Slaker Nadzy. In fact, I've just submitted my application for US citizenship. It'll be a proud day when I finally get the other blue passport."

"And all this was what, ten years ago, when you joined the firm?" Maria was toggling between her notes and the thin files they had on him.

"Twelve actually, I joined as an intern. They backdated my start date when I was promoted from junior analyst to financial advisor." Bronstein's hand was steadier now, Steve noticed. Also, his restless left leg was calming.

"Our files say Tel Aviv is the head office for Slaker Nadzy. Is that correct?" On this, Maria was flying blind. Their files on the firm were flaky to say the least.

"We call it our main office, not head office. We're an international partnership. The partners share the equity and consider themselves equals. I'm told they can get a bit touchy about all this."

"So how come you ended up here?" Maria continued tapping away.

"I was honoured when they asked me to open this office. They've been very good to me and helped in getting the green card. We had an agent working for us in New York for many years. He proved the need to have a presence here. Initially he worked with the Pemberton's to help them raise finance then I took over the account. Corporate life wasn't for him, so he moved on. I can give you his contact details if you wish."

"That would be helpful, thank you." Maria decided contacting him wasn't going to be necessary. It was recent events they were more interested in, but maybe the agent could provide background material.

Steve could see Bronstein was relaxing. Some colour had returned to his cheeks. Dressing this up as a routine investigation was turning out to be a good move and more likely to open things up, especially if he continued to drop his guard.

"So how did Pemberton Electronics come to sell out to a start-up company?" Maria took the nod from Steve to keep probing gently, get his side of the story. He may not be aware of any kidnapping, if, indeed, it ever happened.

Bronstein paused and took a deep breath. "Do you want my official answer or the truth?"

Steve closed the file and looked hard at him. "Don't get clever with us now, Ethan. No corporate bullshit, we want the truth. That's why we're here. If it all stacks up, this conversation doesn't need to go any further. If you're lying to us, you can kiss goodbye to US citizenship. Clear?"

"Perfectly, thank you. It's just that I wouldn't want this repeated outside the room. Client confidentiality is paramount. Can you guarantee that?"

"No guarantees, Ethan, we'll decide what to do with the information. Now spit it out." Steve glanced across at Maria who closed her laptop.

"It was Todd du Prez who asked me to find a buyer. He's not a well man, something he hasn't shared with Connie. The pressure of running Pemberton Electronics was destroying his health but he knew Connie would be reluctant to sell. *My Grandpapa's company*. He thought she might see sense if the offer was right. Greater regulation, more competition and higher development costs were killing them. Todd reckoned it was time to get out."

"But the offer wasn't right, was it, Ethan? The company was worth ten times more and you knew it. The IRS are pissed off, to say the least. Were there any other mitigating factors around this sale?" Steve brandished a copy of the sale agreement. He wasn't going to mention the possible kidnapping at this stage, until they had more proof.

Bronstein had found some backbone. This was his turf, after all. "No other factors, it was all straightforward. A company only has a price if the owner will sell. The value is what someone is prepared to pay. Given the mitigating factors, I think the price they accepted was fair. All their involvement and liabilities ended when they signed the paper. The pressure was off overnight. They'd made good money in recent years. Todd tells me his health is greatly improved."

"So, you saw nothing untoward in the sale?" Maria fell into the good cop role naturally.

"Not in the least. I'd been working with the new owners since they set up shop. Herzl Power Technologies were struggling to develop the type of new products that Pemberton had already created. It was something to do with membranes, as I recall. Putting the two businesses together made perfect sense. It was the wheel turning, bright young guys taking over from the tired, old guard. A win/win situation."

"Steve, I think we need to talk to Todd du Prez." Maria interrupted.

"I agree but I'm still troubled by your role in this, Ethan." Steve wasn't buying this story. He remembered the tears running down Connie's face. This explanation was just too convenient.

"You were privy to confidential information about Pemberton Electronics and used that to help your other client basically steal the company away from them. There are laws against insider dealing."

"Yes, there are. We take such matters very seriously. Slaker Nadzy has an excellent reputation out there for being ethical and professional. We would never risk that, especially in what was, for us, a relatively small acquisition."

"I'm not talking about Slaker Nadzy. I'm talking about you, personally, Ethan." Steve saw his hand shaking again as he picked up the cup of coffee.

"I'm a deal maker. My role is to facilitate, to bring the parties together. I can't force anyone to buy or sell. Of course, I'm privy to confidential information. I only share what is approved by my clients and Todd approved it. My notes are in the file. Nobody stole anything. Both sides were happy with the arrangement but please, don't just take my word for it."

"We won't, Ethan. We will get back to you once we've corroborated what you've told us. In the meantime, don't leave town." Steve looked at Maria and nodded it was time to go but she'd opened her laptop again. There must be something else on her mind.

Maria continued. "One last thing. You told us Slaker Nadzy is an international partnership. Who are your partners and where are they? How is the equity shared between them? This will provide context and help our understanding of how you operate."

His guard shot back up before she'd finished talking, Steve noticed. Clearly this was something he didn't want to discuss. Yet again, Maria had found the right nerve to press.

"I'm sorry, I'm not able to answer those questions. To be honest, I've no idea who the partners are and have never been told. They don't have to divulge their identities or their shareholding. It's always been kept secret. My boss in Tel Aviv might know but he's an employee like me so may not know either. I can give you his contact details too if you like."

Bronstein opened his hands as if to show they were clean, but Steve wasn't convinced. "You said before that the firm has been good to you. Presumably, a decision like sending you to New York to open an office off Wall Street would only be made by the partners, given the importance of such a move and the significant investment involved?"

Although Bronstein didn't seem fazed by his question, Steve noticed the involuntary twitching in his left leg had returned. "I didn't ask. Look, it was the chance of a lifetime for me. My wife wanted to return home. She's now talking about starting a family, at long last. It's a dream come true. Sure, these aren't the best offices in town, but these things take time. We're doing well and we're here for the long haul."

"Well, let's try this another way. Who are Slaker and Nadzy?" Maria took a softer approach.

"I'm told they don't exist. Slaker Nadzy was a creation from the names of the founding partners. It's an anagram, that's all I know. Now, if you'll excuse me, I have another meeting across town."

Maria tapped in the details for the CA and Bronstein's boss in Tel Aviv before saving her work and shutting down. Steve thanked him for his cooperation and the coffee but added they would almost certainly need to see him again.

They retraced their steps down the poorly lit corridor. Steve took a wrong turn trying to find the exit. It seemed to take them ages to get back to the car. Steve was becoming more and more irritable as he could see this fraud investigation was eating up too much of the time they really needed for the homicide.

"The key here is Todd du Prez." Maria offered as Steve struggled to reverse out of the cramped parking space. "He can substantiate the kidnapping story and his conversations with Bronstein about his health."

Steve managed to avoid colliding with the barrier. The ticket machine was asking for a credit card. His were in the trunk. Maria obliged. Steve took a slow breath. They wouldn't get back to the office any quicker if he got angry. "But if there was no kidnapping, why would Connie make up such a story? I still feel we're missing

184

some pieces here, but I don't want to waste time finding them if it's all a wild goose chase."

The traffic was heavy, exacerbated by a power outage at a major junction which had killed the traffic lights. A uniformed officer in white gloves was unsuccessfully trying to direct an onslaught of angry motorists.

"And if there was a kidnapping, where does that leave Bronstein?" Maria reasoned, trying to focus Steve's mind on the task in hand.

"I didn't like the guy or trust him. He's not telling us the whole story. If there was a kidnapper, he had to find out from Bronstein when the deal was done, surely?"

"Or from someone above him."

"You're thinking his boss in Israel?" Steve suggested.

"No, I'm thinking one of these shady partners. Or maybe these Israeli investors. I'd love to know who we're really dealing with here. Bronstein is a puppet. There's someone pulling his strings, I bet."

"I thought you didn't gamble, Maria?" Steve smiled across at her as they ground to a halt again, joining the next tailback.

Steve's phone started ringing. He pressed the hands-free button on the steering wheel, having noticed Lonsdale's name in the lights. As usual, his former boss didn't bother with any pleasantries.

"I had an interesting meeting today at the Palace of Westminster. It took a while to get into their arcane security systems, but it turns out Dr Robert Stannard met two people while he was there last week. Tell me, Detective Sergeant, do you still have a natural aversion to coincidences?"

Steve slammed on the brakes, narrowly missing a pedestrian wearing headphones who had stepped off the sidewalk and hadn't bothered to look. Why did so many people have a death wish these days, he wondered. The resulting drama inside the car didn't help his darkening mood. At least Lonsdale sounded like he was enjoying himself. "I don't think I'm going to like this, sir. Who did Stannard meet?"

"Do you remember in Guildford, some time ago, a dubious case of suicide involving a British national in India? You got an overseas trip out of it."

Steve didn't need this memory test but felt he had to play along. Lonsdale was doing them a massive favour, after all. He started to think back. Yes, he could see faces around a table. It was a young girl, he remembered. Her father was convinced she'd been murdered. The Delhi police weren't interested. There turned out to be a connection to organised crime.

He could picture the interview room at the Surrey Force Headquarters, three faces. Lonsdale at the head of the table, as usual. A well-dressed man and an elegant American woman, both in their fifties. She was angry. The man calmed her down. Military swagger, he'd been a pilot in the RAF. What were their names?

"Yes, I do remember, sir. I can see them."

"The name you're looking for, Detective Sergeant, is former Wing Commander Max Hartley."

186

CHAPTER 21

They skipped breakfast to save time. Hannah packed a bag with water and fruit she'd bought the day before in Lodwar. Josphat met them at the Land Cruiser just after sunrise. Birdsong filled the air. The lake was flat and calm. Not a breath of wind, a sharp contrast to the morning before. The earlier predictions about a storm were another Lake Turkana mystery. It was a stunning morning, but Hannah had no time to lose herself in its stillness.

It took longer than she expected to get around the various locations collecting samples. A herd of goats being driven haphazardly through the village: the road to the lake blocked by a group of men arguing over boats. It was very heated for a few minutes then they all made friends, slowly. No one was in a hurry. African time, Hannah reflected.

Eventually they pulled up outside Agnes's hut. The woman herself was slumped on a rough wooden stool in the shade. Hannah offered *Jambo*, how are you? Agnes replied through Josphat. No better, stomach pains and another sleepless night. She'd not been able to keep any food down and was even having difficulty drinking water. One of her eyes was partially closed and looked very sore. Hannah gave her a hug and promised to do all she could.

They needed two samples now from Agnes's well, then they could get over to the airport. Hannah had the parcel ready to seal and send once the last sample jars were labelled and included.

Snakes or no snakes, Hannah was on a deadline. She set off at a brisk walk. Josphat had asked one of the local girls to come with them. In fact, three came along and a couple of dogs for good measure. The girls found some empty containers to fill while they were there. No point in wasting a visit, one of them said.

They must have gone a different way because Hannah didn't see the rocky area where the snake was yesterday. But then, the terrain did look very similar after a while.

They got to the water pump in less than an hour. The samples were taken from the flow at different times, duly labelled and sealed into the parcel which was already stamped and addressed to Fara at the university lab.

"Hear it now?" Lawrence had mopped his sweaty brow after the gentle exertion of pumping the handle. It was hot, and the flies were persistent.

"Yes. And look, there's the dust cloud." Hannah pointed above the distant trees. "Maybe I couldn't hear it yesterday because of the wind."

"There's heavy machinery. Not too far away either, I don't think. Come on, let's go." Lawrence started moving towards a scrub path.

"Wait, we need to get these samples on that plane. We haven't got time. Let's come back this afternoon." Hannah was checking her watch. It would be tight if the plane was on time.

"It may be too late by this afternoon. If a storm does come in, we may not get back at all." Lawrence insisted. "It could be our best chance to solve this."

"But what about the samples? We need the test results pronto. We're running out of time."

Lawrence's eyes suddenly opened wide, a lightbulb moment. He smiled and turned to Josphat. "Can you drive a Land Cruiser?"

"Yes, Mister Lawrence. All Africans can."

"Could you make sure this parcel gets on the noon flight to Nairobi?"

"Yes, sir. It never on time."

"Settled then. Josphat, here you go. We're counting on you." Lawrence gave him the sealed parcel and a wad of notes in case he needed to pay extra at the airport. "Can you text me when it's on the plane?"

"Of course, sir."

Within seconds, Josphat, the three girls, dogs, and a stray neighbours' goat they'd found, all set off back. The girls were in high spirits, singing at the top of their voices, bright yellow containers rolling on their heads. When they'd all gone, it was eerily quiet, apart from the distant rumble of machinery.

Hannah looked terrified. "Snakes, lions, bad guys, there could be anything waiting for us out there. And we must find our own way back. You didn't tell Josphat to pick us up after he's been to the airport. You're a crazy man, Mr McGlynn."

"Crazy but decisive. Let's go." Lawrence set off at a pace. Hannah wasn't convinced but there was only one way to find out. She had to run to catch up.

The path soon became little more than an animal track. The noise beyond the trees was growing louder with each step. Lawrence pushed aside a thicket of branches then fell to his knees, pulling Hannah down with him.

Two armed guards in military fatigues were patrolling on the other side of a chain-link fence directly in front of them. Thankfully they were too engrossed chatting to each other that they hadn't seen or heard anything.

Beyond the fence lay a large open space in the middle of which stood a collection of new, concrete buildings. A sprawling parking lot nearby was full of cars, heavy plant, trucks, and other industrial vehicles, some loaded with rock. A huge metal tower, maybe twenty or so metres high, Hannah guessed, had pride of place amongst the buildings, rising up into a hazy, dust-filled sky.

189

The guards continued their lazy patrol of the perimeter. Lawrence pulled the bushes back up in front of them to give cover.

"What is this place?" Hannah looked even more worried than before.

"I'm thinking a mine, judging by the slag heap over there and the rocks coming out of that building. From the noise, I guess that's a crusher." Lawrence pointed over to what he presumed was the main gate. "Looks like they're taking stuff away by road in unmarked containers."

"There are no signs anywhere. Not on the guards' uniform, on the fence, on the buildings, even on the trucks, nada." Hannah shrugged her shoulders. "Someone doesn't want anyone to know they're here, doing whatever they're doing."

"It said in the inflight magazine that licences had been granted for mining exploration which they hoped would create jobs and boost the local economy. It mentioned copper but this doesn't look like a copper mine to me." Lawrence added.

"Go on, Sherlock, what does a copper mine look like?" Hannah edged a bit closer to him. This was a scary place.

"I interviewed a guy years ago who'd been a chief engineer at a mine in Australia. He said the cheapest mining operation was open pit. You know, dig a big hole, and keep blasting away until you'd extracted all the good stuff."

"Did he get the job?" Hannah felt conspicuous and wanted to keep moving but didn't know where. Back to the swimming pool at the Lodge would be good right now.

"No, he was way too expensive. His party piece was sinking mine shafts. That's what the tower is." Lawrence nodded towards the buildings. "You sink the central shaft then run horizontal adits off in different directions,

190

usually along the mineral seams. He showed me photographs of shafts he'd sunk. Apparently, it's the costliest method to extract ore. They only do it if necessary."

"Or they're making so much money they don't care about the cost. You must really have been paying attention." Hannah was trying to ignore something that was now crawling up her left leg. She hoped it wasn't a snake, but didn't dare look.

"Let's go round nearer the entrance. We might spot something." Lawrence suggested pushing through the undergrowth. Hannah couldn't resist any longer. She looked down then flicked away a giant crawling insect. Clearly it was immune to the thick coating of jungle gel repellent she'd applied at the Lodge that morning.

Moving sounded good but crawling through dense bush wasn't what she had in mind. Then she thought about Agnes slumped outside the hut with her husband lying under the goat pen. She soon found the resolve to push on.

Having followed the track for a short distance, Lawrence branched off to the left, carefully rounding a thicket of bushes with long, sharp thorns. He tripped and disturbed a flock of brightly coloured birds that scattered into the high branches arched above them. In the background they could hear the relentless grinding of the heavy machinery.

Lawrence reckoned they were getting closer. He whispered in Hannah's ear to stay there while he checked out where they were. She grabbed his arm and assured him he wasn't going anywhere without her.

Suddenly, up ahead, they heard a distinctive ping. It came from the middle of a clump of trees. Someone just received a text at the wrong time, Lawrence whispered.

Hannah watched in amazement as Lawrence threw himself into the trees like a great bear on the trail of fresh meat. A scuffle followed, branches shaking, a woman's voice shouting *let me go, you're hurting my arm,* beautifully pronounced in very clear Oxford English.

Hannah followed in his wake to discover Lawrence holding onto a Kenyan woman wearing a jungle-print dress with wrap-around sunglasses perched in a tangle of thick dark hair. Hannah guessed she was mid-twenties, but she could have been older. She was clutching a mobile phone like her life depended on it.

The woman looked as much out of place as they did. Educated and professional with sharp, brown eyes, her face was wreathed in anger. But Hannah sensed something else. Was it surprise? Shock? Guilt? She wasn't sure.

Lawrence immediately let her go. "Who are you? Why are you following us?"

"I'm not following you. I got lost. I was looking for the water pump." She shifted uneasily, transferring her weight nervously from one foot to the other. Hannah knew she was lying. She wasn't carrying anything apart from a shoulder bag that she slipped the phone into before zipping it up. Another muted ping. Someone was really trying to contact her.

"Where are your water carriers? Why are you here? We want the truth, and we want it now." Lawrence was trying to talk quietly as they couldn't be far from the entrance.

"I'm doing research into water supplies in the region. I work for the university. It's my PhD project. Now I need to go, my colleagues will be worried about me."

Another lie, Hannah decided. She was working alone, her nervous looks giving it away. Hannah was about to step in and ask the woman for some means of

192

identification when she heard shouting coming from behind them, male voices, local accents this time.

Before they could react, a burst from a semi-automatic weapon ripped through the branches above their heads. Birds filled the air and unseen creatures dived for the thick undergrowth.

More shots drilled into the silence sending splinters of tree bark and shredded leaves cascading down from above. The voices were getting closer, more of them now. Military boots pounding the dry earth, heavy bodies crashing towards them.

When Hannah looked back, the woman had gone. They had to go too. She grabbed Lawrence by the hand and started running. A track was taking them away from the gunshots. It narrowed but Hannah didn't care. Sharp thorns tore into her arms and legs, trickles of blood mingled with sticky sweat running down her face.

Lawrence slipped and fell, rolling awkwardly into the gnarled trunk of an old tree. He yelped in pain, clutching his lower back as he twisted onto his side. Hannah yanked him to his feet. Another burst of gunfire ripped into the lower section of a tree just up ahead.

They carried on running until the gunfire ceased. The undergrowth fell silent behind them, all was quiet again. They had reached the clearing, the water pump standing idle, oblivious to their ordeal.

Once they were satisfied the guards had given up, they stopped and held each other, panting for breath. Sweat was stinging Hannah's eyes. She pulled some thorns from her arm and tried to stem the trickles of blood.

"Shit." Lawrence was checking his pockets. "I've lost my phone. It must have been when I fell. It's back there somewhere."

"Well, it will have to stay there, we're not going back now. We must keep moving." Hannah gave him the look.

This was non-negotiable. She wasn't going to risk their lives for a piece of plastic.

"Have you got your phone?" Lawrence had a forlorn look on his face.

"I didn't think I'd need it. It's on charge back at the Lodge. There's probably no signal here anyway." Hannah could feel her heartbeat slowing as she took deep breaths and started to think more clearly.

"Then what do we do?"

"We start walking."

CHAPTER 22

By the time they'd crawled to Agnes's hut, Lawrence's back had stiffened up. He was struggling to walk. Hannah was limping, having twisted her right ankle in some rocks. She thought she'd seen a snake and lost concentration for a split second. It was all it took. Hot, thirsty, and increasingly worried about who might be watching them, they were not in good shape.

One of Agnes's grandchildren took pity and found them a bench to sit on. She brought them a bottle of the mineral water they'd bought in Lodwar the day before. It was refreshing and very welcome. She left some for Lawrence. He swallowed what was left in a single mouthful, thanking her.

Agnes appeared in the doorway looking tired and distant. She sat down next to Hannah who put her arm around her shoulder and squeezed with what strength she had left. Agnes responded by resting her head on it and getting as comfortable as she could. They sat for a few minutes in silence, Hannah reflecting on what had just happened. Very soon her thoughts turned to what they needed to do. If that woman had been following them, she would know where they were.

They had to keep moving but to where? The Lodge was too far away, and it would be dark long before they got there, if they made it at all. Hannah didn't fancy being out after nightfall, not with armed gunmen and puff adders on the loose. Agnes didn't have a phone or any means of contacting the outside world.

"We've got to walk to the village." Hannah concluded, turning towards Lawrence, trying to summon up the strength to stand. "We might get a taxi."

Agnes seemed to understand their predicament. Firstly, she indicated they could stay with her, pointing to one of the huts and resting her head on both hands, held together as if in prayer. Hannah smiled as she thought a prayer might be their best hope.

She thanked Agnes for her kind offer but shook her head. It wasn't safe to stay there for any of them. Then Agnes made an imaginary dialling motion with her finger, pressing her other hand to her ear. "Phone in store."

"A payphone? In the village?" Lawrence struggled to his feet. "I can call Josphat, he can pick us up."

"You got his phone number?" Hannah managed a weak smile. She was ahead of him again.

"Damn. It's in my phone."

"But you got the room key, right?"

Lawrence fumbled in his pocket. The Lodge phone number was on the key. His spirits lifted momentarily. The Lodge could call Josphat or send a car. Then he remembered how far away the village was. Kalokol was only minutes by car but a good hour at the speed they'd be making.

Hannah thanked Agnes and gave her another hug. The woman looked so ill Hannah thought she may not see her alive again. Whoever was behind this would have hell to pay if Agnes joined her husband under the goat pen.

They found the tyre tracks and set off with the dying sun at their backs. The terrain was easier, but each step brought more pain. Hannah needed some distracting conversation as her ankle was very sore and noticeably swelling. "Who was she, then? The girl in the bushes?"

196

"I've no idea but she was definitely following us. I didn't believe that cock and bull story about a PhD or being lost. My guess is she's been following us since we got here, maybe even from Nairobi. Did you see her on the plane?" Lawrence leaned against a tree to stretch his back muscles. His movement looked awkward and painful.

"No, I hadn't seen her before. She looked terrified when the shooting started. No wonder she ran away. Whoever she is, I don't think she's the brains behind this. She's someone's eyes and ears. We must find that someone, before it's too late." Hannah tried waggling her foot to loosen the strain, but it didn't work. There was nothing else for it but to keep walking.

"Too late for Agnes, you mean? You're right, she doesn't have long unless we can crack this open. Talking of which, I hope Josphat made it to the plane on time."

They pushed on but the pace was slowing. They rounded a corner and Hannah spotted the village in the distance. She hoped the store would still be open. She daren't ask Lawrence about having enough change. Somehow, she couldn't imagine the payphone taking credit cards out here. Would the Lodge accept a collect call? They were about to find out.

"She wasn't from round here, I'd say. Her English was too good. She looked more like a big city girl. We certainly scared her." Lawrence added.

"You mean *you* did. I couldn't believe how you threw yourself at her. Promise me you won't do that again. You could have taken a bullet." Hannah stopped and pulled him to her. "Being brave is one thing, being dead is something else. I don't want to lose you. It's taken my whole life to find you. Whatever we're caught up in here just isn't worth dying for. Promise?"

197

Lawrence draped his arms over her shoulders. "I promise. I just got so angry. Here we are trying to save lives yet people around us are playing hide and seek. We get through this. Righting wrongs and protecting the innocent, it's what we do. And we do it together. Now let's keep moving."

They'd reached the outskirts of the village. Thick clouds had rolled in over the lake, causing the temperature to drop a few clicks which Hannah welcomed. A couple of cars had sped past along the way, ignoring Lawrence's attempts to flag them down. Another had stopped about a kilometre in front of them, its headlights piercing the gloom. Lawrence waved to the driver who promptly spun the wheel and headed off in a cloud of dust.

The village was strangely quiet. When they'd passed through that morning, it was a hive of activity. The store seemed to be the focal point with people milling about everywhere, sitting outside, and carrying heavy bags laden with groceries.

As they limped in along the main street, Hannah could see the signs had gone from outside the store. No one was sitting on the low, mudbrick wall near the entrance, and there were no parked cars.

She could see a small group of people standing together further up the street, but they soon parted and disappeared into some ramshackle buildings. A dog started barking from somewhere nearby. A raised voice echoed out, then the dog went quiet.

Hannah didn't want to believe the store was closed. She kept walking, hoping Lawrence hadn't noticed yet. Her mind was spinning as she ran through whatever options they had left.

They reached the front door which was locked and bolted. A sign said they were an hour too late. It would open again at seven the next morning. Hannah peered through the toughened glass. A payphone sat annoyingly on the counter next to a neat stack of cans. Heinz baked beans, English recipe, whatever that meant.

Lawrence had tried around the back. No signs of life or means of entry. Now what? Hannah thought out loud. A night curled up together in a fishing boat. The hut next door to Agnes's place. Bed down in the doorway of the store. None of the options were appealing.

A single light appeared, followed by the buzzing of a motorbike engine. It slowed then turned down the road to the lake before Lawrence could wave it down.

Stillness. Silence. Minutes passed. A black cat was watching them on a wall next to the store. After a few minutes, it yawned, stretched, and slipped away.

Suddenly Hannah heard an engine noise in the distance. Headlights flickered in and out of the trees. A car was coming slowly towards them from the far end of the main street. It was weaving in and out of the potholes. A careful driver must be a good sign, Hannah decided.

She looked at Lawrence. The car was slowing down. Was it the girl from the bushes or the hitmen from the lake? There was nowhere to hide, and they couldn't run. Hannah thought about calling out for help but decided against it. There was no one in earshot. They'd have to front up themselves.

The car stopped right in front of them, the headlights glaring until the driver switched them off. Hannah saw the driver's face in the courtesy light when he opened the door. The beaming smile was instantly recognisable. Josphat. It was their Land Cruiser.

"Are we glad to see you?" Hannah hugged him, much to his surprise, creasing his spotless polo shirt.

Lawrence was pumping his hand. "How did you know we were here?"

Josphat resumed his calm, composed exterior. "Agnes tells me. I try her place first. I call and text many times. You no answer so I come."

"Great logic, Josphat, thank you so much." Lawrence couldn't resist. "Did you get to the plane on time?"

"Yes, Mr Lawrence, plane was late one hour. Parcel gone." Josphat didn't seem to understand what the fuss was about. But then he hadn't been chased through the bush and shot at by armed guards, Hannah reflected.

They piled in and were soon heading back to the Lodge. It was pitch dark when they arrived. They thanked Josphat again and arranged to meet him the following morning.

Back in the room, sweaty clothes were dumped in the hamper, a hot bath was shared which soothed away the pains of the afternoon. Lawrence raided the minibar while Hannah lit the solitary candle. The door was double locked and room service ordered. It felt like they'd reached sanctuary at last.

"There's an email from Fara, looks like the test results are attached." Lawrence was trying not to get grease all over the laptop. He was eating fish and chips with his fingers. He didn't care if the fish was full of mercury, he was hungry.

Hannah appeared in the doorway wrapped only in a short towel, another twisted tightly round her hair. "What's it say? Well done, Fara. We owe her one."

Lawrence was ploughing through the report while Hannah dried her hair and slipped on some casual clothes. She pulled up a chair next to him, pinching chips while he stared at the mass of data on the screen.

"It's in gobbledegook. What's wrong with scientists? You ever heard of *mispickel*? *There is significant evidence of highly toxic arsenopyrite deposits in several samples.* Why can't they write in plain English?"

200

Hannah understood fully. She was used to cutting through scientific jargon and getting to the nub of things. "Arsenic in the groundwater. They're being poisoned by the pump water."

"Deliberately?" Lawrence exclaimed in disbelief. He wanted to flick to other screens and learn more about it. There'd be time for that. They needed to work through this report systematically.

"It doesn't say, of course." Hannah scrolled down. "The samples from Agnes's well have the highest levels of toxicity."

Hannah continued. "The report says the two water samples from her well registered 276 and 297 parts per billion."

Lawrence looked puzzled. "What should it be? How many parts per billion are OK?"

"Ten. They reduced it from fifty some years ago." Hannah read to him the footnote where Fara had helpfully listed the World Health Organisation's recommended safety guidelines.

"Ten? No wonder Agnes is in trouble." Lawrence stifled a yawn.

"It's the build-up of toxins over time in the bloodstream as well as the toxicity of the arsenic itself that causes the trouble. I hope we're not too late."

Hannah wanted to know more. She'd come across arsenic in her medical training. It was both a saint and a sinner, she remembered. It had been used as a medicine in the Middle Ages for certain diseases including syphilis. But it was also labelled the *poison of kings* on account of it being an easily accessible yet untraceable means of murder.

Lawrence finished off the fish and chips then made himself comfortable on the sofa. Hannah said she needed an hour on the laptop. A hunch was forming in her mind as she pieced various bits of information together. First, she needed to check some things out. Lawrence offered no resistance and fell into a light sleep within minutes, while rubbing his lower back.

Hannah wondered how they ever survived in the days before search engines spewed out information at the touch of a button. But, she reflected, the laptop was only as good as the person using it. You only got the right answers if you asked the right questions.

She started going through her list which included copper mining, cures for arsenic poisoning, World Health Organisation reports on safety guidelines for groundwater, the geology of Lake Turkana, even Crown Prince Rudolf and the theft of his prized rock collection.

By the time Lawrence awoke, she was ready to share her hunch. He made them both a cup of tea. She never used to drink tea before she met him, but he'd persuaded her to try it. Tea was a British institution, he explained. It was a lubricant used to calm things down, reflect on situations and help formulate a plan. Mostly it was to buy valuable thinking time while it was brewing.

Eventually Hannah got the taste for English breakfast tea which was the right choice in this situation. Earl Grey was growing on her, but they didn't have any. The instant coffee they'd bought was just shocking, especially considering Kenya was a major exporter of some of the world's finest coffee beans.

"OK, try this." Hannah took a sip then put her cup down. She had made copious notes but didn't need to look at them. "Copper deposits are discovered near the lake. The Kenyan government, hungry for tax revenue, export dollars, and to create local jobs, offers exploration licences to foreign mining companies based on joint venture agreements so they can share in the spoils when it all comes off."

Lawrence finished his tea and joined in. "They lack the expertise and investment funding to go it alone. This way, the mining companies take the risk and do the hard yards with the government mopping up at the end. I'm with you so far."

"A copper mine is opened near Agnes's well. Everyone, including the mining company and the government, want to keep this hush hush in case it doesn't produce anything. They don't want the press spreading stories about foreign companies raping the mineral resources and greasy backhanders to government officials, so the mine is kept out of the public eye." Hannah continued.

"What did Father Kelly call it? *The land of broken dreams for foreign investors?* I'm liking it so far, keep going." Lawrence had a couple of questions simmering but she was in full flow and at her best when thinking out loud.

"A big open pit with huge explosions would be too conspicuous and create media interest, so they choose to sink a mineshaft and tunnel into the rock. Unfortunately - and maybe they don't know this - the mining activity disturbs natural deposits of arsenic pyrites which seep into the local groundwater, poisoning the well. Fara reported above normal levels of poison in the other two wells but not significant enough to cause long-term damage."

"Yet." Lawrence added.

"I agree, yet. There was arsenic in the stool samples we took but nothing in the roots and vegetables or in the lake. Also, no mercury traces turned up in the lake water, so you were fine to eat the fish."

"Too late now, it was delicious. Then what about the miners? If they're drinking the same groundwater as

Agnes, shouldn't they be getting sick?" Lawrence wanted to start with an easy question.

"Good point. Either they are getting sick, and we don't know about it or they're taking water from somewhere else."

Lawrence remembered the article about the huge aquifers recently found, only a few miles away. Maybe they'd built a pipeline directly into the mine. Another question to add to the list. "Go back to the mine itself." Lawrence offered to make more tea, but Hannah hadn't finished hers yet. Lawrence pressed on. "Suppose it's not copper they're digging out. Suppose copper is the cover story for something more lucrative, hence the decision to go mineshaft rather than open pit."

"Why do you say that?" Hannah looked intrigued. Her research into the geology around the lake was inconclusive. It hadn't mentioned deposits of other minerals with higher street value.

"I'm thinking about the rock collection stolen from the museum in Vienna. I don't know but it's my hunch there's something else down there. Somebody wants it badly enough to stop us sniffing around and thinks poisoning a few local tribespeople is a small price to pay."

Hannah's eyes widened. "Poison the wells which drives the local people away. Mining becomes a whole lot easier."

"Easier and cheaper." Lawrence yawned again.

"You have a devious mind, Mr McGlynn, which brings us back to your initial question. Is this being done deliberately?"

"How can we find out?" Lawrence was ready for bed.

Hannah understood. She closed the laptop. "Easy. We ask them."

CHAPTER 23

They'd reached their office in Lenox Hill and were still on the phone to Lonsdale. He had told them about his meeting at the House. Stannard had designed the nuclear propulsion systems for *Comet 5* which Max Hartley had just delivered to St Louis Lambert International Airport.

Steve put the call on speaker. He knew nothing about this race, but Maria was nodding, having seen something on the TV news. She started rooting through the files and triumphantly fished out the handwritten note from Stannard's bedroom.

MH@SLLIA 10.30am.

"I think you've filled in one of the blanks, sir. It looks like Stannard was due to catch up with him in St Louis yesterday. I'll give Max a call. He must be wondering why Stannard didn't show." Steve took down the number from Lonsdale, only to discover it was already saved in his phone, along with Max's private email address.

Lonsdale continued. "I understand both men were to be passengers in the race itself. I suppose it's worth following up but doesn't get us any nearer to who shot him."

Steve agreed but this was fresh information and could be relevant. "I presume, sir, if Max Hartley is over this side of the pond, you must have been told all this by the other person Stannard met. You mentioned two people."

"We'll make a detective out of you yet. Yes, indeed, the other person was none other than Quentin Fitzgerald-Manning, OBE. He was very polished, welcoming, and diplomatic but needed some persuasion to answer my questions. When I told him about Stannard's sudden, violent death, he said, and I quote, that he was *shocked and saddened.*"

Steve knew Lonsdale was testing him again. He'd missed this kind of cut and thrust with his former boss. Try as he might to call him by his real name, to Steve, Lonsdale would always be *sir.*

"*Shocked and saddened.* But what did his eyes say, sir?" Steve could feel his own mood lifting. Things were moving. He sensed progress. This felt more like proper police work.

"I think his eyes already knew, Detective Sergeant. I didn't trust the man. He's hiding something. That's thirty years of experience talking as I have no proof. He's leading a consortium in a ten-billion-dollar race that could project him into fame and fortune, yet, when he learns of the tragic death of the genius behind their entry, Fitzgerald-Manning can only muster *shocked and saddened.*"

"But what *is* the secret, sir? What's he not telling us?" Steve was googling Fitzgerald-Manning while Maria was getting the latest update on the race. Sure enough, *Comet 5* had been granted FAA approval. *The New Spirit of St Louis* already had its certificate of air worthiness. Both planes would be ready for take-off in the next few days. The UN decision on a possible racing start was imminent, CNN reported.

Lonsdale continued. "I've no idea but I'm running some background checks on him. My old friend in HMRC might turn up some dirt. Tax records can be very revealing. Also, I see the Met central computer has a file on him. I'm not cleared to read it, but I know a man who is. Let me attend to the plumbing and report back, Detective Sergeant."

"And did you learn anything more about Stannard, sir? I think you mentioned another contact you had at Oxford

University, when we spoke last." Steve was printing off a lengthy biography on Fitzgerald-Manning. Well at least he thought he was. He'd check the printer after the call.

"As it happens, I'm treating my friend to lunch tomorrow, amongst the dreaming spires. All he could tell me over the phone was that Stannard was an advocate for thorium-based reactors and a living legend at the university. The living bit will have to be updated now, sadly. A life-long bachelor, he drove a 1974 Morris Minor, lived in college accommodation and was a proud workaholic. His passions were real ale, test cricket and crosswords."

Steve saw Maria smile. Were all crossword enthusiasts umbilically tied, he wondered. "There must be someone else in the faculty who understands this propulsion system. It would be good to know."

"He told me Stannard's sidekick is a rather severe woman called Dr Angela Fischer, spelt the German way with a c. The hard g in Angela is quite fitting, apparently. I'm hoping to meet her while I'm there. Maybe she has a softer side and can spill the beans on how this plane actually flies."

Steve had jotted down the name. "We'll continue checking things out at this end. Given what we now know about Stannard's involvement in this lucrative race, I'm struggling to see this as a random street crime. Enjoy your lunch in Oxford."

"I'm told Green's do an excellent Welsh Rarebit. Let's talk tomorrow." Lonsdale disconnected.

Maria returned from the kitchen with two mugs of steaming hot coffee. She teed up the footage from the hotel lobby again and froze the picture when they got to the part where Stannard handed over the envelope. They compared the picture on the screen with the print she'd taken the day before.

The image was quite grainy and not helped by the shadowy lounge uplighting but at least they could make out the man's features.

"As I said, he was one of Stannard's entourage, I saw him at the hotel." Steve was scanning the print while Maria clicked onto the website for the Rokelle International. She quickly discovered Stannard was presenting at the annual conference for the Global Nuclear Forum then followed the link through to their website. The leadership team were all middle-aged, white males, straight from central casting.

Maria compared the images and decided the similarities were good enough. "Dr Logan McInnes is the current President. There's an email address and even a phone number for him, how obliging. They're based in Franklin Park, Cook County, Illinois. He must have been one of the last people to see Stannard alive. I wonder what was in the envelope?"

"Let's find out." Steve dialled the number and got straight through. He moved around the corner to another window where the signal strength was better. He liked to walk when talking, he told Maria once, as it helped him to concentrate.

Maria replayed the hotel lobby footage over and over again then correlated the timings with the other footage from the jewellers' shop camera showing the attack. Using a secure police access code, she patched into the cameras covering the 28th Street Station and clicked through to archive.

The system wasn't easy to navigate but eventually she found the footage showing Stannard exiting an east bound train on the R Line and climbing up the steps onto 28th Street itself. After a few seconds orientation and map checking, he set off down the street towards Lexington, following a handful of people who got off the same train.

His blood-stained map was now entombed in a clear plastic coffin on the desk in front of her. She shook her head. This homicide was becoming more tragic and intimate with every piece of new evidence.

Maria worked out that all the timings fitted together. Stannard hadn't got lost or exited at the wrong station. He was only a couple of blocks from the pub when he met his fate. From what she could see from the outside cameras, the street looked quiet with few passing cars, evidence confirmed by the camera in the jewellers' shop.

"Technical calculations for the thorium rods they're using in the plane's engines." Steve announced as he returned, before slurping more coffee. "McInnes was gutted with the news. He's been friends with Stannard for over 30 years. He couldn't believe anyone could be so cruel. Irreplaceable was the word he used, a huge setback to the clean-up of the nuclear industry. He's going to recommend a memorial service for him."

"And the envelope?" Maria prompted.

"Apparently, Stannard referred to *Comet 5* in his presentation. All the delegates were asking for his calculations. Nothing confidential, just how much neutron irradiation they used to create uranium-233 from thorium-232. Don't ask. He lost me. Apparently, it's the uranium that creates the energy within a molten salt reactor. He said thorium is fertile, not fissile, and quite harmless. *Comet 5* will be safe to fly, he assured me."

"So, his notes were in the envelope?" Maria rolled her eyes.

Steve smiled at her. He couldn't help being curious but realised it must be quite frustrating at times working with him. Thankfully Maria had sufficient patience and determination.

"Stannard only had a hard copy with him. The main university files weren't accessible until the new firewalls

209

had been installed. McInnes agreed to collect the notes from the hotel. Stannard invited him to dinner at the pub. McInnes burst into tears down the phone. *I should have gone with him. This might never have happened.* Poor guy."

"OK, Steve, my turn to be devil's advocate. Do you think these notes would help us? Is McInnes a suspect?" Maria continued, to support her reasoning. "He knew where Stannard was going and that he'd be alone. He knew about the propulsion systems for *Comet 5*. With Stannard out of the way, maybe McInnes is involved somehow."

"He couldn't have known how Stannard was getting to the pub or precisely what time. Stannard was quirky to say the least and more than capable of changing his mind. No, I don't think McInnes is involved. He was genuinely shocked, unlike how Lonsdale described Fitzgerald-Manning. Call it police intuition if you like but I don't think he's a suspect."

"And these notes? Would they tell us anything?" Maria smiled, not bothering with any eye movement this time.

"If Stannard was happy to make them public, I can't see them being much use to us. It will all be mathematical gobbledegook anyway. I'll ask McInnes to send us a copy for the file."

Steve suddenly put down his mug and looked hard at her. "Just replay that devil's advocate bit. I think you may have hit something."

"Which bit? About McInnes?"

"No, about the propulsion systems."

"What about them?" Maria looked puzzled.

"You said, with Stannard out of the way, McInnes could be implicated."

"I didn't, I said he could be involved." Maria corrected him.

"And I said he wasn't a suspect."

"Steve, what's bugging you? You're making no sense."

"Exactly. McInnes may not be implicated but someone else could be."

"Who?" Maria had already guessed the answer.

"Someone desperate to win this race."

CHAPTER 24

Over breakfast on the terrace, Hannah tried to reach Father Kelly but could only leave a voicemail message. If he was still up country or out of range, it may be some time before he returned her call. They couldn't sit around waiting.

They had agreed that Father Kelly provided some insurance in case their plan went wrong. He'd got them into this mess, after all. The least he could do was come with them. Accusing the mine owners of poisoning the well - accidentally or otherwise - was not without risk. But people were dying. It was a risk worth taking. Having a priest with them who knew the local area seemed a sensible precaution.

With Josphat happily strapped into the back seat, they headed for Lodwar to stock up with as much bottled water and groceries as they could muster. Hannah wanted to ask around and see if clean drinking water could be delivered by tanker. She quickly discovered it wasn't possible.

Lawrence suggested rainwater barrels but, with so little rainfall, it didn't seem a viable alternative. Using the other wells could be a short-term solution but they'd need transportation. Hannah decided the question of a more secure water supply for Agnes, her family, and neighbours needed more thought. For now, bottled water would have to do.

Several websites had confirmed there was no direct cure for arsenic poisoning. One talked about vitamin E and selenium supplements helping to counter some of the pathological effects. It sounded like a quack remedy but, if it bought them time, then why not? The main pharmacy

212

in Lodwar had supplies of vitamin E capsules and even bottles of oil, but had never heard of selenium. Hannah bought all the vitamin E they had.

Josphat waited outside while they stocked up at the general store. They were loading the trunk when Hannah's mobile phone rang. "It's Father Kelly, I'll take this."

She moved away to an empty area in the parking lot. Lawrence and Josphat carried on squeezing in all the bottled water, groceries, and vitamin supplements. Bars of chocolate were carefully wrapped in a towel and stored away to stop them melting.

"He's on his way back. He reckons he'll be in his office around lunchtime." Hannah announced.

"That would work for us. We can deliver this lot, explain to Agnes about the well, find my phone and get back here in time. Then we can all go together to confront them. Come on."

Lawrence gunned the engine and dropped the cabin temperature. A welcome blast of cold air filled the Land Cruiser.

"Does he know anything about the mine?" Lawrence kept checking his mirror. Nothing suspicious so far.

"Yes, and he was shocked by our test results. Contamination of their water supply hadn't occurred to him either. The good news is he's happy to share everything he knows if we can save Agnes's life. He didn't want to talk on the phone. He suspects the mine owners are in cahoots with our devious friend in the Vatican. Apparently, the Cardinal twisted a few arms to get them the exploration licence, no doubt for a tasty backhander."

"Who are *they*?" Lawrence flicked his eyes to the mirror. Still nothing behind.

"He thinks there's Russian money involved. The guy who runs the mine is a brute."

"Russian? Is he sure?" Lawrence swerved to avoid some rocks strewn across the road. The groceries were rolling around in the trunk.

"Russian or Ukrainian. Unpleasant people, either way."

"And a name? Did he give you a company name?"

"He thought KMI or CMI, he wasn't sure but would check when he got back to his office. I said we'll be there about one o'clock." Hannah looked across at him. "Lawrence, thanks for agreeing to involve Father Kelly. I'm feeling a bit better about all this now."

"It was you who suggested him. Having him with us will strengthen our case."

Agnes was stretched out in the shade when they got there. Hannah thought they were too late, but Agnes opened her eyes when they approached her. Lawrence brought a thin blanket and a pillow from the trunk as Josphat started to unload. Some of the children rushed over to help, encouraged by the promise of chocolate.

Hannah helped her to sit up. Through Josphat, she told her about the water being poisoned. She didn't speculate about the mining operation, now wasn't the time. Hannah pointed to the stacks of bottled water. It was important for Agnes to drink as much mineral water as possible and flush the toxins from her system. Eating good food and taking the supplements would also help. Agnes marvelled at the sight of the piles of fresh vegetables and fruit they'd brought.

Hannah asked Lawrence and Josphat to tell the others what was happening, then poured away the rest of the contaminated water in the containers. The girls understood immediately and helped Josphat empty them into the ground behind the huts.

214

Lawrence suggested putting a sign on the water pump, but Josphat said it was just easier to remove the handle. It was agreed to do both. Josphat proudly made a sign using marker pens they'd bought in Lodwar and a sheet of cardboard packaging.

Before they set off, Lawrence reminded Hannah to bring her phone with her. She had it in the Land Cruiser. If she sent him a text, his phone would ping, making it easier to find, but he was pretty sure he knew where it was.

There were just three of them making the journey this time. Josphat felt confident he knew the way but did falter a couple of times. Progress was slow. Even with her ankle strapped up, Hannah could only limp along at half speed. Lawrence was even slower. He'd taken some painkillers but had to keep stopping every so often to massage his lower back. The flies made everything more unpleasant.

Josphat took them on a wide detour around the rocky outcrop where the snake had been, using the sign to shield his eyes from the strong sunlight. It took well over an hour to reach the well. When they got there, Hannah was surprised to see a small group of villagers waiting patiently in line to fill their containers. Some of them looked quite ill, she thought.

The villagers quickly dispersed when Josphat told them about the well. He proudly strapped his sign to it as Lawrence removed the handle, which he decided would make an excellent walking stick. He used it to point towards the dust cloud. They continued their journey.

Josphat took the lead, even though he didn't know where he was going. He told them it was his duty to make sure the path was clear of danger. He headed cautiously towards the dust cloud and the grinding noises coming from beyond the trees.

"Wait, Josphat." Lawrence called out as quietly as he could. "It's around here. That's the tree I collided with, I'm sure of it. It must be in these bushes somewhere. Hannah, can you do the honours?"

Hannah typed the word *test* into her phone and pressed send. The signal strength was very weak, and it failed to go. She took a couple of paces into more open ground and tried again. After a few seconds, it sent. Lawrence was listening intently. No ping.

"Josphat, you try over there. Hannah and I will comb through these bushes. Watch out for the thorns." Lawrence placed the metal handle on the ground carefully, trying to make no sound. What little breeze there was had died away. Birdsong could just be heard over the relentless grinding noise coming from the mine.

Hannah re-sent the text. Still no ping. Suddenly a single shot rang out, shattering the silence. Hannah looked across at Josphat whose face had frozen into a look of total astonishment. She watched helplessly as a dark mark on his forehead began to bleed - a trickle at first then blood was gushing down his face.

He was trying to speak, his mouth gaping open, blood coating his silent lips, small bubbles where the words should be. She noticed blood stains had smeared across his precious polo shirt. Within seconds, he fell face down into the dusty earth.

Hannah didn't know where the shot had come from. Lawrence had moved to her side. They held each other, both shaking with fear. There was no time to run and nowhere to hide.

Out of the bushes ahead of them stepped a giant of a man in military fatigues, a black revolver in his right hand. He was a white, Caucasian, male, with broad shoulders and a heavy, muscular build. His long, wavy dark hair, glistening in sweat, was swept back from a

216

swarthy, pock-marked face. The lick of a smile creased across his cruel grey eyes.

In a moment he was flanked by two of the guards from the mine, their rifles pointed straight at them. There was no escape, Hannah realised. How could the guards have known they were here?

In his left hand, the man was holding Lawrence's phone. He waved it provocatively in front of Hannah's face.

"Looking for this?"

CHAPTER 25

The blindfold had been tied so tightly, it was hurting her eyes. Adhesive tape across her mouth meant she couldn't speak and was finding it hard to breathe. Her nose was congested by dust and fumes. Her hands were strapped behind her back and held together with what felt like plastic cable ties. She could feel them cutting into her wrists. Her ankle was throbbing too. And she needed to use the bathroom.

Hannah had been frogmarched by the guards for what seemed like an eternity, stumbling through bushes and over rocky terrain. The heat was unbearable. Rivers of hot, sticky sweat were pouring down her face. Her clothes were wet through and clinging to her body.

Worse still, she didn't know where Lawrence was. Had they shot him too? Was he lying face down next to poor Josphat? And where were they taking her? At least there was some comfort in knowing they had an insurance policy. Father Kelly was expecting them and could raise the alarm.

Suddenly, they all stopped walking. Hushed voices in local dialect were followed by heavy boots fading away across a solid floor. She heard a door close behind her and felt a dramatic change in temperature. She was in an air-conditioned room.

Rough hands on her shoulders pushed her down onto a chair. She felt hot breath on her neck. Clumsy fingers fumbled behind her head then the blindfold was off, a sudden glare of dazzling light. She instinctively closed her eyes, then opened them again gradually.

Hannah yelped as the tape was ripped off her mouth, stinging her cheeks and lips. She tried to move her hands, but they were still fastened behind her, the pain in her wrists being made worse by a dull ache across her chest and shoulders, her arms being stretched back too far. She'd lost the feeling in her fingers to pins and needles.

"Thank you." Hannah mouthed the words to a young woman who wiped her face with a soft towel and held a glass of cold water to her lips. Hannah took a mouthful, her throat parched with exertion and fear. She focused on the face. It was the woman from the bushes. She offered Hannah a weak smile, as if to say sorry.

Apart from the young woman, Hannah could only see the giant who had now positioned himself behind a polished wooden table. He was standing up as he flicked through two passports: one American, one British.

"How come you're Siekierkowski yet you call yourself McGlynn?"

The accent was Midwestern, no nonsense, and very direct. Although his expression didn't change, Hannah sensed he was enjoying the control and savouring the thought of whatever cruelty was to come.

"We got married. I haven't renewed it yet." Hannah's voice was hoarse. She tried clearing her throat. "How did you get them?"

The blow came from someone behind her. She twisted as she hit the floor, the chair falling on top of her. She was looking up at one of the guards. He'd slapped her with the palm of his hand, but it felt like a hammer.

The young woman helped her up and righted the chair. Hannah thought she looked even more uncomfortable in this torture chamber than she had in the bushes. Now wasn't the time to connect with her. She hoped she'd get another chance.

At least Hannah had established there were only four of them in the room. She needed to be patient. There must be a reason why they hadn't shot her as well. But what about Lawrence?

"Speak only to answer my questions and we'll get along just fine." He tossed the passports across the table to the woman. "Shemmy, you'd better call these in. You know they hate surprises. I don't need more earache over this."

Shemmy collected the passports and gave Hannah a quick glance as she left the room. Was that the last time they'd see each other?

Shemmy; her name was Shemmy. He didn't hesitate to call her that. Obviously, he wasn't worried about Hannah knowing. This wasn't a good sign.

"Why are you sniffing around my mine? Don't lie to me. I know more than you think."

Hannah tried to compose herself, find the right words. "Innocent people are dying. Your drilling has poisoned their well. We're here to save lives. I need your help."

He stared straight at her, his grey eyes on fire. He glanced at the guard who had moved to be by her side. She sensed another blow coming but instead the man burst out laughing. "You mean the village people? They aren't worth saving, I assure you. Anyways, the sooner they're gone the better."

Hannah had a thousand questions, but speaking out would only result in more pain. She had to let him do the talking. An American running a remote mine - maybe he was lonely or needed some stimulating company. *You'd better call it in*, he'd said. This couldn't be a standalone operation. He must have a boss somewhere. *Russian or Ukrainian*, Father Kelly had said. Was that true? The Irish priest had been right about one thing. This man was certainly a brute. And a murderer.

220

"You were trespassing on private land."

"We were in scrubland, there were no signs. We were looking for a phone, that's all."

"But you were planning to come in here and shove these test results in my face, right?" The man brandished a wad of papers he grabbed out of Hannah's bag. "Who else knows about this?"

Hannah could see the first flicker of doubt on his face. He may be holding a better hand, but he didn't have all the trump cards. She had to risk the blow to even this up. "What's your name?"

Hannah saw a fist raised out of the corner of her eye, but a shake of his head was enough for the guard to lower it again. The man took a seat, then leaned back in the chair.

"OK, I level with you, you level with me."

"Agreed."

"I'm Joel Chernick, general manager here. I run a tight ship and don't need any interference from the likes of you. Now answer my question - who else knows?"

"I work for the World Health Organisation." Hannah replied, watching closely for his reaction.

"You lie. You work for the Pope. He's probably forgotten all about you by now. People in the Vatican tell me they want you out. You've no friends in Geneva either. You're flying solo on this so I'm asking for the last time."

"You're right, Joel." Hannah thought she'd irritate him by using his first name. "Apart from all the people in my team, the lab technicians at the University of Nairobi, the villagers and the people at the Turkana Lodge, the only other person I can think of is Father Kelly at the Diocese."

"The drunken priest?" Chernick raised his eyebrows in disbelief.

221

"And, of course, all the people he's talked to about our mission here." Hannah pressed on. "Now you answer a question for me. What are you mining here?"

Chernick stood up quickly sending his chair crashing to the floor behind him. He looked at the guard and nodded towards the door. Clearly, he'd had enough of this conversation. Hannah was pulled to her feet. The guard held up the blindfold, but Chernick shook his head. Hannah didn't think this was a good sign either.

She was led down some stairs into the bowels of the building, then through a maze of passageways. The guard unlocked a heavy metal door and threw her inside. It looked like a disused storeroom with no windows. Ceiling-high, empty, metal racking was bolted to the floor and walls. It was cramped, hot and dimly lit. Hannah asked for the handcuffs to be removed but the guard retreated, slammed the door, and locked it.

Hannah usually didn't suffer from claustrophobia but suddenly she could feel her heart racing. She closed her eyes and tried to take slow deep breaths. She focused on the job in hand. They knew about the arsenic in the groundwater. *The sooner they're gone the better*. Was this just the start of their mining exploration? What if other mines were to open around other parts of the lake? Maybe they already have.

More deep breaths. Inhale through the nose, exhale through the mouth. Her pulse was slowing. She was desperate for the bathroom now. The best she could do was crouch in the corner. She felt ashamed as the pressure relented but told herself to convert the emotion into anger and determination. Joel Chernick and his private army would pay the price. Cardinal Maina will regret this. Agnes's husband will be avenged. But for now, she had to get out of this room.

222

They'd removed her watch and jewellery. She'd no idea what time it was or how long she'd been locked up. She was hungry, thirsty, and still in pain. A headache was stabbing behind her left eye. She'd tried calling out to the guard several times with no response. She'd closed her eyes to sleep but kept seeing the astonished look on Josphat's face. She would avenge him as well.

At last, footsteps down the corridor, getting closer. She stood back from the door as it swung open. It was a different guard this time, older but his expression was no less cruel. He quickly checked inside the room then looked Hannah full in the face. In his right hand he was holding a sharp knife. Hannah froze as he spun her round with his other hand. She held her breath as he moved close behind her.

She felt the knife brush against her wrists as he snipped the cable ties with a single upward slash. He stepped back to the doorway and grabbed a crumpled figure propped up against a wall outside. He launched the prisoner into the room, his head banging against a metal shelf, knocking him sideways.

"Lawrence, oh thank God." Hannah leapt over to him as the door slammed shut again, a turn of the key locking them inside.

Lawrence was in poor shape. His head was bleeding from numerous wounds. Both eyes were bruised and badly swollen. There were deep gashes on both wrists where cable ties had been. He must have been so weak that they didn't bother re-tying them.

Hannah wiped the blood from her own wrists and waggled some life back into her fingers. She cradled his head in her lap, kneeling on the floor next to him. His breath was shallow, every movement seemed to cause him searing pain. He'd taken a beating and possibly had some broken bones. One of his fingers was badly misshapen and he could hardly lift his left arm.

His eyes were struggling to open, the corners of his mouth creasing into a weak smile. He croaked out a few words. "I saw a file."

"Stay quiet, we can talk later, you need to rest."

"No time, they're going to kill us. I heard them talking. They threw Josphat's body into the crusher. It jammed the machine, thank God, or we'd have been next. I got free and ran. I was hiding in an office when they caught me. I saw a file on the desk. Oh Hannah, I never…" Lawrence choked back the tears, his voice fractured. "I never thought I'd see you again."

"We'll get out of this, I promise. Father Kelly will help us. You need to rest but tell me about the file." Hannah could do little to ease his pain. She tore off a strip from her t-shirt and dabbed his wounds. It seemed to make things worse. They had to get out of this hellhole. In this heat, his wounds would go septic.

"It was a production report. They do mine some copper but that's the cover story. I know what they're doing but I don't know why. It makes no sense."

Footsteps down the corridor, more boots this time. The door opened and several guards marched in. They used metal handcuffs not cable ties, their arms were locked in front and heavy cotton sacks thrown over their heads. No time for blindfolds. Someone was in a hurry to end this.

The air in the corridor was cooler but still unpleasant. Hannah could hear Lawrence's cries behind her as they were manhandled along the passageways, up staircases, and back outside. They were thrown into a vehicle, with their handcuffs secured to a rail.

"Lawrence?" Hannah was sure she could hear him struggling nearby. She tried tossing her head around to shake off the bag, but it just made her headache even worse.

"Yes, I'm here. Where are we going now, for God's sake?"

"I don't know but I think you're right, they plan to get rid of us."

Hannah could feel the truck speeding up as it crashed through potholes and swung sharply from side to side. It wasn't a long journey. They were slowing down. Hannah could smell fish. They must be at the lake.

"Lawrence, what're they mining? What's so precious they're prepared to kill for?"

They'd stopped. The engine cut off. Hannah could hear voices outside. Somebody was protesting. Sounds of a scuffle, a heavy thud. It went quiet.

"In the report they called it kamacite. It's a metallic rock, there was a sample on the desk. It looks like a shiny lump of lead, nothing special. Can't see what the fuss is about."

Voices, louder this time, the doors at the back of the truck were opening. People jumping inside, sweaty bodies nearby, Hannah heard the handcuffs being unlocked, rough hands on her shoulders, Lawrence groaning. *Hang on in there, Lawrence, we can get through this.*

Despite the inner peptalk, Hannah was beginning to wonder if they would get through this. It seemed like days ago when they were driving over to warn Agnes about the well, Josphat teasing the children with the chocolate. How quickly things change.

The smell of fish was stronger outside the vehicle. She could hear water lapping against the shoreline. The breeze had freshened. A hand grabbed the bag over her head. As it was ripped off, she closed her eyes in readiness for bright sunlight. Instead, it was dusk, with pinks and

225

oranges in the distant sky, the sun setting majestically behind them. Such a beautiful country yet so brutal. There was no time for sunsets.

At the end of a short jetty was a boat like the one that chased them into Ferguson Bay. Sleek, powerful, it was tied up but straining at the leash, the twin outboards impatiently churning out a stream of muddy water.

Hannah could see there were two or three people on board. The spotlights above the cabin were switched off. There were no navigation lights, no lights anywhere. When Hannah looked around, she saw deserted fishing boats strewn along the shoreline but no one in sight. The only movement was a flock of pelicans combing the shallows looking for a meal.

Lawrence was struggling to walk along the jetty which earned him a sharp jab in the ribs. Hannah winced for him, but he made no sound. She stepped into the boat and was greeted by a thin, wiry crew member in a ridiculously thick woollen sweater and a Rasta-coloured, Beanie Hat. He was pointing a revolver at them.

"You no give me trouble tonight." He flicked off the safety catch.

"Where are you taking us?" Hannah demanded.

There was shouting on the jetty as the ropes were untied and thrown on board. The outboards revved to full throttle forcing the bow to swing out into the sinister darkness of Lake Turkana.

Hannah looked back to see the truck drive away, a fading silhouette against the dying embers of a horrible day. No lights. Within moments, the truck had gone. Had it ever been there, she wondered.

They were taken down into the forward hold which was empty apart from a bundle of rags stashed between two boxes. The boat was bouncing around in choppy waters causing Hannah and Lawrence to lose their footing.

"Wait in here. Not long. No funny business." Beanie Hat kept panning the gun between them. Given what we've been through and the amount of pain we're in, Hannah thought, he didn't need to worry. We're in no state to surprise him.

"I want to know where we are going." Hannah insisted.

"Very nice place, you'll love it." A huge grin revealed an impressive collection of pearly white teeth, interspersed with gold and silver fillings. "Not in Lonely Planet. We call it Paradise Alley."

CHAPTER 26

Beanie Hat retreated, locking the door behind him. The violent rocking of the boat made it impossible to stand, so Hannah and Lawrence collapsed against the bulkhead. Lawrence's feet could reach the bundle of rags. He gave it a kick out of sheer frustration. How did things come to this?

To their astonishment, the rags began to move. "Hey, don't do that. I've suffered enough."

Hannah recognised the rich Irish brogue immediately. She looked in horror at Lawrence. *So much for our insurance policy.*

Father Kelly straightened himself up and tossed the rags across the floor. He too was badly beaten with multiple bruises and cuts on his face. There was a great lump over his left eye, clearly where he'd taken a heavy blow from a blunt instrument. His hands were also cuffed in front of him.

"What happened to you?" Lawrence asked.

"The bastards jumped me in the office. Pardon my French, Hannah." Father Kelly replied, struggling to get the words out over a deep split in his lower lip.

"No need to apologise, Father, bastard is the right word." Hannah shuffled round so they could talk in hushed voices.

"Didn't anyone help you?" Lawrence remembered there were other people in the diocese office when they visited last. "And what about the gun?"

"Everyone had disappeared when I got there. I thought it strange, but they may have gone out for lunch. Mind you, I can't say I'm surprised by this. Round here, the

228

local people change sides depending which way the wind blows."

"Or who's paying the most, I suppose." Hannah added.

"And the gun?" Lawrence thought for one crazy minute that he might have it with him. Although ideologically opposed to guns, Lawrence might have been persuaded to change his viewpoint in these circumstances.

"They'd already taken it. I looked. Clearly, I had a spy in the camp."

Hannah knew that there couldn't be much time. At this speed the boat could reach any part of the lake in minutes. She needed answers.

"Did you check the name of this mining company, Father?" Hannah pushed. It seemed heartless given the pain they were all suffering but, knowing something about their enemy, might just save their lives.

"It's KMI, I remembered after we spoke. I think the K stands for Khazi as there's a funny smell about the whole thing. *Khazi Mining Industries* or something like that. I'd put the contact details in my phone. One of my parishioners works there, a young woman from Nairobi, she moved here not so long ago, now what was her name?"

"Shemmy?" Hannah suggested.

"Yes, Shemmy. Shemmy Biwott, thanks for reminding me, charming young girl, come's in every week for confession. Regular as clockwork. Do you know her?"

"We've met a couple of times, put it that way." Next weeks' confession could be interesting, Hannah thought. She saw a puzzled look on Lawrence's face and whispered she'd explain later. If there was a later.

"And the Russian money?" Hannah persisted, trying to squeeze what she could out of the good priest.

"Ah, yes, Ukrainian, definitely Ukrainian. I found some emails. We'd tried to get them to support a

229

fundraising event for the diocese. I'd emailed the local guy, Joel Chernick. American, nasty piece of work, by all accounts. He never replied so I had a go for the parent company, thinking they might chip in. In Kenya they work with a venture capital firm in Nairobi, but the big money is funnelled through an investment outfit in Kiev."

"That's quite common." Lawrence stepped in. "A joint venture with a local firm gets them past the money laundering protocols. The Kiev firm will be a shell company to protect the real owners and provide a tax dodge. Did you learn anything else about them, Father?"

"Sadly not. That's when I got the gypsy's warning from Cardinal Maina. Somebody must have tipped him off. He said I should make any requests for donations through him. He told me he'd helped KMI get their mining licence. Apparently, he's personal friends with the top man at the Ministry. Knowing the Cardinal, there'll be some greasy baksheesh involved somewhere."

The boat was slowing down. They must be in calmer waters as the rocking motion had almost stopped. The hold door opened. Beanie Hat was back, his gun at the ready. Behind him were two of the heavies Hannah had seen when they first came on board.

Beanie Hat motioned for them to follow him up on deck. The heavies had to drag Father Kelly who had difficulty moving.

The fresh air on deck was a welcome relief after being locked up in the hold. By now it was totally dark. A panoply of stars filled the night sky. Hannah saw the first glimpse of a huge moon rising over the brooding mass of a rocky island dead ahead.

When she looked closer, it was two islands with large volcanic cones rising straight up from the ink-black waters. Fingers of moonlight found a narrow channel snaking between them. She reckoned they must be on the leeward side as the breeze had gone.

The boat started to idle towards slack water in the channel between rocky shorelines. Beanie Hat announced there were no other boats on the lake. *No one to help you*, he beamed. He had the underwater lights switched on *so they could enjoy the show*, laughing as he pulled open one of the deck gates. The lights cast eerie shadows into the murky depths.

Hannah looked at Lawrence then across to Father Kelly. They both shrugged their shoulders, resigned to whatever was about to happen. Beanie Hat and the crew moved in unison to get things ready. Hannah could see they must have done this many times before as each crew member knew the drill.

They dropped anchor in the channel. The rope kept spooling and spooling. It was deep, very deep. When they killed the engines, there was silence, just the gentle lap of water against the hull.

"Time to see Paradise." Beanie Hat nodded to the heavies who grabbed Father Kelly and, in one effortless movement, threw him through the open gateway into the lake. He shouted as he hit the water, the words muffled as his whole body submerged, silver-topped ripples catching the moonlight as they splayed out in all directions.

The lights made it seem surreal, like he was moving in slow motion. Hannah could see him trying to surface, kicking out with both legs, struggling with cupped hands to pull the water down.

It took several seconds for his head to break the surface, his legs now treading water. First, he looked for help from the boat. Quickly realising that none was being offered, he turned towards the nearest shoreline, flipped onto his back, and started kicking out as hard as he could.

"You bastards!!" Hannah shrieked which earned a slap to the face, knocking her across the deck. She got to her feet and could only watch in horror as two dark shapes on the far shoreline slithered into the water. The priest was swimming straight for them, their sinister wakes fanning out across the calm waters.

Hannah looked away as the first croc reached him, thrashing the water amid violent screams. The croc let go to fight off the other one, giving Father Kelly a few precious seconds to get away. He tried to swim, but his hands were still cuffed, and his wet clothes made it more difficult. The reprieve was short lived.

The priest's body disappeared momentarily, only to resurface closer to the shore. The first croc was giving chase. Father Kelly was trying to kick it away when the other croc grabbed his upper leg and rolled over the top of him. It pulled him down into the depths, followed quickly by the first.

It was over in seconds, just a dark stain on the surface bearing witness to where the commotion had been.

"They drown you first, jam you under a rock then eat slow." Beanie Hat explained, the evil grin back on his face. "Them crocs not feed for days now. There'll be nothin' left. Don't worry, we find others for you, then you join him in Paradise."

The anchor chain was pulled up and the engines set to idling speed. The channel got narrower as they went further in between the two islands. The rocky shoreline became steep cliffs with narrow strips of beach on either side where the scree had fallen.

Beanie Hat raised his hand and the engines died. The anchor rope spooled out again, deeper this time. In the half light, Hannah could see three or four logs washed up among the rocks. Suddenly one of the logs began to move, followed by the others. They slide silently into the dark water. They must recognise the boat, she thought, like feeding time at the zoo.

Lawrence begged them to stop. He offered them money, but it was no use. The crew waited until the anchor was securely fastened then Beanie Hat nodded to the two heavies. *Ladies first.*

Hannah yelled and kicked out, swinging her arms in an arc to stop them but another crew member came up from behind and wrestled her to the deck, squeezing her breasts gratuitously in the same movement.

Lawrence tried to help but was quickly overpowered. Beanie Hat fired a shot into the air then pointed the gun straight at him.

By now all four crocs were circling the boat in hungry anticipation, their menacing shapes captured in the underwater lights.

Three of the crew positioned Hannah by the open deck gate. She managed to jam one of her feet under the gatepost, determined not to go easily.

She tried twisting towards Lawrence before her foot was yanked away.

Hot salty tears were rolling down his cheeks. They'd been through so much together but there was no way out this time.

An idea flashed into Hannah's mind. If Lawrence dived in after her and they could kick out in unison, could they fight them off long enough to get to the shore? It wasn't that far away. But even if they reached it, they'd never get off the island. The cliffs were too steep. And how many more crocs were there? She had to accept there was no escape from Paradise Alley.

Beyond the shouting of the crew members, Hannah heard the crackle of a two-way radio. It was likely to be the last thing she ever heard as their hands gripped her more tightly, ready to throw her overboard. A voice from

233

the cabin called out to Beanie Hat. He gave the gun to one of the other crew and told them all to wait till he got back *as he wanted to see the bitch die.*

Hannah looked down into the floodlit channel. One of the crocs was huge - well over fourteen feet long, she reckoned - a silhouette writhing and rolling in the slack water. Its dead eyes were fixed on hers. She felt an icy chill run through her.

Raised voices coming from the cabin, then Beanie Hat was back. He was angry. He grabbed the gun and fired off a burst at one of the smaller crocs, hitting it behind its eyes. Blood spurted out, clouding the water which sent the other three into a feeding frenzy. Within seconds the water was boiling as tails thrashed and jaws snatched at anything they could sink their teeth into.

Beanie Hat came over to Hannah, his face burning. She thought he was going to push her over the side.

She braced herself against the gate post.

CHAPTER 27

Steve couldn't see what she was getting at. They'd replayed the hotel lobby footage several times. He knew the dangers of imagining things that weren't there, just because you needed them to be. He admired her dogged determination though. She should have trained as a detective; her attention to detail was remarkable.

"OK, Maria, play it again. I don't see a resemblance." Steve didn't need more coffee when she offered. What he wanted was a tangible lead.

They both watched as Stannard walked past the camera again and disappeared offscreen, towards the elevator. A man entered the lobby shortly afterwards, stayed in the lounge area for a few minutes, made a phone call then exited. His face wasn't all that clear and he mostly had his back to the camera. Steve had to admit there was no apparent reason why he was in the lobby but there could be several plausible explanations.

"And that's the same man in the street outside the window when Stannard meets McInnes. See, he's on his phone again. The same red phone case." Maria zoomed in triumphantly although the enlarged picture was very blurred.

She then cut to the cameras outside 28th Street station. "And there he is walking ahead of Stannard towards Lexington."

"But if he was following him, wouldn't he have waited?" Steve had an idea. If his hunch had legs, they might make a much-needed breakthrough.

"Only if he didn't know where he was going." Maria replied.

"But how could he know?"

"Somebody must have told them. If that was the case, all they didn't know was the time and which route he'd take." Maria surmised. "So, follow him from the hotel until they were sure where he'd be, then commit the crime, having checked out the scene first."

"And you're saying it was the shorter of the two guys who followed him?" Steve asked her to toggle between the screens. He knew this evidence wouldn't stand up in court, but it may not have to, if they could get a name. The figure on the screen during the attack was the same build, wearing similar dark clothing, but he couldn't tell about his hair colour due to the ski mask.

"Yes. See, the jewellers shop camera shows the others from the train walking down towards Lexington, but not him." Maria clicked to a street map of the area. "I reckon, he nipped off down this alley, here, and met up with the tall guy around here, before they came down here and waited for Stannard in the shadows, knowing he'd be along in a few minutes and the street was quiet."

Steve liked the hypothesis but that's all it was. What would have happened if Stannard crossed over, took another route, or even caught a cab? Maria suggested they'd have gone to the pub and found the right moment when he came out. Or gone to his hotel room later, perhaps. As things worked out, they'd committed just about the perfect crime with little chance of being caught, she explained.

Now to play his hunch. Steve asked her to patch back into the 28th Street archive. Sure enough, there were cameras capturing passengers getting on and off trains as well as using the exits. Stronger lighting made the imagery much sharper. Steve spotted their man using his phone in its red case as he climbed the steps. Maria copied the image.

It took three calls to Apicella, a reluctant email confirmation and Steve's countersignature in triplicate on an authorisation form promising not to abuse the facial recognition system before they finally received the access code. It took a few minutes for Maria to feed in the image correctly, then they had to wait. And wait. The cursor continued to blink.

"Of course, he may not be in the database at all. He may not be the guy in the ski mask, in which case, we're back to square one." Steve suggested as he brought back the coffee refills. "Or this could just be another bloody coincidence. That reminds me, I need to call Max Hartley. Wonder if he'll remember me."

He was about to dial Max's number when a file flashed up on the screen. Maria clicked it open. "Michael Abraham Shapiro, answers to Mickey Shaps, born in Brooklyn, age 32, no dependents or close family, there's an address, looks like an apartment block on Pendle Street in Brownsville."

Maria continued, reading off a screen. "He's got previous for burglary, petty larceny, possession of Class C drugs, loitering with intent, car theft, all small-time stuff. He was in Otisville on a three-year stretch, parole for good behaviour and showing remorse, released two years ago, supposedly clean since."

"Where's Brownsville?" Steve had to admit that this was looking more promising.

Maria skipped to another screen. "It's the wrong side of Brooklyn, out east. Used to be an upmarket area once but it's all urban renewal, social housing, and gentrification now, an attractive neighbourhood, according to the council's propaganda."

"Our Mickey was a long way from home then." Steve pulled up a map of the Greater New York area. "Also, a bit out of his depth, by the sound of it. Robbery with

237

violence, manslaughter, not his thing. How did he get mixed up in this, I wonder?"

"Well, to be fair, Steve, he wasn't carrying the weapon. The tall guy fired the shot. Mickey may not have known it would turn so ugly. We don't know what he was told."

"Then let's ask him."

* * *

Maria was driving. Steve had left a message for Max Hartley. They'd decided against calling Mickey Shaps, preferring to surprise him. As they crossed the Brooklyn Bridge heading south, Steve's phone burst into life, caller unknown. "Hello?"

"Is that Detective Mole?"

"Yes, who's calling?"

"We haven't spoken before, I'm Todd du Prez, Connie's husband. She said you were looking into the sale of Pemberton Electronics."

"Todd, you've saved me a call, thank you for making contact, please call me Steve." He was mouthing the name to Maria, but she whispered that she'd already heard it.

"Thanks, Steve, that makes it easier to talk. Is now a good time, by the way?"

Steve confirmed it was and asked him to say what Connie had told him. He needed to make sure the caller was legit. Even assuming he was, Steve wanted Todd to do the talking.

"Connie said you're investigating the sale. I fully understand that. It does look somewhat suspicious, changing hands for well below market rate. I can see why the IRS feel short changed." The delivery was calm, measured, the voice confident and quite assured but with

238

a slight hint of uncertainty, possibly even concern, Steve decided.

"So, in your own words, why did you accept their offer?" Steve had pulled out his notebook and was scribbling away with it balanced across his knees. The traffic was slowing as they came off the bridge, but his notes were still quite illegible. Better than nothing, he decided.

"As Connie told you, we were blackmailed. Someone had kidnapped our granddaughter, Chicory. We had no choice but to sell out."

"Why didn't you contact the police?" Steve wanted to hear his version of events.

"We were told they'd kill her if the police or anyone else got involved. Look, Steve, since talking to Connie yesterday, I've had a change of heart and want to cooperate fully with this investigation. My wife is right. We can't let them get away with this. We must be stronger, better prepared to face any consequences."

"And what about Chicory?"

Todd explained the whole family were booked on a late flight to Europe from JFK tonight and would be staying with friends until this blew over. Chicory would be out of reach. He and Connie had agreed to house-sit a friend's apartment in New York for a few months. It would be safer and make it easier for them to cooperate with the investigation.

Steve asked about the kidnapper. Todd confirmed he had spoken to the man several times. He had a strong Caribbean accent, was well organised, methodical, ruthless, and always seemed one step ahead of them. He'd always worn a ski mask around Chicory, so she hadn't seen his face. They'd never met him.

"I'm curious about how this man knew when the deal was done so he could release her." Steve was getting around to Slaker Nadzy's involvement, hoping Todd would mention them first.

"We never did find out. I don't think anyone in the law firms or Slaker Nadzy were involved. Our contact there is Ethan Bronstein. He's straight, although Connie got upset when she thought they were acting independently."

"And were they, Todd? Acting independently, I mean." Steve probed. This was the crux of what he needed to know.

"Steve, at the beginning of this year, my doctor told me I had to quit running Pemberton, or my heart would give out. I was getting palpitations and stabbing chest pains. The stress was killing me, but I couldn't say anything to Connie. She kept reminding me it was her family's company. That's fine but she wasn't living with the operational problems day to day. We'd overstretched ourselves. It was horrible."

"You mentioned Slaker Nadzy." Give him the rope.

"I'd taken Ethan into my confidence about my state of health. I asked him to keep things quiet but see if he could find a buyer. I didn't want Connie to know, she'd have worried herself even more. And, given the financial headwinds we were facing, I didn't really think anyone would be interested in buying us. How wrong can you be?"

"And what was Ethan's role in the sale?" This story was stacking up. Maybe he'd been wrong about Ethan after all.

"He brokered the deal, very professional, made sure both parties were kept in the loop and handled all the paperwork effectively. I was impressed by him. He showed a lot of maturity and commercial nous for such a young guy. By then, of course, Chicory had gone missing, and our hands were tied."

"And what was the sale price? I need your confirmation, please." Steve flicked over to a clean page.

"Five million. That's what we got. No dealings under the counter. We wanted more, as every owner does, but the situation had changed with the kidnapping. The sale itself had to be above board, or else we'd never have seen her again. I can show you written confirmation." Todd confirmed.

Steve had all the paperwork he needed. The satnav had lost signal and Maria didn't know which way to turn through the backstreets of Brooklyn.

He asked Todd if he'd be prepared to make a statement. He was happy to do so. They agreed to meet in the lobby of the same hotel where he'd met Connie. Steve thanked him for the call, disconnected, then updated his phone with Todd's contact details.

Maria had pulled over and reset the satnav. It chirped back into life as if nothing had happened. They were nine minutes away from their destination.

"Do you believe him?" Maria killed the engine and turned towards him.

"Yes, I think so. It all seems to make sense and, of course, gets Ethan off the hook. The thing that's puzzling me though is why? I can see why Herzl wanted Pemberton. I can see why Todd wanted to sell out, but obviously not at that price. I can see why Ethan put the deal together. But there's another player in here. Whoever's behind the kidnapping wanted something else, something from Pemberton maybe. We're still not seeing the bigger picture."

"But at least we can close off some lines of enquiry." Maria added cheerfully. "There was a kidnapping. A crime has been committed. We have cooperation now from Todd and Connie. Ethan and Slaker Nadzy are not quite smelling of roses but don't seem to have been colluding with the kidnappers. And the IRS were right to pursue this. That's pretty good progress for a few days' work, I'd say."

"I love your optimism, Maria. Now let's see if we can make some progress with this homicide. I wonder what Mickey Shaps is going to tell us."

Maria was just about to turn the key when Steve's phone lit up again. She sat back and unbuckled her seat belt as he pressed the button.

"Max, thanks for returning my call."

CHAPTER 28

Max had heard the sad news about Stannard's death from Quentin Fitzgerald-Manning, but he thanked Steve anyway for letting him know. He was still shocked about what had happened and couldn't believe Stannard would have been anywhere near a dangerous part of town.

"It isn't dangerous, that's what's confusing us. There've been no serious crimes in that area for many years." Steve replied.

It was strange how, with some people, Steve reflected, you sort of pick up from where you left off, as if you only spoke to them yesterday. It was years since they'd had any dealings together, yet Max fell into the category of immediate trustworthiness. Was it his RAF pilot-officer pedigree or his open, honest approach, perhaps it was their shared sense of humour? Whatever it was, Steve knew he could rely on what Max had to tell him.

"I only met Stannard once, in Quentin's office at the House. He was a strange fish, I'd have to say, huge intellect, bit of an acquired taste I should imagine but he knew his stuff. I was hoping he'd come over on the flight with me, an insurance policy I suppose, but he had these meetings in New York." Max explained.

"Why was he needed in St Louis? *Comet 5* can obviously fly without him." Steve wished he knew more about the propulsion systems, then he might be able to ask sharper questions. But, then again, Max may not know the answers, as he was only the pilot.

"I was supposed to meet him yesterday at the plane. Stannard was due to give the salt box a final check, load the other rods and charm the FAA inspectors, if we needed him to. As it turned out, they were just blown away by the technology and issued the certificate there and then. They didn't need any schmoozing, thankfully."

Steve asked for a translation. The salt box was Max's name for the molten salt reactor that housed the thorium rods and sat in what used to be a bulk-head toilet behind the cockpit.

"In the original design, apparently, they were going to put the salt box in the cargo hold, out of the way, 'til someone rightly pointed out the crew might need quick access to it in an emergency." Max continued. "It's about the size of a washing machine and just sits there humming away. A control panel on the facia tells you what it's up to but you can read all that from the cockpit instrumentation."

While Steve was asking about the thorium rods, Max sent him some photos of them. About eighteen inches long and two inches wide, they were silvery metallic in colour and perfectly cylindrical. Max assured him they were very heavy.

"Yes, quite safe to handle. I picked one up and conducted the band with it. I needed both hands, as it was that heavy. An imaginary band, of course, played the Dam Busters theme. Childish, I know, but I got a bit carried away."

Max continued. "What an amazing discovery. Stannard is an absolute genius. Sorry, was. Anyway, the rods only become truly radioactive in the salt box when irradiated with a blast of neutrons. It's all Greek to me but the beauty is that the salt box is leak-proof and the whole process can be easily controlled. Any trouble, Steve, you can just switch it off."

"How do you know for sure?" Steve was scribbling away again.

"Because I did it coming over. We were mid-Atlantic, the plane's lithium-ion batteries were fully charged, comfortable at cruising height, co-pilot asleep, no sweat, so I thought, why not try it? As an old test pilot once told me, best to find out before it's too late.

"Anyway, I switched off the salt box and we flew on batteries for forty minutes. Nobody noticed. The plane just carried on. We'd topped up the batteries well before we landed. Piece of cake." Max then added, in a whisper. "Please don't tell anyone. With all the modifications, the plane's insured for a tad over $400 million. I had to sign a piece of paper and swore an oath not to take any risks."

"You mentioned other rods. What other rods?" Steve could sense that Maria wanted to get moving. Inside the car, it was becoming quite hot and sticky. He indicated to her two minutes, so she turned the engine back on. The aircon was surprisingly welcome.

"The salt box can take up to ten rods. We came across on four. They're manufactured here in the States so the other six were delivered directly to St Louis. Angela explained there's enough fuel in four rods to keep *Comet 5* airborne for years. Now they want to see how the salt box performs fully fuelled during the race itself."

"Angela? You mean Dr Angela Fischer? She's with you?" So, Lonsdale wouldn't be meeting her in Oxford.

"I'm surprised you've heard of her. She keeps a low profile, by all accounts. The boys have nicknamed her the Ice Maiden." There was laughter in his voice.

"My colleague was hoping to meet her in Oxford. She could help us with our inquiries." Steve explained.

"She flew over with me and a few hangers-on from the UN. No dramas, the plane's easy to fly once you've got used to it. She's spent 15 years in the lab with Stannard and wanted to know it worked. Ironically, she's terrified of flying. I saw her crying when I walked through the

245

cabin. She said it was a mixture of joy and relief that their baby had finally flown the nest. I noticed she did manage three large gin and tonics to calm her nerves. The Ice Maiden melted for a while."

Max confirmed that Angela had personally loaded the other six rods, tested the salt box performance levels, and sealed the unit ready for the flying start tomorrow. With Quentin's approval, he'd offered her Stannard's seat for the race, but she declined. Brandon College had called and offered her an Associate Professorship.

Max added. "There's so much going on at the university, she said, she had to get back. Personally, I don't think being locked in a metal tube at forty thousand feet for up to fifty hours quite floated her boat."

Steve made a note. "Strange she's not taking part. A chance in a lifetime, I'd have thought. Honour Stannard's legacy, take some of the glory."

"She's heading straight home after we take off tomorrow. There's a roof-top party at the House when the planes fly over London. Big Ben is Sky Station Seven. Those lazy bastards will take any excuse for a party. She said she might go."

Steve wished Max well for the race. He planned to do a blog from inside the cabin, recording the mood as they flew over each Sky Station. Steve said they'd cheer him on at the Statue of Liberty, which Max confirmed was Sky Station Eight. Maria nodded in agreement that she'd be there. Although this race wasn't intended to be the USA versus Europe, inevitably that's how it was being seen, especially State-side.

"*Comet 5* has the blue belly; in case you're wondering. The Yanks' Boeing is painted red. We must pass each Sky Station at 2,000 feet for the ground observers, so you'll be able to see us clearly. I'll wave to you." Max laughed as he disconnected.

246

Steve needed a few minutes to finish off scribbling his notes. Maria had given up trying to persuade him to save them digitally through voice recording software. For a man only in his thirties, Steve was surprisingly set in his ways and resistant to change, in Maria's view, as she'd told him many times. But, despite his technical shortcomings, she had to admit he was a bloody good cop.

Maria checked the mirror, saw a gap, swung out into the traffic, and headed east towards Brownsville. The satnav was behaving itself again.

Maria glanced across at him. "Were you serious about the Statue of Liberty? The crowds will be horrendous. It said on CNN last night the whole city's going to turn out. There hasn't been this much interest in aviation since Lindbergh flew the Atlantic."

"I've got to be there now; a promise is a promise. Besides, if the first plane over is painted blue, the crowd's stunned reaction will be something to savour." Steve couldn't help the grin.

The traffic had thinned out as they turned onto Pendle Street. The neighbourhood wasn't as Steve expected it to be. Gone were the brick-and-stone houses, low-rise tenements and densely packed apartment blocks as he'd seen in some old photographs. It may have been a difficult place to live but he reckoned people pulled together, as communities, in those days. They helped each other out.

Instead, high-rise concrete and glass towers had sprung up out of the rubble. Urban planners, who grew up playing with Lego bricks, had finally been given a chance to create their dream of an angular, regimented, vertical city, he surmised. Any soul the place had previously was long gone, balled into dust in the name of progress. Brownsville? Nowhereville, he renamed it in his mind, as he got out of the car. He made sure it was locked before crossing the street.

The apartment block was twelve stories high. The website had proudly recorded it was officially opened by the Borough President for Brooklyn only nine years ago. It wasn't aging well, Steve thought. Some broken glass, graffiti, and a smashed door panel greeted them. The elevator was out of use and the sign looked like it had been there a while. Thankfully, Mickey Shap's apartment was only on the second floor.

The concrete stairs looked like they hadn't been swept since it opened. One of the lights in the stairwell was out. Steve saw Maria tense up and lean into the wall as a resident swept past them on the way down, carrying rubbish bags, lost in pulsating, head-phoned rap music. At least they didn't throw the bags out of the window.

Steve had always refused to carry a weapon. Ever since his basic firearms training, he firmly believed he was safer without one. The country would be safer without them. But, right now, a shadow of doubt crossed his mind. Was this the right thing to be doing? Should they have asked for back-up before confronting a known offender on his home turf? One thing was for sure: if there was trouble, they couldn't rely on any help from the neighbours.

They stopped outside the apartment door. Faint sounds coming from inside, a TV maybe. Cracks in the paint, scuffing around the lock, the handle had buckled under immense pressure and there were deep chisel scars in the doorframe like someone had tried to prise it away from the thin, plaster-board wall.

Steve recognised the sweet, musty smell of cannabis drifting around the hallway. It could be coming from any of the four apartments on that floor.

He motioned for Maria to stand back as he knocked firmly on the door. First there was silence, presumably the TV had been turned off. Then footsteps getting closer, stopping behind the door. A few more seconds. The door opened a crack, one bloodshot brown eye appeared in the space. No chain across the gap, Steve noticed.

The eye disappeared and the door started to close slowly. Steve jammed his foot into the crack and pushed hard. The door swung wide open, there was little resistance.

The man fell backwards into the darkened hallway. The musty smell was much stronger in here, almost overpowering. They moved inside and closed the door behind them. Steve tried the light switch, but nothing happened.

To Steve's surprise, instead of getting to his feet, the man flipped slowly onto his stomach and started to crawl away down the hall. Steve had rehearsed an opening gambit and had his identity card at the ready, as did Maria. It wasn't necessary. Steve felt a sense of relief as he watched this pathetic creature struggling to escape. He never did see the point in cigarettes or drugs. Life in the police provided enough excitement for him.

They followed the man to the big room at the end of the hallway and helped him into an armchair. The air was thick with blue smoke rising from an ash tray full of cigarette stubs. Steve put out the one still burning as Maria managed to pull back the dirty curtains and open a small side window. A stiff breeze started to clear the fug.

Steve compared the man's face against the photo taken at 28th Street Station. It was a close enough match, even allowing for his current state of substance abuse, dishevelled appearance, and apparent lack of sleep for several days.

This was Mickey Shaps, his identification confirmed when Maria pointed to his phone in its red case on a side table. She also found a crumpled letter addressed to him from the landlords, threatening eviction for rent arrears.

Should have taken the Rolex as well, Steve mused to himself.

Maria put a pan of water on the stove and searched the cupboards for coffee, without success. At least there was gas. She did find a tin of chocolate powder and managed to make a hot, sticky concoction using plenty of sugar and some UHT milk from a grubby carton at the back of the refrigerator. By this time, Mickey was asleep in the armchair, snoring gently.

"I'll wake him, you pour that down his throat and we'll try to get some answers. I don't want to stay here a minute longer than we need to." Steve explained, moving over to the chair.

"We could take him with us and question him at the precinct." Maria offered.

"I'm not sure we'd make it to the car. Ever since we got here, I feel like we're being watched. We stand out like sore thumbs. I'm guessing Brooklyn police come here better prepared. Maybe we should've told them." Steve couldn't disguise the uncertainty in his voice.

Maria tried to get some liquid into the man's mouth, but it just dribbled down his already stained sweater. Steve started to shake him gently by the shoulders. There was mumbling but the man was out cold.

Steve pinched his nose hoping he'd wake up that way, but Mickey Shaps just started breathing roughly through his mouth. "We may have to take him in. I want to know what he was doing there and who he was with."

There was a noise behind them. The lounge door creaked as it swung fully open. The man in the doorway was huge, well over six feet, thick set, almost bald, clear almond shaped eyes. Steve noticed the row of perfect, marble-white teeth, grinning at him from a face as black as coal.

Then he spotted the gun, pointing straight at them.

Andrew Harris

"I think it's me you're lookin' for."

CHAPTER 29

Steve knew very little about guns but this one looked expensive and very deadly, especially with its silencer attachment. The hand holding it was assured. This man knew what he was doing.

He wanted them to move to the big table and empty out their pockets, including the contents of Maria's bag. It made quite a pile with pepper spray, a taser, phones, car keys and even handcuffs. There must have been a couple of hundred dollars in cash. But no weapons. Steve thought he saw the man smile to himself. He wasn't interested in the cash. Strange for a mugger. Who was he? Had he sensed their naivety?

The man stepped over to where Mickey was sleeping and looked straight down at him. Steve and Maria could only watch as, in one fluid movement, he raised the gun and shot him twice straight down through the top of his head. Sickening dull thuds as he pulled the trigger. The bullets must be lodged somewhere in his spine or even the armchair he was now slumped down into. Blood was pooling over Mickey's hair, temples and down the sides of his face.

Maria let out a gasp but managed to stifle a full scream. She clung tightly to Steve's arm. He scanned the room looking for options. There was only one door, which they would never reach. The side windows were too small to fit through and, even if they could, the drop would surely kill them both.

"Mickey was a problem. Don't need him now. I must go but can't let you follow. Cuff yerselves together. No fancy moves. Nice and slow, where I can see ya." His voice remained calm like nothing had happened. He wasn't wearing a mask or gloves this time. He acted like he knew who they were, almost like he was expecting them.

As Steve snapped the cuffs over their wrists, the man picked up their phones and car keys. The rest of the things, including the bank notes, he casually swept onto the floor with the back of his hand, like they somehow irritated him.

Making no attempt to conceal the weapon, he followed them along the hallway, across the landing and down the stairwell. Outside, he seemed to know it was their car parked across the street and headed towards it. There was no traffic. The few pedestrians further along the sidewalk were too far away to help, even if they'd have wanted to.

Steve looked at Maria then nodded down to his right knee. Her eyes told him she'd noticed as well. The man was limping heavily and struggling to keep up, even though they were walking slowly.

They stopped by the back doors of their car, but he opened the trunk and forced them to get in. It was awkward enough without being handcuffed together. Steve was hoping someone would be watching the debacle from one of the apartments nearby and contact the police. As the trunk slammed shut, a shiver ran through him. This could be the last time they saw daylight.

Pitch dark, their bodies pressed together, he could feel her heartbeat racing away, even faster than his. Trapped inside a metal coffin. Sweat stinging his eyes, gluing the shirt to his body. A sudden panic gripped him as never before. He had to get out. He couldn't breathe, his burning lungs had seized in fear.

The engine started up. Steve tried to kick out with both feet but couldn't get any leverage, the exertion leaving him even more panicky and desperate. He squeezed his free hand into a fist and slammed it against the trunk lid above. It didn't move, the contact cutting his little finger and hurting his wrist. A metallic sound echoed around the confined space.

He was just about to turn on his side and kick out over Maria's back towards the panel next to her when he felt her hand squeeze his.

In a whispered voice, Maria said. "Steve, we must stay calm and conserve what little air we have. He didn't shoot us for a reason. There's a good chance we get out of this alive if we're smart. We should stay quiet and use the time to figure it all out."

Steve squeezed her hand to indicate he understood. She was right. Getting angry wouldn't spring the trunk lid. He closed his eyes, took a deep breath, and held it. He tried to slow his spiralling heartbeat.

He remembered the module of a training course he did shortly after becoming a beat bobby in Cobham. *Coping in Confined Spaces*. It taught them to stay calm and be patient when incarcerated. Compensate for the physical restraint, the tutor said, by expanding your mind. Go inside yourself, give your brain something to concentrate on, imagine you're in a better place, drive the panic away. The only thing to fear was fear itself.

The car was moving now at high speed. Every twist and turn proved painful as they were thrown around, heads banging together, their bodies crushed into the side walls or bounced against the trunk lid. Steve was starting to feel nauseous and disorientated. It was so dark he didn't know if his eyes were open or shut. Whether he was alive or dead.

A few minutes later, the twists and turns stopped. Steve assumed they were heading down a straighter stretch of road. The cloying, sticky air was getting thinner and smelling stronger of stale sweat and desperation. Concerted attempts to slow his pulse were not working. Maria's back was spooned into his chest. Her heartbeat was pounding. They were both holding their breath if they could, releasing the air slowly.

Steve knew they couldn't survive like this. He was beginning to think a bullet to the head might have been kinder. Why didn't he just shoot them? Thoughts in bubbles now, floating around in a sticky, black liquid. He was finding it harder and harder to concentrate. Maybe this man didn't want their murders on his hands. There was a special place in hell for cop killers.

Maybe he would release them in a remote spot, giving himself time to escape. Or maybe he had some gruesome death planned. The man obviously placed no value on human life, that was for sure. Was he alone or acting on orders, Steve wondered, before his mind skipped away into another dark cave as he blanked out.

Steve was floating in and out of consciousness. On the course, the tutor explained that a lack of oxygen resulted in bewilderment and severe dizziness. Eventually, you could expect to pass out as the body shut down prior to death. The tutor's face kept appearing and disappearing. Stay strong. I must help Maria. She had started to sob and was mumbling goodbyes to her husband and children.

Steve had the sensation of the car slowing down. He heard the indicators come on as the car swung right and dipped down onto a rough stretch of road. Increased tyre noise, the car started lurching through potholes and crunching through gravel which was spitting up against the underside. They were sliding around corners, the rear end correcting its trajectory as the rubber bit deeper into the uneven surface. The pace had slowed.

He'd tried to check his watch when they set off, but it was too dark. He'd no idea how long they'd been travelling as he kept passing out, but they could both still breathe, so it can't have been that long. Even so, it was long enough to suffer. Were they nearing their destination? He feared what might be coming next.

Steve decided he might only get one chance to surprise this man. He was no match for him in size and strength but a well-aimed blow as the trunk lid opened, might knock him off his guard.

If, indeed, the trunk ever did open. Banish these negative thoughts. We get through this.

Steve would make a grab for the gun which meant they'd need to move together in unison, given the handcuffs. He gently nudged Maria. She rubbed the moisture from her eyes and shook herself fully awake.

The car had ground to a halt. Gravel sounds had been replaced by trickling water. Steve whispered his plan and they both turned onto their backs in readiness. She squeezed his hand again, this time for luck. He flexed his free hand in and out to make a fist, trying to get the blood pumping.

Steve heard the driver's door opening and closing. Footsteps were squelching closer, round towards the trunk. Two hands gripped the lid. Steve squeezed his fist in readiness and narrowed his eyes to slits in case the daylight was too bright when the lid flew open. He positioned his feet to get maximum leverage. Maria did the same. They were as ready as they could be.

Silence. Nothing happened. The lid remained firmly shut. What was he up to? Was he going to flip it open then step back, giving himself a clear shot? Was he going to shoot them through the lid itself? There was nothing they could do except wait.

They waited and waited. Steve heard a groan outside the car, followed by a low rumbling noise. The groaning stopped as the car started to move. Slowly at first, then quicker as it gathered pace. The engine was off so they must be rolling down a slope.

Or was it over a cliff edge? Steve turned to Maria who must have had the same idea. They braced their legs for any impact.

But instead of free falling or continuing to gather speed, the car slowed again and came to a stop. The sound of running water was louder here. No more footsteps squelching through boggy ground. Maybe they were near a stream.

Slowly, the car felt like it was sinking. It angled down one way then the other. Maria yelped at the first sensation of ice, cold water seeping into the trunk. Now Steve could feel it, trickling in through the seals around the lid and up through the carpeted floor.

He touched a wet seal then licked his finger. Salty water, more saline than true sea water. Wherever it was coming from, they wouldn't have long to escape. The weakening seals were allowing more and more water to pour in.

Instinctively, they both raised their heads up, noses pressed hard against the trunk lid. It was drown or die of asphyxiation. Neither option was appealing.

In desperation, they both started shouting for help and pounding against any metal surface they could touch. The shouting was short lived as the water reached their mouths. Steve kept pumping his fist against the lid with what little strength he had left.

Through the numbing cold, Steve could feel Maria starting to cry again, her body quaking as the water level reached her upper lip. He felt her plunge her head beneath the surface, no doubt to get it over with. He managed to pull her up, tilting her head back as far as it would go.

In the inky blackness, he gently ran a cold finger over her nose. She seemed to respond and nuzzled her face up against it or was that his imagination playing a final trick. A moment of tenderness in a cruel world. He hadn't fully appreciated how fond of her he'd become. It wasn't like his love for Sophia, more a feeling of intimate friendship. Whatever it was, the prospect of losing her still hurt like hell.

Seconds turned to hours in their tortured despair. The relentless tide kept rising. It would not be long now. He pushed his head up as far as it would go, yet still the unseen water kept coming.

He wanted to hold her until they slipped away, to say how sorry he was for getting her into this mess. If she'd stayed in forensics, none of this would have happened. But he could no longer speak. His sorrow would have to go unspoken. His true feelings for her would die with him.

Taking one last deep breath, Steve plunged into the underwater silence, gently pulling her down with him. She didn't resist. There was no escape now. All that remained was to open wide and swallow a big mouthful of salty poison.

It was time to let go.

CHAPTER 30

"It's your lucky day, bitch." Beanie Hat spat out the words as he closed the deck gate.

Hannah didn't remember much about the journey back. The boat was bouncing around, Lawrence was snoring, and she couldn't get comfortable. Every time she nodded off, she was woken by the nightmare screams of Father Kelly, the desperate scene playing out over and over in her mind.

He was a good man, betrayed by those he trusted and murdered because he interfered. His sole intention was to save innocent lives. Hannah knew whoever was behind all this hadn't shown their face yet. *Definitely Ukrainian.* The radio message must be connected in some way. All that was in the future. For now, she was grateful to be alive.

After an uncomfortable journey, they were thrown back into the same storeroom. The stain in the corner was an embarrassing reminder. They hadn't been in the room long when Hannah heard heavy footsteps pounding down the passageway outside. The door swung open, three guards this time. They were manhandled back upstairs to Joel Chernick's office. The air conditioning offered some relief, but Hannah could see Lawrence was moving awkwardly due to severe pain in his lower back.

"Someone really wants to see you suffer." Joel Chernick didn't mince his words. Hannah noticed an empty bottle of Jack Daniels on the desk in front of him. No sign of a glass.

"Personally, I'd have left you to the crocs, but I'm told there's a score to settle. Don't build your hopes up. The outcome doesn't change, only the timing."

"Who has a score to settle? With me? Him?" Hannah pointed at Lawrence. She was angry and tired of this game playing. "What is it with you people, why can't you tell us what the hell's going on?"

"You'll find out soon enough." He went to swig from the bottle, realised it was empty and threw it against the far wall, the glass shattering on impact. Seemingly, in the same easy movement, he produced a full one from the bottom drawer. He unscrewed the cap and took a long pull of the amber liquid which seemed to calm him. Hannah surmised he was losing interest in them. Clearly, he'd been overruled. This was out of his hands now.

"Shemmy, make sure they're alive when they get on the plane. Take Albert with you." Joel nodded towards the guard stood in the corner holding a machine pistol. "I don't want to see them again."

To Hannah's surprise, they exited the building through a side entrance that led to open ground near the slag heap. An unmarked helicopter was blowing dust clouds up into the bright, perimeter lights.

Shemmy settled into the front seat next to the pilot. Albert forced Hannah and Lawrence into the back seats. He had to click their seat belts on before wedging himself alongside Lawrence. With the doors locked and handcuffs on, keeping the machine pistol trained on them seemed to Hannah like an unnecessary precaution.

The chopper took off low over some trees then turned up into a steep trajectory, climbing steadily to its cruising height. Hannah reckoned they were flying north, judging by dawn's first light creeping in through the starboard windows.

260

She whispered loudly in Lawrence's ear, above the noise of the rotor. He concurred with her logic and suggested they must be heading towards Ethiopia.

It was a short flight, certainly less than an hour. As they began their descent, Hannah could make out a huge scar on the landscape below. The headlights of trucks were picking out hairpin bends descending into an open pit like a cancerous sore in the earth's surface. Lawrence reckoned a gold mine. He was fast becoming their mining expert.

They flew beyond the crater and started heading down towards some buildings near one end of a long runway, its pin lights dissecting a desert landscape. Several large transport planes were being loaded and unloaded near where they landed. Lines of heavy equipment and containers sat in neat rows along the edge of the tarmac.

In the gloom, Hannah could make out an army of yellow and orange ants in hard hats beavering away with fork trucks and hydraulic lifts. Their arrival went unnoticed. Soon after landing and before they could get out, a helicopter on the other side of the apron lifted off and spiralled away towards the rising sun. It had two passengers on board and was also unmarked.

As they walked across the apron, none of the ants paid them the slightest interest. Hannah decided the sight of handcuffed white people being frog-marched away under duress by an armed black guard must be a common occurrence out here.

They made their way over to a hangar that housed several smaller containers with what looked to Hannah like air conditioning units strapped to their sides. Shemmy unbolted the one nearest the hangar entrance. Albert forced them inside, locking the door behind them.

Shemmy referred to it as a pod. There were no windows. It was used to move mine workers and engineers around the world quickly, she explained. Hannah interpreted that as using pods, which looked like containers full of mining equipment, to transport people who would not get customs or security clearance. Armed mercenaries and illegal immigrants came to mind.

Shemmy threw a switch. Electric light flooded the pod, revealing an aircraft-like interior with twelve seats in total, three rows of four, two on each side of a central aisle, all facing the front. The seats were basic in design, covered mostly in cheap fabric that bore a kaleidoscope of dried mud and disgusting ochre-brown stains.

Shemmy unclipped a galley door to reveal a row of black, one-piece thermal suits with fur-lined hoods. Beneath them was a rack of industrial boots that had clearly known many feet. Some had thick socks protruding from their mouths. One pair was covered in dried blood and mould, Hannah noticed.

"You'll need one of these." Shemmy produced a breathing apparatus from a box in a cupboard. She demonstrated how to put on the face mask and tighten the straps. She slipped the harness around her shoulders and clipped it at the side. Hannah noticed several torches in the same cupboard. No doubt it went very cold and dark when the power was disconnected.

"How long's the flight?" Lawrence asked, holding out his handcuffs which Shemmy unlocked, having just released Hannah's.

"Long flight, so get comfortable." She managed a thin smile. "There's a toilet and washbasin behind that curtain. I'll check you have enough food and water before I go."

"Does our guard here speak any English?" Hannah asked quickly to see if he reacted. There was no movement. Albert stood blocking the doorway with the machine pistol braced and ready.

Shemmy seemed to understand and shook her head. She led them further down the pod and made a point of showing them a large grey bag which was strapped to the metal wall. It became a life raft, she explained, on impact with water. It was very old and had never been used so she wasn't sure it still worked. There were no lifejackets.

"Reassuring." Hannah replied sarcastically. Now was the chance she had waited for. "Shemmy, they murdered Father Kelly. We saw him die. It was horrific. These people you work for, they're killers. But you're not one of them, are you?"

Shemmy was silent. Hannah could sense the emotions surging through her. Fat tears had formed in the corner of her troubled, dark eyes.

Eventually she moved closer. "He was a good man. Joel said I wouldn't see him again as he'd been called to Rome. A Cardinal in the Vatican had relayed the good news, he said. I didn't believe it. Then one of the guards I know through church said he'd been taken. I don't know what to do. I need this job but not like this. I feel ashamed."

Albert was walking slowly towards them, clearly concerned about this private conversation. Shemmy pulled away and straightened herself. She wiped away the tears, resetting her composure.

"Last question, Shemmy. What is kamacite? Why is it so important?" Hannah probed.

"I don't know exactly. I was told we mine copper. We do, but only in small quantities. Kamacite is our main production. It's very rare, apparently. The richest deposits in the world are to be found around Lake Turkana. The mineral density is very high, and the crystals are unique to this region. Our mine is to be the first of many. Others will follow, much bigger. That's all I know."

263

"But who is buying it? Who wants kamacite?" Hannah smiled at the guard. She made sign language like she was asking Shemmy about what food supplies they had in the pod. They moved back to the galley area where Shemmy started opening and closing drawers, like she was looking for something.

"There are no customers. It's all for internal use within KMI. It's a big project. We need to increase production volumes. Now please, I must go." Shemmy moved quickly towards the door. She looked apologetic. "We must lock you inside. They will disconnect the power and move the pod onto the aircraft. The power will come back on. You will be connected to the flight deck so the pilot can talk to you. He can also hear what you're saying so be careful. Good luck."

"Shemmy, who owns KMI? What do the initials stand for?" Hannah raised her voice. The words echoed around the pod.

But Shemmy and Albert were gone. The door was bolted. A few moments later they heard movement outside. Hannah just had time to grab a couple of torches before the lights went out. The pod began to lift. It swung around before coming down heavily. She felt it being clamped in place. It must be the back of a vehicle of some kind as it slowly began to move.

"OK, it's time for a hunch." Hannah sensed the unease in Lawrence. They had strapped themselves into adjoining front seats, ready for take-off.

It was a big enough space not to feel claustrophobic, but Hannah knew the thought of being trapped in a metal coffin on an unmarked cargo plane that could be going anywhere, would not be filling Lawrence with much hope. She shared his concerns but was trying to tough it out.

They needed to take their minds off this latest predicament. Also, they must get some rest after such a traumatic day. But first, they had to fit the pieces together, before being overheard by the flight deck. A hunch right now seemed like a good place to start.

"I'm listening." Lawrence tried twisting towards her but the stabbing pain in his back was too great. Instead, he leaned across.

"Somehow this mining company discovered rich seems of kamacite in a remote region of Northern Kenya." Hannah began.

"My guess is they came across the rock sample in the museum in Vienna." Lawrence added. "For me, the question is whether they were looking for kamacite and found it in Kenya or if they were looking for minerals with certain properties. When they realised kamacite fit the bill, they traced it back to where the samples were found."

Hannah continued. "At this stage, we don't know the answer to that, maybe we never will. Either way, they want this rock for some big project and started extraction near Lake Turkana. They need to do it in secret, mine quickly, cheaply and in large volumes. The problem is the local tribespeople getting in the way and potential media interest. So, they call in a favour with a high-ranking Cardinal who twisted some arms in Nairobi. That got them the licence, but they couldn't go for an open pit without creating suspicion."

Lawrence suddenly looked puzzled. "Why is it top secret? They have a legitimate licence so why not dig a big hole? If it creates local jobs and boosts the economy, who cares?"

"Presumably someone doesn't want everyone to know about the rock itself." Hannah concluded. "Maybe the project is top secret and knowing about the properties of this rare mineral would give the game away?"

Hannah felt the pod being lifted off the vehicle, swung through the air then anchored again. They must be on the aircraft now. It would be too risky to continue the conversation for much longer.

"Brilliant!!" Lawrence exclaimed. Hannah liked his eureka moments. "They deliberately disturb the arsenic seams to poison the well and drive the local people away. No people mean no prying eyes, no compensation claims, and no restrictions on extending their mining operations."

"But the well only supplies a handful of villagers. These guys must be thinking bigger." Hannah added.

"Didn't you say Lake Turkana was drying up and might disappear altogether in the next decade? You know, becoming saltier, fish moving away, people going to the cities in the south?"

"Of course, the dam." Hannah had her own eureka moment. "KMI puts money into this dam project to block off the Omo River, causing the lake to disappear. When all the people have moved away, they can dig as many open pits as they like, even where the lake used to be. Throw in a few dodgy politicians and slippery church leaders and hey bingo, you've got an ecological disaster that everyone predicted yet no one did anything about."

"Yet another ecological disaster no one did anything about, you mean." Lawrence added.

Hannah continued. "Meanwhile, KMI fill their boots with cheap kamacite and the Cardinal lines his pockets."

"Climate change activists say something should be done and blame the politicians. Lake Turkana becomes the next Aral Sea, and they all say what a shame as they troop off to the next, all-expenses-paid, climate change conference. I like it." Lawrence concluded.

266

Suddenly the air was filled with the sound of jet engines powering up. The pod began to shake and tilt upwards at a steep angle. Hannah tightened her seat belt and checked her breathing apparatus was handy. They could put on the thermal suits once they hit cruising height. For now, the dark, vibrating space around them was still at a comfortable temperature.

"I'm guessing Father Kelly nicknamed them *Khazi Mining Industries* in disgust. I don't think he was telling us the whole story." Lawrence speculated.

"He was bound by the sacramental seal and could never repeat what was said during confession." Hannah explained. "If Shemmy had spilled the beans, he'd never have told us."

Hannah's face suddenly went very pale in the torchlight, all the blood leaving her cheeks. She sat up straight, struggling for breath through the shock of realisation. *Sounds like Khazi?*

"What's up? You, OK?" Lawrence loosened his belt and winced as he turned towards her, placing his hand over hers.

"I think I know what the K stands for."

"Oh, thank God, is that all? I thought for a minute we were in trouble."

"We are in trouble. Big trouble."

They were levelling off. Hannah heard a noise outside. Something was being connected to the pod. The pilots would be able to hear them shortly.

"Hannah, it couldn't be bigger trouble than hungry crocodiles ready to rip us to shreds."

"The crocs are dumb animals. At least we had a chance with them." Hannah made a sign to show they must stop talking now.

Lawrence acknowledged and sat back, making himself as comfortable as he could.

Hannah felt something pressing into her thigh as she swivelled towards him. She rummaged in her pocket and pulled out the lock of braided hair Agnes had given her. *It from my princess. It bring you luck.* Hannah thought she'd left it in the hotel room. Maybe it was a lucky charm after all. They could certainly use some more magic right now. She showed it to Lawrence, who smiled.

In a low whisper, she added. "If this K is who I think it is, she wants my blood."

CHAPTER 31

The offices in his part of the House were deserted. A TV screen showed MPs bunched together in the lobby like lambs waiting for slaughter. He knew the division bell was about to sound. A vote would follow a few minutes later.

Whatever was being argued by the handful of die-hards in the debating chamber would only ever make a footnote in the dusty pages of Hansard. The whips had already decided which way the vote would go. This was British democracy in action, or was that inaction, Quentin mused, before turning it off.

He wasn't sure about making this call but felt he had to express his anger. His instinct said let it go but their actions were seriously out of line. Another mistake like this and the whole thing could blow up in his face.

More importantly than Stannard's death was the fact he was out of pocket. Although his bank account was currently healthy, if he had to pay back some or all the money he'd siphoned off, he'd be staring bankruptcy in the face. This arrangement could be his lifeline. But where was the money?

Quentin made sure no one was in earshot. His assistant had gone home hours ago on the dot of five, as she always did. He was taking deep breaths, trying to remain calm but couldn't quell the rising sense of trepidation. Talking to this woman was like playing with fire.

He keyed in her private number. It was answered on the second ring. Without thinking, he launched straight in. "I can't believe you killed him. For God's sake, we agreed incapacitated, put in hospital, kept out of the way. I wish I'd never told you where he was going."

"They were told to shoot him in the leg. There was a struggle, the gun went off. I've punished them, OK? It's unfortunate, an accident, these things happen. Nothing else has changed." Ice cold, as ever, everything was just so matter of fact to her.

"I've had a police officer here from the Met, a Detective Inspector. He's working with a homicide team in New York. They don't believe it's a random shooting, they're investigating. If this unravels, we're both finished, you realise that."

There was a silence down the line. It seemed to last an eternity. Quentin wished he hadn't said unravels. He was beginning to wish he'd listened to his instinct and hadn't made the call at all.

When the voice returned, it was lower in pitch, slower in delivery and much more ominous.

"This will not unravel so long as you keep your mouth shut and do what we've agreed. People who let me down don't live to regret it. Will you let me down, Quentin?"

He tried to apologise but the wrong words kept spilling out. "And another thing, he's going to Oxford tomorrow. I had to tell him Stannard was working for us, he'd have found out anyway, then the finger of suspicion would point at me."

"There is no suspicion. A man was attacked and robbed in New York. It happens every day. A firearm was discharged accidentally. The police will investigate but draw a blank, as they usually do. Gun crime is routine in a country with more guns than people. There is no evidence that links this back to us. We must keep it that way. Do you understand me?"

"Yes, of course I do. But this policeman was sharp, really sharp. I don't think he swallowed what I told him." Quentin regretted saying swallowed also.

"My sources tell me the investigation has been passed to a junior officer and a forensics girl, both on secondment from the UK. They used to work with the officer who came to see you. It's a lightweight team. NYPD aren't taking this seriously so neither should you, Quentin. We're not expecting any trouble but if they do get in the way, we will deal with it, OK?"

"Deal with it? What, put them in the morgue as well?" Quentin was going to say something about another accident, but morgue just slipped out.

As he was talking, something outside caught his eye. He turned towards the darkened office window. Stannard's haunting face suddenly appeared next to his own reflection, sending a pulse straight through him, like an electric shock. He had to end this call.

She continued. "Anyway, the situation has changed. The race start is imminent. I'm waiting to hear. The police haven't got time to interfere with our plans."

Quentin needed to raise it now. The timing wasn't right, but would it ever be? He hoped he'd pick the right words this time. "Talking of plans, my first payment is overdue. You promised I'd get the money last week. For our agreement to work, we need to trust each other."

Silence again. Why did he say trust? He just wanted the money. No, needed the money. If he had to run, and there was a good chance he would, then the money was essential.

"We agreed a first payment when the wheels leave the ground and not before. The second payment's due when you've delivered. How are the arrangements?"

"All in hand. Tomorrow, I've asked for a final engine test, then *Comet 5* will be ready to fly."

"I hope so, for your sake."

* * *

Zelda disconnected and tossed the phone angrily across the desk. Why couldn't people just do what they were told? She didn't want any dealings with this man but the opportunity he presented was too tempting. When he first approached her, he made it sound so easy. It *was* easy, for fuck's sake. Quentin was the key. She needed to keep him sweet, for now. Thankfully, it would all be over in a few days.

Her phone rang again. She reached over and checked the screen. At last, where the fuck has he been? "Jeremiah. Are they here?"

"No, I told you, plane refuelling. It's picking up some equipment in Ireland."

"Ireland? I want them here, now." This man also irritated the hell out of her but now wasn't the time to fix that. She might need him if the police got too close.

"Tomorrow, arrive tomorrow, be patient. How long you waited?"

"She will pay for what she did. Is everything in hand?"

"Of course. Maintenance teams there now. You'll get yer revenge. I'll come by chopper from airstrip. Be there at midnight."

She disconnected. How long ago was it? She worked out ten years at least, maybe nearer twelve. Her first contact with the Klinkenhammer Foundation had been encouraging. A friend of a friend recommended them. His condition was worsening, their situation was getting increasingly desperate. It was worth a try. Now she wished she'd never heard the name.

On the corner of her desk was a framed photo of him taken after a polo match. Sam was in his late twenties, so

272

fit, so playful, her dashing younger brother, she was so proud of him. Magna cum laude in physics from Berkeley, offers from all the top corporations, a glittering career ahead of him.

He'd already made his mark in industry and was ready for a new challenge when he started talking about a PhD. One day his speech became slurred, he couldn't pronounce PhD, she recalled. The doctor said it was nothing to worry about, drinking too much probably, prescribed some pills. Sam recovered but, a few months later, it returned. This time, along with struggling to speak, he noticed some paralysis in his right leg and had to give up the sports he loved.

The Klinkenhammer Programme Manager promised an effective treatment that would restore all his faculties and repair the damaged nerve cells in his brain and spinal cord. He'd be able to walk and talk again, look after himself and live to a ripe old age. It sounded like a guarantee.

Zelda remembered them telling her how they'd had some success with enzyme replacement therapy for other genetic disorders. Sam's rare form of Tay-Sachs disease was inherited and treatable, they said, despite it being quite well advanced when diagnosed.

Once she'd started feeding their gravy train, there was no end to it. She had to keep putting more and more money in to see any results. With additional investment funding, the Programme Manager said, the Institute could also develop a substrate reduction therapy that would prevent the failure of the metabolic pathway and effectively cure this insidious disease. Other families wouldn't need to suffer.

She believed them and pumped millions into the research. They were always close but not close enough. The Programme Manager kept coming up with excuses as to why the experimental therapies just didn't work. In the end, Zelda had to pull the plug.

When she told Sam, he was heartbroken. It was his last chance for a normal life. There was no cure for the disease and still isn't. By then, other medical research outfits had smelt money on the wind and kept approaching her with the promise of miracle cures. Cord blood transplants, gene therapies, expensive quack medications that had long lists of side-effects, requiring even more expensive quack medications.

For ten miserable years, he suffered. She watched him slowly getting worse, confined to a wheelchair, losing his voice, needing care 24/7. In the end, he took matters into his own hands, while he still could. She didn't blame him for doing it. He had no kind of life. She'd have done the same.

Her dealings with the medical research sector left her shattered and disillusioned. She'd lost faith and felt betrayed.

Standing at Sam's graveside, she vowed his death would not go unpunished. In her heart of hearts, she never expected to get that chance. The Programme Manager had left the Klinkenhammer Foundation. Zelda had tracked her down to Italy. She'd been working on a plan when the call came though from Kenya, of all places. The timing and situation were perfect. The woman was off the grid. Now she could exact her revenge.

A life for a life. Tomorrow at midnight.

"Zelda, I've got the UN Secretary-General on line 2."

Lost in thought. Lost in memories. Lost in anger. She could hear Sam calling to her from the photo. *C'mon, sis, let's play ball*.

Zelda's secretary prompted her again. She snapped back to matters in hand. "Put her through."

Betty Gachuhi was her *naturally effervescent self.* The description had been termed in a Time magazine article on her. No one had ever used that expression to describe a UN Secretary-General. Betty's UN climate change motives behind this race were of no interest to Zelda. It was the doors it could open that made their entry worthwhile. The US$10 billion prize money was just a bonus.

"Zelda, I've got the go-ahead for a racing start. We take off in two days. Both planes to cross the start line together. I'm sending you the revised safety protocols. Please make sure everyone involved is aware."

"Thank you. I'm told we're ready to go. We'll get the passengers there two hours before, as per any normal flight. Security screening, boarding passes, drinks in the lounge, the whole shooting match." Zelda had slipped on her diplomatic face.

"Excellent. All our observers are in position at the Sky Stations. The ones on the plane will board with your crew. We're getting lots of media interest now. They've sold over two hundred thousand tickets for the start. Will you be there?"

"No, I'll watch on TV. I'm not directly involved with the plane itself. I'll let my team take the glory." Zelda replied, wondering why Betty was calling. She could have put this in an email.

"Zelda, I've been asked a question about your entry. I hope you don't mind."

"Not at all, please fire away."

"One of the media companies want to run a feature on your consortium, to coincide with the start of the race. Make it more personal, they said, the faces behind the *New Spirit of St Louis*, that sort of thing. Naturally, we've kept your identity confidential, as you requested. They're offering some free TV advertising space for an exclusive

275

interview. The international viewing audience will be huge. Would you be interested?"

Zelda thought she'd made this quite clear when the entry was submitted: no publicity. Their law firm was the registered address for Lindbergh Aviation Inc. All matters relating to the plane were handled through the project team in Seattle who also dealt with marketing and media campaigns. She had her reasons for wanting to keep her name out of it. That situation hadn't changed.

"I'm sorry to disappoint you, Betty, but I must decline. I'm only one of the financial backers for this venture. We all agreed to let the plane do the talking. Once we've won the race, maybe that will change. For now, I wish you good luck." Zelda disconnected.

Lost in thought again, her eyes fell onto the photo. The senseless waste of his life will not be in vain.

Tomorrow at midnight. I will watch her suffer.

CHAPTER 32

Lonsdale relished the last mouthful of Welsh Rarebit. It was a blissful union of crunchy, buttered wholegrain toast smothered by a rich, creamy cheese topping, delicately laced with Dijon mustard and Lea & Perrins sauce, then flash grilled to perfection.

His lunchtime companion recommended a cheeky, little rosé d'anjou which Green's had just started listing from a family-owned vineyard in the western Loire region. It took Lonsdale several glasses to fully appreciate the unique combination of piquant flavours mixed with the aromatic bouquet of the wine.

This was turning out to be a good day. Lonsdale had had a successful morning at the university, getting statements from Stannard's colleagues and collecting personal items from his rooms, including his PC and a little black notebook containing passwords and usernames. One mysterious six-digit pin might give access to his mobile phone, judging by the scribbled letters BT next to it.

"So, that's all I can tell you about Stannard, I'm afraid, David. Bit of an open and shut case, poor man. He was happy in his own way, I suppose, but he lived to work, not the other way round. Sadly, he missed out on so many joys in life. May he rest in peace."

Lonsdale declined the dessert menu as the plates were cleared. He leaned back and let the scene wash over him. A busy mid-week lunchtime, the café buzzing with excitable students, old and new. Delicious food, stimulating conversation, a clear diary for the afternoon and no top brass chasing him. He decided the delights of cultural responsiveness would have to wait for another day. This was indeed a moment to savour.

"What about this woman, Fritz. Is she an open and shut case?" Lonsdale smiled; his cheeks flushed. Enjoyable as the day had been so far, now it was time for some business. No such thing as a free lunch, even in Oxford. "OK, here's the deal. You spill the beans and I'll pick up the tab."

"Agreed." Fritz paused as a more serious expression swept across his face. He leaned in closer. "Dr Angela Fischer is a different kettle of fish. This mustn't go any further, you do understand?"

"Strictly between us girls, Fritz. My lips are sealed." Lonsdale knew he could rely on the juicy morsels he was about to receive.

Their friendship had been established many years ago. Of similar ages and tastes, including a passion for classic British sports cars, Lonsdale was a Detective Sergeant when he first met Dr Fritz Popper at the University of Surrey.

Fritz proved to be an invaluable expert witness in a murder trial. His testimony helped Lonsdale put a serial killer behind bars. They struck up an instant rapport and had kept in touch ever since, even after the good doctor moved from Guildford to his current, exalted position as Head of Psychology at Brandon College, Oxford.

In the intervening years, Dr Fritz, as he was widely known, had become something of a TV celebrity and the people's trusted voice on the murky world of psychoanalysis. Whenever serial killers were on the loose, Dr Fritz was trotted out in front of the cameras, always wearing his trademark black suit, black shirt, black silk tie and hand-made, red, leather brogues.

He had become so well known that he was awarded an MBE in the last New Year's Honours list, for services to mental wellbeing.

"They couldn't have been more different. Maybe that's why they proved such a winning team. Opposites attracting and all that." Fritz broke off for a moment to sign an autograph for a spellbound psychology undergraduate who'd been plucking up the courage to come over. She beamed as she left the table, proudly returning to show off the scalp to her friends, who were clearly amazed at her new-found audacity.

"How do you mean, Fritz?" Lonsdale got the nod of approval to take some personal notes, having assured him none would be attributable or used in evidence.

"At the College, they're lovingly referred to as the *Odd Couple*. Stannard is a straight-up-and-down workaholic, bachelor-type with little to interest a curious psychiatrist. Fischer is the opposite, a most fascinating and complex woman in every respect, I mean from a psychological viewpoint, of course. You could create a three-year degree course based on trying to understand the inner depths of her psyche."

"So how come you know her so well, if you don't mind me asking?" Lonsdale hadn't expected this level of insight. He had never been entirely convinced about the science behind psychoanalysis. When feeling open-minded, he saw it as a reasonable attempt to explain why criminals did what they did when there was no rational explanation for their wild behaviour.

When feeling less generous or free-spirited, Lonsdale thought it was psychobabble, mumbo jumbo that provided employment for people who would never get a job doing anything else.

"She came to see me, a few years ago. I told her I wasn't a psychiatrist, but she said she just needed some help to understand her own feelings. A close friend had told her she could be suffering from cognitive dissonance, after reading an agony aunt column in a woman's magazine. Fischer wanted to know what it was. That's how it started."

Lonsdale smiled at him. This felt like a mumbo jumbo day. "So, what is it, Fritz? What did you tell her?"

Some years before, Fischer's husband had taken his own life quite unexpectedly, Fritz explained. It rocked her confidence at the time, especially when she discovered he'd been having an affair with one of her best friends.

"Her husband couldn't bear to live without one of them and couldn't reconcile his feelings with the reality he was facing. Ironically, that was probably Fischer's first brush with cognitive dissonance. How could he say goodbye to a woman he wanted to be with? The self-contradiction tore him in half. The poor man decided to deny both women. He found reconciliation in a packet of weed killer, sadly."

Fritz continued. "The following year, their only daughter was killed in an horrific car accident. Fischer never did find out the truth but suspected her new boyfriend was a drug addict. He'd been driving when the car spun off the road and down a cliff face. The daughter was living in California at the time. The coroner's report simply recorded accidental death."

"Poor woman, she has been through the wars." Lonsdale added. "It's hardly surprising she's such a complex character. Coping with one major tragedy is bad enough, let alone two. I suppose our subconscious mind must protect us from all the pain and feelings of guilt. *Why them, not me?*"

"Exactly. Guilt is what she was drowning in. But when we started talking, I realised there was something else, much deeper, underneath all this emotional turmoil. It all became clear in our subsequent conversations. It's something she's wrestled with throughout her career. To be honest, David, she continues to wrestle with it today, in my opinion." Fritz checked his watch. He had to get back for a tutorial group.

They agreed to talk as they walked. Lonsdale dutifully settled the bill. They exited into bright sunshine, a perfect October afternoon, the trees starting to show off their vibrant, autumnal colours. Around them, the ancient, honey-coloured, stone walls of the university were bathed in an amber glow, with exaggerated patterns of light and shade.

"The irony is," Fritz pointed out, as they crossed the High Street and headed up Alfred Street towards the impressive main entrance to Brandon College. "Fischer is a leading authority on nuclear fission. Her forte is uranium-233. She told me once that, fundamentally, she doesn't agree with it. I didn't really understand where she was coming from."

"Agree with what, Fritz? Nuclear fission or working with uranium-233?" Lonsdale would have to commit all this to memory as they walked. Fritz would be disappearing soon, so he earmarked a little café they just passed. Lonsdale would return for some note taking and to gather his thoughts. It was open until five, he noticed. A large café au lait would be most welcome, after a visit to the toilet. It must be an age thing, he mused.

"Both, really. You see, nuclear fission is a human invention, she told me. Although it can occur spontaneously in nature, it's very, very rare. Splitting the atom is unnatural, in her view, a scientific discovery that goes against the natural world. *We shouldn't be playing God with nature.* Those were her actual words."

They'd reached the entrance. Fritz still had a few minutes. Lonsdale was intrigued. "Is this a religious

281

thing, Fritz? Is she a happy clapper? You know, a clash of deeply held personal convictions about God and humanity, that sort of thing?"

"No, I don't think so. She never mentioned anything about God in that sense or any religious cult she's a member of." Fritz explained. "I think she's trying to reconcile her beliefs about interfering with nature and how wrong it is to de-stabilise our world by playing with forces we don't really understand."

"Or can control?" Lonsdale added.

"Precisely. Fischer, of all people, can see the destructive power of nuclear fission, and yet she is directly involved in the creation of highly fissile uranium-233 from something as harmless as thorium. It's a classic example from the textbook on cognitive dissonance theory. How can I be doing something I firmly believe is wrong? It's like a vegetarian eating T-bone steak. A very complex woman, as I said. Anyway, my friend, I must go. Thanks again for lunch."

"It's my pleasure Fritz, good to see you again. Give my love to Annie and the boys."

"Next time, David, come for longer, the weekend, perhaps. I've just discovered a wonderful country pub called The Bull over in Harpwell. Home-made food, terrace by the river, guest beers, real fire, friendly staff, and no muzak. The landlord's a gem, you'd love it. Might get the TR out for a spin if it's like this."

"You bought it? The TR2?" Lonsdale remembered seeing a photo Fritz had shared with him, shortly after moving to Oxford. It was their dream car, in British racing green, a true roadster, sensitively restored to preserve its authentic sporting heritage.

"She's called Wanda, 'cos that's what we do in her." Fritz smiled.

"That's not the reason and you know it. You are a lecherous, old man. You had a crush on Wanda Ventham, I remember now. You bought a boxed set of *The Lotus Eaters* when it came out on DVD. There was a pin-up of her in your locker at the squash club." Lonsdale wasn't going to admit to owning a copy of the same photo.

"You know me too well, David. Don't tell Annie, for God's sake. She's the jealous type, I'm afraid." Fritz was about to turn off into a side corridor. "Good luck with your investigations. Keep in touch."

Lonsdale retraced his steps to the café. His notes were a jumble of statements, comments, ideas, and random thoughts. He was disappointed at not being able to meet this woman today but there would be another time. If indeed it proved necessary at all.

If she and Stannard had worked together all these years - *a winning team*, Fritz had said - and this propulsion system was as much of her creation as Stannard's, it was difficult to see how she could be involved in his death.

Even so, Lonsdale had the distinct feeling Fritz was trying to warn him about her. He obviously couldn't divulge everything she'd told him, but Fritz had dropped enough hints to make it worth following up.

He wrote down *cognitive dissonance* again and underlined it. Was this really so much mumbo jumbo? Sitting alone at a corner table, Lonsdale remembered the scathing words his boss had said when he took this secondment. *Align my outdated values with the more progressive society we now serve.* Maybe he should be more open minded.

He checked the time and decided to give his intrepid, former Detective Sergeant a call. It went straight to voicemail. They'd catch up later.

On the train going back to London, Lonsdale was thinking about a gruesome murder case some years back.

283

The finger of guilt pointed firmly at a known criminal who denied any involvement and even had an alibi for the night it happened.

When the truth finally emerged, the murderer turned out to be the most mild-mannered and introverted social worker who had been supporting the victim through a traumatic time in her life.

One day, the burden of listening to other people's heart-wrenching stories proved too much for him. He finally snapped. None of his colleagues could believe it. He'd never raised his voice or shown any aggressive tendencies towards anyone. An exemplary colleague, a role model for the department.

In his confession, he said he did it for her, to put an end to her misery. He genuinely believed it was an act of kindness. After more than 30 years in the police, Lonsdale was no longer surprised by how twisted and cruel some people could be.

But was Dr Angela Fischer one of them?

CHAPTER 33

Steve could feel the hot sun beating down on his bare chest. The smell of coconut oil was drifting up from her hands as she gently massaged the soothing lotion into his bronzed skin. He opened his eyes to see Sophia smiling at him, a colourful sarong wrapped suggestively over her azure blue bikini and knotted at the front.

"Coming in?" she said, unfastening the sarong and padding off through shimmering white sand to the water's edge. She waded out until it was waist deep then turned towards him, smiling as she slipped off her bikini top.

Steve found himself walking in after her, his feet stirring up little silty clouds that attracted shoals of brightly coloured fish.

She was wading backwards now, out into deeper water. She held out her arms towards him, inviting him to swim into them. *Hold me, Steve, hold me tight.*

He dived headlong into the calm sea, kicking out with his feet. He opened his eyes underwater just in time to see a dark shadow pass over the ocean between them, obscuring his view of her. Where had she gone? The water was colder here.

He stopped swimming and looked around, treading water. The shadow extended everywhere. The sun had disappeared. Day had become night. He looked back where he'd come from but couldn't see the beach. He was out of his depth. He started to panic, unsure what to do, yet he could still hear her siren call. *Hold me, Steve, hold me tight.*

Her voice had changed, still female but deeper. The accent was now American, the grip was much stronger than Sophia's, with more urgency about it. A third hand, then a fourth grabbed his arms as the water receded beneath him.

When Steve opened his eyes, he saw Maria looking down at him. Two police officers were standing next to her, their arms locked onto his. They pulled him out of the trunk and laid him down by the water's edge, turning him into the recovery position.

He tried to speak but only saltwater dribbled out of his mouth. The female officer told him not to move, just breathe slowly, lie still and rest. An ambulance was on its way. He closed his eyes.

Minutes later, a paramedic was shining a bright light into them and asking dumb questions. Steve had regained full consciousness. He knew what day of the week it was, could count backwards from ten and repeated his name and address several times.

The medic seemed satisfied there was no immediate brain damage but wanted to run more tests before releasing them. He was talking to the female police officer outside the open back door of the ambulance.

Steve realised his wet clothes had been replaced by overalls. There was a white towel over his head and a thick woollen blanket around his shoulders. Maria was wearing a similar outfit as she stepped into the ambulance, almost tripping over her blanket as she did so. She looked very pale and tired but none the worse for their ordeal.

"The police officer thinks we should buy a lottery ticket." Maria smiled as she sat down on the bed next to him. "A few more seconds and we'd had it."

"How did they find us? Where are we?" Steve briefly saw the smiling face of Sophia as she faded away into the ambulance window. Hallucination? Guardian angel?

Lovely dream or just wishful thinking? Maybe hope was the last thing to die after all.

"Apparently, the patrol car was responding to a traffic incident on the main highway near here. The driver called in a carjacking at gunpoint. He was dumped on the side of the road by a tall, black man who took the keys and drove off at speed. The car's been found abandoned in the Brownsville area. The call just came in." Maria added.

Steve was struggling to process all this. He hadn't noticed, until Maria started talking, that his head was pounding, a throbbing ache like a migraine. Maybe it was the lack of oxygen. More likely, the relief of staring death in the face then living to tell the tale.

"A police patrol car happened to be on a highway near here, at just the right moment? That's no coincidence. With that limp he couldn't get far, but I'm guessing far enough so's they'd never find us." Steve looked over to where their car had been pulled out of the water, trunk first, by the police car. The lid had been forced open by a crowbar that was covered in weed and lay discarded by the water's edge.

Beyond the open doors, Steve could see the desolation of the surrounding area. It looked like a huge expanse of marshland, with a myriad of small islands dotted amongst the shining waters. There were no signs of habitation as far as the eye could see. And no sign of a highway.

He thought back. It was salt water he tasted. They hadn't been in the car for long so couldn't be that far from Brooklyn. He cursed his lack of knowledge of the area. Worse, each thought was proving painful, the headache deepening. He needed to take the policewoman's advice and get some rest. Wherever they were, whatever had happened, he was just glad to be alive. Explanations would come later.

The paramedic had been joined by his partner. They ran more tests on Steve and Maria, including blood pressure, body temperature, reflexes and looking for any signs of concussion. They were reluctant to give Steve any headache tablets and started quoting safety regulations to him when the female police officer intervened and said she'd take full responsibility. The paramedics acquiesced and gave him some strong paracetamol. The relief was quickly appreciated.

"We'll give you a lift back to the station," she added as they watched the ambulance head off slowly down the gravel track. "Your boss said he'd sort the car out. He didn't sound best pleased. Alpaca, that his name?"

"Apicella, it's Italian. He's no cuddly animal, I can assure you. So, what's he so pissed off about? The car?" Steve wasn't looking forward to that conversation. With hindsight, it did look foolish charging off without telling Apicella where they were going. Even so, he hoped they wouldn't be taken off the case. He had skin in this game now and needed to see it through.

"No, he said they can replace the car. Maybe he's just relieved, some people are funny like that," she replied as they got into the police car. The male officer untied the tow rope, wiped down the crowbar and put everything back in the trunk. He climbed into the driver's seat, started the engine, and pulled away slowly, the tyres struggling to find any grip on the loose surface.

Steve looked over to his car, abandoned half in and half out of the water. The trunk lid was left open. The tide must still be rising as the trunk itself was filling with cold, dark water. Even under the warmth of the blanket, Steve could feel an icy chill run through him. They'd been left to die. That dark hole was meant to be their grave. Whoever he was, he would pay for this.

On the way back to the station, Steve told the uniformed officers about Mickey Shaps and the gunman who killed him. They called it in. A team was being sent over. The officers said they knew Mickey. It would be no great loss to the largely peaceful community, they said.

Maria asked about the carjacking and if they had any new leads. Apparently, the assailant was wearing a ski mask. The gun had a silencer attachment, the victim said. He was badly shaken up but unharmed. Another patrol car was taking him to his vehicle. The keys were still in the ignition. Steve and Maria were happy to provide a full description of the gunman. An APB was to be circulated.

Later that day, they were in Apicella's office. A shower, change of clothing, hot drinks and some welcome sandwiches had lifted their spirits. Maria had some rosy colour back in her complexion, Steve noticed. His feelings of despair had been replaced with a determination to nail this bastard. This had become personal.

"I didn't know where the fuck you where, you know?" Apicella glared at them. On the face of it, he was showing all the signs of real anger, but Steve had worked with Lonsdale long enough to know what anger looked like. This wasn't it. The female police officer was right. Relief was a better description.

Apicella continued. "First rule in my department, it's a team game. You win, we win. You lose, we lose. Capisch?"

They both nodded. Maria stared down at the floor. Steve lowered his eyes momentarily in acknowledgement but raised them again to look straight at him. "I'm sorry, Tony, it's my fault, I should've told you what we were doing. It won't happen again, I promise."

"It won't, I can promise you, or you're both off the case."

"Tony, how did you know where we were?" Steve had to ask. He struggled to call Apicella sir, even though rank awarded him that privilege. They were similar ages. Tony felt more comfortable and Apicella didn't seem to mind.

"I'd been trying to reach you. I called three times, but you didn't respond. I even sent two texts. Nada. I checked with the geek boys, you know, in the GPS team. All cars have tracking devices. I guessed you weren't fishing. They told me a patrol car was close by. Spring Creek Park, Jamaica Bay area. You got lucky. You owe them, big time."

Apicella explained this investigation was now getting attention upstairs. Some big noise wanted them off the case. Their inquiries were making too many waves, stirring up trouble. It's an accidental shooting during a street crime that went wrong. Nothing to see here, move on. For the sake of your career, Apicella was told, close the investigation, and reassign their duties. Better still, send them back where they belong, across the ditch.

Steve looked at Maria. She spoke first. "Is that what you're going to do, Tony?"

"The hell I am. They can fire me if they want, but I need to know what really happened. I'll never find out if you two are bagged up in the city morgue next to Stannard."

Steve brought him up to speed. The body of Mickey Shaps had now been recovered. Steve was waiting for a ballistics report on the bullet that killed him. He was in no doubt it was fired from the same gun that took down Stannard.

"It was murder, pure and simple." Steve explained. "Stannard's killers knew where he was going, followed him from the hotel and lay in wait. They took his wallet to make it look like a mugging but never searched his body. They left behind a watch that cost more than my apartment."

Maria joined in. "We think they used Mickey Shaps to give the cover story some credibility. He didn't know what he was getting into and paid with his life. We looked this gunman straight in the eye. He's a thug, an enforcer, a hitman but no way could he plan all this. There's a missing link here to someone higher up."

Steve added. "Someone with powerful friends, as you've just found out."

"OK, I'll buy it." Apicella leaned back making his chair creak. "What's the missing link?"

"Remember a few years back, there was a craze for those magic eye drawings." Steve smiled at Maria. She'd reminded him on the way over what they were called. She owned puzzle books full of them. "You crossed your eyes and could see three dimensional shapes inside the picture. They're called stereograms."

"Yeah, used to drive me crazy as I could never see it." Apicella replied. "My wife loved them. *There, you schmuck, it's a frickin' eagle.* I'm listening, what's your point, Steve?"

"Our missing link is in the picture, but we can't see it yet. We need to cross our eyes or change the angle, something. We need more time. Stannard's death is somehow connected to this air race." Steve explained, unconvincingly. "The gunman will lead us to the top guy."

"So how do you find this gunman?" Apicella sounded sceptical. "Your leads are all cold. The race starts tomorrow and I'm under pressure. I need something more solid than magic eyes, Steve. I'll buy you what time I can, but this may be taken out of my hands."

They were back at their desks. Maria had coaxed two mugs of fresh coffee from the machine. Steve was staring out of the window, twiddling with his pen, deep in thought. Two new phones were charging up in front of him. Neither held any useful information or phone numbers. They didn't have a name or any photo ID for the gunman.

Steve's old UK phone was in the desk drawer. He pulled it out and recharged it. It contained contact names and numbers, including Lonsdale's. Steve needed some good news. He hoped Lonsdale's trip to Oxford would shed some light on Stannard and the Ice Maiden.

Before catching up with him, there was something else Steve had to do.

"You got Todd du Prez's number somewhere?" Steve asked as Maria handed him his coffee.

"You're in luck. I scribbled it on a note in Connie's diary." Maria flicked through the pages. "Why? What's he got to do with the homicide case?"

"That's what I'd like to know."

CHAPTER 34

Steve cleaned the whiteboard then drew a vertical line down the middle in blue marker pen. He put the words *STANNARD* top left and *PEMBERTON* top right. Underneath Stannard he wrote *Air Race, Comet 5, Nuclear Propulsion, United Nations* and *$10 billion prize money*. He was about to write *Kidnapping, Slaker Nadzy* and *$5million Sale Price* under Pemberton when his phone started ringing.

"Todd, thanks for getting back to me. Look, I've got two questions for you." Steve was pleased he'd responded so quickly. He'd only left the voicemail half an hour ago.

"This is going to sound a bit strange but it's important. Can you find out from Chicory how her kidnapper looked and moved? I know he wore a ski mask, so she didn't see his face but what about his physique, big or small, fat or thin, was he agile, did he move quickly or slowly, that sort of thing? I'd really like to know anything she can remember, even what the gun looked like. Anything."

Steve's second question was more complicated. It concerned the product development programme Pemberton Electronics was working on prior to the sale. He put the call on speaker phone so Maria could join in. He thought her knowledge of electrical engineering would help cut through the jargon surrounding membrane electrolysis, green hydrogen production and power storage capacity in lithium-ion batteries.

Todd couldn't see why this was relevant to a kidnapping investigation, but he successfully answered all their questions. Steve thanked him then disconnected.

Next, he called Lonsdale and listened closely to his report from Oxford University. Again, he put the call on speaker phone. He needed Maria to hear Lonsdale's thoughts on Stannard and Dr Angela Fischer. Maria wrote her name on the board under Stannard, followed by the question, *cognitive dissonance?*

A call from Todd came in while they were talking to Lonsdale. It went through to Steve's voicemail. He hoped Todd had some answers for them about the kidnapper. They might start piecing this together now.

Lonsdale wasn't sure about Dr Fischer. She was due to arrive home in the early hours, day after tomorrow, according to one of her colleagues. Lonsdale didn't think she was involved in Stannard's murder, but he was intrigued by her. *A curious red herring* was how he described her.

In Steve's view, she was too closely connected with Stannard, the propulsion system and the race itself. She might hold a vital clue they were missing. If nothing else, an interview would rule her in or out of their inquiries. It was more of a hunch, Steve admitted. Lonsdale liked hunches and agreed to meet her off the plane at Heathrow when she landed.

There was better news regarding Stannard's passwords and pin numbers. Lonsdale referred to the little black book he'd found in the bedside cabinet. It seemed to be all the security numbers he ever used, including access to his bank accounts, eBay, PayPal, LinkedIn, Pizza Hut and even the membership login for CAMRA, the Campaign for Real Ale, Oxford branch.

While Lonsdale was scrolling through the pages, Maria was able to access Stannard's mobile phone and laptop.

He'd made three calls on the evening he was killed, she announced. They'd already discounted Max Hartley and Logan McInnes. The third name was far more interesting.

Maria wrote Quentin Fitzgerald-Manning on the board. The call lasted eight minutes and three seconds.

Long enough for Stannard to let slip he was off to the *Shine The Light* pub for dinner, Steve decided. He asked Lonsdale if he could pay another visit to the House to see what Fitzgerald-Manning had to say about this conversation, after he'd interviewed the *red herring*. With tomorrow being race day, no doubt the head of the *Comet 5* consortia might be unavailable, but it was worth a try.

After they disconnected, Steve could tell his former boss was enjoying the thrill of the chase once more. Lonsdale's gut feelings and local connections were proving invaluable. It was a big help having such an experienced officer covering the London end of this investigation. More importantly, it was an officer he could rely upon to get to the bottom of things and tell the truth.

The voicemail message from Todd du Prez brought a huge smile to Steve's face. "Chicory described him as a big black man who limped. The square-barrelled gun sounds like the one he pointed at us. Caribbean accent, same colour skin, powerful build, disability in the same leg, armed with a similar handgun, ruthless and yet seemingly dancing to someone else's tune. That's too many coincidences for me. I'm now convinced the kidnapper also killed Stannard. Now we need to figure out who he is and why."

"And who's calling the shots." Maria added.

Steve continued to fill up the whiteboard as Maria launched in. "You're right, Steve, I think the connection is the air race. OK, let's call the head honcho behind all this, Mr X."

"Hold on, it could be a woman." Steve corrected.

295

"Yeah, yeah, or one of the many other genders we have nowadays." Maria smiled. "Let's not get pedantic."

"Agreed. Mr X. Please proceed."

"As I was saying, Mr X wants to win the race, for whatever reason. Lucrative future contracts, prize money, ego stroking, competitive nature, whatever. He needs to eliminate *Comet 5*, leaving his plane, the *New Spirit of St Louis*, to cruise round the world unchallenged.

Maria continued. "He finds out Stannard will be visiting New York. He hires a hitman to take him out and wants it to look like an accident. He knows the police will be slow off the mark and most likely to file it as just another street crime that went wrong. The race will be over by the time we've worked it out."

"If we ever do. Mr X has a friend in high places within the NYPD who can bugger us up, if we're getting too close. I'm liking it but there're a few holes in the story. For example, why kill Stannard now? *Comet 5* can fly without him. Surely the time to eliminate him was before the propulsion system was installed?" Steve argued.

Maria didn't know the answer, but suggested maybe Stannard was getting in the way of something. Perhaps they had only intended to take him out of the picture and his death was a genuine accident. She carried on with her hunch.

"Meanwhile, Mr X finds out Pemberton Electronics can produce green hydrogen from cold water. What did you say Connie called it? An *ecodrivetrain*? You pour water in one end and out comes enough green energy to power a commercial airliner. The only biproduct is pure oxygen. Perfect for the *New Spirit of St Louis*."

Steve picked up the thread. "I guess Mr X was told all this by someone at Slaker Nadzy. They knew the ins and outs of Pemberton's new products. Mr X might be a client or an investor. Maybe he squeezed our friend Ethan to tell the kidnapper to release the girl, once the deal had gone through."

Maria continued. "But Mr X has a problem. He needs to keep all this secret, especially his involvement. He couldn't do that if he was just another Pemberton client. So, he decides to buy the company and get the *ecodrivetrain* that way. But the company wasn't for sale. The owners needed some persuasion to sell out. Their granddaughter's life did the trick."

Steve added. "If he'd paid the full market value for Pemberton, the IRS bloodhounds wouldn't have picked it up and none of this would have been investigated. Connie wouldn't have spilled the beans."

"Leaving us both frustrated, me in forensics and you twiddling your thumbs in fraud." Maria offered a smile. "Clouds and silver linings, I suppose. Dare I say, Steve, without our brilliant teamwork, no one would ever have linked the fraud investigation to Stannard's murder."

"This Mr X must really want to win this race." Steve added. This gave him another idea.

Maria took a photo of the whiteboard in case they needed more space. "By doing things this way, Mr X owns the company and the patent, which will be worth billions when his plane wins the race. As it was him who closed the deal, he could tell the kidnapper himself when to release Chicory. Maybe Ethan is still whiter than driven snow."

"But Mr X doesn't own the company." Steve interjected. "Herzl Power Technology does."

Maria seemed ready for this. "OK, Mr X just wants the patent for the *ecodrivetrain* technology. He doesn't want Pemberton Electronics. Maybe, the patent changed hands around the time of the sale. That way, everyone wins, except Connie and Todd."

Maria reached for her laptop. She accessed the website for the US Patent Office.

"Well, even Connie and Todd sort of win, I suppose." Steve reasoned. "They get their granddaughter back in one piece, Todd returns to full health, they escape any ongoing corporate liabilities, and they bank $5 million for their troubles."

Maria eventually found the right search button and put through her request. A blinking cursor told her to wait.

Steve was on his feet, rolling the marker pen between his fingers. He wiped some space on the board.

"My turn. The race is called the *UN Crystal Clear Skies Challenge*. Let's imagine it works and fossil fuels are removed from the aviation industry. A new generation of planes will have zero carbon emissions. The cost of producing green hydrogen will plummet, benefiting other industries including automotive, power generation, shipping, and manufacturing. Air travel becomes cheaper and pollution free. So, we know who the winners will be. But who will lose out?"

Maria noticed the screen had gone blank. An answer was coming. "Easy one - the oil and gas companies. They've controlled aviation, automotive and the others for decades, making huge profits at the expense of our planet. Even now, they're fuelling the production of grey and blue hydrogen. A breakthrough in creating green hydrogen on an industrial scale would be a disaster for them. This race is the last thing they want."

"Precisely. But public demand has forced their hand. They can't stop the race. Once it's proven you can fly around the world in a commercial airliner pollution-free, with little or no safety risks, demand will be overwhelming. The cost of air travel should also plummet as aviation fuel is replaced by cold water. The next best thing for the oil industry would be to protect its profits by controlling the aviation market in other ways." Steve was happy with his logic.

"Leading to the reasonable conclusion that Mr X runs an oil company." Maria's attention turned back to the screen which had filled with pages of information and links to other websites.

"Steve, according to this, nine minutes after Herzl Power Technology bought Pemberton Electronics, the new owners sold the *ecodrivetrain* patent for an undisclosed amount." Maria reported.

Steve moved round to share the screen with her. "I think I can guess who bought it. Don't tell me, Lindbergh Aviation Inc.?"

"Wrong. Sorry, no cigar, Steve. It was bought by an outfit called ZKI Futures." Maria wrote it on the board under Pemberton.

"Who the hell are they?"

Try as she could, Maria was unable to find out anything about them. No website, no shareholding or ownership information. She kept clicking on numerous links, but they all brought her back to the same unhelpful screen, explaining that ZKIP stood for zero-knowledge proof and was an authentication system used in cryptography. She was no wiser after reading the definition but made a note anyway.

Steve tried through the IRS systems but drew another blank. There was no reference to ZKI Futures. This had been cleverly planned, he decided. They should be able to find out through Ethan at Slaker Nadzy. He must have a contact name. Steve called him but it went to voicemail. He would follow up tomorrow.

It had been a long day. Maria leaned back, finished her coffee, and looked down at the keyboard, dejectedly. "Steve, this is all well and good but it's entirely hypothetical. We've no names, no evidence and no proof.

We don't even know why Stannard was killed or where to look for Mr X or the kidnapper. If our theory is correct, Mr X will get away with this scott-free once the race is over. We're running out of time. There must be something else we're missing. Let's try crossing our eyes again; we need to see that eagle."

Steve considered several options. Flying over to St Louis and confronting the Lindbergh Aviation team seemed plausible and might shake out some answers. But, with the race starting tomorrow morning and all their legal bases covered, he knew their inquiry would just get pinged around like a hopeless pinball, eventually running out of steam and falling down the hole, empty handed.

Going through the United Nations also seemed problematic. No doubt, the anonymity of race backers was protected. It would need solid proof to get them to open their books, even for a homicide investigation. There had to be another way to identify Mr X, Steve reasoned.

Maria was wiping the board clean. "If we could only see a list of backers for Lindbergh Aviation Inc., I think we'll find a connection to ZKI Futures."

"Then let's try to get that list." Steve replied.

"But how?" Maria was gazing at the board. One name hadn't been wiped from the Stannard section. She looked at Steve. He smiled, having reached the same conclusion.

Quentin Fitzgerald-Manning.

* * *

Zelda tried to put the photo down but couldn't let it go. The glass was smeared with hot, angry tears. She kept gazing into Sam's handsome face, a face so full of life and possibility.

300

He would have been 47 tomorrow. Revenge would have to be his birthday present. It wouldn't bring him back, but it might ease the pain of losing him. Just a few more hours to wait.

She'd put the phone on vibrate only. It started humming as it slithered across the desk. She checked the screen. Jeremiah returning her call. She clicked on speaker. Her office was soundproof, no one could hear. She dived straight in.

"You're a fucking idiot!! What were you doing? They fished them out in time. Now the NYPD's on full alert. They close ranks to protect their own. There's an APB out on you." Zelda cleaned the glass and carefully replaced the photo whilst screaming down the line.

"Couldn't you just shoot them?"

"This way was cleaner, leave no trace, no ballistics. Let me fix it."

"You'd better, before they find you. Bring the bodies tonight. This time there'll be no trace."

"It can't be tonight now. Maintenance people say new sensors needed, fix by tomorrow."

Zelda was on her feet, pacing the office. She tried not to look at Sam. More failure, more delays. She had wanted this resolved before the race started. That wasn't possible now. A twenty-four-hour delay was painful, but not disastrous, she concluded.

If she delved too deeply into the maintenance issues, it would make waves. Too many people would get involved. It was best to live with the frustration. One more day wouldn't make any difference.

"Where are they now? Jeremiah, don't lie to me."

"Over Atlantic. What shall I do with them when they land?"

She couldn't risk them being found at the site, especially with maintenance crews crawling all over it.

Best to keep them locked up overnight then use the chopper, after dark, in and out, get it done.

"Hold them at the strip. Bring them at midnight. No, wait. When will the maintenance crews have finished?"

"By 9pm tomorrow."

"Then bring them at 10pm. Time to finish this."

CHAPTER 35

The following day, Steve decided to pay Ethan Bronstein another visit. He hadn't returned any of his calls. Steve believed that, when the sale of Pemberton Electronics went through, Bronstein must have been involved in the transfer of ownership for the *ecodrivetrain* patent, therefore, he must know something about ZKI Futures, the new owners.

Steve was feeling refreshed after a good night's sleep. The drive across town was uneventful. He'd struggled with the replacement vehicle going home last night and had just about mastered the controls by the time he got back to the office. The rear-view mirror refused to stay in the right place, but it was close enough. He didn't have time to fix it now as he knew Maria would be waiting for him.

"It's going to be chaos out there today. We'd better get moving." Maria flicked off the live streaming from St Louis. "They're talking gridlock in all our major cities, with people pulling over to watch the race. They've sold quarter of a million tickets at the start-line and expect a greater TV audience than the Apollo moon landing. Someone on CNN just reckoned the advertising revenue alone would cover the prize money, though I think he was joking."

"When's it start?" Steve stuffed all the papers he needed into a briefcase, grabbed his new phone, wallet and keys then lead the way down the backstairs to the basement parking lot.

"Betty Gachuhi, the UN Secretary-General, fires the gun at 11.15am local time, which is an hour behind us.

The race was her idea so it's only right she gets the honour." Maria reasoned. "Having said that, the build-up's already started. There's no other news, the race is on every channel and media platform. The planes must enter the start box by 11am. *Comet 5* won the toss and will enter first. No one knows if they'll have an advantage or not."

"Sorry, did you say gun? She fires a gun?" Steve had been watching it on breakfast TV at home but had screened out most of the studio talk. He was secretly hoping they identified the race backers by mistake but wasn't that lucky.

"It's a six pounder, pulled out of a local museum and last fired in May 1780, defending St Louis from attack by the British. They must've thought it symbolised future independence from fossil fuels in aviation, though I doubt Downing Street will see it that way. We lost if you remember."

"How'll they hear the gun in the planes? It's all a bit weird if you ask me." Steve pulled open the basement door, just as his phone started ringing.

"The gun fires a flare, then a signal is sent to both pilots. There'll be a 0.0037 second delay, they reckon. Given the race could take up to 50 hours to complete, it shouldn't be a decisive factor. I think the gun is more for the spectators really." Maria added.

She waited by the passenger door while Steve fumbled with the key fob and tried to answer the call at the same time. The screen displayed the caller's name.

Ethan Bronstein. About time.

He apologised for not getting back sooner, there'd been an illness in the family, which Steve didn't believe. He put the call on speaker as he gunned the engine and made his way round towards the exit.

Bronstein was his usual, unhelpful self. He was aware of the change of ownership for that patent, did not know who ZKI Futures were and had no contact details. He believed the transaction was handled by his boss in Tel Aviv, but he wasn't sure. His boss was taking annual leave around the Yom Kippur holidays and wouldn't be contactable until the end of next week.

While Steve was struggling to get any useful information out of Bronstein, Maria was able to access the US Patent Office records. ZKI Futures was using the Slaker Nadzy address in New York as their registered office. When she pointed this out to him, Bronstein just said it was standard practice. Many of their clients used their address, to avoid unwanted media attention.

"And if an inquiry was made about this transaction, how would you handle it, if you don't know who your client is, this ZKI Futures?" Steve was getting impatient which wasn't helping his driving. Twice he'd had to brake suddenly, and they hadn't left the 19th Precinct parking lot yet.

"My official answer would be, in this hypothetical situation, that ZKI Futures wasn't our client. Our client was Herzl Power Technologies, and it was their decision to sell the patent rights. This was not a decision we advised upon and, therefore, couldn't comment. If such an inquiry was ever to happen, I'd refer it to Tel Aviv and let them answer it."

Maria tried a different approach, given that this was starting to look like a wasted journey. The clock was ticking, and the race start was getting ever closer. "Ethan, do you have a contact at the Patent Office we could talk to? Someone must keep the records updated."

The line went silent. Maria looked across at Steve who was busy fighting with the automated barrier. Finally, it lifted. She knew he'd need some directions when they came out onto East 67th Street. She put the Slaker Nadzy office address into her phone and placed it where he could see the screen. It may not be where they would end up, but at least it was a starting point.

"Their main offices are in Virginia, I think. I've never been and don't really have much to do with them." Bronstein replied, apologetically. "As I explained when we met, we specialise in corporate mergers, acquisitions, and capital investment projects, mostly. Sorry, I'm not being very helpful, am I?"

Steve managed a wry smile. He looked across at Maria who'd spotted it too. The synaptic gap before answering, the subconscious clue in the specific words he'd chosen, the caution in his voice. *Their main offices are in Virginia.*

"Ethan, I'm about to contact the Intelligence Unit at the IRS. If they tell me the US Patent Office has a place here in New York, and we subsequently find out you knew that, it will mean you're lying to us and obstructing our investigation. I don't need to tell you what the consequences would be, for you personally, I mean."

The traffic was thickening up. Steve needed to concentrate on this call and decided to pull over. He saw a gap outside a liquor store and swung in. Taking a deep breath, he switched into his most threatening 'you're making a life changing decision here' voice.

"We'll ask you again, Ethan. Do you have a contact at the US Patent Office, here in New York?"

"Let me check, I might have."

Maria opened her laptop and was ready to tap in the details. She didn't have to wait long.

"Sorry, yes, I've just remembered. I did have to register a patent for a client some time ago. The person I dealt with was very helpful. Of course, she may have moved on since then, so I'm not sure her contact details are still relevant." Bronstein's voice was quieter, less assured.

306

"Good, Ethan, now spit it out. We need her name, job title, office address, phone number, email, the works. I'm not interested in dropping you in it with Tel Aviv or anyone else. As I recall, Yom Kippur is a time to atone for your sins. If you help us get what we need, consider yourself cleansed, end of story."

Bronstein reluctantly read from his screen, while Maria tapped in the details. Angelica Seyvic was Archiving Services Lead, based in an office block near the Flatiron on West 22nd Street.

As if by a miracle, Bronstein's memory was getting clearer. "I went there once. It's on the 3rd Floor. There's no signage. A heavy oak door, near the elevator, I seem to remember. They don't like visitors. They may not let you in."

"Ethan, they'll let us in. We appreciate your cooperation. Enjoy the race." Steve disconnected then nosed back out into the traffic.

Maria tapped in the new address. Her satnav estimated 45 minutes but even the quickest route was showing delays. Steve handed over his phone and she punched in the number. Angelica's voicemail said she was in meetings most of the day and not contactable.

That meant she was in the office, which was all Steve needed to know.

CHAPTER 36

It took over an hour to reach the office block. A sign on the wall near the entrance proudly announced that The Thomas Willett Building was named after the first Mayor of New York, who died in 1674. The same sign also listed the myriad of companies occupying the twelve floors, except there was no mention of the third floor. We've come to the right place, Steve commented.

Ethan had been right. Two doors down from the elevator was a solid, oak door. No signage, just a buzzer. Steve pressed it. They waited. He pressed it again. On the fourth press, the door creaked open slightly. An eye peered out suspiciously, quickly followed by a 'wad d'ya want', in best Manhattan brogue.

Steve flashed his ID and pushed the door open at the same time. Maria flashed her ID as they breezed in. They found themselves in a small reception area, offering three dusty chairs clustered around an empty coffee table. On the unattended reception desk stood a dead cactus in a dirty, old plastic tub, next to a sign inviting any determined visitor to *press the bell for attention.*

After verbal interchange and some direct persuasion, they established Angelica Seyvic sat behind the fifth door on the left, down a long corridor that must have had ten doors on either side. Having been forced to surrender this information, the woman who let them in scuttled back into the first office on the right and quickly closed the door. Steve thought he heard a key turn.

Thick, beige carpeting ran the length of the corridor. It wasn't really needed to deaden any sound, Steve quickly realised. The place was like a well-lit morgue. No pictures

308

on the walls. No sound of voices or phones ringing. No movement at all. It was the land that time forgot.

After the third knock on the fifth door down, Steve depressed the handle and surprisingly found that the door opened. They entered a tiny box room with no windows. Behind a clean, white desk, angled across the opposite corner, sat a middle-aged woman with untidy, grey hair. She peered out from behind a large computer screen, her startled expression clearly visible through rimless glasses.

There were no other chairs in the room. Steve asked Maria to hold the fort and headed back to reception to grab a couple. Maria was doing her best to allay the woman's fears when Steve returned.

"This is most irregular. I never have visitors. You do not have an appointment. Who did you say you were?" Angelica had moved to the side of her screen but, in doing so, had inched further back into the corner of the room.

With Steve and Maria having to sit directly opposite, they inadvertently blocked off her escape route. This only heightened her anxiety. "I'm afraid I must ask you to leave. Whoever you are, I can't help you."

"This will only take a few minutes, Angelica, thank you for agreeing to talk to us." Maria explained, which made Steve smile. He guessed what Angelica would say next.

"But I haven't agreed. Now, if you don't leave, I will call the police."

Steve noticed there was no handset in the room, nor any sign of a mobile phone. He decided to launch in before the woman had a panic attack.

They both held up their ID Cards. Steve tried a softer approach. "Angelica, we are the police, please relax. We need your help with a routine investigation. It concerns the change of ownership for a patent you were dealing with earlier this year. Do you remember a company called

ZKI Futures? They acquired a patent from a firm called Pemberton Electronics. Ring any bells?"

It took a few seconds for the woman to register what he had said. She slid her chair over to the keyboard and started tapping away, all the time muttering to herself about their impertinence to barge in like this.

"I have it here. ZKI Futures acquired the patent following the sale of Pemberton Electronics to a company called Herzl Technologies. This type of transaction is quite common. Patents are traded all the time. My job is to maintain the records and ensure our archives are updated regularly. I hope that answers your questions. Now please close the door on your way out."

Steve pressed on. "We believe ZKI Futures can answer some questions for us that could eliminate them from our inquiries. Do you have their contact details, please?"

Maria slipped gently into the good cop role, even offering a smile for reassurance. "Angelica, if you can help us, we will happily leave and not come back. This conversation is off the record, there'll be no further involvement, I promise."

"Very well, I understand, but it is highly irregular for us to divulge classified information, even to the police."

Steve was about to show his frustration when Maria restrained him with a slight shake of the head, before adding. "We're not looking for any classified information, Angelica, just a name and contact details."

"I have it here. ZKI Futures is registered to the offices of Slaker Nadzy. The contact's name is Ethan Bronstein. Would you like his office number and email address?"

Steve rolled his eyes to the ceiling, but Maria took a different angle. "When a patent changes hands like this, how are you notified?"

Angelica explained the extensive bureaucratic process required, including the protocols surrounding proof of

310

ownership and transfer of the undertaking or intellectual property rights. She swivelled her screen round so Maria could see the various steps that had been followed in this case. Steve didn't move from his chair. Instead, he checked his watch. The race would be starting in less than an hour. They were getting nowhere.

"And are there any fees involved in this transaction?" Maria asked, innocently.

"Yes, of course, our services are not entirely funded by the public purse. It costs between eight and ten thousand dollars to register a patent, depending on the circumstances."

Steve couldn't resist. "What circumstances?"

Angelica looked taken aback. She wasn't used to direct questioning and inched deeper into the wall. "It depends on the complexity of the patent, the financial resources of the inventor or owner and other factors. We use an algorithm to determine our charges."

Steve considered the reference to an algorithm as universal code for *we make it up as we go along.* He continued. "But this wasn't a new patent, merely the transfer of ownership on your files. Do you charge for that?"

"Yes, we do charge a small administration fee." Angelica replied.

"And how was that paid, in this case?" Maria again.

"By credit card." Angelica announced, after some serious key depressions.

"In the name of?" Steve realised where Maria was going with this. He sat up straighter.

"ZKI Futures, of course. They requested the ownership change, so we charged them. I can print you a copy of the receipt if you wish. Then you must leave."

Minutes later, grasping a hard copy that had materialised, as if by magic, from an unseen printer in the bowels of her desk, they thanked Angelica and picked up their chairs. At the door, Steve turned to ask one last question but thought better of it when he saw the look of relief flooding across her face. He closed the door quietly as they left.

Back at ground level, the atmosphere on the street had changed. Race fever was filling the air. It was party time.

There was gridlock in both directions. Horns were blowing, the street was alive with singing and dancing. What looked like colourful samba schools were making congas between lines of stationary cars, their movements pulsating to the beat.

Crowds of people were milling about, some obviously on their way to fancy dress parties, others must have taken the rest of the day off to watch the race in a bar or at a friend's apartment.

Many people were decked out in red, white, and blue. The *Stars and Stripes* was everywhere, tied to lampposts, hanging out of office windows, even one big flag was strung across the street. Some people were carrying banners saying, 'Go Lindbergh', 'USA Rules', 'It's The Air We Breathe', '*Spirit* Move Us' and even 'Clean Those Skies'.

A big screen outside an electrical store was belting out commentary and live pictures to a swelling crowd. One intrepid hot dog vendor was doing good business.

Steve realised they weren't going anywhere in a hurry. It took a few minutes to cut through to their car. Once inside, Maria started making notes on her laptop while Steve punched a number into his phone.

"Jerry, yea Steve, listen, I need a favour. It's urgent. I want the name and address behind a credit card number. Could you find out and call me back, pronto?"

Steve had worked with Jerry Carmichael on a fraud investigation last year. He was a senior auditor for one of the top credit card agencies and was loyal to the cause. He didn't need convincing to help and asked Steve to wait. It only took a couple of minutes.

"Thanks Jerry, I'll just repeat that so's my colleague can take it down. The card's in the name of ZKI Futures, registered to Suites 5 - 12, Level 9, 1350 6th Avenue, New York. You're a star mate, I owe you one." Steve disconnected.

While Maria was tapping away, there was a loud bang on the front passenger window. A group of singing revellers clearly didn't think they should be working on such an auspicious day. One was wearing a hat in the shape of an airliner. Steve never did understand how people could get so drunk that early in the morning.

"There are twenty-five companies listed in that building. It doesn't specify who's on which floor." Maria reported. "I'll narrow it down to the most likely. Somehow, I don't think Manhattan Joke Books Inc. is what we're looking for."

"If our hunch is right, it must be the HQ or Finance Department for an oil or gas company." Steve folded the receipt and added it to the papers in his briefcase.

Maria suddenly stopped tapping. A huge smile swept across her face. For a minute, Steve thought she was going to kiss him. After the life-or-death traumas of the last few days, some warm, female contact would have been most welcome.

"Look what we have here." Maria beamed as she turned the screen round for him to see. "The Krasny Petroleum Corporation, founded by Aharon Krasny in Chicago, 1910. The family fled to America to escape persecution during the Odessa Pogrom of 1905. They'd made their money in the Galician oilfields of Western Ukraine and had moved to upmarket Odessa for health reasons, according to this article."

313

"Ukraine was in turmoil even then." Steve added. "What else does it say?"

Maria continued reading out loud. "Although the parent company has diversified its interests since the 1930's into gas exploration, plastics, financial services, healthcare, mining, consumer packaging and other manufacturing sectors, the main income generator remains petroleum products."

Maria was trying to find their latest audited accounts, without success.

"Impressive. They've lived the American dream. So why move from Chicago to New York?"

Maria flicked over to other screens, trying to find a chronology. When the answer came up, she couldn't restrain herself this time and gave Steve a huge hug and a kiss on his right cheek. "The company HQ moved to Manhattan in 2010 when the new President took control from her father, Saul Krasny, who subsequently died in 2012, after a long illness, it says."

"*Her* father?" Steve looked surprised. "Mr X is Mrs X?"

"Yes, indeed. Well, Ms X, I don't think she's married. The current President of The Krasny Petroleum Corporation is none other than Ms Zelda Krasny."

CHAPTER 37

It was too far to walk, especially with the streets crammed with happy revellers. They abandoned the car and made for the subway. Steve commented that, if the car had gone by the time they got back, they'd have set a record for losing police vehicles in the 19th Precinct. Maria didn't see the funny side.

They were on the F line heading north towards 57th Street Station. The subway was busy, but they managed to get seats in a corner where they couldn't be overheard. Steve was reading what little biography there was online about Zelda Krasny. Maria had found some scrap paper in her bag and started doodling with the letters. They'd already worked out that ZKI Futures must be the Krasny investment arm, but Maria's antennae were twitching.

"Steve, Slaker Nadzy is an anagram of Zelda Krasny. Very clever. I'm guessing she owns the whole firm. No wonder we couldn't find the other partners. There aren't any. She's Ethan's ultimate boss, whether he knows it or not." Maria added.

"So, Krasny must have known about Pemberton Electronics for years and may have funded their product development programme. She might even be the mysterious Israeli investor and funded the $5million for Herzl Power Technologies to buy Pemberton, for all we know."

"Or, at least, planted their seed capital to get them started. But why does the head of an oil company want to develop technology that will ultimately destroy their fossil fuel business?"

"Why? So they can make sure it doesn't succeed. Given regulatory requirements, health and safety legislation, quality standards, financial controls and all the other plethora of project milestones new products must satisfy these days, it's a wonder anything new ever reaches the market."

This had been one of Steve's bugbears for many years. He refrained from boring Maria with his views about how progress was being stifled and humanity was stagnating, if not already going backwards.

As usual, it was Maria who brought them back on point. "But, if she is Ms X in our theory, we need to link her to the American entry in this air race and the bastard who murdered Robert Stannard."

Steve checked his phone. The signal was poor, but a text would still work. He told Lonsdale about Zelda Krasny. After interviewing Dr Angela Fischer at Heathrow, they needed him to find any connection between Zelda Krasny and Quentin Fitzgerald-Manning.

The race was due to reach Big Ben, Sky Station 7, around ten tomorrow evening, local time. Quentin must surely be hosting the *Comet 5* party, Steve reasoned. It was being held in the new roof garden at the Houses of Parliament, with a very select guest list, so Max had told him.

They got out at 57th Street Station and walked into a seething mass of gyrating bodies on 6th Avenue. The police had given up trying to keep the road open or control the crowds who were mostly good natured. People were going in every direction. Reggae music was pumping out. Street food vendors were doing their best to feed everyone. It was a carnival atmosphere.

A silent protest on a street corner was trying to persuade the crowds that climate change was a politically motivated hoax and current temperature rises were

316

nothing more than the orbital cycle of heating and cooling going through its next phase. An argument had broken out with one of the protestors that threatened to turn ugly. Uniformed officers were moving in as placards were torn down.

Behind the protest group, down a side street, Steve noticed a small café that seemed quite empty, despite a window full of delicious bagels and subs. A large, flat screen TV occupied a far wall. Like all the others, it was tuned to the race. Depending on how the next meeting went, it could be a good place to regroup and watch the start.

By contrast to the quiet sanctuary of the US Patent Office, Steve and Maria found The Krasny Petroleum Corporation more like a true commercial operation. One of the three receptionists smiled and made them feel welcome. She acknowledged their request and sent a message to Zelda's EA who, she politely assured them, would be with them in a few minutes. Maria sat down but Steve felt too restless, for reasons he didn't quite understand.

Maria was reading through a selection of corporate brochures that had been carefully placed on a large, wooden coffee table. When the receptionists weren't looking, she sneaked spare copies into her bag. One brochure caught her attention. It showed the genealogy of the Krasny family, dating back to sixteenth century Europe.

More relevant was a diagram showing the current family tree, complete with thumbnail biographies. Zelda must be in her fifties, Maria estimated, having graduated from Princeton in computer sciences in 1989, before going on to complete a master's in advanced algorithm design in 1992, also through Princeton. Maria wondered

317

what Steve would make of that, given his dismissive view of algorithms.

The family history went on to say that Saul and Ruth Krasny had a son called Samuel who was born sometime after Zelda but there was no biography on him. She scribbled a note to follow this up later.

Meanwhile Steve was looking at the numerous business awards, certificates and old sepia photos adorning the walls of the spacious reception area. From the outside, it certainly looked like a large, well-run corporation with fingers in many pies and a full suite of accolades from the worlds of commerce, academia, education, industry, and science.

"Detective Sergeant, how may I help you?"

Steve spun around and was looking into the attractive face of a smartly dressed businesswoman who could have been Sophia's twin, but with jet black hair. She didn't offer her name or position in the company, but it was clear by her aura that she was not to be underestimated.

Her sharp, inquisitive eyes were taking the measure of him, searching for signs of his true intentions, or possible weaknesses. There was an air of confidence about her that was also fiercely protective. Steve wasn't sure what approach would work so decided to play it straight.

"We're here on official police business and would like to ask Zelda Krasny some questions. We believe she can help us with our inquiries. Is she available now? It shouldn't take long." Steve launched in with an opening salvo.

"What type of inquiries, may I ask? Ms Krasny is very busy, as you can imagine." Each word was barbed.

"That's between us and Ms Krasny." Steve had been joined by Maria who had filled her bag with brochures and rearranged the others to make it seem like nothing was missing.

318

He continued. "I appreciate this may not be the best time, but it should only take a few minutes. Is she in her office now? We can wait if you'd like to check."

"I'm afraid it's not possible. Could one of her board colleagues help you instead? I believe Mr Lipman, our CFO, is in today. I could ask him, if you feel it appropriate, although he is due in conference around now."

Because the reception area was in the middle of the building, it meant people had to pass through to reach other offices. As their conversation became more animated, heads were turning. Steve wondered if one of the receptionists had already let slip that they were from the NYPD and were asking for Zelda.

Sensing the growing levels of interest, the EA took them into a small meeting room just off the reception area and invited them to sit down.

At first, Steve thought she was going to ask Zelda to join them. Instead, she explained that her boss was not actually on site today and her diary was solid for the next two weeks. If they'd really like to make an appointment, she will see if a meeting can be arranged, but it was unlikely. Could she schedule a telephone conversation instead, perhaps?

Maria took the lead. "I'm afraid this won't wait. Our investigation is nearing completion, and several other agencies need our findings. Are you sure we couldn't speak to her? A phone call might do it if you can let us have her number."

"Out of the question, I cannot divulge that, even though I'm sure you wouldn't –"

"Abuse the facility?" Steve finished the sentence for her. He'd heard enough. "Alternatively, we can return with a search warrant and a team of investigators who will take away any material we consider relevant, including

319

her phone number, personal computer, and home address, which we will also visit. And if we want to speak to Mr Lipman, we'll subpoena him, thank you, whether he's in conference or not. Am I making myself clear?"

The woman's composure had slipped. She tried to speak but her mouth kept gasping for words, like a fish lying on the sand. Maria came to her rescue. "If we know where she is, we will talk to her there. If we can't, we'll call you and see if something can be arranged. Please forgive our directness, only, like you, we're under some pressure here."

They were escorted back to the reception area. A small cluster of people had gathered round the receptionists. Steve scowled at them but was secretly delighted they'd created quite a stir. News of this was bound to reach Krasny, whether she was in her office or not.

"You said she was off-site today." Steve managed to catch the woman's attention as she turned to leave. "She wouldn't be here, by any chance?"

Steve was pointing at an aerial photo of a huge oil refinery, hung near the main entrance.

"Only it's in New Jersey, so maybe she stayed local today, due to the congestion out there."

The woman froze. Lightning flashes danced across her eyes. Another synaptic gap before the inevitable stalling answer about not being able to say, for reasons of privacy and security.

But there was no denial. The light in her eyes was diverted inwardly, while she tried to come up with a plausible yet non-committal answer.

Back in the hallway, Steve nodded to Maria while they waited for the elevator. It was their sign that all further discussion should wait until they were well clear of the building, and any potential surveillance monitors.

Minutes later they were in the bagel café. Steve ordered a double toasted with bacon and mozzarella cheese while Maria changed her mind about not having anything to eat and opted for gravlax with sour cream. The coffees came piping hot.

"You think she's in New Jersey? How did you deduce that?" Maria only just managed not to dribble melted butter over her jacket.

"I didn't. I just wanted to see her reaction. If I was a betting man, I'd say there was a 60:40 chance Krasny's at the refinery. We've nothing to lose by going over there, once the streets clear. I've never been to a place like that. We might learn something about the Krasny family."

"Yeah, and how they make gasoline. I've often wondered how they separate out gasoline from kerosene, aviation fuel, bitumen and all the other refined products. I guess it's the engineer in me." Maria added.

The café had filled up. Everyone was watching the big TV. The two aircraft had taken off and were circling outside the start box. The gun was loaded and ready, as the clock ticked down towards eleven, St Louis time.

Steve heard a text come through. It was Lonsdale. He was in meetings at New Scotland Yard for the rest of the day but got the message. Dr Fischer was landing at 5.10am at Heathrow. He would go to Westminster after the interview.

In the text, he admitted looking forward to squeezing Quentin Fitzgerald-Manning, especially now he'd received some juicy titbits from HMRC about his tax arrangements. Steve texted thank you and turned back to the big screen in the cafe.

* * *

There were TV cameras everywhere, including both cockpits, amongst the passengers and with the observer teams in the air and on the ground. Steve caught a glimpse of Max Hartley as the camera panned round the cabin of *Comet 5*. He was sipping champagne, chatting to the blonde woman next to him and looking quite relaxed.

After briefly going back to the studio, the TV coverage cut to the Golden Gate Bridge, Sky Station 1, which was closed to traffic and already packed with thousands of spectators and well-wishers. The race wasn't due to reach them for at least six hours but that wasn't going to stop the party.

A commentator cheerfully recalled how 300,000 people crowded onto the bridge in 1987 causing it to sway and flatten out in the middle. San Francisco Police were valiantly trying to prevent the same thing happening today. It didn't look to Steve like anyone was counting.

"If Quentin opens up - either voluntarily or otherwise - and we can link Krasny to the race, I think we'd have enough to bring her in for questioning." Maria sounded hesitant. "But what about our assassin, Steve? How do we prove a connection there? In fact, how do we find him?"

Steve turned to face her. "The jungle drums are beating. Making a scene with Krasny's Executive Assistant will have repercussions. This guy will know we're getting closer. He found us last time."

"And your plan is what, hope he finds us again? We may not survive next time, Steve."

"We need to be careful, that's all. Remember, this guy makes mistakes, thankfully, or we wouldn't be sitting here eating toasted bagels and watching TV. I guess we keep turning over the rocks until he slides out."

Maria asked for refills of the coffee and ordered two more bagels. "Steve, didn't you say you'd spoken to the transport department about your other car?"

"Yes, they brought it back from the water's edge and checked it over. It was clean, nothing inside. There were only our fingerprints. Why?" Steve had seen this look of curiosity on her face before.

"So, the killer took our mobile phones that were both switched on, presumably to stop us calling for help." Maria made room for the plate of fresh bagels being brought over.

"And you're thinking they might still be switched on, in his jacket pocket or somewhere?" Steve was already keying in the number.

It only took the NYPD tech support team a few minutes to connect with their comms supplier and call Steve back. They confirmed both phones were still active and located them using a telecoms tower nearby. Steve noted the address.

"I guess the refinery can wait?" Maria finished the bagel, but the coffee was too hot to drink.

"Krasny Petroleum owns a private airbase in Westhampton, Long Island. Perfect for getting people in and out of the country unnoticed. I wonder if our assassin is planning a trip overseas for a while, back to the Caribbean, for example?" Steve added. "It's about a couple of hours by road from Manhattan, once the traffic lifts."

"You think that's what he's doing out there?" Maria had gathered her things and was ready to move. She could check out this airstrip online when they got back to the car, assuming it was still there.

They stopped near the doorway to let more people into the café. Their empty seats weren't empty for long. The noise level was ratcheted up when the TV screen filled with Betty Gachuhi taking the podium amid wild cheering. The canon was being prepared to fire on her command.

The UN Crystal Clear Skies Challenge was about to start.

* * *

Zelda Krasny was agitated. She'd visited the refinery early that morning but found herself getting bogged down in the maintenance schedules, production delays and the minutiae of SCADA control systems, for which there was an endless list of excuses why they didn't work.

She was assured the new parts had been fitted, everything was being tested and that all systems would be ready for start up again by nine pm. She drove home to an empty house. She'd left three messages for Jeremiah and was about to try again when he finally returned her calls.

"Landed two hours ago. They smelled pretty bad, so taking showers. I got them clean clothes and hot food. Chopper will be here on time."

"We had a visit from the police earlier. Your two cops have found out who I am. They're smarter than we thought. They'll take the bait and come to you. I want no mistakes this time. Bring them with you tonight." Zelda barked her orders.

"Chopper only seats four. Ain't no room."

"I don't want them seated. I want them in body bags."

PART TWO

"It is impossible to suffer without making someone pay for it; every complaint already contains revenge."

Friedrich Nietzsche

CHAPTER 38

Max Hartley, Comet 5, Blog 1, Over St Louis.
They said it would be cloudy, but St Louis has done us proud!! The weather gods were smiling as we took off, bathing the huge crowds in glorious, early autumn sunshine. The atmosphere on board is electric. All of us, including the cabin crew, are peering out of the windows. We just passed over The Gateway Arch and Downtown St Louis, for the third time, with the Mississippi River beyond, shining like a ribbon of glass two thousand feet directly below us. I can see ships and pleasure boats of every shape and size dotted up and down the waterway and along the banks, their flags and bunting waving in the breeze.

We are six minutes before the start, according to the special chronometer installed at the front of the cabin. It will count us down, show our flight time, distance to go and estimated time of arrival at each Sky Station. Next to it is a big screen showing atmospheric readings inside the cabin, including air quality, temperature, and radiation levels. Captain La Fontaine called it our canary in the coal mine *and told us all not to worry about it. He reassured everyone that he will know if there's a problem with the propulsion system long before we do and will shut it down if it can't be fixed. A warning bell will ring if radiation levels are rising. If that does happen, we have enough battery reserves to get down safely. I know that for a fact!!*

I'll report in from Sky Station 1 over San Francisco. Meanwhile, I need a refill of champagne and canapes. May the best plane win!! Max Hartley, over and out.

Hannah could feel a flood of tears mixing with the torrent of hot water powering out of the oversized shower head. Never in her life had scrubbing herself clean felt so good. Her skin had begun to itch through the borrowed thermal suit and all the smeared-on dirt. Her scalp felt horrible and greasy. Her hair had lost any life or bounce. A combination of stale sweat, grime from the boat, prison cell and helicopter ride, together with the recycled air in the container, had proved too much. Her relief was palpable.

They had been blindfolded before landing. The air felt warm outside the plane as they were led down the metal steps and across the tarmac into a large, industrial building. Two armed guards removed the blindfolds. They could have been any nationality under their protective clothing. Hannah noticed the corridors inside the building were all internal, with no natural light or glimpse of the outside world. There was no signage or other clues as to the local language or time.

The mirror in the shower area had given her a real scare. Days of fear and lack of sleep had etched deep lines across her forehead and round the corners of her eyes and mouth. There were more streaks of silver grey in her hair than she remembered.

She'd felt relieved when they got off the boat. At least they'd avoided a confrontation with the hungry, Lake Turkana crocodiles. Now the dryness in her throat was back, born out of the gnawing fear of what was to come.

When she turned off the tap, she could hear Lawrence singing in the next cubicle. He had been a calming influence during the flights. His English humour and bulldog resilience had managed to keep them both sane. Their relationship was still in its infancy, but she had to admit she'd be lost without him.

327

During the last flight, Hannah could see he was just as uncomfortable and worried as she was, but he always managed to keep her spirits up. *We will get through this* he would say, over and over. She was even starting to believe him, although whatever fate was being planned for them must be close now, judging by all the attention they were getting.

Hannah had no idea where they were or how long they'd been locked in the container. They had landed and taken off several times. The lights would go off while they were being switched to mains power or generators or the container itself was being taken off a plane or moved to another location. Those precious minutes gave them some time to talk openly without being overheard.

Twice, teams of ground staff appeared to re-stock the fridge, change towels and provide fresh clothing. Each time, the crews were dressed in what, to Hannah, looked like chemical hazard suits, complete with masks, breathing apparatus, heavy white gloves, and sealed boots. It was impossible to tell their ethnicity. A supervisor, usually armed with a machine pistol, kept an eye on everything from the door which was locked behind them on entry and exit.

Given the length of their journey, she guessed that Kiev or central Europe was out of the question. America was firm favourite, but it could be the UK, Canada, in fact any destination was still possible. She hoped it wasn't the USA. She didn't want to see that woman again.

Lawrence joined her in the drying area. Rivulets of water dripping off his naked, corpulent body made small puddles all over the floor. She flicked him with her towel and struck a pose, flashing him with a brief glimpse of her nudity. They fell together in giggles of laughter which attracted the attention of the guards, suspicious of whatever it was they found amusing.

328

They had slipped into clean industrial overalls and were escorted back to a cell, barely large enough for two chairs and a table. Still no windows or any connection with the outside world. But at least they were together and could talk openly without being overheard.

"Tell me again, Hannah, I'm still a bit hazy about all this." Lawrence repositioned the furniture so they could talk face to face yet keep an eye on the door. He checked round and convinced himself the room wasn't bugged. "You think this Zelda Krasny woman blames you for her brother's illness? Did you say his name was Simon?"

"Samuel, not Simon. She called him Sam." Hannah got comfortable. "It's years ago, I was the Programme Manager leading the research."

"Before they made you CEO?"

"Yes, I was one of ten programme managers. I'd had more experience in degenerative diseases, including some work for another client on Tay-Sachs Disease. It's hereditary. I was confident of finding a cure for Sam."

"And I guess you didn't, so that's why this woman is angry with you?" Lawrence concluded.

"Well, yes and no. Krasny pumped millions into our research which did produce positive results. Mind you, she had the money to play with. She liked the idea of helping her community, or so she said. I think she pulled out too soon, but I'm sure she doesn't see it that way."

Lawrence looked puzzled. "So why are we here now? If she's borne a grudge against you for all these years, why take her revenge now and not at the time?"

"I really don't know, unless something has changed, with Sam perhaps. It wasn't common knowledge that I moved to the Vatican from New York, but I'm sure she could still find me, even though my name changed when we got married. Maybe she's not been looking for me. I really don't know but I suspect we're about to find out."

The footsteps were growing louder. Two or three guards, Hannah surmised, just outside the door.

The first guard into the room was huge, well over six feet, dead eyes, and skin as black as night. Keeping his machine pistol levelled straight at them, he indicated for them to follow the other two guards back down the corridor. He locked the door behind them. Hannah noticed he was limping heavily on his right leg.

"Where are you taking us?" Hannah demanded, when they'd gone through some double doors. She didn't see the slap coming. Her face was stinging. Lawrence immediately reacted which earned him an elbow to the stomach. They crumpled together onto the floor and held each other briefly before being told to get up. The effort twisted Lawrence's back making it even worse.

Suddenly, dead eyes' face burst into a cynical smile, an array of clean white teeth on full display.

"An old friend wants to see you again."

CHAPTER 39

Max Hartley, Comet 5, Blog 2, Sky Station 1, The Golden Gate Bridge, San Francisco.

I've never seen so many people on that Bridge!! Although the vast majority are waving Stars & Stripes and supporting our competitor, it's still a glorious sight and makes your heart feel good. All of humanity wants an end to the disasters of climate change, and this race is playing a small but significant part in that transformation.

Our onboard chronometers are telling us that The New Spirit of St Louis *is in the lead and crossed Sky Station 1 just over 14 minutes ahead of us. They took a more aggressive approach to the Rockies which gave them a slight advantage.*

Forecasts are saying some big storm systems are brewing up across the Pacific, so weather could play a factor in reaching Sky Station 2, the Rainbow Bridge in Tokyo. Our Captain is confident we can make up the time and take the lead before getting to Asia. We are increasing speed, although I'd better not say by how much. We're now cruising at 40,000 feet. This will take us above some of the turbulence off the coast.

The plane is handling well, with mostly smooth conditions so far. The propulsion system is behaving itself with no discernible traces of radiation. Our batteries are fully charged in case we need them. Fingers crossed we can snatch the lead back.

The lady next to me wants to celebrate her birthday in style tomorrow. The bubbles are on ice. Everyone on board is loving the concept of this air race. We really do feel we are making history today. One to tell my grandchildren someday. For now, we're flying into the setting sun and wondering what adventures lay ahead. Max Hartley out.

* * *

Steve and Maria were making good progress across Long Island, now that the euphoria over the race start had subsided and the roads had cleared somewhat. The satnav estimated they should be at the Krasny airbase in less than twenty minutes.

"This is a serious *piece of work*, as they say round here." Maria was reading off her laptop as Steve overtook a truck that had pulled out suddenly from a side road. "The main runway is over 13,000 feet which means they can get the big planes in. I'd imagine it's mostly for cargo and equipment, but it means Krasny could run her own private airline."

Steve swung a right off the main highway and slowed to a T junction. In the distance, a plane was slowly sinking out of clear afternoon skies into strong landing lights. There were no markings on the tailfin. The gleaming white fuselage had no windows. A cargo plane from nowhere, Steve concluded. Not far now.

They reached a perimeter fence that could have surrounded a maximum-security prison. Double banks of razor wire ten feet high were interspersed with look-out towers and floodlighting. Security cameras were everywhere. As they drove along looking for the entrance, Steve noticed armed patrols with attack dogs checking the grassed areas around the airstrip.

Another white plane was taxying towards them, the two pilots clearly visible. Slowly, the plane turned onto the runway and, without stopping, the engines roared into full throttle. The plane accelerated past an orange and white windsock, before launching into a steep climb, taking it through some wispy, light cloud and away towards the North Atlantic.

"So, what do we do when we get there, Steve?" Maria closed the laptop and stored it in her bag. "We don't have a name to ask for."

"Leave the talking to me." Steve replied. "This bastard tried to kill us. I don't have time for names. I want him cuffed and locked into the back seat when we leave here."

The perimeter road was taking them towards some low-rise buildings. There was no signage anywhere to indicate who owned the place. They came across the main entrance by accident. A small road led them towards the buildings. A cluster of bigger buildings lay in the centre of the complex, surrounded by numerous aircraft, none of them with markings. Orange lights flashed on vehicles speeding backwards and forwards.

The fencing here was much higher and four rows deep. Warning signs blared out about private property, no unauthorised access, armed security patrols and trespassers will be shot on sight. Security cameras swivelled towards them in unison.

The entrance barrier was just the first layer of deterrent. Electrified gates lay beyond. Suddenly, the road around them flooded with white light as they approached. Steve could see movement behind the smoked-glass windows of the fortified gatehouse.

"Friendly." Maria commented as she squirmed in her seat. "You sure about this?"

Before Steve could answer, a tannoy demanded them to stop the car, turn off the engine and place their hands on the steering wheel or dashboard where clearly visible. Three armed guards emerged from the gatehouse as the barrier lifted. One stayed near the building and levelled his machine pistol directly at the car while the other two walked cautiously over to the driver's door, weapons drawn. Steve followed their instruction to lower the window.

"This is private property. Turn your vehicle around and leave immediately." The guard didn't even remove his reflective sunshades.

Steve had his badge to hand and raised it slowly. "We are NYPD police officers investigating a homicide. We have reason to believe important evidence was removed from the crime scene and is being kept in this complex. We need to collect it. Please allow us access."

The two guards withdrew, indicating to the third to keep his eyes on them. Sunshades was talking into a lapel microphone while pressing a bud deeper into his ear as another plane took off up the runway behind him.

"It's a bit thin, Steve. Without a search warrant, we'll never get past the first barrier." Maria suggested. "And I'm too old to hop over the fence and outrun the Dobermans."

"You won't have to. I think they'll let us in."

"Ever the optimist."

After a few minutes, the three guards grouped together by the open barrier. Sunshades waved them through, indicating them to drive round to a secure compound behind the gatehouse once the electrified gates had slid open. As they did so, Steve noticed the rows of surveillance cameras recording their every move.

"Too easy." Steve whispered as he pulled in and switched off the engine. One of the guards indicated he should leave the keys in the ignition and get out. "I smell a rat."

"Steve, we haven't got anywhere yet. Let's see what they have to say." Maria let out a deep sigh of relief. "Thinking about it, they need to stay on good terms with the police. I don't expect to be offered afternoon tea. I think our request for access will be politely declined."

"You got the co-ordinates for the two phones?" Steve made a final check around the vehicle before unclipping his seat belt and slowly exiting.

"Yep, in my bag. Maybe they'll just hand them over." Maria replied, trying to share his optimism.

Steve was expecting to be shown into the gatehouse, but, instead, an airport jeep swung round into the compound and stopped in front of them, an orange light flashing on the roof. Two more armed guards in the same colour uniforms jumped out and sandwiched them into the back seat. No need for seat belts, Steve reflected, they weren't getting out past these goons.

The jeep sped off towards the centre of the complex, past rows of equipment and containers. Bowsers, emblazoned in Krasny Aviation signage, were refuelling two aircraft. There were heavy lifting hoists and, what looked to Steve like dismantled parts of an offshore oil platform. It was highly organised, efficient and none of the ground crew paid them any attention.

The jeep pulled up at an unmarked door in the side of a large building in the centre of the complex. They were escorted inside and shown into a room. Strong smell of disinfectant. The two guards positioned themselves across the entrance. Steve noticed the air conditioning was quite fierce in the small reception area, causing Maria to shiver as she stood next to him. In front of them was an empty, square table.

A balding, somewhat dishevelled-looking man appeared from behind a screen, wearing civilian clothes and wire glasses. He took them off slowly, wiped a tired hand over his grey face and indicated for them to sit.

They waited while he got some papers in order. The interview was short and concise: who were they, why

335

were they here, the nature of their business and who their contact was, a question that Steve studiously ignored.

Forms were completed, photographs of each of them were taken along with copies of their NYPD identity cards. They even had to supply fingerprint and DNA samples which made Steve want to protest, although he thought better of it, after getting the nod from Maria.

The man asked to see evidence that the two phones were in the building which Maria handed over. He added this to his paperwork, gathered everything together into a clear plastic folder and returned behind the screen, leaving them to the tender mercies of the two goons, who remained ramrod straight, facing forward and still blocking the only doorway.

Steve wanted to talk to Maria but knew it was best to stay quiet. A security camera was pointing directly at them from above the screen. Too late to discuss tactics.

The man returned and told them to follow him. The goons parted, opened the door then brought up the rear. They walked slowly to a room three doors down a well-lit corridor. Inside was a full body scanner and a metal detector like the ones at an airport only more sophisticated.

Two more guards in uniform called them forward. Steve and Maria emptied everything into a tray. Maria's bag was searched. They wanted to confiscate her laptop and their new phones but, after a few minutes' argument, their protests were reluctantly accepted, although all the batteries were removed.

Back in the corridor, the balding man explained the evidence they had requested had been found and placed on a table in the next room. He pushed open a door to what Steve assumed had been an aircraft hangar but was now being used for storage. Their footsteps echoed across the vast space as they walked over the concrete floor. The man and the guards remained outside. Steve heard the door lock.

Sure enough, their two old phones were sitting proudly on a small table in the middle of the room. All around were crates and boxes of every size and shape. Small containers, equipment in metal cages stacked on top of each other. It was all laid out in neat rows, yellow and white markers on the floor. Three forklifts stood over by the open hangar doors recharging.

Steve noticed the light outside was fading, long shadows dappling the sides of a white cargo plane stood on the apron beyond. A maintenance crew seemed to be dismantling one of the two engines. Again, no heads turned. It was as if they were invisible.

They stopped in front of the table. As Maria grabbed the phones, she noticed their batteries had also been removed. There was no calling for help. She put them in her bag. "I don't like this."

"Maybe, as you say, they must cooperate with us. We're still on American soil, we have jurisdiction, they can't just ignore a request from the police." Steve was scanning the room. The only way out he could see was through the main hangar door.

Suddenly a man appeared from behind some packing cases, around forty feet in front of them. He was tall, dressed all in black with a black ski mask covering his head. He took two steps forward, limping heavily on his right side. A machine pistol was pointed straight at them.

"I knew you'd be back. You can't leave it alone, can you?"

The gun burst into life, bullets crackling past their ears. Steve felt a tug on his left arm as Maria dragged him down onto the floor. They crawled behind a big metal crate. More bullets shattered the table and splintered the concrete floor behind them.

337

"The hangar door's our only chance." Steve struggled to catch his breath. The gunman knew they were unarmed. He could take his time to kill them. They were sitting targets in a shooting gallery.

"Steve, that's what they want us to think. They could have shot us at any time. He deliberately missed to panic us. He wants us to run that way. There must be another door. C'mon." Maria was already on the move.

They crawled further down the line of metal crates and packing cases. Steve noticed one was full of drill bits. He did think about grabbing one, but it seemed a futile weapon against a machine pistol in the hands of a known assassin.

They got to their feet and started to run, only stopping at a main junction, wondering which way to go. They could hear footsteps moving towards them. He was taking his time, flushing them out. Steve wondered if the maintenance crew outside heard the shots and would come to their rescue. It seemed a forlorn hope, in this regimented world where everything was tightly controlled.

"Through here, quick." Maria had spotted a fire exit with a push-down handle.

They ran at the door which burst open. It led into a wide corridor no more than fifty yards long, no windows. It was poorly lit and clearly not used on a regular basis. It ended in large, double doors. There were no other entrances, doors or passageways leading off. If the double doors at the end didn't open, they were trapped.

"Remember the sign at the gatehouse?" Steve was breathing heavily. Sticky sweat was stinging his eyes. "Trespassers will be shot on sight. Maybe that's the idea. But they'll have to prove we've trespassed first."

"I don't care who can prove what, Steve. We need a miracle. C'mon, this way."

338

As they'd reached the double doors, they heard the fire exit door behind them slam shut. Steve turned to see the gunman blocking their route back. He ripped off the ski mask and burst into laughter. "Keep running, little rats, this trap won't let you go."

More gunfire ricocheted off the walls and floor around them, some bullets making holes in one of the double doors. Steve could see what was left of the daylight peeping through. The doors were made of plywood and had to open.

Steve tried the handle. Locked. He pushed the doors. They rattled but wouldn't open. Behind them, the gunman was limping slowly down the corridor towards them. He sprayed more shots above their heads, causing streams of dust and debris to shower down from the ceiling panels.

"Right, fuck this." Steve took two steps back then launched himself at the doors, his shoulder smashing a hole big enough for them to climb through. They both struggled through as more shots peppered the air around them.

Outside, Maria spotted an open door in the side of the building opposite. As they ran across the apron, several security lights came on, illuminating the surrounding area. Steve could hear vehicles revving up in the near distance, the sounds quickly drowned out as another plane took off.

Steve was able to lock the door behind them this time. Strip lights flicked on as they moved cautiously down the first corridor. Again, this building was being used for storage, although the clouds of dust that kicked up as they ran suggested it was more of a long-term facility or archive maybe.

"It's him, Steve. You were right, he found us. He used the phones to draw us in. They want us to run then shoot us for trespassing." Maria announced.

"We've no choice, we have to run." Steve opened a door that led into some changing rooms and shower area. It had been used recently with wet towels strewn on the floor. "Trap or not, I'm still going to nail this guy."

Steve closed the door and tried to get his bearings. Which way now? They only had seconds to decide. Steve remembered a police training course where the instructor told them how important it was stay calm and collected in a tight spot. It seemed easy in the training room.

As Maria started to explain where she thought they were in relation to the gatehouse, muffled cries for help came from down another corridor. They looked at each other briefly then started to run in the direction of the voices, lights flicking on above them as they went.

The door this time was heavy metal, double locked with mortis keys and a padlock for good measure. Whoever was in this room was staying in the room. There was a sliding panel covering a peep hole at eye level, around two inches square.

Steve peered into a prison cell with bare walls. A table and two chairs sat in the middle of the room. On the chairs sat a man and a woman in their fifties. They wore clean industrial overalls and appeared terrified.

Steve called out to them. He thought the woman looked strangely familiar.

CHAPTER 40

*Max Hartley, Comet 5, Blog 3, Somewhere Over The
Pacific Ocean*

*What a storm!! I've been flying all my life and don't
remember a storm so prolonged or violent!! Our Captain
asked us to buckle down as it would get bumpy. He wasn't
wrong!! The turbulence went on and on.*

*We increased altitude to 42,000 feet, obviously hoping
to fly over the top. Well, the windows were rattling at one
point, then we fell several hundred feet into an air pocket.
Two passengers were injured, and many were sick,
including a UN observer and a member of the cabin crew.
The lady next to me was clinging to my arm for dear life.*

*Thankfully, we came through mostly unscathed,
although I think we did take a couple of lightning strikes
along the way as our cabin lights did go out briefly. The
thunder was deafening, and the light show on both sides
of the plane was amazing. The sooner we reverse climate
change and stop messing about with Mother Nature the
better I say.*

*Anyway, the good news is that we have made up some
time. Our competitor turned south to avoid the bad
weather. Also, they are now facing stronger headwinds
which are piling in to fill the area of extreme low
pressure. For now, we've found a favourable tailwind.*

*All going well, we should have snatched the lead back
by the time we reach Tokyo. Max Hartley out.*

* * *

Steve was trying to place the two prisoners. He felt he had met the woman previously, maybe in his Surrey CID days.

"Did you say Mole? Detective Sergeant Mole?" the woman repeated, rising to her feet, and moving towards the peep hole. She was tall. "Is it really you, Steve? I thought you'd still be in Guildford."

Steve looked at Maria. He hated coincidences but for this one he'd make an exception. It all came flooding back. Her American accent, the gritty in-your-face approach, her height. He'd met them both before. Hannah and Lawrence. She'd been in the room in Guildford with Max Hartley. The CEO for a medical institute in New York. He was British, a project manager or something like that. But they were seriously out of context. What were they doing locked up in this godforsaken airbase?

As Hannah started to explain about her connection with Zelda Krasny, suddenly the air was filled with the sound of loud voices. Heavy boots running over a concrete floor. The noise was coming from the door Steve locked when they entered the building. They had to go.

"Steve, she's going to kill us." Hannah had tears in her eyes. Lawrence put his arm around her, "You've got to get us out of here."

"Sit tight, we'll come back for you. Trust me, Hannah." Steve thought the words sounded as empty as he was feeling. They were in no position to make promises. Their own lives were at stake.

Steve slid the panel shut, closing off two dejected faces. They took Maria's route down a series of passageways and dark corridors until they finally reached another exterior door with a toughened-glass panel showing what lay beyond.

The apron outside was floodlit. The sky above the blackened buildings was painted in sunset pinks and

342

oranges. More clouds had drifted across the warm skies and the first stars were glinting into view.

There was no sign of anyone around. No planes, no vehicles, nada. In the distance, searchlights were scanning the perimeter fence. Steve could see a patrol with dogs heading back towards a watch tower.

Behind them the voices were getting louder. Doors were opening and closing. Another burst of gunfire. The sound was different this time, more like a heavy machine gun than the drilling woodpecker shots from before. Whoever was coming obviously meant business. Maybe their plan had changed, Steve wondered. Just kill them both and we'll face the consequences with the police in due course.

Whatever the reasoning, the only chance they had was out through the perimeter fence but the double bank of razor wire had looked formidable. They'd have to resolve that problem when they got there. Crossing the taxiways and grassy areas was not going to be easy. There was nothing else but to make a run for it.

Steve turned to Maria. "I'm sorry to keep doing this to you. Please believe me."

"Steve, it's what we do. The stakes have just increased. We must escape to save Hannah and Lawrence. Now we have enough evidence to bring this woman down."

"And our limping friend. I'd like to see him behind bars. What did Connie call him? Papa Doc?" Steve added.

"Papa Doc, good name. I don't think we've seen the last of him yet. Let's go." Maria pushed open the door and started to run across the apron towards the distant fence.

They hadn't made the first grassy area when suddenly three airbase jeeps swung out from behind a low building in hot pursuit, headlights on, orange lights flashing. Papa Doc was standing up in the passenger seat of the middle jeep, holding a roll bar to keep his balance. He raised his machine pistol and fired a quick burst that ripped into the concrete surface ahead of them.

Steve grabbed Maria's arm and started to veer off towards a small plane. It was covered in a tarpaulin and might give them some cover. It didn't help. More gunfire from another jeep shredded the tarp and the windscreen of the plane underneath. After another prolonged burst, the plane exploded, sending hot shrapnel fragments high into the darkening skies.

The gap between them was closing now. At this rate, they weren't going to reach the fence, Steve realised, and there was nowhere to hide. Their only chance was to keep running and pray for a miracle.

With the burning plane behind them, they dashed over a grassy area and found themselves running across a wide taxiway. This strip was better lit than the others which made them more conspicuous.

Steve was scanning the perimeter fence as he ran, looking to see if one part was any more accessible than another. He spotted the silhouette of a car parked on the perimeter road beyond the second fence. Maybe someone would see them and call for help. It was worth a try.

"Steve, they've stopped. Look!!" Maria managed to swivel her head round as she ran.

Steve looked back. Not only had the jeeps stopped in the middle of the grassy area, but Papa Doc's jeep had disappeared. Only two orange lights were flashing now.

"Come on, there's a car by the fence over there. Let's head for that. Quick."

Steve didn't hear the transport plane approaching. Suddenly the tarmac around them was flooded with white light as the plane made its final descent. Maria just had time to grab Steve by the legs and rugby tackled him to the ground. The front wheels missed his head by a whisker and screeched on touch down.

They were blown back along the runway by the rush of air over the top of them, combined with the hot thrust from the jet engines. An overpowering smell of burning rubber filled their nostrils when they finally stopped rolling. The plane continued to disappear into the streams of coloured, runway lights.

"They're coming again. Let's go." Steve pulled Maria to her feet and set off towards the parked car. More shots rang out as the two jeeps hurtled across the runway. They were both running flat out. As they got closer to the first fence, Steve could see that it was his car they were running towards, conveniently parked with the front doors left open.

Not only that, but the double bank of razor wire had already been cut, allowing just enough space for them to climb through if they should reach the fences in time. It looked like it was cut from the outside, with the jagged edges pointing towards them.

Who could have done this? Steve was trying to think when another burst of gunfire rang out. This time a bullet grazed his right leg, ripping through his trousers and cutting across the flesh, just below the knee.

Steve yelped in pain but didn't stop running. When he looked down, he could see by the perimeter lighting that blood was pouring from the wound. He would have to stop and tie a ligature. But they couldn't stop.

As he looked again towards the car, Steve spotted a strong white light in the sky just above the horizon. It seemed to be zigzagging towards them. He couldn't hear anything above the noise of the plane that had just landed which was now taxying towards the main building complex.

More shots, the jeeps were almost upon them now. One bullet ripped into Maria's bag, pulling it out of her hands. She turned as if to go back and collect it, but Steve grabbed her arm and told her to keep running.

Suddenly the distant light was upon them, the noise of the rotor blades whining as the helicopter banked sharply then decelerated to a hover position, fifty feet above the perimeter fence. A powerful beam of white light filled the area and a voice boomed out from loudspeakers under the cockpit.

"Police. Drop your weapons."

The two jeeps screeched to a halt only yards behind them. Steve and Maria slowed to their walking pace, both panting for breath and glistening with sweat. Steve saw one of the guards talking into his lapel mic, no doubt asking what they should do.

Another guard raised his weapon. A single shot from a marksman in the helicopter hit his trigger hand causing the weapon to clatter onto the hood of the jeep. The man slumped into his seat, yelling in pain. Another guard helped him to wrap a cloth over the wound.

Steve and Maria picked their way through the two fences, taking great care not to brush up against the razor wire. As they cleared the second fence, two police cars, sirens screaming, with red, white, and blue lights flashing, raced towards them along the perimeter road. Steve slumped down onto the grass by the roadside while Maria tried to stop the bleeding. She ripped some cloth from his shirt and was about to tie a tourniquet when the first police car reached them.

Two officers jumped out, one dressed in full body armour and carrying an automatic rifle. He took up a kneeling position and pointed the weapon at the jeeps through the open rear door.

The second was a woman police officer who brought a first aid kit from the trunk and took over tending to Steve's wound. Maria collapsed on the ground next to him. She was holding her hands to her face, uncontrollable sobs mixed with short gasps for more air.

A second police car pulled up behind the first. The four police officers crossed quickly through the fence and were detaining the guards in the two jeeps. There was no further resistance.

"You OK, Steve?" Apicella was walking towards them from the rear of the second car. "Good job you called this one in, for once."

"I learn from my mistakes, Tony, you know that. Anyway, we're mighty glad to see you guys. You've saved our necks. Another five minutes and we wouldn't be having this conversation." Steve had managed to stand and was able to put some weight on his leg. It was sore but the bleeding had stopped. He'd live, was his prognosis.

"What about the guy who murdered Stannard and his sidekick, Mickey Shaps? Is he amongst them?" Apicella was pointing towards the group of guards who were now being handcuffed and charged.

The woman police officer had retrieved Maria's bag from the grassy area beyond the second fence. Maria thanked her when she returned with it. The bag was a mess. Bullets had ripped the guts out of her laptop and shattered most of the phones.

"He was but he disappeared before the plane landed." Steve explained.

"What plane?" Apicella looked confused. He'd also just noticed it was Steve's replacement car that was parked by the fence.

"Never mind, it's a long story. Anyway, he's holding two prisoners over there." Steve pointed towards the buildings at the centre of the complex. "I know them. They're good people. Their lives are in danger. I promised we'd get them out."

Apicella took a deep breath as he considered his response. "Normally, I'd say we need a search warrant but I'm getting a little pissed with this Krasny woman, you know."

Apicella called over to one of the officers from the second car and asked them to request back-up. This could be a long night. "How'd your car get here? You told me you were going through the front gate?"

Maria took over as she could see Steve was flagging. The adrenalin rush had gone, leaving blood loss and fatigue to take hold. She was feeling quite tired and emotional herself, but they were a good team and must cover each other's backs. "They moved the car here and cut their own fence. I think their plan was to shoot us as trespassers then plead ignorance about us being police officers."

Apicella continued. "And after all this, did you get the phones back? That's why you came here, right?"

"Yes, we have them, they're a bit chewed up. No doubt they'd have taken them off our corpses at some point. They used the phones as bait to get us here. The whole trap was carefully planned. They just didn't expect the NYPD to show up." Maria added.

Steve was about to explain who the two prisoners were and why he believed they were in danger when another sound filled the air. Not a plane this time but another helicopter which hovered out from a hangar in the middle of the distant complex and started to climb.

Remembering the binoculars in the glovebox, Steve dived into his car and pulled them out, just in time to catch a glimpse of Papa Doc in the front passenger seat of a black chopper. He seemed to be pointing a gun at the passengers in the rear seats. Steve couldn't see their faces.

The black chopper swung high up above the complex, dipped its nose then powered away towards the centre of New York. Steve just had time to call out the registration number on the tailfin which Maria scribbled on a piece of paper.

"That's him. I think he's got Hannah and Lawrence in the chopper. We've got to go." Steve looked at Maria who nodded, she was ready. They'd come this far. Twice this man had tried to kill them. He wasn't getting away now.

Apicella looked even more confused but at least he'd worked out they didn't need a search warrant to rescue the prisoners, as the prisoners just flew off. He'd also calculated that, by the time Steve and Maria had driven back to New York, these prisoners were likely to be dead meat.

He grabbed Steve by the arm just as he was about to climb into his car.

"Take the police chopper."

CHAPTER 41

Max Hartley, Comet 5, Blog 4, Still Somewhere Over The Pacific Ocean.

We've just had great news - we're in the lead!! It may only be eight minutes but it's the first time since we left St Louis. Confirmation came from the UN observer team on board who've had an update from UN Race HQ in New York.

Our competitor stuck to their southerly route, which is shorter as the crow flies, but they miscalculated the weather forecast. Headwinds have really slowed them down. Even so, they have the prospect of clearer skies than us all the way to Tokyo. We are approaching another storm front so things will get bumpy again.

An update on our propulsion system brought a standing ovation from everyone including the cabin crew. Not only are the thorium rods performing at ninety-three percent efficiency but, more importantly, there is no radiation leakage at all.

Our backup batteries are fully charged, giving us nearly seven hours flying time if we need it. Comet 5 is humming along. I just wish Robert Stannard was here to share in the glory. I hope he gets the posthumous recognition he deserves after we win this race. Nuclear-powered commercial airliners are here to stay!!

Although it's still the middle of the night here, technically it's already my travelling companion's birthday. I managed to sneak a bottle of bubbles out of the fridge and a few of the left-over canapes she really enjoyed. Why does contraband always taste that much sweeter?

Anyway, I'll report in from Sky Station 2. Max Hartley saying Sayonara for now.

* * *

Betty Gachuhi was back in her office at the UN. The press conference earlier that afternoon had been her best since taking over as Secretary-General. The public response to the race had been overwhelming. Even the most cynical journalists heaped praise upon her for taking such a bold initiative. Instead of reacting all the time to crises created by others, the UN had done something proactive and truly worthwhile, they reported.

She'd even had a handwritten note from the Pope himself who thanked her for addressing such an important issue. She was giving hope to all humanity that we can pull together and resolve one of the big challenges we face today, He said.

This mirrored the sentiments she'd picked up on the internal flight from St Louis to New York after the race had started. Betty always insisted on travelling economy class so she could interact with the public, much to the annoyance of her security guards.

People at both airports had hugged her, given her flowers, and shaken her hand so hard that it had begun to ache. One well-wisher even said she'd achieved more than any other Secretary-General in the UN's history, and she was only weeks into the new job.

As she was reading through all the congratulatory emails from world leaders, Betty's personal phone chimed into life.

"Henry, what a lovely surprise. How are you? How's Fara and the kids? Phoebe still as lively as ever?"

"We're all fine thanks, sis. It's been a while since we spoke. I know you're off to Europe tomorrow so I thought

351

I might catch you before you leave." Henry explained. "How're you doing? You must be delighted."

"I passed delighted weeks ago, Henry, it's like a dream come true. For years I've wanted to make a difference. I couldn't believe it when they asked me to be Secretary-General. My predecessor saw the job as a reward for keeping his nose clean in public service, with no real agenda for change. He tried to put me off, as others have. This race is just the start. I almost feel like I have a mandate now to shake things up. It's very exciting."

"Well, I just wanted to give you the feedback from home. You've made the whole country proud, sis. Everybody's talking about you and the race. The newspapers are full of pictures of you firing the gun. Pity you couldn't have made Nairobi one of the Sky Stations. Millions would have turned out to watch. Maybe next time. Lots of people are lobbying the government to include you in the next honours list."

Betty was blushing. "I've received an email from the President himself. It was glowing. I'm so proud to be Kenyan and represent my country at the highest levels. I hope my luck holds."

"It will, sis, it will. I love you; we all love you. Please keep up the great work and don't let anyone stop you. Let me know if you're coming home at Christmas, it would be good to see you."

"I will try, Henry. My love to Fara, Giles and darling Phoebe." Betty disconnected. She was still beaming with pride when Chantelle brought through two mugs of earl grey tea, extra hot, and a plate of her favourite oatmeal biscuits.

"We've had more offers of financial support for the race from Sweden, Saudi Arabia and Indonesia." Chantelle was reading from her notepad. "We're in profit now, with pledges totalling well over the $10billion prize money."

"That's incredible. Maybe there is still hope for humanity." Betty snaffled a biscuit.

Chantelle flipped over a page. "Also, Spain, Chile and Nigeria have asked if they could be included in any future race or other such UN initiative. The email from the Nigerian President said he would like to fire the gun next time and would fund all the prize money, if the event was staged in Abuja."

"Please thank them all on my behalf. I'd be delighted to help in any way I can. I'm so pleased we've managed to get this race off the ground. Who's winning, by the way?"

"The American plane was leading until they reached the Pacific, now the Europeans have snatched it back. Media interest is huge. They've estimated a viewing audience of just under three billion watched the start." Chantelle smiled.

"Wow. Why do you think it's proving so popular? The race doesn't go near so many countries like Sweden or Nigeria." Betty reasoned.

"It's about time people could see a world leader stand up and do something positive to reverse climate change." Chantelle put her pad down, reached over and kissed her on the cheek. The hug that followed was from the heart. "We're tired of politicians droning on about being carbon neutral by 2050. There won't be a 2050 unless we act now, for Christ's sake."

Betty moved back to the screen on her desk and clicked into her diary. "What's the latest on my trip to Europe. Am I meeting the British PM or the Foreign Secretary tomorrow?"

Chantelle ran through the changes. Betty was meeting the British PM in Downing Street. An invitation to join

Quentin Fitzgerald-Manning at the Houses of Parliament had been accepted. It was to be held in the roof garden, giving a photo opportunity to watch the planes fly over Sky Station 7.

"You fly to Paris the next morning for a meeting with the French President then you're speaking at the European Conference on the Refugee Crisis." Chantelle handed over a draft copy of the speech for Betty to personalise. She liked to add her unique touches to the content. "I've yet to confirm your TV appearance in Berlin. They want to interview you about the race. We should have a result by then."

"My fingers are crossed both planes get back safely. What about going to Warsaw. Is that happening?"

"The Polish President will meet you in Berlin. His email said he loves what you're doing and wants to tell you personally." Chantelle had printed off a copy.

Betty was checking through the schedule on her screen. "I see you've pencilled in some free time for me before the roof garden event at the Houses of Parliament. You're not match making again I hope, Chantelle."

"Merely responding to a request from one of our entrants, I assure you." Chantelle was grinning like the proverbial cat. "In his email, Quentin argued that, by starting the race in the US, they believed the UN was giving an unfair advantage to the American team. He wants you to share your vision for addressing climate change with key figures in his consortia. Well, that's what he said."

The phone on Betty's desk started to ring. Chantelle reached over and answered it. She smiled as she handed the receiver over. "Talk of the devil."

"Betty, good evening, I hope I'm not disturbing you?" Quentin's voice positively purred down the line.

"Not at all, Quentin, how may I help you?"

"Firstly, I just wanted to offer my congratulations on the race start. We're very pleased with the way it was handled. It was compulsive viewing this side of the ditch, I can assure you. We're even more delighted we've stretched our lead to nineteen minutes, but there's a long way to go yet."

"Thank you, we're getting a very positive response so far." Betty was wondering why he'd called.

"Secondly, I just wanted to explain about your visit to the Houses of Parliament. As you know, the planes are due to reach Big Ben, Sky Station 7, around ten pm tomorrow evening, our time. We've invited some VIPs to join us in the new roof garden for a little celebration. It's right under Big Ben so we should get great views. The press will be there. You're very welcome to bring some media people with you, just let me know the numbers."

"Yes, I'd like to do that. We want full media coverage for this event. Chantelle will email you with the numbers."

Quentin continued. "We're delighted you can join us. For the meeting beforehand, it will be a small gathering, maybe eight or nine people only. Just the big-name backers for our consortia. No media. A private room. You'll be amongst friends, I assure you."

"Quentin, I'm looking forward to it and to meeting you in person. I'm scheduled for an hour; I hope that's enough time?"

"Plenty of time, I'll make sure it's well spent. Thank you, I'll see you in London." Quentin disconnected.

Chantelle gently removed the handset from Betty's grasp and replaced it. Betty herself was lost in thought, gazing at hot air balloons rising over the Serengeti.

A meeting with members of the *Comet 5* consortia? A private room in the House, no media?

What was Quentin up to?

CHAPTER 42

When the police helicopter touched down near the cars on the perimeter road, Steve expected the marksman to jump out. Instead, he continued to sit in the front passenger seat, buckled in and nursing a rifle across his knees.

As soon as Steve and Maria had strapped themselves into the rear seats and put their headsets on, the chopper spiralled up into clearing skies and set off towards the city centre. From high above the airbase, Steve could see the glow over Manhattan in the far distance. The last rays of sunlight had gone, leaving them flying through a patchwork of dark pools and neon lights of every colour.

"Sir, my name is Officer Doyle. I've been assigned to protect you on this mission." The voice from the marksman sounded quite metallic and distant through the headsets, yet he was sat only three feet away.

Steve looked at Maria who managed a smile. After the drama of escaping Papa Doc and the cargo plane, to have some help at last was most welcome. Steve was curious. "Who assigned you?"

"Detective Apicella but I think he got clearance from upstairs. He said you don't believe in carrying weapons and he was getting tired of digging you out of the s-h-1-t, sir."

They all laughed out loud, including the pilot who was listening in. Steve soon established that their bodyguard was third generation Irish, the family originally from Galway. His father had been a beat cop in the NYPD all his life. It was the only career choice Officer Doyle considered after leaving school.

They agreed to drop the formalities and use first names. Connor Doyle proudly told them how he'd been attached to the Aviation Unit last year. He was training for a pilot's licence, had perfect 20:20 vision and was overall in great mental and physical shape. The fact that he finished top of his year in marksmanship was a bonus, as Steve had already discovered.

While Steve was explaining to Connor about their mission and the risks involved, Maria was talking to the pilot about where they were going.

"Maria, the airspace over New York is tightly controlled. Nothing gets through without permission. Not even us. Since 9/11, everything is monitored. I'm told they got fighter aircraft on permanent standby, ready to intercept any unidentified aircraft. My boss reckons there are surface-to-air missiles in silos within Manhattan, but I'm not so sure about that one."

"Well, I hope you're right. All we have is a tailfin registration number. Can you radio air traffic control and see if they have it logged? We don't want to lose them now."

"We call them N90. They control the skies over the Big Apple."

The pilot cut their conversation while he talked to the control centre.

A few minutes later, he reported back. The black chopper was making a routine trip to the Krasny Oil Refinery in New Jersey. Maria requested the same destination.

They logged in their flight plan with N90 then tapped in the coordinates. Flying time should be fifty minutes, it estimated, and flying conditions were good with little turbulence and a seven-knot tailwind.

"My guy at N90 said Krasny have six identical black choppers they use for ferrying people to and from the

357

airbase. They're regular customers and always play by the rules. Sometimes they go to other Krasny sites in the area. He said there's a helipad on the roof of their main office on 6th Avenue." The pilot announced.

"We'll settle for the refinery, thanks." Steve chipped in.

"And when we get there, you know I can't land. It's private property, nothing I can do, sorry." He sounded adamant.

"This is a murder investigation. We're after a known assassin who's already taken out two people. More lives are in danger tonight. We must save them. If you need permission to land, I suggest you call someone." Steve snapped back. "And can you speed up please, our timeframe is short."

The pilot cut the feed again while he was talking to someone out of earshot. When he came back, his position hadn't changed. It wasn't possible to put the helicopter down at the Krasny Oil Refinery without their permission. Did Steve want to try them himself?

The one piece of good news was that he'd increased speed and reprogrammed the navigation system to take them on a more direct route but still avoiding hot spots over the city, as he called them.

Steve was about to give the pilot's headset a roasting when Maria intervened. "Is it possible to hover over their helipad without touching the ground? We can jump out and you can return to normal duties."

The pilot gave this some thought. In the circumstances, he reluctantly agreed to her request. Although it was still a breach of their privacy, he could live with the consequences. Steve settled back in his seat with some relief. Lives were at stake, yet we seemingly must tick compliance boxes.

They changed course a few times to avoid some tall buildings and were making good time. Soon the Krasny Oil Refinery was looming large through the windscreen. Despite seeing the aerial photo, Steve hadn't imagined the site would be so big. It was lit up like a Christmas tree, with mile after mile of pipelines, towers, and storage tanks.

Thankfully, the helipad was clearly visible in the middle of the complex. The landing lights had been left on, almost like they were expected.

As they made their descent, Steve felt his hand being squeezed. He turned to Maria who was looking tearful again and quite worried. He saw her lips moving but couldn't hear what she was saying. He assumed she was praying. He squeezed her hand in return and nodded to give her some assurance. We got this, he mouthed.

They were dropping in alongside a deserted black chopper. Steve checked the registration number. It was the one they'd seen at the airbase. But where were the occupants in this sprawling complex?

The pilot carefully positioned the police helicopter to hover two feet off the illuminated helipad. When he gave the signal, all three of them jumped out and crouched well below the rotors.

Steve heard a single shot ring out, quickly followed by a short woodpecker burst from a machine pistol. It seemed to be coming from a metal platform overlooking the helipad. The platform was connected to a raised walkway which disappeared behind rows of metal pipes.

They had dived for cover as more shots rang out. The helicopter powered up and started to climb steeply. Another burst of fire was aimed at it, tracer bullets slicing into the fuselage and sparking off the nose.

In one almighty blast, the windscreen of the helicopter shattered, sending a thousand crystal fireflies up into the air, only then to fall as shattered glass on the surface of the helipad.

Steve could see the pilot had been hit in his left shoulder and was wincing in pain. He still managed to keep control and narrowly avoided crashing into some power lines that ran close by.

Suddenly all the lights went out onboard. The helicopter melted into inky blackness overhead. Another burst of fire flashed up into the night sky, but the helicopter had turned sharply and made its escape.

Now the gunfire was directed back towards the crates they were sheltering behind on the edge of the helipad. Hot fragments of shrapnel were singing past their ears. Steve weighed up the odds. They'd need to cover over thirty yards of open ground to reach the safety of the nearest building. He could see an open door with a well-lit corridor inside.

Staying where they were wasn't an option. They'd come to rescue Hannah and Lawrence. Cowering by the helipad wasn't what Steve had in mind. In his limited research on oil refineries earlier that day, he knew most of the production processes were fully automated.

This meant there would be a minimal number of staff on site. He never got as far as discovering what the production processes were. Steve remembered the ground staff at the airbase totally ignored them. He guessed the employees on this site would do the same. No point in waiting for help. They'd have to figure this out themselves.

"Connor, could you keep him pinned down while we make a dash for that door?" Steve was secretly thanking Apicella for sending his best marksman with them. It gave them a good option.

"I got a better idea, sir. Sorry, Steve." Connor slowly moved into a firing position on one knee. He produced a telescopic sight from beneath his Kevlar body armour and clipped it into place. Then he inched his way round the side of the crate and made himself comfortable, the rifle pointing up towards the platform.

While he was doing this, shots continued to rain down, tracer lighting up the ground around them. If anything, the firing was getting more erratic, with stray bullets pinging off some metal cannister and a spaghetti of pipework.

Steve reckoned it was coming from a solitary machine pistol, but he wasn't prepared to risk it. There could be other gunmen waiting for them anywhere.

Connor stayed perfectly still, despite incessant fire coming perilously close to his helmet. He reminded Steve of a heron, poised over a riverbank, patiently waiting for the right opportunity to strike.

When the single shot was fired, it hardly registered as a dull thud, the silencer extension doing its job. To Steve's amazement, Connor immediately stood up and put down his weapon. He reached over and unclipped the sights as he turned towards them.

"He won't be causing us any more trouble, Steve."

They looked up to see a man half hanging over the platform edge, part of his brain shot away. Dark patches, Steve assumed was blood, were splattered over the wall behind him. His machine pistol lay silent, just the barrel protruding.

When he looked again, to his amazement, Steve saw the man move one of his hands, trying to grasp a railing. "Nice shot, Connor, but he's still alive. Let's go."

Maria worked out how to get to him. A series of metal stairways linked to a gantry platform, all illuminated by strong white lighting. Steve asked Connor to keep his eyes peeled for other threats as they climbed up the stairs.

He twisted awkwardly and banged his sore leg against a rail. The wound starting bleeding again.

By the time they reached him, Papa Doc had managed to haul himself back onto the platform. His eyes were closed. The machine pistol had slipped from his grasp and clattered down into some pipework. He was in bad shape, a pool of sticky blood oozing from the wound. Exposed patches of brain tissue were mixed in with splinters of bone and skull fragments.

"He's trying to say something." Maria moved across and knelt by his side. She couldn't bring herself to comfort him, knowing what he had done. Even so, she hated to see a soul in torment and hoped the suffering would soon end. There was nothing she could do to help him now.

In one last act of defiance, Papa Doc's eyes flared open as he summoned all his remaining strength to sit up. "You'll all die in the flames of hell."

With that, he slumped down onto the platform, eyes closing and slowly slipped away. As Steve checked his pulse, he had a look of confusion. "Strange last words. What do you think he meant?"

Maria suggested the man might have had some religion in his background before he went to the side of evil. Maybe he knew he was heading to the fiery place and looked forward settling the score with us down there.

"Anyway, we've got to keep moving. But moving where? They could be anywhere in here. It's like a metallic rabbit warren." Steve felt another twinge of pain. He pulled up his trouser leg and tightened the blood-soaked bandage.

There was nothing else for it. Time was slipping away. He drew a deep breath and remembered the forlorn look on Hannah's face as he closed the peephole. They must save them if it's not too late.

"We could split up and cover more ground that way, but I don't like it. This place gives me the creeps. There could be people hiding everywhere and we'd never even see them. Besides, our best chance to save Hannah and Lawrence is to stick with our marksman here." Maria squeezed Connor's shoulder which made him smile.

"I suggest we drop back to ground level and take the main path deeper into the complex. We need another one of your miracles, Maria." Steve started to move towards the first staircase when Connor spoke up.

"Steve, I visited an oil refinery in Texas on a school trip once. We were studying gasoline production in our science class. It was awesome. They gave us a little bottle of crude to take home."

Maria's curiosity was roused. "So how *do* they make gasoline, Connor?"

"They use a distillation column. The lighter oils, like gasoline, have a lower boiling point and rise to the top of the column when they turn to gas. The heavier oils, like bitumen, stay nearer the base of the column. It was fascinating." His eyes were shining as he explained.

"You mentioned boiling points. How does that work?" Maria probed. She nodded to Steve to stay patient as she sensed this was their best chance to find Hannah and Lawrence.

"They raise the temperature of the crude oil until it vaporises. Then all the different products separate out on cooling, so we get gasoline, LPG, kerosene, aviation fuel, and all the others." Connor explained.

"And where do they heat the crude oil, Connor." Maria was thinking back to Papa Doc's prophetic last words.

"In the fire box."

CHAPTER 43

Hannah hadn't slept well for days. The chance to shower and put on clean clothes was fully appreciated, even if they were ill-fitting overalls. The cell at the airbase proved to be quieter but no more comfortable. Therefore, it was no surprise she drifted off in the helicopter on the way over.

They had been blindfolded by guards and led to the aircraft. The tall man with the strong Caribbean accent seemed to join them and dismiss the guards. He made sure they were buckled into the rear seats. Hannah had travelled in helicopters many times and knew the familiar sounds of the rotors and vertical movements. The man poked them both with the barrel of his gun as a reminder not to give him trouble.

Although not asleep for very long, the dream was unforgettable. She was back in the village near Lake Turkana. Agnes was performing another healing ritual. The patient was a young boy who was very sick. When Agnes went into the trance, Hannah could see all her ancestors crowding into the room behind her. They stood in silence, looking down at the boy.

Suddenly Agnes stopped gyrating, turned to Hannah and gazed deeply into her eyes. At the same moment, all the ancestors looked up and stared directly at her. The strength of their presence was very powerful and left Hannah feeling shaken, even though she knew it was a dream.

While Agnes held her attention, she started to speak in her native tongue. The words were spat out with real venom. There was fire in her eyes. After she'd finished,

364

Agnes explained that she'd put a curse on the mining company for taking the lives of so many local people, for poisoning their well and for stealing their minerals from the good earth. The gods would make sure they didn't profit from their venture and bad luck would come to anyone who touched the crystals.

Hannah woke up as the helicopter touched down. She was able to hold Lawrence's hand briefly as they exited the aircraft. They were frog-marched along some concrete walkways, their footsteps echoing as they went. The pilot must have disappeared somewhere.

Hannah could tell there were only the three of them now, meaning their Caribbean guard was alone. He told them to walk more slowly. Hannah figured he must still be limping heavily on his right leg.

Eventually they were led into a room and told to stand still. Their hands and feet were tied with coarse ropes that chaffed her wrists, causing the skin to burn. She was standing up with Lawrence standing next to her. He complained the ropes were too tight, but it fell on deaf ears.

When the blindfolds were finally removed, they were in a very unusual room with a high ceiling. The floor was concrete and had six round metallic discs set into the middle of it. The discs ran in a straight line across the full length of the room, spaced around six or seven feet apart. The one nearest them was only two feet away.

Hannah twisted her head round and could see they were tied to rows of horizontal pipes that ran round all the walls, right up to the ceiling. Even the ceiling itself was crammed full of these metal pipes, all about three inches wide and set two inches apart, running in the same direction as the wall pipes.

The room was poorly lit by emergency lighting, set into the walls behind the pipework. Eerie shadows fingered out onto the unforgiving floor. She found it difficult to see the wall at the far end. It was a soulless and sterile place with no distinctive smells. The room was making her feel very uneasy.

Hannah realised they were alone. The tall guard had limped away through a heavy metal door next to them and bolted it from the outside. They both tried to free their hands, but the knots were too tight. Hannah thought it strange he'd used rope this time instead of handcuffs. They both started calling for help but the walls were soundproofed by extensive brickwork to which the pipes were attached.

Using all her strength, Hannah tried to wrench one of the pipes out of the wall, but the metal fasteners were too strong. Even using her legs proved unsuccessful, as none of the pipes would budge. They could only hope that Zelda Krasny would show them mercy, or that someone would rescue them. Both outcomes seemed very unlikely. How could Detective Sergeant Mole know where they were when Hannah herself didn't even know?

"What kind of a place is this?" Hannah was panting for breath after her desperate exertions with the ropes.

"I've no idea. Those metal discs worry me, especially this one." Lawrence nodded his head towards the nearest disc. "I can't image they emit gas as they would be in the ceiling. And as for what's running through these pipes, goodness only knows. Anyway, I think we're about to find out."

Muffled footsteps outside stopped abruptly at the door. A bolt was sliding back then the door slowly began to open. The figure of a woman, dressed all in black, slipped silently into the room. Hannah couldn't see her face due to the shadows. But she did see the gun that was pointing straight at them. The woman was not taking any chances.

The woman stopped three paces in front of Hannah and turned towards her. She stepped forward into the light. Zelda Krasny was barely recognisable from the woman Hannah had met at the Klinkenhammer Foundation, all those years ago.

She had not aged well. Her fair hair was cut very short, giving her an aggressive, almost masculine appearance that didn't suit her. Deep lines were etched over her forehead and round her eyes which had dark patches beneath them. Clearly sleep was a stranger to her as well.

She was much slimmer than Hannah remembered, the sweater and trousers almost hanging off her protruding bones. Her complexion was difficult to tell in the poor lighting, but the impression was someone decidedly gaunt, with hollow cheeks and red-rimmed eyes. Had she been crying? Hannah couldn't determine but the one thing she was in no doubt about was her demeanour. The steely look in her eyes and the red flushes over her neck. This woman was angry as hell.

The silence was broken by a soft, low voice full of vitriol. "You're in my house now. My grandfather installed this pipework by hand over a hundred years ago. It's still one of the most efficient furnaces in the world."

Hannah swivelled her head towards Lawrence who was looking down at the nearest metal disc. At least it answered that question. A burner so close would mean no chance of survival.

It also explained the ropes rather than handcuffs. There would be no trace.

Hannah was about to speak when Lawrence shook his head and whispered for her to stay quiet. Let's see what this woman has to say for herself. Maybe they would get some clues as to what was eating away at her.

Krasny continued. "We call this the fire box. It's the start of the process to separate out the products we make from crude oil. I've just had this fire box fully serviced, in your honour. You'll be the first to experience it. All the fire bricks have been replaced. The performance of the gas burners has been enhanced. Sadly, you won't be around to tell me."

It was Lawrence who spoke first. "Why are you doing this?"

Krasny didn't seem to hear him. She returned to her prepared speech. "The temperature will reach nearly one thousand degrees centigrade, hotter than any crematorium. You will both be dust after I open the valves. Say your goodbyes now."

Lawrence could see Hannah had started to cry. Her body was shaking as hot tears rolled down her cheeks. All the fighting spirit had seemingly drained out of her. Maybe she was right after all. At least they'd have had a chance with the crocodiles. This woman wasn't going to change her mind. She was holding all the aces.

He tried a different approach. Try to get her talking, distract her, play for time. "Zelda, what's happened to your brother? Hannah told me Sam was a lovely guy. She tried to help him. Is he OK?"

This time Krasny registered what he said. She looked straight at him. "My brother took his own life. He couldn't live with the pain any longer. I miss him every day. It still hurts. I promised him the guilty would be punished. Now it's time to settle this."

Silence. Hannah noticed Krasny had also started to shake, her trembling finger poised over the trigger. Hannah's voice came as a whisper. "I'm sorry to hear about your loss, Zelda. We tried our best for Sam. As we discovered, the odds were stacked against him."

Krasny exploded. "How dare you say that!! All along, you said you would cure him. I believed you, my whole family did. He deserved the very best, yet you failed him.

You failed me. Now you'll pay the price for that failure. A life for a life."

Hannah continued. "You want revenge. I'm the one you want, not Lawrence. Let him go. He's got nothing to do with this. This is between you and me. Please, Zelda, he's a good man."

"Too late for that. He's here now, he's part of you. He must die as well." Zelda turned towards the door.

Hannah had one last card to play. "Did Sam tell you the whole truth about his condition? About the other illness, the reason why our treatment didn't work?"

Krasny stopped. "What other illness? You'd better not be lying to me."

Hannah explained that, after the initial trials using the treatment they'd developed, they were getting some unusual test results. Sam had been diagnosed with Adult-Onset, Tay-Sachs Disease but further investigation discovered another genetic disorder in his body, also caused by an enzyme deficiency. It was known as Gaucher Disease.

"He was born with Gaucher's, but it went unnoticed. Very often the symptoms never actually appear. In Sam's case, when he got Tay-Sachs later in life, the two diseases combined to destroy his major organs, spinal cord, and the nerve cells in his brain." Hannah could see she had Zelda's attention. Clearly this was news to her.

"I told Sam this and showed him the evidence. I also sent copies to his doctor who thanked me for letting him know. I'm guessing Sam never told you because of the longer-term implications."

Zelda's eyes were looking down dejectedly. The convulsions had started again. Thankfully the gun was now pointing at the floor, but Hannah knew the woman was dangerously unstable and capable of snapping at any moment.

369

Slowly Zelda raised her head. "What implications?"

"Gaucher's is the highest genetic risk factor for Parkinson's Disease. Sam had extensive damage to the nerve cells in his *substantia nigra,* the area of his mid-brain that controls the production of dopaminergic neurons. It is the death of these neurons, we think, that causes Parkinson's, although the research continues. Either way, his quality of life would suffer a rapid deterioration which I'm guessing might have pushed him over the edge. I'm deeply sorry he didn't tell you."

"Why didn't you tell me at the time? I was paying for everything." Zelda seemed a little deflated but just as determined.

"I couldn't, under our strict protocols regarding patient confidentiality and privacy. Paying for the research doesn't give you the right of access to such personal information." Hannah explained. It was the truth but sadly she could see the truth wasn't what this was about. Zelda wanted revenge and Hannah was the chosen target. The situation hadn't changed.

"For years my brother suffered. Whether he had Parkinson's or not, you failed to help him. Now you both pay the price." Krasny didn't stop or turn this time. She exited through the door, bolting it behind her.

Hannah heard the footsteps fading away. "I'm out of ideas. We've reached the end of the road this time. I just hope she makes it quick."

"I'm not finished yet. Please keep believing. We'll get out of here, I promise." Lawrence was twisting his hands so hard there was blood staining the rope. It wasn't working. The ropes would be incinerated with them.

Hannah looked on in horror as a small but intense blue flame appeared in the centre of each disc, starting with the one furthest away. The heat from the disc closest to them was minimal but the threat was terrifying.

370

"They're pilot lights. As soon as she opens the main valves, the burners will ignite." Lawrence surmised. Hannah had already worked this out but thanked him for his analysis. She tried to lean over far enough to kiss him, but the gap was too wide.Instead, she told him how sorry she was it had to end like this.

Lawrence was trying to say how much he appreciated her trying to get him released when the burner at the far end of the room ignited.

The rush of heat to their faces was almost overpowering. Hannah screamed and twisted away from the powerful blue flame that almost reached the ceiling. The ropes bit deeper into her wrists, drawing blood this time. She managed to take a deep breath and hold it, bringing some degree of calmness into her. But the rising panic beneath the surface wasn't to be silenced.

Then the second burner ignited.

CHAPTER 44

After Zelda Krasny bolted the door behind her, she moved away from the fire box and clicked open her phone. She alone could override the Command Centre which was based on the far side of the refinery. She didn't want anyone else involved in controlling the ignition systems.

Even before she lit the pilot lights, she received a message from the Centre asking her to confirm she was taking full responsibility. At least someone was doing their job. She acknowledged and confirmed, then manually opened the gas valves that fed the six burners.

Satisfied all systems were functioning within acceptable parameters, she gave the command on her phone to light the first burner. The failsafe mechanism didn't allow all six burners to be ignited simultaneously in case there was a problem in the exhaust systems which could lead to an explosion. Besides, she was revelling in the delicious thought that they were going to die a slow and painful death. Revenge wouldn't bring him back, but it sure tasted sweet.

As she pressed the button on her cell phone to light the second burner, Krasny heard gunfire coming from the direction of the helipad. She smiled to herself as she assumed that part of the plan had worked. When Jeremiah told her what had happened at the airbase, Krasny knew the two British detectives would follow in the police helicopter.

The trap was laid. And, with their bodies already on site, it would be easy to incinerate them in the fire box.

372

No trace would remain, the NYPD could never prove anything.

But the gunfire continued longer than she expected. She lit the third burner. A nagging thought kept flickering in her mind. What if Jeremiah didn't take them out. What if they took him out. What if the police had arrived in force, leaving her standing there with the murder weapon in her hands.

Taking manual control of the ignition systems meant she could ignite the remaining burners from anywhere. It was time to get moving. Let them suffer a few minutes longer. The heat inside the firebox would be building. She could imagine the look on Hannah smug face. No amount of tears would extinguish those flames.

Krasny started to run towards the helipad. When she turned a corner, she saw three figures coming tentatively towards her. One looked like a police officer and was carrying a weapon. She dived down in time not to be seen, then crawled over to a different pathway. It ran parallel, through a forest of pipework.

She found a spot that gave her a clear view of the other path and crouched behind a pump casing. She singled out the police officer when the three of them came into view. She fired several rounds in quick succession and the officer went down. The other two dived for cover. There was no return fire.

Keep moving, there's no time to lose. Krasny ran towards the helipad, zig zagging even though she didn't sense being followed. The helipad was covered in broken glass. There was no sign of Jeremiah. They may have hidden his body, or he may have fallen behind some pipework. Whatever the case, if he was still alive, she knew he wouldn't betray her.

Krasny climbed into the pilot's seat of the black chopper and powered up the engines. She feared they may have disabled it, but the engines sprung into life as normal. She'd got her pilot's licence whilst at Princeton and had been flying helicopters and light aircraft for many years.

She took off into the clear night sky then radioed N90. She gave the 6th Avenue address as her flight destination. That would keep them satisfied until she was at cruising height and speed.

The chopper was accelerating as she flew over the outer rim of the refinery. She looked back in admiration for what her family had achieved. It was an amazing success story. The refinery was a money-making machine, sitting right in the heart of New Jersey. The site alone had been valued at several billion dollars.

She clicked onto her phone and ignited the fourth burner. A ping shortly afterwards confirmed it was fully lit and functioning normally. She'd estimated they couldn't survive more than a few minutes with three burners. The fourth meant death was certain.

She radioed N90 again as she skirted round Manhattan. There had been a change of plan, she told them. The new destination was the Krasny Airbase. They acknowledged and confirmed her new flight path was logged in. Her navigation system estimated she'd be there in less than thirty minutes.

Krasny called the airbase and asked them to make the necessary arrangements. Then she lit the fifth burner.

From under her sweater, she pulled out the photo of Sam. She looked at it lovingly, kissed him lightly on the lips and wedged the photo behind the control panel, in full view.

"This is for you, bro." She said out loud, unable to hear her own words through the headset. Picking up her phone again, she couldn't hold back the tears as she lit the sixth and final burner.

374

Steve heard the gunshots moments before Connor plummeted to the ground. He grabbed Maria's arm and dived for protection behind some heavy pipework. He could only watch as Connor dragged himself to safety, crying out in pain as he did so.

When he fell, the rifle clattered to the ground nearby. Now it lay silent in the direct line of fire. It couldn't be reached. Furthermore, they couldn't protect themselves if the gunman walked over and shot them dead.

They held their breath for a few minutes. No more shots. Steve called out to Connor. There was no reply.

The silence was finally broken by the sound of running feet. Steve guessed the gunman was heading towards the helipad. He had a decision to make. Pick up the rifle and go after them or continue the search for Hannah and Lawrence. He told Maria what he was thinking as they moved over to where Connor was lying.

"Steve, we came here to save them. There may still be time. We can track down the gunman later." Maria was adamant.

They quickly established that Connor had taken several bullets in the chest, but his Kevlar jacket had done its job. It was the two bullets in his right thigh that caused him to collapse. They managed to get him to sit up comfortably. His radio was still working so he could call it in.

Steve retrieved the rifle and propped it up near his right hand just in case the gunman came back. Maria did her best to tighten a tourniquet round the top of his thigh and put a cloth over the bloody wounds.

Connor managed a nod of appreciation for their help. "Look for smoke rising from the stack."

Steve and Maria continued at a quicker pace. They stopped looking for gunmen lurking in the shadows. It was too late for that now. They could both have been shot dead only a few minutes before. They had to keep going.

"There." Maria pointed to a large oblong box on stilts up ahead. White smoke was pouring out of a tall, metal stack above it. Steve thought he could hear muffled voices nearby.

They ran up some steps to a heavy metal door. It was bolted. Thankfully, the bolt wasn't padlocked. Steve tried to pull it back, but it was stuck fast. He could feel the heat coming from inside. It must have expanded the metal. The bolt lever itself was quite hot.

He tore off more of his shirt and wrapped it round the lever. They both put their hands over it and pulled with all their strength. Slowly the bolt began to move. Now they could hear the voices more clearly. They were screaming for help.

With one last pull, the bolt came all the way back and the door swung open. A blast of hot air scorched over them, knocking them backwards. They managed to grab hold of a handrail at the top of the metal steps, just in time.

When Steve narrowed his eyes and looked deeply into the furnace, it was like looking into the fires of hell. Three high columns of blue flame were searing the pipework in the ceiling. The temperature inside must be unbearable but that's where the voices were calling from.

"Wait here." He called over to Maria, but she was having none of it.

"Together, let's do this together." Maria grabbed *his* arm this time. Slowly they pushed themselves into the fiery heat.

Once inside, Maria went to Hannah's ropes and Steve to Lawrence's. The knots were very tight. Steve managed to pull open the rope around Lawrence's hands, but Maria was struggling. He left Lawrence to untie his own feet. Steve and Maria between them managed to pull Hannah's

376

hands free while Lawrence attended to the rope around her feet.

Hannah collapsed into Steve's arms as she came free from the pipes. Sweat was pouring from her face, which was bright red and badly scorched. She didn't have the strength to stand, so Steve and Maria helped her out of the furnace. They laid her down gently on the cool metal walkway outside. She was gulping down lungsful of cold night air.

"Where's Lawrence?" Maria shouted over the top of the noise coming from the burners inside the room.

They found Lawrence sprawled out on the concrete floor, the rope still in his hand. His face was blistered. Sweat had made rivulets over his forehead, cheeks, and neck. He was seemingly unconscious.

They tried to rouse him but there was no movement. They tried to pick him up, but he was too heavy. Steve looked at Maria. They may have to leave him here. The heat was too intense. They couldn't survive for much longer inside this inferno.

To Steve's astonishment, Hannah appeared in the doorway. She was standing upright but swaying a little. She'd tied some cloth over her hands and was using the doorjamb to steady herself.

Hannah stepped into the room and knelt beside Lawrence's head. She bent over and whispered something in his ear. Almost immediately, his eyes opened. Seconds later, the three of them were helping him to his knees. He was able to crawl. Clumsily, they all staggered out, just as the fourth burner burst into a tower of blue heat. The increase in temperature was overpowering.

With Maria's help, Steve was able to close the door. The relief was instantaneous. The raging fires were now contained within the fire box. In the minutes that followed, Steve heard the fifth then the sixth burners being ignited. It was that close. They could all have perished.

It took nearly half an hour for Hannah and Lawrence to recover enough strength to move. They were both in pain and felt dizzy. Throats were parched, faces were hot and stinging. But the nightmare was over.

Steve told them about Connor and the firefight at the helipad. Hannah's voice was very weak, but she was able to croak a few words about Krasny and her hunger for revenge. Steve was going to ask revenge for what when Maria suggested there would be time for that later. For now, they had to get the hell out of the refinery and find a doctor.

When they met up with Connor, he was on his feet and trying to walk using the rifle butt to balance himself. He winced in pain with every step but managed to make it back to the helipad.

Hannah, Lawrence and Connor collapsed on the edge of the pad while Steve and Maria went into the nearest building. They found some bottles of water and a first aid kit. As they were carrying them out, Steve could hear the rotors of a helicopter getting closer. He froze. "We must take cover. It could be Krasny coming back."

They ran outside, dropping the first aid kit. The helicopter was making a rapid descent, a search light adding to the landing lights, illuminating the whole area. Steve called over to the three of them to take cover. It was Connor who shouted back.

"This guy's our best pilot. He'll bring it down, no problem."

As the skids touched down, Steve could see the white and blue markings of the NYPD emblazoned along the fuselage. He let out a huge sigh of relief.

Although it was a different chopper, it was identical in size. It only had four seats, but they all managed to squeeze in, two plus the pilot in the front and three in the back. Steve was the last to board. As he did so, he could hear people running towards them, excited voices carrying over the steady drone of the rotors. All the pandemonium must have attracted the attention of the refinery night shift. Steve didn't want to hang around to see if they were friendly.

The helicopter sprang up into the darkness and veered away sharply towards the centre of Manhattan. Steve found himself sitting next to Hannah. There weren't enough headsets to go round. Only Connor, sitting in the front, put them on so he could talk to the pilot.

Very quickly, Lawrence fell fast asleep. Hannah's eyes were also closing when Steve whispered to her. "What did you say to him?"

"Who?" Hannah was settling into the seat.

"Lawrence. Back in the furnace. I thought we'd have to leave him behind. Whatever you said did the trick." Steve was feeling very tired himself now.

"Move your ass." Hannah replied, her chapped lips creasing painfully into a smile.

"Really?" Steve whispered in amazement.

"Well not exactly." Hannah was almost asleep. "I said the words I knew would get through to him."

Steve waited, his own eyes slowly closing, as the chopper powered up. They were heading for the New York Star Of Bethlehem Hospital. The illuminated helipad on the rooftop was shining at them like a red and white target through the front windscreen.

Steve didn't need to prompt her. He'd already guessed she used the three most powerful words in our vocabulary.

"I love you."

CHAPTER 45

Max Hartley, Comet 5, Blog 5, Rainbow Bridge, Tokyo, Sky Station 2.

I wish you could see this!! Thousands of people on both decks of the Rainbow Bridge (or Tōkyō Kō Renrakukyō, to give it its official name) and crammed onto the approach roads as far as the eye can see. All road and rail traffic has been stopped, which will bring the city to a standstill. I can see the police are out in force, doing their best to marshal the crowds.

Looking straight down, I can see all kinds of flags fluttering: Japanese, American, British, European, Chinese, and more. Everybody here is just as excited to see an end to climate change, especially as Japan has been so badly hit with wild weather in recent years. The global support for this race is truly amazing.

According to our chronometer, the local time is coming up to 1.00pm on Wednesday. The most important time factor though is twenty-three minutes - that's the current lead we have over our competitor. I'm told by one of the UN observers that they suffered some problems with their propulsion system and lost time over the Pacific.

Thankfully, our propulsion systems are behaving normally, although the thorium rod performance has decreased to ninety percent. Captain La Fontaine assures us it's not a major issue, but he is monitoring the situation closely. There are still no radiation leaks.

We are setting course now for Tiananmen Square in Beijing where we expect to see the biggest crowds. This race is hotting up!! Still a long way to go. Max Hartley out.

* * *

Zelda Krasny started her descent into the airbase on schedule. She could see her instructions had been carried out. The Gulfstream G280 was waiting for her on the apron. As she got closer, she could see the steps were down and the engines running, with streams of hot air funnelling out of the twin jets into the cold night air.

The plane had been built in Israel to her personal specifications. It had more powerful engines, a luxurious cabin design and extra fuel tanks, giving it an enhanced range of well over four thousand nautical miles. This brought Western Europe, Central and South America within reach. Tonight's journey would be much shorter.

Although she enjoyed flying on local trips, she had arranged for Michael, her most trustworthy pilot, to take this one. She needed time to think and let her emotions settle. Tonight's revelations about Sam's state of health had been unnerving.

Michael waved to her through the windscreen as she came into land. She was flying almost on autopilot as her mind wandered. Try as she might, she couldn't remember his surname.

She was feeling confused and upset. Revenge suddenly felt hollow somehow. The same questions kept taunting her. Why didn't Sam tell me? Why didn't anyone tell me? She kept imagining him sitting there, all alone, making his final decision. All hope gone. The only way out, he could see, was to end it all. She felt so helpless, so useless. Why didn't he call me? I never had a chance to say goodbye.

Zelda was fearful that her memory of Sam would fade away. While the desire to avenge his needless death was still there, it somehow kept a closer connection with him.

381

Knowing that the woman who failed him was still alive, meant this was unfinished business. Sam was owed a debt that Zelda would ensure was repaid. A life for a life.

But it just had been.

And in that one act, now that Hannah was dead, Zelda felt a fire within her had been extinguished. Once the anger, hatred and hunger for revenge had fully dissipated, the bonds of love and connection with Sam's memory would dissipate also. Her churning emotions had left her exhausted. She needed to rest. There was only one place to go.

Zelda needed to drop off the radar until the race was over and the NYPD had lost interest in the events of recent days. There was no better place than the Popeli Estate, bought by her father in the 1950's and renamed after the little village in Western Ukraine where the Krasny family originated. She remembered happy summer holidays there as a child.

Since she became head of the Krasny Corporation, Zelda had bought the whole island of Petit St Therese in the Southern Grenadines, employed many of the locals to work on the estate and keep the chateau in pristine condition. It was her special place. She valued her privacy there above all else and rarely invited any guests.

She had extended the only airstrip which could now handle the Gulfstream and some larger jets quite comfortably. It was, of course, a private airstrip, entirely for her use. She wanted to visit the island more often but running the corporation had been very demanding. Maybe it was time to change all that.

Over the years, Zelda had negotiated certain privileges with the local governing body, not least being awarded the Freedom of the Grenadines. Although she knew an extradition treaty was technically in place between the islands and the US Government, it was not always upheld.

They valued their independence fiercely. She believed they would offer her some protection if it was needed one day.

And that day may just have arrived.

She landed on the apron near the Gulfstream and powered down the rotors. She'd asked for some ground crew to meet her so they could take care of the chopper, but no one appeared. She didn't have time to find out why.

She put Sam's photo back under her sweater, exited the aircraft, stooped her head well below the spinning blades and ran over to the Gulfstream. She didn't have or need any luggage as the chateau was fully furnished with an entire wardrobe.

She entered the cockpit and sat down in the co-pilot's seat. Michael welcomed her onboard and closed the external door automatically. He re-confirmed their destination, having received the instruction earlier. He knew the route as he'd done this trip many times before. He was looking forward to relaxing for a few days in a beach hut himself if she'd allow it.

The Gulfstream was fully fuelled and ready for take-off. Michael checked the instruments as a matter of routine as they nosed their way towards the end of the runway. All other inbound and outbound flights had been delayed until they were airborne. Two cargo planes were stacked well to the south until the airspace was clear.

They cruised past a plane on an adjacent taxiway that had been held back. Michael waved to the pilots as they did so before turning onto the main runway itself. Their own air traffic controller confirmed they were clear to go.

Zelda rewarded herself with a secret smile as the twin jets powered up. The g force was exhilarating, pushing them back in their seats. She watched all the instruments come alive, a colourful array of digital information spinning across the control panel and ceiling above their heads.

She was keeping a close eye on the take-off speed. They accelerated past the windsock, with the main building complex sliding by out of the side window. The runway ahead was clear with guiding lights running like tracer bullets, tapering into infinity.

Suddenly Zelda saw red, blue and white flashing lights appearing from behind a low building. The convoy of vehicles was moving towards the runway ahead of them. She counted six police cars travelling at full speed. One by one they stopped in line, making a solid blue and white wall, blocking their take-off.

Michael was told to abort by their air traffic controller. This was under instruction from the NYPD. He looked across at Zelda. She had heard it also through her headset. He wanted to decelerate but she overruled him. When he took his hand off the throttle, she switched control to her position and pushed the throttle as far open as it would go. The plane responded with an immediate surge in acceleration.

Zelda did a quick calculation. They should get to take-off speed before they reached the police cars. It would be close, but they could clear them in time. She whispered a silent prayer and kept looking at the spinning numbers.

The police officers from all the vehicles moved away and took up kneeling positions in the grassy areas on either side. All except for one man who remained stationary in front of his car, right in the centre of the runway.

The gap between them was closing at alarming speed. They were just seconds away now. Once airborne, she would give Michael a piece of her mind. Just a few more seconds. They were almost on top of them. The man on the runway was crouching down but he didn't move from the spot.

Zelda wasn't expecting the hail of bullets that flashed out towards them. Some sparked off the two windscreens, some clipped the wings. She started pulling back the yoke. The plane responded. The nose was lifting.

Suddenly the plane lurched to the port side as bullets shredded the tyres under the wing. Try as she might, Zelda couldn't control it. Michael joined in but it was no use. They skidded off the runway and were heading straight towards a group of police officers. They ceased firing and ran back onto the runway for dear life.

The Gulfstream careered over the grass. Zelda threw the anchors on, but the plane was gathering momentum.

Up ahead was an extensive apron that was mostly deserted. The area was floodlit and ran all the way to the perimeter fence.

The Gulfstream was screaming now, the port wingtip had sheared off and sparks were flying from the damaged wheel strut that looked ready to collapse.

Zelda was glaring at the control panel. The numbers were dropping. The plane was slowing down at last. She looked up through the windscreen. That's when she saw it. She tried to scream but no sound came out.

Dead ahead was a large tanker, the words Krasny Aviation Fuel emblazoned down the side. They would be the last words Zelda and Michael would ever see.

Both plane and tanker exploded on impact. The tanker was knocked over fifty yards across the apron spilling fuel as it did so. The Gulfstream disintegrated, its own fuel tanks disgorging hundreds of gallons of aviation fuel directly into the inferno.

Fire engines raced to the scene but were unable to control the fire for quite some time. Flames powered up into the night sky, one explosion quickly followed by another as all the fuel burnt off.

Detective Apicella stood upright and walked slowly from the middle of the runway over to the edge of the apron. The heat was too intense to get any closer. Foam was being sprayed over the raging fires from four appliances. Slowly the flames were decreasing.

A colleague brought him a cup of weak coffee. "What a mess, Tony."

"Sure is. I had some questions, you know. Now she can talk to the angels."

"You think she's gone up there? With her track record?"

"Probably not."

CHAPTER 46

Max Hartley, Comet 5, Blog 6, Tiananmen Square, Beijing, Sky Station 3.

I was right, they were the biggest crowds so far. At first, I thought the Square was deserted. Then I realised people were packed in shoulder to shoulder so they couldn't move. There were no flags, no banners, and no bunting. Even so, as we swooped down over the square, everyone was waving to us most politely. It was an incredible sight.

We've heard through the UN observer team that our competitor is gaining on us again. They estimated our lead is now only fourteen minutes but that will be confirmed once they cross Sky Station 3. Apparently, they have fixed the problem with their propulsion systems and have speeded up. Also, we think they found some favourable weather conditions and took the 'tiger line' to narrow the gap.

The only major problem we've experienced on this leg is boredom and sitting still for too long. The lady next to me has joined an impromptu yoga class towards the rear of the cabin. I'm also told a pensions adviser on board is going to give a talk on planning for retirement. If it's free, I might join them.

Otherwise, our propulsion system performance dropped to eighty eight percent efficiency at one point but has since stabilised at ninety percent, which is well within normal parameters.

Anyway, lunch is being served. I think we have chicken and cashew nuts with pak choi and yangzhou fried rice. I might be tempted by a small glass of Riesling. Tough work this air race participation but someone must do it. Max Hartley saying Zaijian from Beijing.

* * *

Detective Inspector Lonsdale had slept well and was ready to do some real police work again. Having spent the previous day in meetings about the implementation plan for the Police's new policies on cultural responsiveness and diversity, he was itching to get his hands dirty in the field. Today, he had two formal interviews as part of the murder investigation. That was more like it.

He decided to skip breakfast, due to the promise of a Heathrow bacon sandwich washed down by a mug of builders' tea. A former colleague from Guildford Force Headquarters, Inspector Ken Hutchinson, was now based at Terminal 5 and promised to look after him. Getting through airport security on time would be so much easier.

He'd only been to Terminal 5 once since it opened in 2008, mainly because he preferred to fly budget airlines these days. Lonsdale found British Airways a bit too stuffy and expensive.

Although the Aviation Security Operational Unit at Heathrow was technically part of the Metropolitan Police Service, and therefore blood brothers, Lonsdale always believed they saw themselves as an elite force and, therefore, a law unto themselves.

He had been offered a transfer there many years ago, before he moved into CID, but the work didn't appeal. Too operational for his liking, especially the unsocial hours they worked. The growing emphasis on firearms training also worried him.

He had no regrets about that decision as he'd enjoyed his time in Surrey CID. The role in Guildford kept him on his toes for many happy years. Whilst he understood this recent transfer to the Met opened doors for him career-wise, he still missed life at the sharp end.

Dr Angela Fischer's BA flight from JFK had been delayed and was now due to touchdown at Heathrow at 0705 local time. Lonsdale decided to take the Heathrow Express from Paddington as he would be heading back to Westminster later that day and the traffic would be awful. He left the car proudly occupying its new underground parking space, a symbol of what can be achieved in the face of obstinate bureaucracy.

The previous evening he'd tried to read a paper Dr Fischer published some years back on nuclear fission and the principles underlying irradiation in the manufacture of uranium 233. He thought it would give him some insight into her work and provide context for their interview. If he could relate to what she did and talk her language, it might help to open her up and get to the truth. Sadly, the paper was impenetrable.

Ken Hutchinson hadn't changed at all. If anything, he had become even more evangelical since the last time they met. A card-carrying bachelor, his life was full of fresh starts, exciting adventures, and new beginnings. Advanced weapons training, anti-terrorism courses and meeting the threats of cybersecurity were just some of the latest feathers he'd added to his police career cap.

Outside work, Ken was now an instructor, specialising in advanced Ashtanga yoga, the most strenuous and repetitive he could find. This had been added to his Pilates, weights, spin, and boot camp sessions each week. He had just returned from two weeks at an exclusive ashram in Rishikesh. The book he was compiling of raw food recipes was soon to be published.

Lonsdale tried to breathe in as he savoured the delights of his greasy bacon sandwich with white bread. He resisted the tomato ketchup, after Ken told him how much refined sugar was laced into it. Smashed avocado on wholegrain toast, no butter, was Ken's preference.

"I thought you'd given up police work, David, and joined the indoctrination lobby. What is it - cultural responsiveness? I bet that goes over well in Snig Hill." Ken took a mouthful of jasmine tea.

Lonsdale had forgotten Ken was originally from Sheffield. His accent was now pure Windsor. "I haven't been further north yet than Corby. Let's not talk about this, it depresses me. At least for today, I'm back where I belong."

"Agreed. Then tell me about this woman you're meeting. You said on the phone it was a murder inquiry."

"I can't say too much but she's a colleague of a professor at Oxford University who was recently killed in New York under suspicious circumstances. I just need to ask her a few questions. Talking of which, we need to get moving. I see her flight just landed ahead of schedule." Lonsdale was gazing at the monitor in the police canteen.

Ken managed to get them through security without any delays, made easier by the fact that Lonsdale wasn't carrying any weapons. An interview room near the gate had been booked for him and discreet arrangements were in place to have Dr Fischer gently escorted from the plane.

A bleep on Ken's phone told him he must attend an incident in another part of Terminal 5. He apologised profusely.

"I'll catch you before you leave, David. Good luck. If you need anything, just press zero." Ken pointed towards the handset on the wall behind a drab metal desk. Three straight backed chairs sat silently nearby. There were no windows. More like an interrogation cell than an interview room but it would do, Lonsdale reflected.

390

After the door closed, Lonsdale arranged the furniture as best as he could to make the room more conducive to conversation. He read through his files and jotted down a list of key questions he wanted to cover. Then he waited. And waited. He paced the floor, re-read his notes, rehearsed his questions, checked his watch again, and waited.

The plane had landed forty minutes ago. What was the delay? Suddenly the door flew open. Ken was breathless and had obviously been running. Tiny beads of sweat glistened on his perfect brow. Maybe he was human after all.

"David, you'd better come with me."

A few minutes later, they emerged from a hidden corridor close to the arrivals gate. Ken flashed his badge to the cabin crew as they stepped off the airbridge and onto the plane. All the passengers had gone. There was a small crowd of BA staff gathered around a window seat in the first cabin.

As Lonsdale drew nearer, he could see a woman's head slumped against the window. From the photos he'd seen of her, he recognised Dr Fischer.

A member of the cabin crew took them to one side and explained. "We thought she was just asleep, but we couldn't wake her. She has a pulse but it's very weak. She'd been drinking gin and tonic all the way over. She said she was afraid of flying and gin calmed her nerves. We stopped serving her after six but then we found these in the seat pocket."

Lonsdale was presented with an empty half bottle of gin bought at JFK duty free. More worrying was the empty bottle of prescription sleeping tablets. "How many did she take?"

"We didn't see her take any. It was a busy flight, and we didn't have time. I've called the paramedics. An

391

ambulance is coming. I hope she's alright. She was muttering in her sleep. It must have been nightmares, she sounded quite upset."

It seemed to take an eternity to get Dr Fischer into the ambulance and on her way to hospital. In fact, it took so long that her suitcase had been fished out of baggage reclaim and was now sitting with her carry-on bags by the rear doors of the ambulance. Lonsdale sat opposite her, talking to the paramedic.

"She's unconscious, breathing normally and in a stable condition. That's all I can tell you. Her pulse and heart rate are both very weak. You'll have to ask the medical team for an update after they've run some tests." The paramedic explained in their usual, non-committal tone.

The journey gave Lonsdale time to think. This was an intelligent woman. The gin he could understand but an overdose of sleeping tablets as well? She would know the risks.

The staff at Hillsdown Hospital were very well organised on arrival. Dr Fischer was wheeled through to a private room and a medical team attended to her straight away. Lonsdale saw a doctor enter the room shortly afterwards.

He was left in a waiting room nearby with all her luggage. He was going to read through her file again but thought it would be a waste of time, today at least. Dr Fischer would be in no condition to answer any of his questions. He wanted to know she was OK and thought he'd better stay, for a while at least. He still had time to get over to Westminster for his next meeting.

He waited nearly an hour before the doctor emerged. "Detective Inspector Lonsdale?"

Lonsdale showed his ID card and began to explain who he was and why he was there, but the doctor obviously knew already and was prepared to continue.

392

"I've some bad news for you, Detective Inspector. Dr Fischer passed away ten minutes ago despite our best efforts to save her. She'd taken a massive overdose of narcozepam, the strongest antidepressant we can prescribe. I'm surprised her doctor recommended them as sleeping pills. Anyway, the combination of the high dosage with the alcohol was too much for her heart. I'm deeply sorry."

The doctor disappeared back into the room. Lonsdale slumped into the chair and took a deep breath. Only twice before in his long career had a suspect taken their own life. On both occasions, it left him deeply scarred. It took many years afterwards for the feelings of guilt to stop haunting him.

As he gazed down at the floor in quiet reflection, he noticed her handbag squeezed between the black leather carry-on and her suitcase. The zip was open. He thought it best to close it up before the bags were taken away. That's when he noticed the envelope with a BA logo on the front.

It was addressed to him. He opened it tentatively. It was written on BA headed paper.

Dear Detective Inspector Lonsdale,

My colleagues at Oxford enjoyed meeting you. They tell me you are a good man. I believe you are planning to interview me at Heathrow in connection with Robert's death. I'm sorry you've had a wasted journey.

For your records, I know nothing about how he died. It was just another tragedy in a lifetime seemingly full of tragedies. He was both a kind and generous man. He taught me many things and became like a father figure to me. His untimely death was a huge shock. I hope you find his murderer and bring him to justice.

393

As I watched the planes circling over St Louis before the start of the race, I had tears in my eyes. In many respects, Comet 5 *represents the pinnacle of my life's work. Robert and I spent many hours experimenting with different fuel types and propulsion methodologies. His decision to go with thorium was a stroke of genius. My knowledge of uranium 233 helped us develop a new concept for commercial air travel.*

In doing so, we have created a monster. Whether Comet 5 *wins the race or not, the danger remains. Once it is proven that nuclear-powered aircraft can provide a cost-effective, safe, and reliable form of aviation transport, pandora's box will be wide open.*

Nuclear fission is not natural. It is the most dangerous invention humanity has ever created. In my heart of hearts, I cannot allow this to happen. One day I firmly believe it will prove to be the biggest tragedy of them all.

Please forgive me, Detective Inspector, but I do know what I do. It will be my final act of conscience. I helped create this bastard child, now I must destroy it before it destroys everything we hold most dear.

Rest assured, my heart and mind will now finally find the peace I have craved for so many years.

Sincerely Yours,

Dr Angela Fischer, Brandon College, Oxford University

CHAPTER 47

Max Hartley, Comet 5, Blog 7, Gateway to India, Mumbai, Sky Station 4.

I can now correct the last blog. THESE are the largest crowds so far!! It's an ocean of faces, flags, flares, dancing, I've never seen anything like it. Surrounding the Gateway to India monument, all along the sea front in both directions, on the roof of the Taj Mahal Hotel and other buildings nearby, a flotilla of boats big and small in the harbour, just an amazing spectacle.

I can see musicians and bands playing, just wish we could hear them up here. The colours in India are always an inspiration. Today is no exception, it looks like an enormous street party. Mind you, the Diwali Festival is not too far away. Maybe they're just warming up!!

We are still in the lead but only by eight minutes. There were a few bumps on this last leg, mostly going over the Himalayas. I noticed we altered course a couple of times to avoid the worst of the storm fronts. Captain La Fontaine said it should get quieter on the next leg up to Cairo. It is currently clear over the Great Pyramid with settled weather. He said we're expected to extend our lead again, but he didn't say what he had in mind.

The impromptu yoga class has gained in popularity so there are now two classes. My suggestion to try laughing yoga fell on deaf ears. Still, it's keeping people active and might be the future of air travel. Yoga must be a good way to stave off deep vein thrombosis. The pension talk was deadly dull, so I made my excuses and left. Note to self: keep buying lottery tickets.

Our thorium rods remain at ninety percent efficiency which gives us peace of mind. Overall, we are in a good place and hope it continues. Max Hartley signing off from Mumbai.

* * *

Steve hadn't intended to stay with Hannah and Lawrence at the hospital. A doctor saw him limping and asked to examine the bullet wound on his leg. He vaguely remembered someone putting stitches in then it was all a blur.

He was woken by the sound of a tea trolley trundling down a corridor outside. The English breakfast tea was stewed and not too warm, but it was very welcome. A plate of crunchy toast reminded him they hadn't eaten since the bagels, well before the adventures of the previous evening.

"Save some for me, please." A voice drifted out from a pile of blankets on a day bed in the corner of his private room.

Steve was amazed to see Maria's sleepy head emerge. Dishevelled clothes and hair a mess, her face was still quite red and puffy but otherwise she seemed OK.

"I thought you were going home last night?" Steve offered her a mug of tea and a spare plate. She declined the serviette and tucked right in, smearing honey over every square inch of buttered toast.

"So did I. The chopper got called away. I was going to get a cab but waited until Hannah and Lawrence had been seen by a doctor. I was worried about them, especially Lawrence who looked quite badly burnt. They're just down the corridor. I was nearly out of the door when they told me you were being stitched up. When I came in here, you were dead to the world. I threw a blanket over you then sat on the day bed for a few minutes. I must have crashed out."

They ate all the toast and drained the tea pot. Steve had managed to get a spare phone battery from the chopper pilot last night. He'd put it in then switched the phone to airplane mode before he passed out. When he checked his messages, he'd just missed a call from Apicella. He called him back.

"She's dead, Steve. Plane crashed on take-off. We warned her, you know, and blocked the runway but she didn't listen. Irony is, she smashed into one of her own gas tanks. It just blew up."

A million questions were racing through Steve's mind. He picked one at random. "What were you still doing there?"

"After we arrested the guys in the jeeps, we planned to leave. The other guys on the base just pissed me off. I don't like private armies. They were obstructive as hell. So, we did some digging. And guess what? Your friend Zelda was leading the consortium behind the American plane in this air race. She's in bed with some real big noises, you know. No wonder there was heat coming down from upstairs."

"And is the heat still on?" Steve probed, suspecting he knew the answer.

"No, strangely enough, it's all gone quiet. They approved you having the chopper. It's totalled, by the way. Still, we got one of your cars back this time, that's something."

"But how did you know she was going to the airbase? And where was she flying out to?" Steve was delighted to see Maria had found a pot of fresh tea and more toast.

"My spy in the camp. Officer Doyle called me. He's OK. They took the bullets out last night. Some physio and he'll be as good as new, they said."

"I'm pleased to hear it. He'd lost a lot of blood. We'll look in on him before we leave. We owe him big time. And you, come to that. It was a good move sending him with us. Thank you."

"Anyways, he said she'd taken the Krasny chopper. We tracked her through N90. Then the chick hopped into her private jet. Nice. She owns an island in the Caribbean and was planning a little vacation while we were cooling our heels. Gotta hand it to her, the kid had style."

"Style?" Steve spluttered into his tea. "Murder, kidnap, extortion, tax evasion and we haven't even got to the other stories yet. She was a nasty piece of work, private island or not."

"Look, Steve, I wanted you to know you've got upstairs interested. They like what you're doing so you're getting help with the investigation." Apicella sounded almost apologetic.

"Now we know she's connected with this air race; I've been told to dig deeper."

"What does that mean, Tony? Are you taking this off me?" Steve looked at Maria who flashed him an angry look. "I mean us, taking it off us?"

"No, nothing like that. Let's just say, the investigation is being taken more seriously. That means, more resources, greater airtime. Anyways, I got a cousin in the SLMPD. He's sending a team over to St Louis Airport to sniff around in these race camps. Something smells funny and I wanna know what it is. I'll let you know what they find." Apicella disconnected.

Steve updated Maria as they went looking for Hannah and Lawrence. They'd been moved to the Burns Unit. According to the nurse, they'd not slept much and hadn't eaten anything that morning.

Hannah had bandages over her face and arms. She was sitting up in bed and looking very sorry for herself. In the next bed, Lawrence was asleep and snoring gently. He also had bandages covering most of his face. Some of his hair had been shaved off when they examined his head. They'd both been given sedatives. Hannah was still lucid, but obviously in some pain.

"I never got a chance to thank you both last night." Hannah whispered, her voice still quite hoarse. "You saved our lives."

"All in the line of duty, ma'am." Steve mimicked the New York accent which helped break the tension. They all managed a smile. "Now we need to know the whole story. Did you say you were in Kenya?"

Hannah started to relate the events of the last week. When she got to Father Patrick Kelly, she was overcome with emotion and broke down in floods of tears. The nurse came and needed some persuading Hannah was well enough to continue their conversation.

"We discovered Krasny was running a mining operation near Lake Turkana. They're extracting kamacite, a rare alloy deposited on Earth by meteorites. It's very rich in minerals used to make high performance lithium-ion batteries, phones, EV's, whatever." Hannah had banished the images of Father Kelly being torn to pieces. She needed to continue as she wanted to know how it all fit together.

"That makes sense now. Krasny bought the rights to a green hydrogen propulsion system. It's in the American plane." Steve picked up their part in the story. He could see Hannah hadn't realised the race had started. "Hydrogen recharges the batteries which power the plane. That's where the kamacite must come in."

"But their mining operation disturbed arsenic deposits that poisoned the groundwater. Many people were sick and dying. That's where we came in.

"We discovered Krasny was in cahoots with corrupt Kenyan ministers and Vatican officials. If they could drain the lake, and make it look like climate change, it would drive local people away and allow more extensive mining operations. Before we could expose them, they brought us here." Hannah was getting tearful again. Steve offered her a glass of water and suggested she get some rest, but Hannah wanted to continue.

"You see, Steve, Zelda Krasny blamed me for the death of her brother. It's a long story but it wasn't really my fault. She didn't want to know the truth about his medical condition. She just wanted revenge. After we moved to Vatican City, she lost touch with me. Then, by chance, Lawrence and I turned up in one of her mining operations in Kenya. She flew us here for the sadistic pleasure of killing us herself. Her plan would have worked if you and Maria hadn't turned up. I can still feel the heat from those burners."

Maria had been sitting quietly, taking it all in. "So, what are you going to do, now you've ended up in New York? I mean, after you've both made a full recovery."

"As it turns out, Maria, I'm due to give my first speech at the UN as Papal Legate, sometime next week. I can't remember when, but my office will know. After this ordeal, I got things to say." Hannah tried to smile again but the pain in her cheeks was too great. Her eyes looked very tired.

They decided to let Hannah get more rest. Lawrence had stop snoring but was still fast asleep. Steve commented it was nature's best healer. That and time.

Steve and Maria were heading back to collect their things when Steve's phone chimed into life. It was Lonsdale. Steve remembered he was due to meet Dr Fischer that morning. It suddenly felt quite irrelevant now that Stannard's murderer and the woman behind it all

400

were both dead. Still, it was one of the loose ends that needed tidying up.

"Sir, thanks for the call. How did it go with Dr Fischer?" Steve found an empty room and put the call on speaker.

"I'm sorry to say, Detective Sergeant, Dr Fischer is dead. She took her own life on the plane coming over. They couldn't resuscitate her. She left me a suicide note. It's all very worrying." Lonsdale sounded more perturbed than Steve could ever remember.

"Took her own life? What did the letter say?" Steve was trying to process this latest news. Another untimely death. They were starting to tally up.

"That's what's so worrying. Firstly, it was written on BA headed paper, meaning it was probably a last-minute decision. The balance of her mind was clearly upset but, in my experience, most suicide letters are written well before the deed is done." Lonsdale explained.

"Do you think she was forced into it?" Maria suggested. Steve nodded; he'd had the same idea.

"No, I don't think so. In the letter, she states she had nothing to do with Stannard's death. Curiously, she refers to his *murderer* and hopes we catch *him*. We've never called it a murder except between ourselves. And how did she know it was a man that did it? I think she knew more than she was letting on."

"Or wanted to know?" Steve prompted. "Sounds like she became embroiled in all this *after* Stannard's death."

"Indeed. I feel her conscience was carrying a heavy burden regarding her former boss. Add that to her conflicting beliefs about nuclear fission and you've got one truly mixed-up individual." Lonsdale surmised.

"But that's not all, sir, is it? I sense there's more." Steve knew Lonsdale of old. He always saved the best until last.

401

"Very perceptive, Detective Sergeant. Let me quote her actual words. *Please forgive me, Detective Inspector, but I do know what I do. It will be my final act of conscience. I helped create this bastard child, now I must destroy it before it destroys everything we hold most dear.*"

"Crikey, what does that mean?" Steve looked at Maria who was shaking her head.

"I've absolutely no idea, Detective Sergeant, but I think we have very little time to find out."

CHAPTER 48

Max Hartley, Comet 5, Blog 8, The Great Pyramid At Giza, Cairo, Sky Station 5.

I'm always amazed by the Pyramids. From the air, their symmetry, scale, and symbolism are truly awesome. How on Earth did the Egyptians manage to build them? The Pyramids prove they were a remarkable race of people.

But for all their size and majesty, it's the Sphinx that still draws my admiration. There's something magical and mysterious about it. I'm sure our aircraft was caught in a magnetic wave as we flew over. I know it's not very scientific these days to talk about spiritual powers, but this place always invokes in me the need to think more deeply about such possibilities.

Anyway, Captain La Fontaine was right. We've increased our lead but only by three minutes since Mumbai. Our competitor is eleven minutes behind which is too close for comfort. Conditions were very smooth on this leg. We must cross the Mediterranean next where anything can happen weather-wise.

Our propulsion system is hovering around ninety percent efficiency. The radiation level did increase slightly but we were never in danger, and it has since settled down.

The mood on board is buoyant with a bridge club well established and a mini-golf competition heating up through the inflight entertainment system. The big winner, though, remains yoga and meditation, with three competing groups now vying for new devotees.

Paris next then London. The finish line is a short hop from there across the ditch. This race remains wide open. Max Hartley signing off from the desert.

* * *

If anything, Lonsdale's mood had darkened by the time he reached the Houses of Parliament. He kept thinking about Dr Fischer and the torment she must have been facing. Her words haunted him. *It will be my final act of conscience.* He was hoping Quentin Fitzgerald-Manning could shed some light upon what she insinuated. *Attack was the only option.*

After being left to stew in the waiting area for twenty minutes, Lonsdale took decisive action. Kicking up a fuss with the security team brought an instant response. A trouser-suited assistant appeared bearing a tray of coffee and biscuits, apologising profusely that Quentin had been detained unexpectedly and would be free in a few minutes. Lonsdale showed his irritation but knew it wasn't her fault. He gratefully accepted the tray and settled down again, having made his point.

"My sincere apologies, Detective Inspector. Please come through." Quentin himself escorted Lonsdale through the labyrinth of corridors and passageways to a grand meeting room on the second floor. It offered sweeping views over the Thames. The room could have seated twelve in comfort. More coffee and biscuits awaited them, but Lonsdale wasn't going to acquiesce to any more soft soap treatment.

"Dr Fischer is dead." Lonsdale watched for Quentin's reaction. More of a shock this time than over Stannard's death but still not total surprise. *How deep does his involvement go?* Lonsdale needed to find out.

404

"She took her own life. There was a suicide note, addressed to me. Clearly, she couldn't live with the consequences of her own actions. The letter makes certain allegations. I'd like to discuss these with you." Lonsdale fixed him with a cold stare. He had the upper hand with the contents of the letter but knew it wasn't enough to rattle a seasoned political animal like Quentin Fitzgerald-Manning.

"I'm not sure what you're implying, Detective Inspector. Are you saying I had something to do with her suicide?" A few feathers ruffled but otherwise comfortable.

"Yes, that's exactly what I'm saying. I can see she was dragged into your plans at the last minute. You put her under enormous pressure. What you made her do must have pushed her over the edge. I'm holding you directly responsible. I want to hear everything. It's your last chance to avoid a very long prison sentence, so start talking." Lonsdale was bluffing but he had nothing to lose.

If it all came out that he intimidated a suspect, he may have to make a humbling apology and receive a slap on the wrist. Some garden leave on full pay pending further investigation? Well, it couldn't be worse than turgid hours spent in the implementation of policies promoting greater cultural responsiveness and diversity.

Besides, time was against them. Whatever Dr Fischer had done must be imminent, otherwise why end it all now?

"What plans? What the devil are you talking about?" Fitzgerald-Manning had raised his voice for the first time. He'd stopped pacing the floor and was standing with his back to the window. The light reflecting off the river gave him an undeserved halo, leaving his face bathed in sinister shadow. "I only met the woman twice. She dealt

405

mainly with the engineering team. Before you come in here accusing me, you need to get your facts right."

Lonsdale opened his briefcase and pulled out a wad of documents. He carefully laid them out on the table in front of him but managed to keep the confidential source names covered up.

"I'm glad you mentioned facts, so let's start there. Your tax affairs have been worrying the Inland Revenue for many years. Suddenly, all arrears were cleared with a single lump sum payment from a numbered Swiss bank account. Do I have your attention, Mr Fitzgerald-Manning?"

A silent nod. Fitzgerald-Manning lowered himself slowly into his chair. The conversation had clearly taken an unexpected turn.

"Earlier this year, the Serious Fraud Office were alerted by an informant about your reckless gambling debts." Lonsdale fingered another buff folder, as if to say it's all in here.

"An informer? Who said this? I do not have a gambling problem. How dare you say that."

Lonsdale ignored his weak protestation and carried on. "Magically, all debts to the casinos, bookmakers and online betting sites have been cleared in recent days. I'm waiting for a report on how those payments were made, but I think I can guess. Your offshore accounts have been active."

The tension in the room was palpable. Lonsdale took a few moments to study his face. He wasn't seeing genuine anger, not 'this is an invasion of my privacy', not 'how dare you', not even a 'you'll be hearing from my lawyer'. No, this was quick thinking for the benefit of damage limitation. Fitzgerald-Manning was trying to work out how much Lonsdale knew. It was controlled panic. What had that bloody woman put in the suicide note?

For all that the SFO and HMRC reports contained damning information, Lonsdale knew they proved nothing and would not stand up in court. A good defence lawyer would drive a bus through Lonsdale's arguments. He needed more proof. Time to play another card.

"My colleagues in the NYPD have applied to the court for access to Zelda Krasny's private phone records. If you were to tell me how many times you spoke to her recently and what those calls were about, it might shorten your sentence. We can prove collusion. Your career is over. You're going to prison. The question is, for how long. More importantly, from your point of view, what will happen to you when you're behind bars. Life can be tough for people like you if you get my meaning."

Fitzgerald-Manning was staring silently at the table, lost in thought. Was he regrouping, weighing up his options, preparing to fight back?

Lonsdale didn't want to give him time to decide. "You were the last person to speak to Robert Stannard. According to his phone records, the call lasted eight minutes, plenty of time for him to tell you where he was going that evening. You're implicated in his murder, and I want to know why?"

Silence. If he was ready to fight back, he wasn't showing it.

It was time to play his hunch. Lonsdale was past the point of no return. A confession was his best outcome now. "This is about money, isn't it? You're a greedy, grabbing bastard, with expensive tastes and an ego that won't tolerate second best. You're above all that. Creaming off the top from your own consortia wasn't enough. You've done a deal with your competitor to throw the race, on condition they cut you in on the winnings."

"That's preposterous!! I've personally invested thousands in this bloody race." He was on his feet again.

Lonsdale was encouraged by the lack of any retaliation. He pressed on. "Stannard wouldn't play ball, so you leant on poor, confused Dr Fischer. She was too weak to stand up to you. Now she's paid the ultimate price for getting involved with a snake like you."

"Where's your proof, Lonsdale?" The voice was little more than a whisper. His castle walls were crumbling.

"Yesterday I spoke to one of your consortia members. He called me and sounded quite upset. He's asked you several times for an audited set of accounts. Each time, you've denied him. He thinks you've had your sticky little fingers in the till, Quentin, and are playing for time. You think if you win, prize money paid, everyone happy, no more questions. But you're wrong. The questions are already being asked." Lonsdale lied.

He saw Quentin flinch. Time to go for the jugular. "And if you lose, you'll be long gone by the time the holes appear. Which tax haven do you have in mind, by the way? One without an extradition treaty with the UK, no doubt. Northern Cyprus, Honduras, Belarus? Or maybe you fancy a new life in Japan, Russia, or Cambodia."

"If you're so sure of yourself, Lonsdale, then arrest me." The first look of defiance swept across his face. He stood tall, like someone was pulling strings attached to the top of his head. Maybe they were.

Lonsdale was prepared for this. "You'll be arrested when I've stopped *her final act of conscience*. I want to know what you made her do."

A quiet tap on the door. Fitzgerald-Manning responded to the entrance of Trouser Suit, who reminded him his next meeting was about to start. Also, the UN Secretary-General was on schedule and looking forward to meeting him later. He smiled at her, thanked her for the interruption and asked her to show the Detective Inspector out.

Lonsdale gathered up the papers and put them back in his briefcase. "I understand there's a party tonight in the roof top garden. You're welcoming the race to Sky Station 7. I will see you then. Please don't think of going anywhere. We need to finish our business."

"Sadly, you won't get in. It's invitation only and there are no more places available, Detective Inspector."

"We'll see about that."

CHAPTER 49

Max Hartley, Comet 5, Blog 9, The Eiffel Tower, Paris, Sky Station 6.

I don't care what anyone says, I think the Eiffel Tower is one of the wonders of the modern world. Iconic, imaginative, elegant, a breath-taking spectacle from any angle and a stunning feat of engineering. The Eiffel Tower has become synonymous with the City of Light.

On this memorable day, we've been afforded a magnificent view that Gustave Eiffel himself could only have dreamt about, looking down from the window of a passing aeroplane. It is fitting in a way that the race should come here as Paris has played such an important part in the history of aviation.

When Charles Lindbergh landed at Le Bourget Airfield at 10.22pm on Saturday 21st May 1927, he'd been flying solo, non-stop for thirty-three hours across the Atlantic. Paris was his dream destination.

A crowd of well-wishers, estimated at 150,000 strong, pulled him from the Spirit of St Louis in jubilation and carried him shoulder-high around the airfield. The whole world was united in celebration. Lindbergh became a household name.

Today, I estimate nearly double that crowd is lining the streets surrounding the Tower and spilling out along the banks of the Seine. Again, the world is watching, all eyes are on Paris. Can humanity pull together to eliminate fossil fuels from our skies? Yes, of course we can.

Lindbergh was competing for the Orteig Prize. What's at stake now seems much more important. The prize this time is our survival as a species.

Unlike for Lindbergh, we have a true race on our hands. Our competitor has overtaken us. Apparently, they followed a more northerly route from Cairo and caught a favourable jet stream over the Balkans.

They swept into the lead after we crossed the Alps. According to the UN Observer team on board, they flew over Sky Station 6 four minutes ahead of us and are now heading for London.

There's no chance for us to catch them up before Sky Station 7. To pass them again, in compliance with all the safety regulations, we'll need to get clever somewhere mid-Atlantic. For now, we can't let the gap widen. Captain La Fontaine is confident we can still win this.

Onboard, our party mood has gone. No one wants to come second. The yoga classes have moved more towards meditation and reflection. Things will be tense until we know how we stand at Sky Station 7. London calling, Big Ben next. Max Hartley out.

* * *

They were walking towards the Manhattan hotel where Steve first met Connie Pemberton. As they moved in and out of shadows along the sidewalk, a relentless sun climbed high above the tallest buildings into a sparkling blue sky. At street level, the air remained sticky and unseasonably warm for an October morning.

Todd du Prez was much taller than Steve had imagined him. Connie stood a good six foot in her designer jeans and suede pumps, yet Todd towered six or seven inches above her. Together they made a formidable couple. Todd's handshake was solid, unwavering, and very deliberate. He looked like a no-nonsense, tell-it-straight sort of guy which Steve liked. He was pleased they'd agreed to the meeting.

411

Connie had chosen the same booth off reception and ordered the coffees and water. As they sat down after the introductions, Steve reflected on how different this meeting felt than the first time he'd met her. Tearful, angry, frightened, Connie had been so reluctant to talk about the kidnapping. Today, a more composed, relaxed and determined woman sat before them.

"His full name was Jeremiah Winston King. He was a retired soldier, semi-professional heavyweight boxer and part-time security guard. He was working as a bouncer at an exclusive nightclub in Kingstown when they met some years ago." Steve explained as Maria passed over a photograph of the man, minus his ski mask.

"What, Kingston, Jamaica?" Connie enquired. "I knew his accent was Caribbean."

"No, Kingstown in The Grenadines." Steve was referring to his notes. "Zelda's family owned one of the islands. She made as many enemies as friends. Someone took a shot at her outside the nightclub where he was working. Jeremiah got caught in the crossfire. A bullet shattered his right knee. Zelda took him under her wing and made him Head of Security for Krasny Petroleum. That's when he relocated to New York."

Todd looked puzzled, as he handed the photo back. "I don't get it. Why would a billionaire corporate animal like Zelda Krasny get involved with a low-life thug like this guy?"

"For the very reason we're all here, Todd." Maria jumped in. "She wanted an enforcer, someone to do her dirty work. She'd invested in lithium-ion batteries with the intention of screwing up any new developments. Then, this air race came along. A fossil-fuel free aviation industry suddenly became a reality. So, if she can't stop the race, she might as well corner the market for green technology. But there was a problem."

412

"You mean us?" Todd leant over and squeezed Connie's hand.

"Exactly." Maria continued. "She knew you wouldn't sell, after testing the water through Slaker Nadzy. Instead, she went for blackmail. That's where Jeremiah comes in. Zelda's plan would have worked, had not some bean counter at the IRS spotted a possible fraud and alerted the NYPD."

"Which brings me to one of the questions I wanted to ask." Steve topped up the water glasses. "Do you want your company back? I don't understand your legal position, but you have our full support if you try. We know you were forced to sell, which goes against my sense of justice."

They looked at each other for a few moments before Connie explained they'd considered it and decided to leave things as they were. She'd moved past the anger and injustice. She was just relieved their family was safe and well.

Also, she explained, they'd jumped off the corporate treadmill of constantly worrying about cashflow, regulatory pressures, competitor dirty tricks, trying to run the business and wondering when the next crisis would bite them.

"Todd's been given a clean bill of health. We've got a new life to look forward to. I know my granddaddy wouldn't approve but he's not here anymore. We've investigated legal action but don't have the stomach for it. If our technology can help save the planet, that'll make us both very happy."

"I do understand. I would imagine going down the legal road would be slow, expensive, and emotionally draining." Steve had expected their decision but wanted to make sure. They looked so relaxed and happy together.

Clearly their new lifestyle suited them, without the stresses and strains of Pemberton Electronics.

"It's kind of you to ask but I'm guessing that's not why you set up this meeting, is it Steve? I think I know how you work now." Connie glanced at Todd then pushed back deeper into the sofa. "You mentioned kamacite on the phone."

"Am I that transparent?" Steve offered a smile. "OK, we need to know the technical implications of what we're dealing with here. Some industry insight would be appreciated. What's your take on kamacite?"

Todd stepped in. "Connie told me you were interested. I'd never heard of kamacite, so I did some digging. As everyone knows, there's huge demand for the raw materials needed to make lithium-ion batteries. Alumina, lithium, nickel, cobalt, manganese, they're all in increasingly short supply. This kamacite stuff could be a God send. According to my research, it's packed with high grade minerals, everything a manufacturer needs. Also, there's new crystals in it we know little or nothing about. Kamacite could be very important. A game changer, in fact."

"Important enough to kill for?" Maria had started tapping notes.

"You betcha." Clearly Todd had been thorough with his homework. "Our technology is still in its infancy. With climate change, we're being pushed into finding better ways to produce and store energy. Lithium-ion batteries are a clumsy, expensive, and environmentally unfriendly solution. Maybe kamacite could open new markets, but it poses some big questions."

"Like how much kamacite there is on Earth, given that it only got here in meteorites?" Steve chipped in.

"Well, I was thinking more about finding the source." Todd leaned forward and lowered his voice, even though no one was in earshot. "It sounds like science fiction, but those meteors must have come from somewhere. Maybe there's a planet out there full of kamacite. Find that, secure the mining rights and bingo, no more supply problems. Just a thought."

"An interesting thought. The mining rights on this planet have caused enough trouble." Steve had got the answer he needed. No wonder Zelda Krasny had invested so heavily in her Kenyan mining operations. Steve nodded to Maria. It was time to leave, but she had a final question.

"Todd, you mentioned some other crystals in kamacite. What exactly did you mean?"

Todd initially brushed off the enquiry, but Maria persisted. Clearly there was something else on his mind he was reluctant to talk about. Eventually, after an exchange of glances with Connie, he offered a simplified explanation.

"Electricity came of age in the nineteenth century. The first electric streetlights appeared in the 1870's. Edison patented the lightbulb in 1880. Electricity remains fundamental to our thinking about science today. Indeed, here we are discussing how to generate and store electricity quicker, cheaper, and cleaner. My belief is that science hasn't moved on."

Maria looked puzzled. "Moved on to what?"

"Exactly." Todd looked delighted with her reaction. "I don't think we're searching the unknown for new discoveries like Faraday, Edison, Swan, or Tesla did. Today, it's all about money. We're staying with what we already know but trying to make it more cost-effective. Maybe kamacite could open our minds to new ways of thinking, as electricity did for nineteenth century scientists."

"So, you're saying we still think electricity as the answer to our prayers instead of finding new forms of energy?" Steve could see more than a grain of truth in his argument. Money, fear, and greed all lay at the heart of Krasny Petroleum.

"Until scientists stop being accountants and return to being explorers, we may never take the next step in our evolution." Todd explained. "Everyone's excited about this air race, yet there's nothing new about the science behind it. Maybe our answers will come from beyond the stars."

Steve had put his phone on silent at the start of the meeting. The illuminated screen told him he'd just missed a call from Apicella. It was soon followed by a text marked urgent, call me. They really did have to go.

Connie insisted on paying for the drinks. Steve noticed tears rolling down her cheeks as they said their goodbyes. On reflection, a certain kind of justice had been served. The criminals hadn't got away with it. Their intervention had been worthwhile.

Outside on the street, he found a quiet doorway and called Apicella. It was answered on the first ringtone. He put the call on speaker for Maria to listen in.

"I just heard from the search team in St Louis." Apicella sounded anxious. "They went over everything with a fine-toothed comb. The American base was clean, although they did find some incriminating evidence we could've nailed Krasny with. Too late now, you know."

Steve didn't like where this was going. Apicella didn't spook that easily. His voice was thick with worry. "Tony, what *did* they find?"

"That's the thing, they didn't really know what it was, at first. It was so well hidden, they got suspicious and checked it out."

Steve's mind was racing back to conversations about *Comet 5*, Stannard's murder, the nuclear propulsion system, Dr Fischer's suicide. She sealed the molten salt reactor unit. The chilling phrase in her letter to Lonsdale. *It will be my final act of conscience.*

"Steve, they found a thorium rod. It's one of the rods intended for the propulsion system in the plane. You're Fischer woman didn't insert it. What was she playing at?"

Steve looked at Maria, who whispered that the rod itself wasn't radioactive, in that sense. There was little risk to human life, or any danger of the airfield being contaminated. But what about the plane and the performance of the propulsion system, Steve suggested, if one of the rods was missing? Is that why she left it out? To ruin their chances of winning the race?

Maria reminded him that *Comet 5* flew across the Atlantic with only four rods and that it had enough nuclear fuel onboard to stay airborne for years. The fuel capacity didn't affect the plane's speed or performance. They were told the extra rods were only inserted so they could analyse engine output and efficiency back in the lab.

All this seemed to tally with Max Hartley's blog, which had been talking about the engines working at ninety percent capacity. If one of the rods was missing, maybe that explained the reduced performance. None of this answered Apicella's question.

"Tony, did they find any paperwork about the reactor?" Steve tried a different angle. He had a hunch, but it was too horrific to contemplate.

"Sure, it's all in order. The reactor was sealed, tested, and signed off. The FAA were happy. The plane was legit and cleared to fly."

Maria suddenly looked shocked. The colour drained from her face. Steve realised his hunch was catching.

"Tony, if all the cylinders in the reactor were full when it was sealed, yet one of the rods was missing, what did Fischer put in its place?" Steve checked his watch. The planes could only be minutes away from Big Ben. One person must know the answer. His name was still on their whiteboard. *Quentin Fitzgerald-Manning, OBE.*

Maria's whispered voice was cracked but still managed to find the words. "This was planned before the race. They knew Stannard wouldn't cooperate. It was down to him to sign off the reactor. That's why he was taken out of the equation. Then they pressurised his sidekick, Dr Fischer. She was already battling her own demons. *Cognitive dissonance* had weakened her resolve. Her conscience had gone AWOL. What else did Lonsdale say she put in her letter - *I helped create this bastard child, now I must destroy it.*"

"What're you guys talking about?" They'd forgotten Apicella was still on the line.

The only chance now was Lonsdale. Steve had to get off this call.

"Tony, we're talking about a nuclear disaster."

CHAPTER 50

Max Hartley, Comet 5, Blog 10, Big Ben, London, Sky Station 7.

They must really have been pushing it. We increased speed over northern France but couldn't get near them. Apparently, we're at least fourteen minutes behind but will have that confirmed when we both pass over Big Ben, Sky Station 7. We're not far away. I can see the glow of the city up ahead. Flying over London at this height will be exhilarating, to say the least.

Things are going well for us. Our engine performance is stable at ninety percent with no radiation leakage. This race has proved the technology works. Stannard and his team have created a miracle. We're at the dawn of a fossil-fuel free future for aviation, whoever wins the race.

Captain La Fontaine has done his best to boost morale. More champagne and canapes have certainly lifted the mood. He reminded us that we still have an Atlantic Crossing to make. I'm not sure the significance of Rod Stewart's Sailing *played over the speakers was fully appreciated by some of the younger passengers, but my lady travelling companion and I enjoyed singing along.*

More importantly, the captain reminded us that they have the same crossing to make and the gap between us was not that great. They must be stretching their engines to the limit. It isn't over yet!!

I always get a lump in my throat when I see the Houses of Parliament. I suppose it's a spiritual homecoming for me. Then, of course, there'll be the Thames, Big Ben, London Eye and Westminster Abbey. The skyline of London will be a welcome sight this evening, despite our race position. After so many hours of tedium, this race is now full on. Max Hartley out.

* * *

Lonsdale had taken the call from Steve and Maria and was updated about the missing thorium rod. Between them, they'd narrowed the explanation down to three options. Firstly, Dr Fischer could have inserted a bomb with a timing device, set to go off at a certain location. This seemed unlikely as the timings weren't guaranteed given the length of the race. And surely, it would have gone off by now.

The second option was a detonator that could be triggered remotely, perhaps by a signal from a mobile phone. This was more plausible and gave the perpetrators greater control over timing and location, presumably for maximum impact. Even a small ignition within the reactor would be enough to cause a nuclear explosion, Maria reasoned, although she confessed to not being an expert.

Thirdly, this could just be a hoax or a red herring. The empty cylinder may be stuffed with newspaper, or a toxic letter Dr Fischer had concocted about the evils of nuclear energy.

Lonsdale wasn't taking any chances. He seconded two police officers from the Specialist Firearms Command Unit to accompany him to the House and requested a back-up team to be on standby.

Also, he established a control room in New Scotland Yard to which he was connected through a headset and microphone taped to his cheek. The controller would keep the line open, stay connected to Steve and Maria, and keep them all updated on developments in the race.

Lonsdale didn't have time to sort out the politics between the Parliamentary Security Department and the Metropolitan Police. Who was in charge, who had the final say, when was authorisation needed to proceed. He was happy to leave all these thorny command issues for a more senior Met officer to handle.

He quickly discovered one of the two firearm specialists was also an advanced driver. Lonsdale tossed him the keys. Soon they were speeding through the London nightlife, blue lights flashing, their siren drowning out the noise from the busy streets.

Hanging on to the front-seat grab handle for dear life, Lonsdale was starting to feel queasy as they swerved in and out of the lines of traffic, narrowly missing taxis, cars, buses, trucks, pedestrians and even, at one point, a pavement stall selling magazines.

In need of some mental distraction, Lonsdale started running through various scenarios. What about contacting the plane. Maybe they could open the reactor and remove the detonator. But there was a snag. Then do what with it? Throw it out of the window? Besides, there wasn't time, the plane was only minutes away from Big Ben. Such a call could create panic, or even cause the plane to crash, right into the heart of London.

Or they could divert the plane far enough away out of signal range. But if it turned out to be a hoax, and *Comet 5* was disqualified from the race for not crossing over Sky Station 7, there could be a $10 billion lawsuit on his desk next week.

Then what about the signal itself. What if it wasn't coming from the Houses of Parliament at all. Maybe the perpetrator was somewhere else, around Greater London or even waiting for them by the Statue of Liberty. Or nowhere. The detonator could be triggered from anywhere in the world over the internet. The possibilities were endless. This was becoming too much mental distraction.

Thankfully they had arrived at the main security entrance to the Houses of Parliament. Lonsdale was relieved there was no more time to think. Whatever scenario they were facing, he was confident one man knew the answer. Quentin Fitzgerald-Manning.

And, as the security team on site soon confirmed, that man was ensconced in the recently opened Roof Garden, in the shadow of the iconic Elizabeth Tower, home to Big Ben. His guest list included the glitterati from royalty, politics, media, sports, business, stage, and screen. The guest of honour was none other than Betty Gachuhi, UN Secretary-General.

A small contingent of Parliament security guards led the way. Lonsdale could hear loud music pumping into the clear night sky as they stepped out of the lift onto the roof. The cold night air was thick with the tempting smells of barbecued food. He turned a corner and saw the party was in full swing, people straying out along the roof terrace, trying to get a better view.

The officers inched their way through the shadows and were nearly at the entrance when the music stopped. Excited voices were hushed.

An announcer invited the guests to look across the river in the direction of St Thomas's Hospital. At first there was silence. Dozens of expectant eyes were scanning the night sky.

Then someone spotted the plane.

A small dot at first but growing larger as it hurtled towards them. A quick flash of its landing lights drowned out the red and green pinpricks on its wingtips.

Excited cheers rose to a crescendo as the plane swooped down to the allotted two thousand feet for identification. Lonsdale saw the team of UN observers

422

poised in one corner of the roof garden: cameras and recording devices at the ready.

The cheers became muted when the plane came into full view, spotlights catching its red underside, confirming it was the American entrant. A handful of guests leapt for joy, waving the *Stars and Stripes*, chanting U-S-A.

New Spirit of St Louis waggled her wings triumphantly as she flew directly over Big Ben. Lonsdale heard a boom as the first of ten chimes rang out, just before the engines roared, taking the plane up and away out to the northwest at full throttle.

Quentin Fitzgerald-Manning was introducing his guest of honour to a small group of dignitaries over by an illuminated water feature. He looked up as Lonsdale approached, flanked by the two Met officers and the Parliament security guards. His face was quite flushed, a combination of alcohol and anger, Lonsdale assumed. Or was it a guilty conscience?

"What's the meaning of this?" Fitzgerald-Manning thundered, causing a ripple of embarrassment to spread amongst his guests.

"I need you to answer more questions. It's urgent. We can talk here or at New Scotland Yard. The choice is yours." Lonsdale noticed a bulge in his jacket pocket. Was that his mobile phone or another type of signalling device?

"I'll do no such thing. I've had enough of this harassment. You'll be hearing from my solicitor. I've told you everything I know. Now, get out." Quentin's right hand slipped into his pocket.

Before Lonsdale could react, Fitzgerald-Manning threw his left arm around Betty Gachuhi's neck and pulled her to him, shielding his body behind her back. She tried to scream but her windpipe was being throttled. Her startled eyes searched for help among the stunned faces around her. One of the guests yelled out as she joined the others running for the exit.

Lonsdale noticed Fitzgerald-Manning's right hand was now clutching a Glock 19. The ugly square barrel of the black handgun was pressed hard into the side of Betty's throat. One of the two Met officers raised his firearm, but Lonsdale waved it down, trying to calm the situation. The weapon was lowered.

The Parliament security guards withdrew and cordoned off the area. One called down his lapel mike for more resources while another started to shepherd the remaining guests towards the exit. The other Met officer also withdrew to a safe distance and called up his control room.

As they left, some people were capturing the scene on their mobile phones. Lonsdale was worried that footage could already be uploaded on social media. The situation needed to be resolved quickly.

Despite the mayhem, nobody had contacted the announcer who was continuing with his running commentary on the race. *Comet 5* was now speeding through the darkness towards them. Lonsdale watched in horror as the plane flashed its landing lights to announce its imminent arrival over Big Ben. He'd run out of time.

More worrying was the fact that Fitzgerald-Manning had switched the Glock into his left hand, the barrel still pressed hard into the other side of Betty's neck. A large welt had bloomed on her skin, such was the pressure he was exerting.

In the same fluid movement, Fitzgerald-Manning had reached into an inside pocket and pulled out his mobile phone. He was busily manipulating the keys with his right thumb. Lonsdale assumed he must have practiced this many times as he made only split-second glances down at the screen. Otherwise, his eyes were fixed on Lonsdale, Betty Gachuhi, and the security personnel around him.

At one point, a rue smile flicked across his lips. He must have found the right app, Lonsdale concluded as he weighed up his options. None were feasible without major bloodshed. This was no time for heroics, and he wasn't ready to meet his maker. Not just yet.

"Not Cambodia, Lonsdale, but the Caribbean." Fitzgerald-Manning's rue smile had broadened into a full-on grin. He was shouting over the background noise and tightening his grip on Betty's throat, the Glock being thrust deeper into her glistening skin. "I've a friend with a private island to rent, not that rent money will be an issue when the race is over, and the Americans have won."

The *Comet 5* was almost upon them, its blue undercarriage illuminated by powerful searchlights raking the darkness above the rooftops. The UN observers were recording the moment for posterity. Lonsdale prayed history would only remember the thrill of the race and not some cataclysmic human tragedy.

"You'll never get out of here alive. None of us will. Come to your senses, Quentin. Remember where you are." Lonsdale added for good measure.

"I know exactly how to escape from here. There's a fast boat waiting for me on the Thames. But then again, will I take one of the tunnels out of here? There's one that connects to Westminster Abbey. I don't want to make it too easy for you to follow us, Lonsdale."

"Us?" Lonsdale could see he was getting ready to move.

"Sorry Betty, you're coming with me. I suppose it's a form of life insurance." He had started backing towards an exit door.

The next few seconds, Lonsdale was to recount later, happened for him in slow motion. It was triggered by a strange voice in his ear. He'd momentarily forgotten about the headset, that they were all connected, and each officer could hear his whispered comments.

The voice turned out to be a senior commander from the anti-terrorist unit who just happened to be sitting in a nearby office at New Scotland Yard, watching the race live on TV. He was listening to the pilots through the voice recordings from both cockpits. Lonsdale never did find out how he got clearance but was grateful that he did as his intervention proved most timely.

"Tell him the American plane is pulling out. They have engine failure. They've requested an emergency landing at Dublin Airport. Irish Air Traffic are clearing the air space. It should be on the news shortly."

Lonsdale didn't remember saying Fitzgerald-Manning would be a fool to blow up the winning plane or commenting that this shock news might give them the distraction they needed. Instead, he saw Fitzgerald-Manning had his thumb hovering over a big green button on the screen, the sickly light reflecting in his steely, distant eyes.

Comet 5 was virtually overhead now. The faces of the excited passengers were clearly visible in the porthole windows. The pilots and cabin crew were waving to the thousands of onlookers crowded onto the streets around the House, over Westminster Bridge and right along the Embankment.

"Stop, Quentin!! The American Plane's pulling out. They're landing in Dublin. *Comet 5* will win. You'll get nothing from the Americans. It's over. Look." Lonsdale was pointing to one of the huge TV screens. They were all flashing out *Breaking News* in big, bold red letters. Someone thought to turn the sound up.

426

Fitzgerald-Manning stopped moving. His eyes were averted for a split second. He was trying to keep his grip on Betty and process all the information. He seemingly didn't believe his eyes or ears. It could be a stunt to throw him off guard.

Lonsdale was standing no more than ten feet away. Fitzgerald-Manning turned directly towards him. He made his decision. There was no other way out. His eyes of cold, green ice didn't flicker as he went to press the button.

His thumb never reached the screen. A red mark appeared in the middle of his forehead. It momentarily reminded Lonsdale of the bhindi his Hindu colleague in the cultural diversity team was wearing, in celebration of Diwali.

The similarity didn't last as the red mark on Fitzgerald-Manning's forehead soon started to bleed profusely. Everything went very still. His expression was more akin to surprise or confusion rather than pain or defeat. His grip on the Glock loosened. Slowly his arms fell to his sides. Betty was able to prise herself free and run to the safety of the nearby UN observer team.

As Fitzgerald-Manning slumped to his knees, the phone tumbled out of his right hand, landing harmlessly in the soft earth of a flower bed. The green button was clearly visible, below a signal showing detonation strength at full capacity. Lonsdale picked it up, cleared the screen and switched the phone to airplane mode. He thought it appropriate somehow, given the circumstances.

The single, deadly shot had come from an Enfield Enforcer 7.62 calibre sniper rifle. It was preferred for its accuracy over the Heckler & Koch 93 by the second police firearm specialist. He had taken up a kneeling position in the herb garden, which nestled in the corner next to a small shrubbery and was sheltered from the cold breezes off the Thames by handwoven hazel-twig fencing.

A thick rosemary bush had provided perfect cover, only the barrel protruding through the dense, green foliage. Lonsdale recalled that rosemary was for remembrance for those who died. As he looked down at the crumpled figure of Fitzgerald-Manning, he was grateful this greedy, arrogant man proved to be the only human casualty that night.

Suddenly, above him, the giant shape of *Comet 5* filled the sky. It also waggled its enormous wings as it climbed steeply into the darkness. By now, Lonsdale assumed, the passengers onboard would have heard the news about the other entrant withdrawing. The party will have started.

He reflected that they would always be blissfully unaware of what might have been.

CHAPTER 51

Max Hartley, Comet 5, Blog 11, The Statue of Liberty, New York City, Sky Station 8.

Well, I know the race is effectively over AND it was just after midnight local time, but even so, given the importance of this race to help save our planet, I'd have thought a few more New Yorkers could have done the decent thing and turned out to wave us on. It's supposed to be the city that never sleeps, after all!!

There were some Union Jack's, European flags, and plenty of happy partygoers around the Statue itself, otherwise our arrival at the last Sky Station passed unnoticed. The disappointment wasn't shared on board here, I can tell you!! If we'd have had tables, we'd have danced on them. Someone called it Boogey Yoga. One of the cabin crew told me we've drained all the alcohol on board. Best party at forty thousand feet I've ever been to.

The word is that our competitor suffered a double whammy crossing the Irish Sea. They overloaded their green hydrogen plant and lost propulsion in both engines. Also, their lithium-ion batteries started leaking charge. The new technology couldn't handle the demand. They'd considered landing at Shannon on the west coast. As it turned out, they only just made it to Dublin.

Meanwhile, we've got plenty of time now to make the comparatively short trip to St Louis. I don't expect the crowds there to be any bigger than here when we land. We don't need to be carried shoulder-high around the airfield, just a drop more Moet or something harder. And maybe some cheese on toast? With Lea & Perrins, of course. We are British, after all. And proud of it!!

Captain La Fontaine has just announced we'll be landing in a couple of hours. Nothing else to do now but bask in our glory and grab some sleep. A last word about Comet 5 *for all you nuclear sceptics - she flies beautifully!! Max Hartley out.*

* * *

Max Hartley, Comet 5, Blog 12, St Louis Lambert International Airport. Final Report

As predicted, our arrival in St Louis was something of an anti-climax. A few thousand people braved a light drizzle, cheering as we walked across the tarmac and went through to our short debriefing session. No sign of Quentin Fitzgerald-Manning or any of the Comet 5 *management team. I thought Dr Fischer might have made an appearance. Still, we're more than capable of celebrating for them.*

For the record, we landed at two thirty-one a.m. We made the circumnavigation in thirty-nine hours, sixteen minutes, and eight seconds. This was well within the fifty-hour maximum time limit. There were sixty-four passengers and crew on board and nearly three thousand kilos of cargo.

Having complied with all the race protocols and safety regulations, we were officially announced as the winners of **The UN Crystal Clear Skies Challenge**.

A cheque will be presented in New York next week by Betty Gachuhi, UN Secretary-General, just before a meeting of the full UN Security Council. She was supposed to be in Europe all week but has changed her plans, I'm told. Good for her!!

It's been a pleasure and a privilege to take part in this historic air race. I can genuinely say that nuclear powered commercial airliners are safe to fly, eco-friendly

430

and will become part of our everyday lives in the future. Comet 5 is a beauty!! I'm looking forward to flying her back to Bristol in the next few days.

I very much hope you have enjoyed my anecdotal blogs. Now I must go as my lady travelling companion has promised me the best waffles in St Louis for breakfast and I never keep a lady waiting. Max Hartley signing off.

CHAPTER 52

Hannah was nervous. It was a much cooler day, more in keeping with October, yet the palms of her hands were sticky.

She'd been inside the UN Building on East 42nd Street many times, for conferences, receptions, dinners, even a wedding. This time there was more at stake. She knew that addressing the UN Security Council wasn't just putting her in the spotlight. As Papal Legate, she'd be speaking on behalf of the Pope, and, by association, the Roman Catholic Church. It was only a ten-minute slot, but it had to be right.

Being back in New York so unexpectedly felt very weird. They were staying at the residence of His Eminence, the Archbishop. He'd visited them in hospital and brought with him the blessings of the Pope himself. *Mi casa, Su Casa.* He wouldn't accept any other arrangement.

The Archbishop was a charming and gentle man, originally from Tijuana. He spoke perfect English, having lived in the Big Apple for many years. He had two golden retrievers that Lawrence immediately fell in love with. It was good therapy, Hannah decided, as he was obviously missing Trigger, his faithful companion who was still languishing in kennels back in Rome.

Hannah was in a ground floor washroom at the UN Building. She was staring into the tired eyes of a woman putting on a brave face. Most of the redness and blistering had gone. Her makeup was trowelled on thicker than

432

usual to cover any remaining blemishes. What it couldn't cover were the emotional scars from their recent ordeal.

She ran her fingers through the long, dark hair and tossed it around. There were yet more silver flashes. Her body was rebelling against the stress and fatigue. Despite the best conditioner she could find, it still looked dull and lacking any sheen.

Next, she practiced a smile. The cherry red lipstick was glossy enough but there was no warmth, no sparkle. Sunken cheeks, with tiny lines around her mouth, betrayed her exhaustion. For now, this was the best she could manage.

Lawrence was waiting for her in the corridor outside. They walked through the building to the lobby of the Security Council Chamber, hand in hand. He said how great she looked. Bless that man. God loves a trier, she thought, and this man had tried so hard to reassure her over the last few days.

He had sat patiently in the store while she prevaricated over what dress to wear. He had read his paper for hours in the café across the street from the hairdressers. He never tired from telling her why he was so proud of her. It was good to hear, but she wasn't really taking it in.

They had been amongst the revellers at the Statue of Liberty when *Comet 5* flew over. Lawrence waved his Union Jack with gusto. Hannah joined the conga as it snaked around the monument. Even the music and dancing couldn't take her mind off things.

"I spoke to Steve Mole." Lawrence was standing with his back to a huge globe in the middle of the lobby. "He'd heard from one of the race officials who examined the American plane. They couldn't find anything wrong with the propulsion system or the lithium-ion batteries. They literally just stopped working."

Hannah caught the end of what he said. "Don't mess with witch doctors and the spirit world. That's the moral of this story. Talking of which, Agnes is fine. I spoke to Father Kelly's successor yesterday. He'd paid her a visit. They're piping water from another source until the well clears. The drilling's stopped so things should go back to normal."

"Normal for the well but what about the water in Lake Turkana?" Lawrence asked. "The mining company had bigger plans, you said."

"The lake's still drying up. Father Michael said it was too shallow last week to get any boats in or out." Hannah noticed a woman weaving her way across the crowded lobby area towards them. It was Betty Gachuhi's Executive Assistant, Chantelle Holmes. Hannah recognised her face from the website. She was carrying a portfolio.

"Father Michael? Who he?"

"The replacement for Patrick Kelly. Apparently, Father Michael's a good man, so my team tell me, despite him being in the pay of Cardinal Maina. That man has fingers everywhere. He's spreading rumours Father Kelly's in rehab and that the Church is footing the bill. Every inch the caring cardinal."

"Nice touch. With colleagues like that, who needs enemies?" Lawrence was gently shaking his head.

When Chantelle reached them, she gave Hannah a big hug, squeezed her shoulders and kissed her on the cheek, much to her surprise. Even more surprising was that she did the same to Lawrence. He went to rub her lipstick off but changed his mind. He didn't get much attention these days from the opposite sex, Hannah reflected, let him enjoy this moment.

"We're so proud of what you did for the villagers in Kenya." Chantelle gushed. "Betty's been talking to her brother. He was singing your praises. She can't wait to meet you."

"It was nothing, really. I was just doing my job. It was a team effort." Hannah took Lawrence's hand. His contribution had proved invaluable, so it was only right he got some of the recognition. "Once we found the cause of the problem, the rest was easy."

"Oh, I don't think so. You're being too modest, Hannah." Chantelle suddenly looked horrified. "So sorry, is it OK if I call you Hannah? It's just I feel like I know you."

"Perfectly. We're Hannah and Lawrence."

"Not old enough to be Mr and Mrs McGlynn, thank you." Lawrence beamed.

Hannah asked about the modesty comment. Chantelle explained that a senior officer from the NYPD had been in touch and told Betty how Zelda Krasny had tried to kill them in the fire box. The officer believed their involvement had scuppered Krasny's plans to cheat over the air race. The police now had proof of collusion between the two entrants.

Chantelle continued. "Of course, Betty was on first name terms with Zelda and Quentin. I can't believe they're both dead. They seemed such nice people, especially Quentin. I'd nicknamed him 007, what with his good looks, British accent and the DB5. Betty said he held a gun to her throat. Just shows, you can't trust anyone these days."

"It's all about money." Hannah explained. "Our police contact told us an automated payment of five hundred million dollars was to be credited to Quentin's Swiss account once your prize money was received. Even nice people can turn evil for that sort of money."

Chantelle checked her watch. It was time to get moving. She handed Hannah the portfolio which

435

contained the run sheet for the day. Betty was due to make a short speech about how successful the air race had been in the quest for a fossil-fuel free aviation industry.

She would then hand over a large presentation cheque to the CFO of the Comet Aeronautics Group. The actual prize money had been transferred that morning. Once the photographers and journalists had gone, Betty would then introduce Hannah.

"Couldn't the journalists stay for Hannah's speech? They might find it interesting." Lawrence suggested, adding. "Only if Betty approves, of course."

Hannah looked daggers at him. She'd rehearsed the speech over dinner last night. He never mentioned suggesting the media should be present.

"I think Betty would be delighted. I'll ask her and let you know." Chantelle was leading the way into the Security Council Chamber.

The room was packed. Extra seating had been set up round the sides of the large semi-circular table and across the back of what has been described as the most important room in the world.

Chantelle asked them to wait near the podium while she went over to where Betty was chatting to some of the African nation delegates. As soon as Chantelle whispered in her ear and indicated where they were, Betty came rushing over. She threw her arms around them as if they were long, lost relatives.

"Hannah, Lawrence, at last. I'm so happy you're here. I've been hearing all about your adventures in my home country. I'm relieved you're both looking so well. Welcome to the United Nations."

"That's very kind of you, thanks for inviting us and allowing me to speak." Hannah replied on their behalf.

"Chantelle was asking about the press. Yes, yes, of course, I'll invite them to stay. They'll have to leave before the council meeting starts, but we normally take a short recess beforehand, so that'll work out fine."

Shortly afterwards, the meeting was called to order. Betty was an excellent orator and made an impassioned speech about reversing the disastrous effects of climate change. She saw the air race as being a small, yet important, piece in the jigsaw. She promised the UN would not rest until the planet was saved. Her speech got a standing ovation.

The presentation that followed went smoothly. It wasn't everyday a cheque was written for ten billion dollars, even a fake one. The photographers snapped away and ad hoc interviews took place. Hannah whispered to Lawrence how young she thought the CFO looked. He dismissed it, saying it was just another sign of aging. She punched him lightly on the shoulder.

Betty invited the media to stay for Hannah's speech. Most of them did, with only a few deciding they'd got what they came for and headed for the exit. Hannah joined her at the podium. Her speech was on autocue, but she was at her best when she spoke from the heart:

Every human being wants the same thing. Our needs and desires haven't changed for thousands of years. We all want to live a long, healthy and happy life: to provide for our families and be financially secure: to share joy and laughter with the people we hold most dear: to feel safe in our own homes and in society at large: to live in peace without fear of injury, injustice or discrimination: to be free to express ourselves without recrimination: to feel a sense of belonging, pride, fulfilment and contentment.

There is no reason why we can't have all these things. We've accumulated the knowledge, developed the science and technology, amassed a wealth of resources, and acquired a depth of experience so we can create a world where everyone can live in peace.

So why isn't it happening? Why do we have wars and crime? Why do we tolerate poverty and hunger, disease, and destruction? How can we allow a handful of people to spoil things for the majority? Regarding healthcare, why are we looking for treatments instead of ways to prevent illness? Why do we always rely on others - our leaders, politicians, governments or whoever - to do the right thing, for the sake of us all?

My name is Dr Hannah McGlynn, Papal Legate to the World Health Organisation. I'm privileged to be an adviser on healthcare, having spent a lifetime in medical research, here in New York. Today I want to share a true story with you, to demonstrate the importance of our work.

Agnes lives in a small village near a big lake in Northern Kenya. Her ancestors have lived there, mostly in peace, for hundreds of years. The lake always provided an abundance of fresh fish. The land was bountiful, with regular rainfall and plenty of rich soil. They grew crops, raised cattle, and kept goats, sheep, and chickens.

Agnes and her family should be living long, healthy, and happy lives, safe in their home with everything they need. Sadly, that is no longer possible. Why? Because of recent interventions from the outside world.

It is a world run by many people hell-bent on exploitation and greed. Where decision makers don't take responsibility for their actions. Where those in control simply don't care about the damage they cause or the people they harm.

This outside world is our world.

Agnes lost her husband, two children and two grandchildren earlier this year. Nine other local people also died from poisoning when their water supply was contaminated by an American mining corporation extracting rare minerals. This has now been exposed and stopped, but for how long?

The lake is drying up. A hydro-electric scheme in a neighbouring country is strangling the river which supplies eighty percent of the fresh water. Fish stocks are declining. Within ten years the lake will be gone. This will create an ecological disaster.

Hannah paused to take a sip of water. She looked out over a sea of faces. She certainly had their attention, but many were shaking their heads. Several journalists closed their laptops and notepads. One was overheard saying, *another bleeding heart.*

Undaunted, Hannah continued. *Then there is climate change. The rains do not come. Temperatures are rising in the blazing sun. The land can no longer sustain cattle nor provide the nutrients for arable crops. What was once fertile ground is rapidly becoming a desert. People are moving away to urban slums or seeking a better life overseas.*

Agnes may have to join this migration, leaving her ancestors and way of life behind. She is frightened, worried, and confused. It is difficult for us to understand how our carbon emissions can be destroying our planet. Try explaining to her that the rains no longer come because of coal-fired power stations belching out carbon monoxide on the other side of the world. Agnes has never seen a power station.

Of course, there are consequences for all this that we must live with. Refugee crises, humanitarian aid, children dying from illnesses we have the means to prevent. Or watching them starve while we send tons of good food to landfill.

Agnes has no voice. She can't protest or make her opinions known. She can't protect her family from the

439

evils being inflicted upon her by people she has never met. She has suffered injustice, and it is wrong. She just wants to live a long, healthy, and happy life, like the rest of us. Is that too much to ask?

I put it to you that WE are her voice. We must speak on her behalf, and millions like her.

The United Nations, acting through its agency, the World Health Organisation, has the stated objective of the attainment by all peoples of the highest possible level of health. I have two recommendations to help us achieve that objective.

Firstly, we must focus on the words, <u>by all peoples.</u> To paraphrase Abraham Lincoln. "That we here highly resolve that the dead shall not have died in vain. That we, the people, shall have a new birth of healthcare for all. And that government of the people, by the people, for the people, shall not perish from our earth."

We are the people to deliver healthcare for all. Change is achieved from the bottom up, not the top down. We cannot wait for our leaders to do the right thing. We must shake the tree until it bears fruit.

But how? My second recommendation is that we appoint the best people into the important roles that can make the difference. We all know what must be done, yet we get frustrated by political double-speak and lack of progress.

It's time to remove the vested interests, the game playing, the political shenanigans, the profiteering. It's time to let the 'person in the street' decide.

Let me thank you for your attention and leave you with a question. If you've not come here to help Agnes and the millions like her, then why are you here?

Hannah smiled as she moved away from the podium. The applause was polite yet lukewarm. A handful of people jumped to their feet, inspired by her words. The synaptic gap seemed elongated as translations were filtered through the many sets of headphones around the room.

Hannah felt tired and a little angry. The large bouquet of flowers that Betty presented to her was appreciated but didn't much lift her mood.

Lawrence continued clapping long after the room had descended into general murmur, in preparation for the council meeting.

He put his arms around her. "That was wonderful. It needed to be said, whether they were listening or not. Much more powerful than the rehearsal. I love the Gettysburg Address bit. Very clever."

Hannah had tears in her eyes as they made their way towards the exit. A hand on her arm caused her to turn. It was Chantelle. "Hannah, I've just spoken to Betty. She wonders if you have a few minutes."

Hannah looked quizzically towards Lawrence. He shrugged his shoulders and confirmed they were in no hurry. Lawrence took the bouquet and said he'd wait for her by the globe in the lobby.

Chantelle led Hannah to a small meeting room off the main chamber. She explained that the Council was taking a recess before the meeting. Betty wanted a word in private.

"Hannah, thank you so much, your speech hit all the right notes." Betty was sitting on a bright yellow sofa against the far wall. She invited Hannah to take one of the armchairs facing her across a highly-polished coffee table. Hannah declined the offer of a drink, somehow feeling she hadn't earned it.

Betty continued. "Let me come straight to the point, Hannah. I've been so impressed by your determination to do the right thing, even if it meant putting your own life in danger. Most people would have ignored Agnes and

441

stayed in Rome. You went out on a limb for her. You were incensed by the injustice. I admire your courage."

Hannah was trying to read her face but couldn't get beyond the effervescent smile and infectious enthusiasm. Where was this going?

"What's more, I could tell your speech today came from the heart. I agree with you. We need people in top jobs who will stand up and be counted: who will say what must be said and - more importantly - do what must be done, for the good of us all, which includes Agnes. I've been to her village by the way. I know what's happening to the lake. It makes my blood boil."

"I'm delighted someone was listening." Hannah managed a smile. "What can I do to help you?"

"The time for political game playing is over. The world is on the precipice. I need someone I can rely on." Betty picked up a folder and pulled out a single piece of paper. It was a letter, obviously signed with a flourish in blue pen. Hannah could make out the watermark and UN letterhead on the reverse side.

"Hannah, I'm restructuring the World Health Organisation. I need to strengthen its credibility. There are too many accusations about collusion with various governments and global corporations." Betty handed her the letter. It was her flamboyant signature.

"I'd like to appoint you as CEO, with operational control for the day to day running of the organisation. It's a new role with full management and fiscal responsibility, reporting to the WHO Director-General, with a dotted line to me. Well, not so much dots as very thick dashes." Betty beamed one of her electric smiles. "If you follow my meaning."

"I do indeed." Hannah felt herself blushing. She hadn't expected this. "Betty, I don't know what to say. I'm surprised and honoured you think I could do it."

442

"Hannah, you don't need to say anything. You can do it. I want you to do it. No pressure." The beam continued.

Hannah said she'd need to think about it and talk it over with Lawrence. Betty told her to take her time and asked if she could let her know next week. She confirmed it would involve moving to Geneva for a three-year contract, ideally starting early in the New Year.

Details of the remuneration package would be provided when she indicated her acceptance.

The package would include accommodation, relocation expenses, an executive car, and a generous salary, along with other benefits.

Hannah folded the letter and slipped it into her bag. She was about to offer Betty her hand when she found herself inside a warm, squeezing embrace. This was not how things were usually done at the UN, Hannah reflected. And she loved it.

The kiss on the cheek left Hannah feeling even more lightheaded as she made her way out towards the lobby. Lawrence was standing by the globe empty-handed. He had asked Chantelle to look after the bouquet and their briefcases.

He took her arm, guided her to a nearby café and grabbed a corner table, well out of earshot. He ordered the coffees and sat down waiting for a full report. Hannah's silence told him wheels were turning.

"OK, good news or bad news?" Lawrence made space for the lattes.

"Unexpected news. Good news, I think."

"You think?"

"I've been offered a job."

"Another job? You're in demand, Dr McGlynn." The coffees arrived. Lawrence thought about a lump of brown sugar but resisted.

443

"She wants someone to shake up the World Health Organisation. It's three years in Geneva, with all the trimmings. Start in January." Hannah sipped the latte, spilling some into the saucer.

"And?" Lawrence was at hand with a paper napkin.

"It's tempting but I don't feel I've done this job yet. The Pope would be hugely disappointed. The Legate role was his idea." Hannah could feel the light headedness darkening into a headache.

"I hear that but let me ask you a straight question. Will you ever be allowed to do the Legate job? Remember the threats from Cardinal Maina. The Pope seems to have influence but not day to day management control. Willingness to change isn't the Catholic Church's strongest suit. I fear they'll freeze you out."

Hannah told him she needed to walk and get some air. They finished the coffees and found themselves strolling through the grounds outside the UN building. A fresh breeze off the East River made all the flags dance to keep warm. Boxed hedges lined the paths round the side of the main complex.

One gravel path led them to a bronze sculpture entitled *Let Us Turn Swords Into Ploughshares*, depicting an Adonis type figure wielding a hammer. A sign explained that the piece symbolised our desire to end all wars by transforming the tools of destruction into implements for the benefit of all humanity. It was donated by the USSR to the UN in 1959.

"Somehow appropriate, given your speech, don't you think?" Lawrence was admiring the craftsmanship in the twisted shape of the huge sword.

"Indeed. When the world needs harmony and peace, we get hypocrisy and symbolism." Hannah blew out her cheeks in disgust.

444

Lawrence gently pulled her towards him. "There's something I want you to know, Dr McGlynn. New York, London, Rome, Geneva, or Timbuktu. I don't really care where we live so long as I'm with you. My PhD isn't dependent on location, so I can carry on my research. Fara came back while you were with Betty. She'd be delighted to help in my research into Parkinsons. The pieces are fitting together. Whatever you decide, count me in."

Hannah had been squeezing the lock of braided hair in her pocket that Agnes had given her. *It from my princess.* She felt in need of another slice of good fortune right now. There were just too many life-changing decisions for one week.

Something clicked inside. She threw her arms around him. "I'll need to do some homework. There're people I want to talk to. If Betty's serious about doing this, it could be an exciting new challenge. Are you *sure* about living in Geneva?"

"Why not? I make a really great fondue."

THE END

ACKNOWLEDGEMENTS

Sky Station 7 is a work of fiction. It is the fourth book in *The Human Spirit Series*. There will be six books in total, each addressing the biggest questions facing humanity. The characters, events and storylines are simply the result of an overactive imagination. The locations, however, and scientific background to the story are very much in our world. Fictional characters in a factual setting.

I have always been - and will forever remain - an optimist. Good will always triumph over evil. The reader can rest assured that the goodies will come out on top. I strongly believe we are amazing creatures that can achieve anything we set our minds to, providing we have the right attitude.

Whilst *The Human Spirit Series* is a celebration of what we have achieved over the last hundred years or so, through advancements in science and technology, inevitably the books explore what I believe is holding us back. Why haven't we removed fossil fuels from the aviation industry, for example? Announcing we hope someone else can solve the problem by 2050 doesn't cut it for me.

Today, it is very encouraging to see critically important issues such as climate change, desert lakes drying up, destruction of the natural environment, and human rights issues taking centre stage in our political awareness.

History tells us that politicians don't change the world - people change the world. Politics follows the will of the people, not the other way around. It is my strongest wish that this series of books will add to the debate about saving the planet and making the world a better place by pinpointing what is holding us back.

Sky Station 7 is designed to be provocative, informative and entertaining. I very much hope that's how the reader will feel about it and be prepared to take action as a result. It can, of course, just be read as an action thriller/adventure story, without reading between the lines.

The history of aviation is not a long one. From the Wright Brothers taking to the skies in 1903, we have created a global industry with over 15,000 commercial airliners airborne every single day, along with countless military, cargo, research, private and other aircraft.

The industry is one of the biggest polluters of the atmosphere and, despite improvements in performance, engine efficiency and decarbonisation, it remains one of the major contributors to carbon emissions. Yet surprisingly, there doesn't seem to be any urgency to resolve this crisis.

The history of aviation has been driven by competition, with technological advancements being created in response to competitive pressure. I suppose war is the ultimate competition: innovate or perish. Either way, we have marvelled at the advancements in aviation which have taken us ultimately into space travel and the prospects of exploring our universe. But we can't rest there. It must become a clean, green aviation industry.

I remain an optimist. If this book sparks new ways to reduce carbon emissions and make the world a cleaner, safer and better place to live, I'll feel it's all been worthwhile.

In writing this book, I am indebted to countless people who have encouraged, inspired and stimulated ideas along the way.

Three stand out. My thanks go to **Mickey Mestel**, the author of *Wandering Turkana,* distributed by Lucita

Publishing. The book provided granular detail on what has been described as the **harshest terrain on the planet**. I was truly fortunate to speak with Mickey who was most helpful in providing background to the story.

Kevin Hanson is a British intellectual property lawyer with a unique insight into the US Patent and Trademark Office. Although the scenes in the book are purely fictional, it is reassuring to know that an actual IP lawyer has given them a tick for credibility.

Lynne Holmes has been a tower of strength, encouragement and technical help with the manuscript throughout the project. It is as much her book as mine and would probably have never made it to print without her guidance and support.

In addition, I've used countless reference books to make the story as authentic as possible. Notably **Lindburgh** by A. Scott Berg proved very informative. I had hoped to visit Lindbergh's grave in Maui to pay respects to a much-maligned adventurer and someone who did change the world.

Another useful source was **Turkana: Kenya's Nomads of the Jade Sea** by Nigel Pavitt. It stimulated my imagination and provided essential cultural and historical context. The colour photography and imagery are stunning.

From a writing perspective, it was a delight to work again with my structural editor **Ian Critchley**. The book is all the better for his critical comments and sharp attention to detail. Every crime fiction novelist needs someone like Ian behind them to say the things they may not want to hear. In my experience, not all editors are as kind and supportive as Ian, which is why he is a joy to work with.

And a genuine thank you for **Dawn Martin**, my copy editor and eagle-eyed proofreader who was a real pleasure to work with. It is a long and complex story made all the better for having the grammar corrected, the spelling checked and the right punctuation in place.

Finally, although the story is fictional, many of the moving parts are factual. Prince Rudolf funding the 19th century explorations of East Africa, Lake Turkana potentially becoming the next Aral Sea, mineral-rich kamacite being deposited on earth by meteorites and even nuclear-powered planes are all based in fact (see **Project NEPA**).

Sky Station 7 closes with Dr Hannah McGlynn on the horns of yet another dilemma. Will she, or won't she? The answer will come in the fifth book in *The Human Spirit Series*. I hope you enjoy finding out. Thank you.

Andrew Harris

THE
HUMAN
SPIRIT
S E R I E S